Juno Rushdan is a veteran US Air Force intelligence officer and award-winning author. Her books are action-packed and fast-paced. Critics from *Kirkus Reviews* and *Library Journal* have called her work 'heart-pounding James Bond-ian adventure' that 'will captivate lovers of romantic thrillers.' For a free book, visit her website: junorushdan.com

Bestselling author **Anna J. Stewart** honestly believes she was born with a book in her hand. After growing up devouring every story she could get her hands on, now she gets to make her living making up stories and fulfilling happily-ever-afters of her own. Her dreams have most definitely come true. Anna lives in Northern California (only a ninety-minute flight from Disneyland, her favourite place on earth) with two monstrous, devious, adorable cats named Sherlock and Rosie.

Also by Juno Rushdan

Cowboy State Lawmen: Duty and Honor
Wyoming Mountain Investigation

Cowboy State Lawmen
Wyoming Winter Rescue
Wyoming Christmas Stalker
Wyoming Mountain Hostage
Wyoming Mountain Murder
Wyoming Cowboy Undercover
Wyoming Mountain Cold Case

Also by Anna J. Stewart

Honor Bound
Guarding His Midnight Witness
Prison Break Hostage
The PI's Deadly Charade
Deadly Vegas Escapade
A Detective's Deadly Secrets

The Coltons of Roaring Springs
Colton on the Run

Colton 911: Chicago
Undercover Heat

WYOMING RANCH JUSTICE

JUNO RUSHDAN

HUNTING COLTON'S WITNESS

ANNA J. STEWART

MILLS & BOON

First Published in Great Britain 2024
by Mills & Boon, an imprint of HarperCollins*Publishers* Ltd
1 London Bridge Street, London, SE1 9GF

www.harpercollins.co.uk

HarperCollins*Publishers*
Macken House, 39/40 Mayor Street Upper,
Dublin 1, D01 C9W8, Ireland

Special thanks and acknowledgment are given to Anna J. Stewart for her contribution to *The Coltons of Owl Creek* miniseries.

ISBN: 978-0-263-32242-2

0824

This book contains FSC™ certified paper and other controlled sources to ensure responsible forest management.

For more information visit: www.harpercollins.co.uk/green

Printed and Bound in the UK using 100% Renewable Electricity at CPI Group (UK) Ltd, Croydon, CR0 4YY

WYOMING RANCH JUSTICE

JUNO RUSHDAN

For all the first responders. Thank you for your service.

Prologue

Tuesday, September 17
10:39 p.m.

He'd waited as long as he could, holding back the urge until it took control. Tonight, he would sate the dark hunger gnawing at him and find some sense of relief.

Watching her, he licked his lips, excited and eager for their hookup. He had it all planned. Everything was in place and ready. The SUV. The syringe. The intimate hideaway where they'd have lots of privacy and time for him to play. She looked stronger than the others. Maybe she'd last more than a day or two. He had high hopes for this one.

Jessica logged off the computer in the university lab and began packing up her things.

Now. He threw a book in his backpack, slung it over his shoulder and hurried to beat her to the door without looking like he was rushing. The key to pulling it off, he'd learned the hard way, was in the timing. If he left behind her, then she'd be on the defensive, wondering if he was following her.

Leaving the place first—whether the lab, the café, the rec center—and then luring his prey to come to him had consistently been easier than shooting fish in a barrel and always got him his quarry without fail.

He pretended to hobble on the foot he'd Velcroed into the immobilization boot on his left leg. Shoving through the front door of the Southeastern Wyoming University computer lab, he stepped out into the cool late-night air. No worries about leaving his fingerprints; the seamless flesh-colored gloves solved that problem. He bent his head away from the camera and lowered the bill of his cap pulled over a shaggy ginger-colored wig.

Plenty of traps everywhere, but he was vigilant. He was prepared.

Making his way to the SUV he kept prepped for these special nights, he slowed down when he heard her leave the building and the door clicked shut. Anticipation slithered through him.

She was only a few feet behind him, drawing closer. He limped to his vehicle parked at the far end of the lot, near the alley she liked to use as a shortcut to the bus stop, where she was headed now, rather than take the long way around the block.

Dropping his bag and decoy keys on the ground, he swore loudly. He bent over and feigned struggling to pick up his keys, which he had slid beneath the car with his foot.

"Oh, man." Another curse flew from him as he glanced around, catching her eye. "Hey." He gave a quick wave with his right hand, ensuring she could see his other arm tucked in a sling like a broken wing, and she slowed. "Would you mind helping me a second?" he asked, and she stopped. He pushed the nonprescription glasses up on the bridge of his nose and limped a couple of steps, giving her a clear view of the medical boot. "If I get down there, I might not be able to get back up." Flashing a gentle smile, he fought the impulse to scratch the top of his lip, which itched from the fake mustache. He was anxious to shed the disguise. Even the colored contacts irritated his eyes.

Jessica glanced from side to side, then looked between the sling and the immobilization boot, deliberating.

She was perfect. Precisely his type. White. Slim. Blond. Dark eyes. High cheekbones. Pretty mouth. Only twenty-years-old. Easygoing. Not too wary.

He'd considered a few others, but she was his top pick for his next hookup. This was going to be his lucky night.

"This is what I get for trying to ride my bike more and do my part to save the environment," he said lightly, raising the sling. "Someone not paying attention hit me. I'll owe you one."

With a nod, Jessica headed toward him, making the mistake of thinking he wasn't a threat. "I'm the same. Even though my parents offered to help me buy a car, I either bike or take the Secure Ride," she said, referring to the public transportation bus service offered by the university.

Little did she realize that she'd never make it to the bus tonight.

"I would've taken the Secure Ride myself," he said. "But at the closest stop, there isn't a bench, and I'd have to stand while I wait for the bus. The doc told me to keep pressure off my foot." As she drew closer, he pulled the grin wider. His excitement over the risk of grabbing her was liquid fire in his veins. The burn was good. "I appreciate you helping me." He hid his right hand behind his leg, and the sling covered most of the other. Up close, someone could tell he was wearing gloves if they looked carefully. "Can I pay you back with a coffee or something at the Wheatgrass Café?"

Stepping within his reach, she flicked her hair over her shoulder, kicking up the sweet scent of her perfume. The smell reminded him of a previous hookup.

"No need." She narrowed her eyes at him for a second. "Hey, I know you. You're in my Mythology 101 class. I nearly knocked you down the other day." Her shoulders immediately relaxed. A smile tugged at her rosy lips.

Another key to success was to pick one of their classes. The larger, the better, where he could blend in, disappear. Simply sit in once or twice while in disguise. Orchestrate a meeting where they bump into him or vice versa. That first connection, the initial spark, made this moment when he snatched them so much easier because once they remembered him, it lowered their guard.

"Oh yeah," he said, filling his altered voice with pleasant surprise. "I didn't recognize you." The truth was, he'd memorized her face, the shape of her body, the way she moved. Fantasized about tonight a hundred times. "By the way, I'm Theodore Cowell. Just call me Theo." Introductions put them further at ease.

"Jessica Atkinson."

His next steps flew through his mind. *Take hypodermic needle from sling. Dose the girl. Grab her. Quick tussle*—they always fought and lost. *Pop trunk. Toss her in the vehicle. Handcuffs. Leg irons. Gag. Drive.*

He could do it in under a minute. His best record was twenty-two seconds. None had ever gotten away. By the time he got behind the wheel and sped off, the ketamine would hit her system, keeping her quiet for several hours. Once she woke up, then they'd party.

"Thanks again." He smoothed his palm over the slight bulge of the compact handgun tucked in the pocket of his lightweight jacket. He only carried it for insurance. Not that he had a problem killing an animal or a person by pulling the trigger—he was a hunter in every sense of the word and was even a long-range deadeye, capable of hitting a target one mile away. But using a gun to wrangle his prey would be cheating.

"Sure. No problem." She got down on her hands and knees and reached under the car for his keys.

Always worked like a charm.

Time slowed to a crawl. He looked around, sweeping the area once more, ensuring no witnesses lurked nearby. It was just the two of them. His heart throbbed with anticipation as he pulled out the hypodermic needle.

Chapter One

Tuesday, September 17
10:46 p.m.

Hannah Delaney got off the Secure Ride bus operated by SWU, surprised it had arrived four minutes ahead of schedule. Hitching her backpack on her shoulder, she headed for the computer lab to work on a project.

At least, that was what she wanted people to believe.

Her police chief had given her the undercover assignment at the last minute after the University Killer suddenly resurfaced ten days ago, taking the life of twenty-one-year-old Madison Scott. For nearly the past decade, the murderer had struck on and off, always claiming three lives within a month, using the same MO before disappearing again.

Hannah had pored over the routines of the previous victims, zeroing in on things they'd had in common, and tried to recreate their lifestyle. She'd moved into on-campus housing, enrolled in a myriad of classes, frequented the Wheatgrass Café, rode the Secure Ride bus at night, hit the gym at the Sweetwater Recreation Center, biked during the day to downtown, shopped at the farmers market and caught live music at the local bar, the Watering Hole.

She still hadn't had a chance to swing by the computer lab at night on a regular basis like some of the victims had done in years past. Fall semester had only been in session for less than three weeks. With all the new student events and socials, where a predator might be lurking, there simply hadn't been enough hours in a day to cover everything. She had to prioritize. The lab wasn't high on the list, since Madison Scott had never been there. Quite honestly, Hannah didn't understand why many students would use the campus computer lab these days when most had a personal laptop.

Time was running out. The killer was going to snatch his next victim soon. Only twenty days left for him to claim two more lives. Hannah only hoped she was doing enough to catch his eye. She'd do anything to spare someone else from being violated and murdered. Stopping monsters was her life's mission, the only way for her to atone and silence her demons. It drove everything she did—why she got up in the morning, became a detective, even why she kept everyone at a distance.

You'll find him. You have to.

Dressed in jeans, an open flannel button-down with a tank top beneath it, hair in a high ponytail to make her appear even younger, she blended in with any other student. The only thing to set her apart was the concealed gun in her inside-the-waistband holster at the five-o'clock position between her back and hip, and the small knife that was a part of her belt buckle.

She took the alley, a shortcut to the lab. There was no way for her to know for sure if any of the other victims had ever used this same route at some point leading up to their murder. It was smarter and safer to walk around the block to get to the lab, using the well-lit sidewalks, where a passerby might see something. Yet young people, not considering the fragility of their lives, tended to trade security for convenience.

People showed you who they were in subtle ways by their choices and preferences, which were almost as telling as a Myers–Briggs personality test if you watched someone for weeks on end. Whether they were cautious or carefree. Skeptical or trusting. Selfish or caring. Predictable or impulsive.

All the slain women had been described as kind, thoughtful, naive. Somewhat of a loner. Most importantly, creatures of habit.

Despite being the right physical type, this was where Hannah was at a disadvantage. Less than ten days wasn't long enough to establish a consistent routine, a pattern the University Killer could rely on. He not only chose his victims for their appearance, but she suspected he also stalked them to know precisely when and where to strike.

Two more women were going to die soon if she couldn't lure him in as the bait.

A soft scuffling sound came from the other end of the alley near the outskirts of the computer-lab parking lot. Whatever it was, it was bigger than a rat.

Hannah's gut tightened. She picked up her pace down the alleyway, sticking to the shadows of the wall. Straining to see in the dim light, she caught sight of a dark SUV, the back end of the passenger's side.

The trunk door popped open.

Someone grunted. More scuffling noises.

"What are you doing?" a woman asked, her voice frantic.

Two people stepped into partial view, but the dark SUV partly obscured them. A man wrestled with a blond woman, possibly in her early twenties. The man hit the blonde in the face, dazing her, and hauled her to the back of the vehicle.

Dropping her backpack, Hannah rushed forward. She drew her weapon from the holster.

"Police!" Hannah called out, holding the Glock in a two-handed grip, sighting down the barrel.

He whirled, pulling the woman up in front of him like a shield, one arm locked under her chin, pressed against her throat. With his other hand, he wrenched one of the blonde's arms clutched behind her back. An empty arm sling swung back and forth along his side. His gaze darted to the open trunk, and Hannah realized how close he had come to getting the young woman inside it.

"Let her go!" Hannah ordered. "Right now!"

Keeping the woman held tightly in front of him, he scurried backward around to the driver's side, dragging her along with him. Her nose was bloody. Her eyes were wide with fear. She clutched the arm over her throat, her feet shuffling in the direction she was being forced.

Easing around the rear of the vehicle, Hannah glimpsed inside the trunk. A chill ran through her. The interior of the cargo compartment was padded. A plastic tarp was laid out. Handcuffs and leg irons each dangled from a chain that had been bolted to either side of the trunk. On the breeze, the biting scent of bleach hit her. No license plate.

She rounded the back side, coming face-to-face with him. One clean shot was all Hannah needed.

"Release her, or I'll shoot." A complete bluff. Although an excellent markswoman, she didn't have a clear shot with the blonde being used as a human shield.

Between the shaggy hair, mustache, glasses and the way he hid his face behind the young woman's head, Hannah couldn't make out enough details to identify him, much less find the clearance to pull the trigger.

Yanking the woman another foot or two toward the driver-side door, he released the arm wrested behind her back and pulled something from his pocket. A semiautomatic pistol. "Drop your gun," he demanded, pressing the muzzle to the young woman's side. "Or I'll shoot her."

Hannah held her ground, keeping her weapon aimed levelly. "This isn't what you want," she said, taking a calculated risk. Killing his victims slowly after raping them was his MO. Taking her life in an impulsive act wouldn't satisfy him. Not only that, but he'd also lose his only leverage. "I don't think you're going to pull the trigger and kill her."

He eyed the car door. "Who said anything about killing her?" He jammed the muzzle into the woman's side so hard that she winced. "Drop it, or I start putting bullets in her."

Hannah hesitated. The need to put this monster down and end his nine-year-long killing spree was an ache in her soul. She might not get another opportunity if he slipped through her fingers now.

"The first one goes in her stomach," he promised.

Getting this woman out alive was the only thing that mattered at the moment. Hannah glanced over her shoulder at the dumpster near the entrance to the alley. If he tried to shoot at her, she could make it there and duck for cover. She raised her palms with her gun vertical, barrel pointed up. Slowly, she set it down on the ground, never taking her gaze off him and the girl.

"Do you think I'm stupid? Kick it under the car."

She did as instructed, sending her weapon sailing beneath the SUV, only deepening the nasty twist in her gut spiraling into fear. Fear for the life of the young woman.

"Open the door," he snapped at the blonde, tightening his arm over her throat.

No matter what, Hannah wasn't going to let him get away with another victim. Worst case, if he managed to get the girl into the car, she'd pull her backup weapon from her boot and blow out his tires. He wouldn't make it far.

With a shaking hand, the young woman grabbed the handle and opened it. Her eyelids grew heavy, and she swayed in his grip.

Was the hold on her throat choking her, cutting off her airway?

"Let her go!" Hannah took a tentative step forward. "She can't breathe."

"Don't you move. Not another step." He backed up, using the woman's body to block him. His arm loosened around her throat as he climbed into the vehicle, keeping the gun pointed at her side.

The woman swayed again, her head bobbing like she was going to keel over any second.

She'd been drugged. He must have dosed her with ketamine already.

The car engine roared to life while he kept the gun pointed at his hostage. "You'll have to choose. Me or her."

Choose? What does he mean?

He pulled the trigger, shooting the blonde in the side, and peeled off.

No!

The young woman staggered and slumped to the ground. The SUV sped across the parking lot, hitting the street. He turned the corner and sped away, tires squealing, as Hannah raced over to the young woman, knelt beside her and checked the wound.

Thankfully, the bullet had missed her stomach, but it had

struck her just above the hip. The woman's brown eyes fluttered closed—a combination of the drugs and shock.

Hannah took off her shirt and applied pressure to slow the bleeding. "Hang in there. You're going to make it." She whipped out her cell phone and called 911.

Once she heard sirens approaching, she wondered which campus officers would arrive on the scene.

She'd readily deal with any of them except for one—the SWU police department chief.

Matt Granger.

Chapter Two

Tuesday, September 17
11:19 p.m.

Behind the wheel of his pickup truck, Matt Granger sped to the university campus with his teeth clenched. Since waking up that morning, he'd had a familiar tingle prickling his spine that forewarned him to prepare for trouble. It was his day off from the SWUPD. The bad feeling niggling him had made him consider going in, but he had coordinated a full load of work on the ranch with his cousins. Before he could relax with an ice-cold beer, a sergeant had called with news he'd been dreading.

A young woman had been shot during an encounter with a man they suspected to be the University Killer, and somehow a detective had been on the scene.

Trouble indeed—a subject in which he had plenty of experience. Truth be told, he was drawn to it...or rather, trouble was drawn to him. Good at seeing it coming and neutralizing it, a talent that had served him well during his time in the army as a Special Forces Operator. His job had been training and planning for the worst and then making sure it happened—to the enemy. After seeing too much carnage, he'd returned to his family's ranch, set between Laramie and Bison Ridge. The transition to the Laramie police force and later to campus law enforcement felt natural, even easy. He'd mistakenly thought that in the two small towns, where neighbors helped one another and everyone was so welcoming with open arms, things would be slower, quieter. Safer. Instead of bloodshed and loss, he'd finally find peace.

But whether he was in the army, with the LPD or the campus police, there was no escaping trouble and the death that always followed.

Matt pulled up to the headquarters of the SWUPD, located on the west end of campus, threw his truck in Park, and hurried inside. The department occupied five thousand square feet of the first floor of a parking garage, providing a modern, spacious facility for the law enforcement agency. He nodded hello to a couple officers.

One looked him over with raised eyebrows, making Matt consider how he must appear after sixteen hours of hard manual labor.

It had been his idea to expand his family's sources of revenue by designating a modest portion of the property to big game hunting. He'd taken the lead on building small cabins that could be rented to those looking to hunt or simply relax. Earlier, he and his cousins had been working on Sheetrock and wall texture since the wiring for the electricity had been finished.

Taking off his dark brown cowboy hat, he wished he'd had time to shower, or at least had the foresight to change his sweaty shirt, wash his face and grab a sandwich for the ride over.

Sergeant Lewis stood in Matt's office, talking to a woman—presumably the detective—seated in a chair that faced the desk. Lewis looked up, catching sight of Matt, and opened the office door for him.

"Evening, boss," Lewis said.

The woman pivoted in the chair, glancing over her shoulder at Matt and meeting his gaze. He swallowed a sigh.

Lewis gestured to her. "This is Detective—"

"Hannah Delaney," Matt interrupted, letting the spike of annoyance leak into his voice. The woman was the walking, talking epitome of trouble.

"Oh, you two know each other," Lewis said, surprise stamped on his face.

"Yeah." Hannah gave a curt nod to the officer while keeping her stare leveled at Matt. "We worked a case together before he quit being a detective with the LPD to hide out and play cop over here."

Matt tamped down a retort. He'd been through this rigmarole before, where a cop—usually a detective—hurled an insult at him for taking this position and he, stung by the icy disdain, inevitably went on the defense.

Little good it ever did him.

For some reason, when it came to Hannah, all her taunts teased in a way that reminded him he was not only a cop but also a man. "I forgot you could be so…" He let his voice trail off, realizing that finishing his statement wouldn't help the situation.

"Candid?" she offered.

He measured his words to mitigate the tension in the room. "I was going to say *blunt*. Hard-hitting." *Like a sledgehammer.*

He had no idea why he found that kind of sexy.

Lewis stood still and quiet, shifting an uncomfortable glance between them.

"Would you excuse us, Sergeant?" Matt guided Lewis to the door and closed it behind him. "What are you doing on my campus?" With Hannah, there was no telling. He crossed the room and dropped his hat next to his computer. Leaning on the edge of his desk, facing her, he noticed bloodstains on her white tank top. "And how are you involved in tonight's shooting?"

Sergeant Lewis had given scant details, as he hadn't had a chance to interview Hannah yet before he'd called Matt.

"For the past ten days," Hannah said, crossing her lean legs, "I've been on campus, pretending to be a new student named Helen Davis, in an undercover op to catch the University Killer."

Undercover? He had not seen that one coming.

"I'd been following the routines of the previous victims," she continued, "and came across him attempting to take his next. According to her student ID, she's Jessica Atkinson." Hannah ran through the events leading up to her 911 call.

The student was now being treated at the university hospital. Over the phone, Matt had instructed Lewis to send an officer to watch over her while she recovered.

"Where's your partner?" Matt asked.

"I'm solo on this."

The benefits of having her assigned to a case like this with a partner were obvious and numerous. So why was she working without backup?

He stiffened, hoping she hadn't gone rogue, taking it upon herself to do this outside official channels. If he had to describe Hannah in one word, it would be *firebrand.* And true to that nature, she was incendiary.

The only reason they had been put together on a case was because no one else wanted to work with her and he had lost his previous partner. To this day, he blamed himself for his death, even though the inquiry had found him not guilty of any wrongdoing.

"Why did they pick you?" He folded his arms across his chest. "And why alone?"

She narrowed her eyes at the questions.

Not that he meant them as an insult. One thing he didn't question was Hannah's extensive experience working undercover. If anyone could immerse themselves in a different world, become a different person—quickly—it was her. Yet something else about her that made him uneasy.

"The chief picked me," she said, meaning the chief of the Laramie police department, Wilhelmina Nelson. "She thought I would make the perfect bait."

Now that she mentioned it, Hannah did fit the profile of the previous victims—blond, trim, petite, dark eyes. Although she was twenty-eight, the right clothes, combined with her girl-next-door look and small stature, would make most guess she was no older than twenty.

"You should've notified me about your undercover operation." Matt scratched at the stubble on his jaw. "It's called *professional courtesy*."

"Wasn't my decision not to notify you. Only following orders. If you have a problem with that, take it up with Chief Nelson."

The not-so-polite suggestion was only made to irk him. They both knew he wasn't going to go crying to anyone about this. "Any idea why you were given an order to cut me out of an op on my campus?"

"Three different campus police chiefs have tried and failed to catch this guy."

"And the LPD assumed I'd be the fourth?"

She gave him a one-shoulder shrug. "The University Killer has stayed two steps ahead of your department and evaded capture for almost a decade. There's a reason for that."

"What exactly are you implying? That the perp could be someone in the campus police department?"

"I didn't *imply* anything. I merely stated a fact. You have personnel who have worked here for ten-plus years. Three sergeants and a dispatcher. Everyone else in your department either attended SWU or has lived locally long enough to be a suspect. Have they been investigated?" she asked pointedly.

He flicked her an impatient glance, not caring for the second implication belying her tone. Did she think he was incompetent? "Of course they have, including the support staff."

Ten women had been violated and murdered over the years. The killer hadn't bothered to wear a condom when he'd raped his victims, leaving behind his DNA, and had put a queen of hearts playing card with the eyes scratched out on their corpses.

Matt had only recently taken over as chief. Still, the department's failure to find the killer weighed heavy on him. He'd hoped that the killer would be dead by now or too old to resurface. But as soon as the body of Madison Scott had been discovered—the first under his watch—it had taken him a week to investigate every single person in the department.

"I took the added precaution of getting everyone to take a polygraph test." It wasn't admissible in court and wasn't foolproof, but merely asking them to take it told him a lot if any refused. Mostly it gave him another opportunity for someone to slip up. As a detective, he'd even had a suspect confess once when questioned about how nervous he'd been during the test. "All their alibis have been checked, but two officers didn't have one," Matt admitted.

Hannah narrowed her eyes to slits. "Who are they?"

Hesitant to share that information, he knew not disclosing it would only further raise her suspicions.

"Officer Laura Jimenez," he said, and the tension in Hannah's face eased slightly at the mention of a woman. "And Officer Carl Farran. He would've been twelve at the time of the first murder, and he readily agreed to DNA testing when he didn't have to." Matt had cleared every other employee in the SWUPD. "I realize Chief Nelson suspects there are bad apples in every department, but I hope you don't share the same tainted view." He was willing to make an exception for Chief Nelson. She'd been brought into the Laramie Police Department for the express purpose of cleansing it of all the corrupt officers, and there had been plenty buried deep. More than enough to require help from the division of criminal investigation—the DCI—under the Wyoming State Attorney's General Office. No one was prepared for the vile things that case brought to light, such as a crooked lieutenant who sold the personal information of every officer in the department, endangering families, putting the lives of kids at risk. The worst part was, the seller had never been tracked down. "My officers aren't dirty, and they're certainly not serial killers."

"My, my, Matt, you seem a bit touchy regarding the subject."

To say he was sensitive on the issue would be an understatement. Not only had he worked for the LPD and had friends who had turned out to be crooked, but his cousin, Holden Powell, had gone through a scandal after his boss, the previous sheriff, turned out to be the worst of the worst when it came to corruption. For a long time, Holden had to deal with people gossiping, giving him the side-eye, wondering if he was guilty by association or how he could be so blind as to miss it.

It lit a fire under Matt to ensure his department was above board. "A dirty cop, much less a murderer hiding behind a badge, is a subject that should make any officer worth their salt touchy."

Her jaw hardened. "The campus police have turned up no leads, no solid suspects and no matches to the DNA the killer left behind. He just keeps slipping through your fingers like grains of sand."

Frustrated by the same thing, Matt had submitted the killer's DNA to a publicly accessible genetic-genealogy-testing service. More than one hundred users had matched as a distant relative, possibly as close as a third cousin. It would take four to six months of research to narrow it down to a pool of people who could be the University Killer. He had a retired investigator from the DCI working on it, unbeknownst to anyone in his office. He was keeping this information on a need-to-know basis. Eventually, the murderer would be caught; it was simply a matter of time, which he didn't have.

"You're not faring much better on your own," Matt said. "He slipped through your fingers tonight, didn't he? You're always the daredevil, but this was reckless. And what do you have to show for it besides a wounded victim?"

She jumped to her feet, still not coming eye level even with him sitting on the edge of the desk. Putting her hands on her slim hips, she drew closer, grazing his knee with her thigh. "Better wounded than dead. That's what she'd be if I hadn't been here undercover. This op was dangerous, sure.

Not reckless. Maybe you've been playing cop too long on campus to remember the job can be hazardous."

He took a breath, not wanting to argue with her, especially when she had a legitimate point: Jessica Atkinson was alive and safe thanks to Hannah. "If you'd had backup, we might have him in custody."

"Backup would've meant a partner tailing me. This guy is really good. His setup was sophisticated. The fake arm sling and leg boot. Padded trunk to muffle noise. Handcuffs and leg irons. Which were just an added precaution because he drugs his victims before he even gets them in the vehicle. And the trunk reeked of bleach. A sign he's careful not to leave behind DNA in the vehicle. He would've spotted a partner. Maybe even sensed I was undercover as bait to trap him if someone had been shadowing me."

Hard to disregard Hannah's instincts or the fact that she had gotten more details about the way this guy operated than anyone else had in nearly a decade. Not that he liked how Chief Nelson had made Hannah bait, left to fend for herself with no backup, and had cut him out of the loop about an op on his campus. But whether it had been reckless or clever for her to be out there alone, he was no longer so sure.

"The killer never used a gun before that we know of," he said, looking for a way to get on better terms with her. "Thanks to you, we'll have ballistics."

"If only I'd had a little more time to lure him in," Hannah said, the regret in her voice palpable. "I'm sure he would've gone for me."

Half of him hoped that wasn't true despite the need to put an end to the killings. No victim had escaped the University Killer. Until tonight. The idea of this twisted psychopath setting his sights on Hannah, regardless of her training, had unease stirring in his blood. When they'd worked together and he'd seen firsthand the cavalier risks she took, which had ironically also made her successful, it'd triggered his protective instincts. Something she had made clear she didn't appreciate.

Not that he could help it or was sexist in any way. The military had programmed him to protect his country, his teammates and those in need, and to be merciless in that endeavor.

He got up and went around to the other side of his desk, putting ample distance between Hannah and himself. "Well, your cover is blown now since he got a good look at you. I trust you're not going to request to be taken off the case."

Her honey-brown eyes sparkled with a definite challenge. "You'd trust correctly."

One of the things he admired about Hannah was her spirit, her *never back down no matter what* attitude. It also worried him because one day it might get her killed.

He dropped into his chair, physically exhausted while adrenaline kept his mind sharp. "My department is going to continue investigating as well," he said. "To avoid wasting resources and duplicating effort, it only makes sense to work together from here on out. We'll make better headway faster. Besides, you could use a partner on this."

"Don't you mean, *campus police* could use a detective?"

Swallowing another sigh, he grinned. "My *advancement* to chief doesn't make me any less of a detective."

She rocked back on her heels, her face wary. "I hope you're not suggesting that you and I work together."

In his mind, there was no question about it. "As a matter of fact, I am. Is there another officer in my department who you think is more qualified? Who can keep up with you?" *Who won't let you run roughshod over them?* "Or who you can trust to have your back despite your brash risk-taking tendencies?"

Averting her gaze, Hannah smoothed a hand over her ponytail.

That was the first time he'd ever seen her speechless, and he relished being the one to have caused it. "What do you say? Unless you need to get permission from your chief before you can decide."

Straightening, she looked up at him. "I'm authorized to do what's necessary to get this guy, but I think it would be better if it was me and another *full-time* detective working this case."

Three irksome implications in one conversation. She was really trying to strike a nerve. Getting close, too. Maybe she wanted him to concede and turn over the case to the LPD.

Never one to shirk his duty, no way that was happening. The killer was targeting women on his campus, making it his responsibility. Detective Delaney would just have to deal with him.

"I'm not rusty." He'd been in the position of campus police chief for only a year. "I'll have Sergeant Starkey, my number two, manage the day-to-day stuff here, and then you'll have me all to yourself full-time," he said, knowing it was the last thing she wanted.

Her eyes flashed with annoyance, but a slight flush colored her cheeks.

Did he get under her skin the same way she did his?

For a few seconds, she just stared up at him. "The less time I spend with you, the better."

As he suspected. He wished he could say the feeling was mutual. She was a tough nut to crack. But the more she gave him a hard time, the more he itched to break past her shell to understand her better.

Being around her had him questioning whether he'd gotten it wrong. Maybe he was attracted to trouble.

"I get I'm not your first choice, or even on your list of choices." He wondered if anyone would make the cut on who she'd want to work with. She was such a loner. "But I thought we made a pretty good team on the cartel case."

A branch of a notorious Mexican cartel had set up shop practically in their backyard, processing and distributing fentanyl and methamphetamine. They had managed to find it and shut it down. No easy feat, with both of them nearly dying in the process, but she couldn't deny they'd been effective.

Hannah frowned. "Yeah, I suppose we did," she said, as if agreeing to eat a bowl of broken glass.

Good thing he didn't have a fragile ego. "I want this guy as badly as you do." Probably more. Every woman taken from his campus, violated and murdered, was one more to keep him up at night. "I think we can stop him. One more case together?"

After a long moment, she nodded her acquiescence. "Fine. I guess we're partners again. Stuck together for the sake of the greater good."

Could she look any less enthused?

Then again, of course she could. This was Hannah Delaney.

"Lucky me." His voice was thick with sarcasm. "Look, the sooner we catch this guy, the sooner you can go back to working solo."

"Just the way I like it." She stuffed her hands in her pockets. "But let's get one thing straight—I'm not following your lead or playing it safe this time."

As if she had before. Refraining from rolling his eyes, he gave his head a little shake in disbelief.

"To nail him," she said, her demeanor turning steely, "we have to do it my way."

Why was he not surprised? "I would expect nothing less."

But following her lead didn't mean he was going to abandon his good judgment.

This time around, he'd make sure they compromised and acted like partners. It was the only way for them to avoid another close call with death.

Chapter Three

Wednesday, September 18
6:00 a.m.

For the past several hours, he'd been unable to sleep. Unable to eat. All he could think about was Jessica. Her sweet mouth. Her pretty face. Her perky breasts. Her lean legs. He pictured her stripped of all her clothes and having his way with her.

But he'd lost her because of that devious cop. She'd ruined his hookup. And he'd needed it so badly.

Anger and frustration ran riot inside him, tangling and swelling into a seething mass until he trembled from the force it. He'd been denied his satisfaction. The release he craved.

Swearing, he pounded a fist on the wood railing of his front porch and stared at the flames in the firepit. His head was throbbing. Maybe he should call in sick today and lick his wounds, even though it was better to stick to a routine the day after nabbing one of his dates.

Tried *to nab but didn't quite make it.*

Last night was a mere setback. Not defeat. He was not a loser, and he would not sulk.

He was going to fight for what he wanted. Take it with no remorse.

But missing a painstakingly planned hookup stirred other emotions inside him, ones he knew for certain he shouldn't dare entertain. Like finishing what he'd started with Jessica.

No, no. No! Too risky.

He had to focus on the next step. Moving forward.

But this growing need could destroy him if he didn't do something—and soon.

His mind careened back to the cop. The slender blonde. With dark eyes. Curves in all the right places. The one who had been undercover, acting like a student. He'd noticed her. How could he not? She stood out. But he'd had others on his carefully cultivated list.

Yes, the list. Stick to the others already chosen.

He'd take a different girl. With everything going on around campus, this week was best. The timing would be perfect.

But what about the pesky cop?

He had to teach her a lesson. Punish her for the sin of disrupting his process. Toy with her. Torture her.

Then he'd kill her, too.

Smiling, he walked down the porch steps, over to the firepit, and squeezed more lighter fluid onto the flames. The fire roared higher. Smoke curled around him. He picked up the disguise he'd shed from the ground and tossed it into the blaze.

Sometimes less was more, anyway. Glasses and contacts weren't necessary. One thing he was good at—had always been quite skilled at, even as a child—was becoming a chameleon. Though the loss of the sling and orthopedic boot hurt. He'd grown accustomed to using them to lure in his prey.

He'd gotten lazy. Complacent. Now he'd have to come up with a new way to capture his birdies. He went back up to the cabin's porch.

Settling back in a rocking chair, he stared out over the woods that ringed the edge of his property. He loved the forest. Being out here alone never failed to calm him, to steady his thoughts. Rocking in the chair, taking in the green landscape, he considered the best way to achieve his goals.

Cops hated losing. Getting bested by the enemy. He smiled, now knowing exactly how to proceed.

Not only would he beat that harpy at this sport, but he was also going to humble her, break her, make her wish she had never messed with him. The thought of it gave him such sweet satisfaction.

First, he had to figure out who the hell she was. Wouldn't be hard.

With no idea that he was coming, it'd never occur to her that she should be the one hiding from him.

Chapter Four

Wednesday, September 18
10:05 a.m.

Regret flared inside Hannah as she watched the forensic artist finish a drawing of the University Killer. Last night's events replayed in her head. Bleach. Handcuffs. Plastic tarp. How close she had gotten to stopping him but had ultimately failed.

Now that psychopath was still on the loose, looking for his next victim.

The forensic artist turned the sketch pad around to show Jessica Atkinson. "Is this him?"

"Yes, that's what he looked like," the young woman said from her hospital bed, staring at the sketch of her attacker. "You got all the details right." A shiver ran through Jessica, and she pulled the blanket up to her neck with a wince.

According to the surgeon, if the bullet had hit her two inches higher, she might not be alive. Once she recovered, and after some physical therapy, she'd be able to walk without a limp. In her bloodwork, they'd found the drug GHB, gamma-hydroxybutyrate, also known as liquid ecstasy. Not only was it a common, illegal date-rape drug, but it was also the same one that had been found in Madison Scott's system. Now they knew the University Killer used GHB in the abduction of his victims as well as throughout the time he held them captive up until he murdered them.

The forensic artist, who worked freelance for local law enforcement, lowered the sketch pad. "You did great, Ms. Atkinson. I only drew what you described."

Hannah took a quick picture of the drawing with her phone.

"You can drop it off with Sergeant Starkey at the station," Matt said to the artist. "I want to get his image out there for everyone to see before noon."

Little good it would do them. "It's a disguise," Hannah said to Matt, keeping her voice low. "He's only going to change it."

Jessica grimaced at the comment.

Hannah sighed. Guess her voice hadn't been as low as she thought.

Cupping her elbow, Matt ushered her off to the side of the room. His grip was firm, and the heat of his palm seeped through the sleeve of her blazer. She gritted her teeth to keep from squirming.

Across the room, the artist uttered something comforting to the young woman that made her nod, her eyes brightening with hope.

Hannah couldn't remember the last time she'd *felt* hope, much less inspired it.

Once they reached the window, she jerked her arm free of his hand.

At six-five, Matt stood a foot taller than her. Dark haired. Overly muscled. A rough-looking part-time cowboy.

They'd worked together when he was a distinguished detective with the Laramie Police Department. Although they'd solved a tough case, he'd rubbed her the wrong way the entire time.

Two words described him best. *Too much.* Too big. Too tall. Too broad. Too self-righteous. Too smart and shrewd to be a university campus cop.

Even his energy was too disquieting. His blue eyes too piercing. All that bundled in a package that was simply too handsome.

There was no denying the last part, no matter how hard she tried, but even thinking it made her skin prickle.

Matt Granger's perfect facade was infuriating.

Too good to be true. Everyone around him believed it was real. Not her. At fourteen, she'd learned that sometimes the devil pretended to be a saint. The pretense so convincing, so calculated, that even those closest couldn't see the evil lurking within.

"Yes, it's probably a disguise," Matt said. Wearing a black T-shirt that was too tight—the only reason he purchased that size was to show off his physique—blue jeans, badge clipped on his top, walkie-talkie hooked on his utility belt and a dark brown cowboy hat, he glanced down at her with one of those disapproving looks she'd grown to despise. "But it'll take some thought and maybe a day or two for him to change it. In the meantime, not only do we have his current disguise but also his MO. We'll make sure every student will be wary of anyone wearing an arm sling or a walking boot or even asking for physical assistance."

Something was better than nothing. Hannah nodded. "We should also encourage a buddy system of some sort."

"When I took over as campus police chief, there had been an uptick in thefts and sexual assault. So I helped the university form a student organization to promote safety. I'll call an emergency SAV meeting, and we can talk to them about it. They'll spread the word quickly."

"'SAV'?" she asked, vaguely remembering seeing a flyer with the acronym.

"Students Against Violence."

"Good idea—forming the organization and talking to them." Maybe he *was* making a difference on campus. Still didn't change the fact that he could make an even bigger one working for the LPD.

He flashed a wry grin. "Did you just pay me a compliment?"

Not on purpose. Her guard had slipped. She had a tendency to go soft around him and usually overcompensated for it by turning more surly than normal. "Don't let it go to your head. I'm undercaffeinated. I had expected a delicious flat white from your fancy, expensive-looking espresso machine when I showed up this morning." Clearly, his department had a healthy budget.

"Sorry about that. It's on the fritz. My office manager is working on getting it fixed."

She'd spotted Dennis Hill fiddling around with the machine. He hadn't really seemed like he knew what he was doing. Not that she was an expert in the handyman department.

"I'll buy you a cup of coffee in the cafeteria on the way out," he offered.

She needed a triple shot of espresso at this point, but if he was buying, then she'd even take the mediocre java from the hospital.

Matt took out his phone. "I better send Sergeant Starkey

a text letting him know the sketch is on the way and what I want him to do with it."

The artist finished packing up his things and waved on his way out of the room.

Hannah went over to Jessica's bedside. "I know talking about all this is difficult, but it's important. We only have a few more questions for you." After Jessica nodded, Hannah proceeded. "Do you have a personal laptop?"

"Yeah. Of course."

"How often did you go to the computer lab?" Hannah asked.

Jessica pressed a palm to one of her bruised cheeks, resting her face in her hand. The bandage over her swollen nose—at least it wasn't broken—tugged at her pale skin. "Every Tuesday, Thursday and Saturday."

Matt stepped closer, coming up alongside Hannah. "Why only on those days?" he asked.

"I started going the first week of school. On the days when I have my engineering class—Tuesdays and Thursdays. I go on Saturdays now, too, to keep up with the workload."

Hannah made a note in her pad. "Why did you use the lab at all since you have a laptop?"

"Modeling software the university paid a license for is loaded on the computers in the lab. To use it on my personal laptop, I'd have to buy it. Costs a small fortune. Besides, my computer doesn't have the gigs to run it without the software glitching, anyway. The ones in the lab are a lot more powerful. And they offer free printing but don't advertise it. Those who know go there all the time just for that. I had planned to print out a paper for my Comm. 1 class." Tears welled in her eyes. "But I ran out of time because I wanted to catch the bus."

"You're slated to graduate next spring," Matt said. "Most students take Communication 101 during their first year. Why did you wait so late?"

"I wanted to balance some of my more challenging coursework with easier classes. Thought it would be less stressful that way."

"Which one were you enrolled in?" Hannah asked. Comm. 1—as most students on campus called it—was offered twice that quarter: either Monday, Wednesday and Friday for an hour at three p.m. or Tuesday and Thursday for an hour and a half at nine a.m. The registrar's office was going to email a copy of Jessica's class schedule to Matt before noon, but the more ground they could cover now, the better.

"The one that's three days a week," Jessica said.

A chill slithered down Hannah's spine. They'd been in the same Comm. 1 class. Hannah didn't remember seeing Jessica, but the auditorium had been packed with students, many of them blond females.

"Besides the supposed bike accident, what else did you talk about before you were attacked?" Matt asked.

Jessica shrugged. "I don't know. Everything happened so fast. One second, he was helpless and nice. Kind of sweet. Like a wounded puppy. The next thing I knew, I felt the pinprick of the needle before I was even upright from the ground, and then he snatched the keys from my hand."

Victims sometimes had trouble recalling information, not wanting to relive the trauma of the assault. "We need you to try to remember anything else that he said or did that might help us." Hannah held her watery gaze, her heart breaking for the woman and all the others who had been killed. "Any detail, no matter how small or insignificant, could be the key to stopping him before he has a chance to go after someone else."

Jessica nodded miserably and closed her eyes. A moment later, she said, "He offered to pay me back for helping him."

"Pay you back how?" Matt asked.

"With coffee at the Wheatgrass Café."

Hannah and Matt exchanged a look. She turned back to Jessica. "Did you go to the Wheatgrass often?"

"I usually grabbed lunch there. Since it was a short walk from the quad, it was convenient." Jessica's eyes flew open. "There is something else. Last night, while I was talking to him, I recalled running into him once before. I mentioned it to him."

"Do you remember where?" Hannah asked. "And when?"

"Mythology 101. But what day?" She shrugged. "Honestly, I don't know. Maybe when we had the lecture about the Titans. Last week, Tuesday or Thursday. I can't say for certain. But the class was from four to five."

"Are you sure you were the one who remembered him and not the other way around?" Matt asked.

"Yeah. I'm positive. He claimed not to recognize me."

A blatant lie after stalking her for days, weeks—who knew for how long. "To get you to lower your guard," Hannah said, thinking out loud.

"It worked." Jessica closed her eyes again for a second, just long enough for a shudder to shake her. "That's when he introduced himself. Told me his name was Theodore Cowell."

An alias, surely, but Hannah wrote it down anyway. Once they dug into the name, it might lead to something if they got lucky. She turned the page in her notebook, quickly going over all the places the other victims frequented. "Did you ever use the Sweetwater Rec Center?"

The fitness center was popular among the students. Those who took at least six credit hours a quarter received free membership.

"My first year. I took a tour and the HOPES class."

"'HOPES'?" Hannah asked. She'd seen a brochure about it but had been focused on other things.

"It stands for Healthy Options for the Prevention and Education of Substances," Matt said. "They teach students to make healthy choices."

"The class wasn't preachy or judgmental at all." Jessica rubbed her arms. "I learned a lot."

"Do you remember who gave you the tour or who led the class?" Hannah asked.

"It was the same person—Perry Slagle."

Hannah made a note. She remembered the guy. He had approached her, offering to give her a tour, but she had declined. Perhaps that had been a mistake. "How often did you go back to the rec center?"

"I go swimming once a week. Great pool. Nice facility. But I honestly use the rec center more to decompress. I make appointments a couple of times a week to use the relax-wellness pod or the massage chair."

"Appointments online?" Hannah asked, writing it all down.

"Sometimes. You can also go to the Athletic Training Room the same day to see if they have any openings. Other than that, I bike everywhere during the day to keep the pounds off. At night, I always used the Secure Ride shuttle. I heard it's supposed to be safer."

The service was separate from the normal school bus, which ran a preplanned route on campus. Secure Ride only operated on weekdays from six p.m. to two a.m. and all day on the weekends. Students could also use the Secure Ride app to be picked up or dropped off at any location within the town limits during those hours.

"It is safer and has cut down on the number of DUIs and alcohol-related accidents," Matt said. "My department highly advises all students to use the free service."

"How long has the university had the program?" Hannah asked.

Matt met her gaze. "About twenty years."

Hannah arched a brow at him with a knowing look. They needed to investigate the drivers. He nodded in silent agreement.

Jessica wrapped her arms around her midsection. "Do you really think the guy who attacked me is the University Killer?"

"Yes." Hannah gave a solemn nod. "We do."

"I can't believe I fell for his act." Jessica's shoulders sagged as tears fell from her eyes. "How could I be so stu—"

"Hey, don't do that to yourself," Matt said, cutting her off, his voice warm and soothing. "What happened wasn't your fault. This guy is a predator. A cold-blooded killer who preyed on your kindness."

Hannah recognized the guilt swimming in Jessica's glassy eyes. She knew better than most how easy it was to allow an encounter with darkness to snuff out your own light. "Is there anything else you can remember?"

"No." Jessica sniffled, and Matt handed her a tissue. "I'm sorry."

So was Hannah. "You should seek counseling on campus. Talking to someone about what you went through could help you heal and move forward."

Therapy had helped Hannah make sense of her past. Of

discovering her father was a monster. But no amount of counseling had stopped her from building walls around her heart. Or had changed her mind that love was a game for the foolhardy.

Matt scrubbed a hand over his jaw with a distant look like he was thinking about something. Hannah made a mental note to follow up on it. He wasn't the type of partner to withhold information, but it could slip a person's mind to mention it.

"I'll have an officer posted outside your door twenty-four-seven until we catch this guy. We'll keep you safe," Matt said. He had assigned campus cops to stand guard in twelve-hour shifts, from nine to nine.

"Try to focus on rest and recovery." Hannah pressed one of her cards into Jessica's cold hand. "If you remember anything else, please give us a call."

On their way out, the assigned officer, who was seated in a chair beside the door to the room, jumped to his feet. Carl Farran.

"You don't have to get up every time I pass you," Matt said.

Farran stood ramrod straight at attention. "Yes, Chief."

Hannah and Matt made their way down the hall.

She slipped her notebook into her blazer's pocket. "I don't think it's a good idea to have him on guard duty until his DNA results come back officially clearing him."

"Duly noted," Matt snapped, and the know-it-all hotshot kept walking without a glance at her.

"That's it? You're not pulling him?"

"No. I am not." As she opened her mouth to protest, he raised a hand, silencing her. "When the first victim was murdered almost ten years ago, Carl was twelve and weighed ninety pounds soaking wet. I know that because I checked with his former pediatrician. Does that sound like the rapist and murderer of a grown woman? Or one with the knowledge to cover their tracks?"

She looked back at Officer Farran over her shoulder. He had sat down and was watching them walk to the elevator. Lanky and unassuming and baby faced, he didn't look like a twisted killer. But neither had her father. "No, it doesn't, but you're the one who likes to keep everything clean. Having a suspect, who hasn't been formally cleared guarding our witness is messy. Not to mention reckless." She'd been itching to throw that word back in his face. It had hurt when he'd called her that.

With anyone else, their insults and judgments didn't bother her. For some reason, only Matt got to her. She hated that he thought she wasn't good at her job and wasn't a smart detective.

"Label it what you want," he said, not looking the least bit fazed. "Carl is not a suspect. He's a person of interest at most, and even that is a stretch. I've got to use my people efficiently. In order to prevent this guy from snatching another woman, I need my most experienced officers patrolling campus. Not babysitting."

"You agreed to do this my way."

Stopping short, he pinned her with a stern look and nudged the brim of his cowboy hat up with a knuckle. "I did. And I will. But on this, don't push me. We've got plenty of reasons to fight. A common-sense decision shouldn't be one of them."

Matt was a stickler for the rules and playing things by the book. His motto was *No such thing as too careful*. This approach was out of character for him. Then again, she'd never seen him in charge of a team or a department with people to manage. Either way, she wasn't going to push this, since Farran was too tall—only a couple of inches shorter than Matt—to be the man she had encountered last night. The guy they were looking for was between five-ten and six-foot, possibly five-nine. Footwear could alter height an inch or two. "We need to see if there's surveillance footage of the Mythology 101 class."

"Not sure how much help it will be, since he was wearing his disguise, but I'll have Starkey look into it, along with a list of drivers working when Jessica and Madison Scott rode the Secure Ride," Matt said.

"Our perp mentioned the Wheatgrass Café for a reason. All ten victims frequented the place." She'd made an effort to swing by the café twice a day while undercover.

"Might just be because it's familiar to everyone on campus, but I think we should check it out, too. Let's grab coffee there instead of the cafeteria," he suggested.

"We also need to speak to the Comm. 1 professor," Hannah said. "Every victim took the same class."

"Right along with every other student. It's a prerequisite to graduate, regardless of your degree."

"Even more reason to talk to him."

"The only problem is that over the past nine years, the instructor has changed four different times. Other than the syllabus, the classes have nothing in common."

Frustration bubbled up in Hannah. "Great." Bye-bye to a possible lead.

"Except for one thing." Matt pressed the call button for the elevator. "The location."

"Go on," she said, gesturing for him to elaborate.

"The auditorium is right across the hall from where Dr.

Bradford Foster has held his classes for the past eleven years. He teaches two popular courses. Psychology of Crime and Justice and Psychology of Serial Killers. That's not all—one of the victims from the last time the University Killer surfaced was a student of his."

"His field of expertise would enable him to know how to be a serial murderer without getting caught."

"My thoughts exactly."

The elevator chimed.

"When we were wrapping up with Jessica, you got that look in your eye," Hannah said.

"What look is that?"

The doors opened, and they stepped on.

"Like you found a piece to the puzzle."

He shook his head. "I wish. After that poor girl almost blamed herself for what happened, I thought about how different serial killers go after their victims."

Hannah hit the button for the lobby. "There's more to it than that." She could tell by his strained tone that he was filtering his ideas. "I hate it when you hold back." Only his thoughts. Not his criticism.

"It's nothing, really. A few nights ago, I streamed a movie about Ted Bundy. I was thinking specifically about him. The ruses he used to lure his victims to the vicinity of his vehicle. A plaster cast on a leg. A sling on one arm. Sometimes hobbled on crutches. Then he asked for assistance in carrying something to his vehicle. Our guy did practically the same thing. Almost as though he'd watched the movie and had taken notes."

"You're right." Hannah's mind churned over what Matt had said. "His MO is pretty similar." She took out her cell phone.

"What is it?" Matt asked.

"You might be on to something," she said, typing into the search engine. She hit Enter, pulled up the page she was looking for and scanned it. Two paragraphs down, she found it. "That son of gun." She turned her phone so Matt could see the page. "Ted Bundy was born *Theodore* Robert *Cowell*."

"The name he gave Jessica."

The elevator stopped, and the doors opened once more.

"This is some kind of game to him," she said, getting off the elevator with Matt. "He puts the queen of hearts playing card on the body of his victims." She kept her voice to a whisper as they headed for the outer doors. "He is bold enough to rape them without a condom, leaving behind his DNA."

"He's not afraid of getting caught. Brazen. Must be confident that he's not in any database."

"Not yet, anyway," Hannah agreed. "But the amount of bleach he used in the vehicle is a sure sign he didn't want to leave DNA there. On his victims is fine, but not in the car. Why?"

"Control, is my guess. The body he discards, while the car is his domain, a part of his hunting ground. He spends a lot of time in it and wants to keep it clean. Hence, the bleach."

She was impressed by his insight. "Makes sense." Further proof he was wearing the wrong badge. Working with him had been a challenge on multiple levels, but they had closed one of the toughest cases of her life. Maybe together they could do it again.

With a whoosh, the outer doors opened, and they stepped outside into the brisk morning air. She shivered against the crisp breeze and glanced at Matt's bare arms. "You're not chilly?"

"I run hot."

"Why does that not surprise me?" Everything about the guy was hot. Matt Granger definitely had raw physical appeal.

Shake it off, she mentally chided herself.

"You're one to talk," he said with a smug expression. "All I get from you is fire or ice."

She couldn't deny it and wouldn't apologize for it. "We all deal with stress differently." Even the stress of sexual tension, but her current source was about this case. "I feel like there's this clock in my chest, counting down to when our guy makes his next move." They only had twelve days left in the month for him to claim his next two victims. "He's been so slippery for so long." She was terrified of failing yet again.

"I bet he didn't plan on firing his gun. He only did it because you surprised him. It was a mistake. Ballistics will be back tomorrow. It might turn up something."

The murderer using the university as his hunting ground strangled his victims, which wasn't quick or easy. The act was personal and didn't leave ballistics traces.

Matt put his hand on her shoulder, giving it a light squeeze, and she found his touch reassuring even though she wished she didn't. "No matter what game this sicko is playing, we're going to make sure that in the end, he doesn't win."

Chapter Five

Wednesday, September 18
12:25 p.m.

As Matt opened the door to the Wheatgrass Café, his cell phone buzzed. He took it out of his pocket and glanced at the caller ID. "It's Starkey," he said to Hannah. "Order me a large black coffee with two pumps of vanilla syrup."

She made a gagging face over the amount of sugar. "I thought you were buying."

He whisked out his wallet and tossed it to her. "What's up?" he said, answering the phone and walking away from the entrance.

"Flyers with the University Killer's likeness have been made and printed."

"You included the warning at the bottom in bold, red font?"

"I read the text you sent, Chief. It's done. The flyers are being put up all over campus as we speak, starting with the quad since it gets the most traffic. I sent a copy to the news station. It'll air within the hour and from there around the clock. I also emailed a copy to Erica Egan."

Matt's blood pressure spiked at hearing the name. "I don't

want my department dealing with her. She only writes sensationalized articles with flagrant disregard for the feelings of innocent people." The woman had written stories that had wounded members of his family. Mostly his cousins Holden and Sawyer and his new wife, Liz. "My department doesn't do her favors. You got it?"

"Sorry. But we wanted a copy to go the *Laramie Gazette*, right?"

"To the *Gazette*. Not to Egan. Send it to the editor in chief next time."

"She slipped me her card one day and said if I had anything for the paper that it should go directly to her. What's the problem?"

Pinching the bridge of his nose, Matt shook his head over the sergeant's naivete. "Did she slip it to you one day or one night over drinks while she was cozying up to you in a bar?" Dead silence on the other end of the line was the only answer he needed. "May I remind you that you are a married man? With kids?" Granted, they weren't little, but even at eighteen and twenty, they'd feel the impact of an affair. "Don't mess up a good thing."

"I didn't go home with her. Only a little harmless flirting," Starkey said, but Matt knew there was nothing harmless about that viper. "She's nice."

Matt huffed out an annoyed breath. "And pretty. And sexy." The kind weak men found irresistible. "And willing to cross any line to break a story and see her name in the byline below the headlines. Stay away from her. Do we have an understanding?"

"Sure do. I'll get the flyers disseminated."

"Hold on. I need you to find out if there are any surveillance videos of the Mythology 101 class last week on Tuesday and Thursday. I want to know if there's any footage of our guy interacting with Jessica Atkinson. Also, get with transit services about the Secure Ride app. We need them to give us a list of drivers who picked up or dropped off both Atkinson and Scott."

"Roger that."

"Where's Dennis?" Matt asked, needing his office manager to handle something for him.

"He's still tinkering around with the espresso machine."

"I want him to call everyone on the SAV contact list and set up an emergency meeting at six o'clock in the lobby of the Student Union." Most of them would be done with their classes by that time, and the building was adjacent to the quad, making it easy to get to the dorms for those who lived there.

"I'll tell him."

"And I want of stack of flyers waiting for me there so I can pass them out at the meeting."

"We'll make it happen, Chief."

Matt disconnected, tucked his phone in his pocket and headed back inside the café. Hannah was at the counter with two large to-go cups and a couple of protein bars in front of her, notepad out, and talking to the manager, a woman in her fifties or sixties.

"Ma'am." He tipped his hat at the manager and read her name tag: Barbara S.

"This is my partner, Campus Police Chief Matt Granger," Hannah said.

"I'm aware." Barbara offered a pleasant smile. "The school paper did a wonderful piece on you. As I was telling Detective Delaney, you're looking at my usual crew. They work flex hours between them Monday through Friday, five a.m.

to six p.m. I work at the register on the weekends. It's a lot slower when classes aren't in full swing. Other than that, they fill in when they can." She gestured to her staff.

Matt looked over at the workers. Four of them—two girls and two boys. They were barely twenty years old. One guy had braces, and the other—at two hundred pounds and five-five—didn't meet the physical description. "How long have they worked for you?"

"A couple of them since last year," Barbara said. "The other two are new hires that started right before the quarter began."

"Does anyone run deliveries for you?" Hannah asked.

"We only deliver to the university hospital and the campus police department. Otherwise, I'd need a dedicated runner. As it stands right now, I send one of them to make the deliveries and I handle the register while they're gone."

Matt picked up his cup and a protein bar. "Thank you for your time."

Sipping her coffee, Hannah strolled out of the café ahead of him. Her long blond hair was loose, swaying a bit as she walked and catching the late-day sunlight when she stepped outside.

On the sidewalk, he faced her. She wore a navy blazer over a fitted V-neck tee, jeans, booted heels, her badge clipped to her belt and her gun holstered on her hip. Even though she still had a dewy glow to her complexion and appeared younger than her age, without the ponytail, there was no hint of a girl. Standing in front of him, she looked formidable—all woman.

He held up the protein bar. "Is this supposed to be a power lunch?" he asked, wondering what happened to the woman who loved hearty meals.

"More like a power snack. I remember you need sustenance every couple of hours, or you get cranky. And trust me, I prefer it when you're not cranky." With a hint of a grin, she handed him his wallet. "I'm surprised you trusted me with it."

"Why?" He took the leather bifold and slipped it back in his pocket.

"Who simply hands over their wallet?"

"You're my partner, not a stranger. It's not as if you're going to steal my credit card number. Plus, I don't have anything to hide." He opened the protein bar and bit into it.

Tipping her head to the side, she studied him for a long moment.

"What is it?" he asked, her silent scrutiny making him uneasy.

"Nothing. Just trying to figure you out." She took a sip of coffee and put her bar in her pocket. "Peel beneath the *perfect* outer layers."

Perfect? The way she'd uttered the word didn't sound like a compliment, but he was the first to admit that he wasn't without flaws. "I could say the same."

A quirk of a smile played around one corner of her mouth. "If you want to know me, you're wasting your time. There's nothing more to me than this—a woman with a badge and a gun, determined to put the bad guys away no matter the cost to myself."

How grudgingly she let go of bits of herself. "Maybe that's all you *want* there to be, but there's more." *A lot more.* And he was going to do some peeling of his own.

"Believe what you want." She threw on a pair of sunglasses and looked away. "I say we speak to Slagle next."

"The Sweetwater Rec Center is only three blocks over," Matt said. "Want to walk and stretch our legs?"

"We may as well. I need to burn off some energy. Besides, the College of Arts and Sciences building is right across the quad from the fitness center."

Matt ate his protein bar and finished his coffee on the fifteen-minute walk. He chucked his trash in the waste receptacle near the front doors of the rec center. "Do you know what this guy looks like?"

"Buzz cut. Dark hair. Brown eyes. Clean shaven every time I've seen him." She opened the door, and he walked in behind her. "Lean and wiry. Easy to tell he works out a lot. A bit under six feet. Looks like he could be in his late thirties. Real chatty. I found it off-putting. And he's very enthusiastic."

The facility had been renovated and expanded a few years back. At twenty-thousand square feet, it was massive and state-of-the-art. If Matt had time to indulge, he'd use the equipment here, but plenty of work on the ranch kept him fit.

"Can I help you?"

He turned his attention to a woman sitting at the reception counter behind a stack of towels.

Hannah flashed her badge. "We need to speak with Perry Slagle. Is he around?"

The woman's smile faltered as she looked at the badge prominently displayed on Matt's shirt. "Sure." She picked up the phone and pressed a button. "Hi, Perry. The police are here to speak with you." She listened for a moment. "Okay. I'll let them know." Hanging up, she glanced at them. "He's about to get someone set up in the CryoLounge Recovery Chair. He'll come out front as soon as he's done."

"Will he? How nice of him," Hannah said. "Where can we find him?"

"In the Wellness Room." She pointed over her shoulder. "Back through there."

Hannah stalked off like she knew where to go.

Matt trailed along, his gaze darting around. Glass, mirrors, sleek equipment and sweaty bodies as far as the eye could see.

They passed a large sign that read *Wellness Room*. It didn't take them long to find Perry standing beside a student the size of football player, who was reclining in what appeared to be a comfortable space-age lounge chair.

"I've got it programed to gradually decrease the temperature since it's your first time, buddy. But trust me," Perry said, talking a mile a minute, "you're going to feel incredible afterward and even better over the next few days. Say goodbye to muscle fatigue. This is just as effective as an ice bath, without the inconvenience of getting wet."

Hannah sighed. "What did I tell you?"

"Maybe he'll talk himself into a confession."

"Perry Slagle," Hannah said, and the guy turned toward her. She held up her badge. "We need a word with you."

"After thirty minutes, you'll be good to go." Perry patted the student on the shoulder. He came over to them with a pleasant smile, his eyes bright and sparkling with energy. "I told Mindy I'd be out front in a sec." No hint of an attitude in his friendly tone.

"We didn't feel like waiting," Hannah said, guiding him out into the hall.

"What can I do for you?" Squinting, he stared at Hannah. "I know you. You refused to take a tour last week. Didn't even want to see the fifty-two-foot rock wall. Everyone wants to take a gander at that thing, even if they don't ever climb it. I thought you were a student."

"I'm Detective Delaney. This is Campus Police Chief Granger. We're investigating the murder of a student, Madison Scott."

"Oh yeah. I read about that in the *Laramie Gazette*. So sad."

"Did you know her?" Matt asked.

"We weren't friends, if that's what you mean, but I remember her. Talking to her. Seeing her here."

Hannah took out her notepad. "Did you happen to give her a tour?"

Perry shrugged. "I don't know. It's possible. We don't keep records of tours, but I give them all the time. I love getting people excited about the facility and fitness."

"Do you know if she took your HOPES class?" Matt asked.

"As a matter of fact, she did. Last month. Sweet girl. She also brought along her roommate. I encourage the more, the merrier for my HOPES class. Unlike some substance abuse–prevention programs that rely on a fear-based approach and promote a *just say no* message, HOPES takes a more positive approach and focuses on harm reduction. I recognize that college students are young adults, who have the intellectual capacity to make responsible, informed decisions about their substance use. Heck, I've an eighteen-year-old enrolled here myself."

Hannah looked up from her notes. "Do you keep records of who attends those classes?"

"We have to. The class is mandatory for all first-year students, as well as those who transfer in with less than sixty credits and those who are twenty-one years of age and younger."

Matt and Hannah exchanged a quick glance. That would've been every victim.

"The gym is open from five in the morning until ten at night," Matt said. "What's your work schedule?"

"I'm usually here during the weekday from nine to three, but I also do personal training outside of those hours. I'm off on weekends, unless I have a one-on-one class."

"Must be nice to have such a flexible schedule," Hannah said.

Grinning, Perry folded his arms, his T-shirt exposing rock-solid biceps and powerful forearms. "My wife certainly appreciates it. She's a nurse at the university hospital. Works nights. I pick up the slack with the kids. And when Tina is off, I get extra me-time."

"'Kids'?" Matt asked. "You only mentioned you have a kid going to SWU."

"He was our surprise baby when we were seniors here ourselves. We decided to wait to have more. Our other son is twelve and our daughter is ten."

Three kids. Sounded stressful. "Where were you eleven nights ago, on Saturday the seventh, between twelve thirty and one thirty in the morning?"

They didn't know the precise time Madison Scott had been taken, but they did have a time of death.

Perry's gaze darted around as he thought about it. "That was Labor Day weekend. My wife took the younger ones to Boise to visit her parents. On Saturday, I was home, watching the football game. SWU versus Las Vegas. Started at eight forty-five. Didn't end until almost one in the morning. Went into overtime. Good game. Our star quarterback,

Linder, is going to be a first-or second-round draft pick—mark my words."

"Did you watch the game alone?" Matt asked.

"Yeah."

Hannah finished writing. "Where were you last night between ten and eleven p.m.?"

"I was home with the kids. My wife was at work."

"What time do they go to bed?" Matt asked.

"Eight thirty, if they've got school the next day. Otherwise, ten."

"Are your children good sleepers?" Matt gave an easy smile to keep the guy from getting guarded. "Any trouble with them getting up in the middle of the night asking for water? Nightmares? That sort of thing?"

"I'm lucky. I've got sound sleepers. I cut off liquids one hour before bed. And don't tell my wife, but if one is acting restless or cranky, I give them a kiddie sleep gummy."

No alibi for Scott's murder, and he could've easily snuck out last night while his kids had been asleep. Now for the hard part. "Would you consent to giving us a DNA sample?"

Perry's smile fell. "Why? I'm not a suspect, am I?"

"We're looking at common connections between the victims," Hannah said, "and you happen to be one of them. The sample would take thirty seconds. A buccal swab. We brush a Q-tip on the inside of your cheek. That's it. Then we can cross you off our list."

Perry nodded, unease glinting in his eyes, his jaw tightening. "Yeah, yeah. That makes sense. But kind of sounds invasive, too."

"It would be really helpful," Matt added.

"I want to help. I do. I've got nothing to hide, but I still don't see how I figure into the equation."

"Of course you don't, and the sooner we don't have to look in your direction, the better for everyone. How about you come by the station after work today?" Matt asked. "It'll only take a second. I promise."

"I can't." Perry lowered his head, his gaze shifting around. "Today isn't good." He looked up at them. "I think I might want to talk to my wife and a, um, a lawyer first. Is that okay with you?"

They'd lost him. He would never voluntarily give a DNA sample after speaking with a lawyer.

Hannah stiffened, probably sensing the same. "Sure."

"Am I free to go now?" Perry asked.

Matt nodded. "You are. If we have any additional questions, we know how to find you."

Perry hurried away down the hall, not glancing back at them.

"All the victims have the HOPES class in common. They have *him* in common." Hannah pointed at Perry.

"Not to mention he had opportunity with Scott and Atkinson." It was difficult to ask people to recall where they were two to three years ago, much less nine.

"Maybe we give him a couple of days to squirm. To worry. I doubt he'll talk to a lawyer and certainly not his wife. Raising the subject with her could cause marital strife. Then, when he doesn't think we're still looking at him, we speak to him again. Lean harder—and next time we'll bring the buccal-swab kit with us."

"Let's go talk to Dr. Foster." Matt turned for the entrance. "We might have better luck with him."

Chapter Six

Wednesday, September 18
1:45 p.m.

At the College of Arts and Sciences building, Dr. Foster's class was still in session.

"What time does it end?" Hannah asked, staring at one of the SWUPD flyers that had already been taped on the wall.

Along with the drawing of the suspected University Killer was other pertinent information: Male. White. Approximate height. Medium build. His use of medical devices and request for assistance as a ploy. The vehicle driven, a dark SUV—possibly a Chevy Tahoe or GMC Yukon, after she had reviewed plenty of makes and models and had narrowed it down.

At the bottom, in bold, red text, was a warning:

Be advised that the suspect is most likely wearing a disguise and his physical appearance may change. Stay alert. Use the buddy system.

"Two thirty," Matt said.

Hannah glanced at her watch. They'd have to wait forty-five minutes.

She spun around and faced the large auditorium doors across the hall. "His class ends right before Comm. 1 begins. He could easily watch students flowing into the room. It's usually packed. I'd say two hundred, maybe more. Fifty-three percent of the student body is female." Hannah fished out her notebook and flipped through the pages. "The Mythology 101 class that Jessica took was Tuesday and Thursday at four p.m. Do you know if Dr. Foster has a class at that time?"

"Easy enough to look up." He grabbed his phone and did a quick search of Foster's classes. "He doesn't teach on those two days this quarter."

Pivoting on her heel, she eyed the doors to Foster's room. There were two ways to approach it. Wait until the doctor was finished with his class and then catch him off-guard. If they went in now, they'd lose the element of surprise—but by the same token, their presence might rattle him. "Why don't we sit in and listen to his lecture? We might learn something."

"It's your call."

On the walk over, to keep the chitchat with Matt to a minimum, she'd read the professor's bio, getting up to speed on him. Divorced. Two kids. Both attended SWU. He'd written a couple of books, worked as a consultant for the Seattle Police Department before he relocated from Washington to Wyoming. Now she was ready to see him in action.

She pulled the door open and crept inside. Matt followed behind her into the dimly lit room. Unlike the auditorium across the hall, this one was much smaller, seating fewer than fifty.

Dr. Bradford Foster was at the front of the room, standing before his presentation as he clicked on to the next slide. His gaze flickered up to Hannah and Matt as they found seats in the top back row.

"The making of a serial killer is never clear, and every case won't fit inside the same box," the professor said. "Many factors can lead a person to become a violent adult, from causality to mental illness. There is so much variation between each serial murderer, one cannot generalize them beyond the simple definition that they have killed at least two victims with a cooling-off period between those murders, ranging from hours to years. With that being said, there tends to be common characteristics that can be found in the psychopath personality disorder. Lack of remorse and empathy. A strong impulsivity. The need for control." Foster walked around the front of the room, using lots of hand gestures. "Not every psychopath is a serial killer, but rather, various serial murderers present some psychopathic traits. A charming personality. Pathological liar. Like to think of themselves as all-knowing. Have great self-esteem but also some antisocial traits." He brought up the next slide. "Now, let's look at causality before we dive into today's notorious killer."

The students were absorbed in his lecture, their gazes following his every movement more than looking at the slides. Most seemed to be recording the class on their phones and laptops rather than taking copious notes.

Hannah had to hand it to him—Dr. Foster was an engaging orator. He had a fluid way of dissecting the minds of psychopathic killers, identifying their uncontrollable urges, anger, excitement or the need for attention as the drive for the offender's behavior. His style lessened the danger and with that, the degree of fear one should have regarding a brutal monster.

"I like to alternate between examining serial killers of the past with those more recently brought to light. Last time, we looked at Jack the Ripper. Today, Edward Ressler."

Hannah stiffened in her seat, her blood going cold.

Dr. Foster clicked onto another slide, bringing up a picture of her father. Suddenly, it was like all the air had been sucked out of the room and she couldn't breathe.

Matt leaned over, bringing his mouth close to her ear, putting a gentle hand on her forearm. "Are you all right?"

Frozen, she couldn't immediately respond. Matt must have sensed or seen her distress but didn't know the cause. No one knew Hannah's real identity, that she was Anna Ressler, the daughter of a serial killer. Not even Matt.

She stared straight ahead at the image on the screen, right into the familiar dark eyes, and nodded.

"Sure?" he whispered, the concern in his voice tugging at her heart.

Hannah cleared her throat. "Yeah. Fine." She was anything but fine. She wanted to run from the eighteen-by-twenty-four picture enlarged on the screen, out the auditorium, through the front doors of the building and keep going until she forgot she was the spawn of pure evil.

"Even though he targeted mostly women in his county in Colorado, he was known as the Neighborhood Killer. He tortured and murdered more than forty people," Foster said, a burning ache building in Hannah's chest. "Ressler was known as an upstanding pillar of his community, who attended church weekly. A good husband. A devoted father."

Hot bile rose in her throat. It was all true. Before he was caught, her childhood memories had been fond ones. Standing on his toes and twirling around in the living room, listening to folk-rock music. Hiking in the Rocky Mountains. Church on Sundays. Weekend fishing trips. Grilling in the backyard.

Heart-wrenching images flooded her, and she struggled to push them away. She tightened her hands into fists, her nails digging into her palms.

"His wife, Mary-Beth, was married to him for twenty years and claimed she never suspected a thing. After he was arrested, he later admitted that when he got married, he stopped killing for a while—that cooling-off period—because of his wife. He was able to bury his alter ego. You might be asking yourselves, *Then what happened to make him start up again?*" A dramatic pause for effect. "He became a father," Dr. Foster said with a chuckle.

Some of the students laughed along with him.

But the words were a blistering hot knife in Hannah's chest. She'd heard it all before, but each time, the emotional wound reopened as though it had never healed.

"Ressler claimed the stressors of parenthood drove him to release his rage and thirst for blood once again," the professor said. "Ironically, it was his daughter, Anna, who led to his capture and arrest."

Sweat rolled down Hannah's spine. Her heart raced with dread. To have her father, her life—*her misery*—dissected like a lab rat, the intestines picked at and examined under a microscope as a lesson for these kids who had no concept of what it meant to live with and love someone truly evil.

Finding it hard to breathe, she pressed her fingertips to the base of her throat. Her pulse thrummed under her skin. Unwelcome fears of betrayal and loss tangled together and curled around her chest like choking vines.

Dr. Foster pivoted and glanced at the clock on the wall.

"Okay, guys, we're going to stop here today because we're out of time."

The class groaned in unison while Hannah exhaled a breath of relief.

Foster went to the wall and turned on the bright lights. Hannah squinted against the harsh glare. Students began packing up their things.

"Are you sure you're okay?" Matt asked, putting a palm on her knee. "You're pale as death. Look like you've seen a ghost."

What were the odds that Foster would lecture on her father today?

Hannah unclenched her hands. "I'm nauseous." That was putting it mildly. She wanted to puke. "Probably just low blood sugar." Another lie.

"Well, that's because you didn't eat that four-course lunch you bought us with my money," he said, joking about the protein bar. "You want to eat before we talk to Foster?"

Unable to stomach anything, she shook her head. Better to get this over with and then get some fresh air. "Come on." She gave his shoulder a tap, got up and headed down the stairs, passing the students filing out.

Once she reached the bottom of the stairs, a thought filled her with dread. What if Foster recognized her? Who she really was? Anna Ressler, spawn of the Neighborhood Killer.

The pictures of her in the media were of a fourteen-year-old girl. Surely Foster had refreshed his memory, going over everything about her father before the lecture.

She slowed, letting Matt walk ahead of her.

Matt gave her another concerned glance before approaching the professor. "Excuse me, Dr. Foster, we'd like a word with you. I'm Campus Police Chief Matt Granger, and this is my partner, Detective Hannah Delaney."

She would've preferred it if Matt hadn't mentioned her first name, even if it had been slightly changed. She went by her mother's maiden name, and *Hannah* was close enough to *Anna* for Foster to piece it together if she looked familiar to him.

Searching Foster's eyes for a reaction to her name, she spotted a flash of recognition, but then it was gone. It must've been nothing.

"Good afternoon, Officers." Bradford Foster switched off the projector. "What can I do for you?"

The professor stood around five feet, ten inches tall and, for a man of fifty-two, was extraordinarily fit. His polo shirt hugged firm biceps and a trim waist. He had a full head of thick hair feathered with gray. His smile was gleaming white and friendly, his teeth straight.

"We'd like to speak to you about the resurgence of the University Killer," Matt said.

"Really?" Foster grabbed a blazer hanging on the back of his chair and pulled it on. "Would you like to take a look at the case and consult? I did a little freelance work for law enforcement in Seattle before I took the job here. They found my insight invaluable."

Another wave of nausea swamped her, and she put a hand on the side of the desk to steady herself. "We're aware of your freelance work—but no, that's not why we're here."

"Then what is it?" Foster asked, his face tanned and glowing like he invested in good skincare products.

Hannah took out her notepad. "Did you know Madison Scott?"

A slight frown crossed his face. "The young lady who was murdered a few days ago? No, certainly not."

"She took the Comm. 1 course right across the hall from this room," Matt said. "You may have seen her in passing, in between your classes. May have even spoken to her."

Foster straightened. "If so, I don't recall."

Matt reminded him of the date of her death. "Where were you that night between two and four a.m.?"

"I was home. Asleep. Alone," Foster said in an arrogant tone, like it was a challenge.

"Did you know Isabel Coughlin?" Matt asked.

Isabel had been the University Killer's last victim almost three years ago. Thirty months, to be precise.

Foster considered the question. "The name rings a bell."

"It should," Matt said. "She was one of your students before she was murdered. You gave her a C in this course."

"I can't remember everyone. Perhaps she should have paid closer attention to my lectures." Foster closed his laptop and tucked it inside his leather messenger bag. "I do my best to empower my students with the tools necessary to spot psychopathic tendencies and avoid danger."

Hannah tightened her grip on her notepad at his callous tone.

Matt mentioned the day and time of Isabel Coughlin's death. "Do you recall your whereabouts?"

"I do not. It was a long time ago."

She hadn't bothered to jot down any notes because she could tell how this would go. "What about last night? Where were you between ten thirty and eleven?"

"Why? Was another woman abducted or attacked? If you let me take a look at the case file, I'm sure I could be of help."

Matt pulled on a tight grin. "Just answer the question. Where were you?"

"Home. Watching TV."

"Alone?" Hannah asked.

"As a matter of fact, yes." His confidence didn't waver for a second.

Hannah put her notepad away. "What were you watching?"

"A cooking show." Foster flashed a self-assured grin. "I think I'll try making the beef Wellington with truffle mashed potatoes and pairing it with a nice Bordeaux. More than enough for three. I could have you two over, and we could discuss the case like colleagues while I give you input."

A hard pass on dinner with this smooth talker. She wasn't sure she'd be able to stomach a meal with him.

Matt stepped closer, invading his personal space just a bit. "What vehicles do you own?"

"I drive a light blue BMW Z4. Why?"

Winters in Wyoming must be tough for the professor with a Z4. Next to impossible to drive through more than five inches of snow. Accumulations of ten to fifteen inches or more for a single storm weren't uncommon. Most people around there who had a little sports car also had a second vehicle, something a bit more rugged.

"Would you consent to DNA testing?" she asked. "Simply to rule you out so we can move on to real suspects."

"I think not." Foster picked up his messenger bag and slung the strap on his shoulder. "The idea of my DNA sitting in a database makes me uneasy."

She bet it did, but she also reminded herself that even innocent people were cautious.

"How about letting us take a look at your vehicle and where you keep it?" Matt suggested. "I'm sure it's a beauty and you like to park it in the garage."

The point was to get in the door with consent and then

push the boundaries of their exploration a bit to see what they might find.

Foster chuckled, showing his pearly whites. The smile was more feral than friendly. "How about you get a warrant, and then you can take a look?"

Hannah heard the bitter defensiveness in his tone and knew then that it was time to pivot.

The professor brushed past them, going toward the stairs.

"We didn't mean to offend you," Hannah said, starting after him. "We're just following procedure." He kept walking. "On second thought, discussing the case over some wine and beef Wellington sounds like a good idea."

She still didn't want to break bread with the man, but the idea of having access to his home and getting a sample of his DNA was appealing.

Foster stopped on the steps and turned around slowly. "So one of you can tiptoe off to my bathroom, find my comb and put some of my hair in an evidence bag? Or pocket a fork I used?" He shook his head. "Do you take me for a fool, Detective Delaney? The opportunity to graciously accept my assistance is gone."

Matt came up alongside Hannah. "Only a guilty person or someone with something to hide wouldn't cooperate with us," he said.

"Au contraire. If a person is innocent, there is no obligation to prove it to the police. Every smart citizen should take this approach. Trying to convince the authorities to reverse their suspicions only exposes a person to considerable risk with little to no benefit. It's one of the things I teach in my Psychology of Crime and Justice course. You two should enroll. I guarantee you'd both learn plenty."

Hannah stepped closer to Foster, drawing his smug gaze.

"You don't have an alibi. Probably because of your antisocial traits despite your great self-esteem. Charming?" She didn't think he was, but his students seemed to. "Check. All-knowing? Check—at least, *you* think you are. Need for control? Check." She didn't mention *pathological liar*, but given enough time with him she could probably check that one off, too.

They stared at each other until his face turned from cocksure to uncomfortable.

"My students love my charm and wit, and my controlled nature has served me well," Foster countered. "I see no reason to apologize for being an expert in my field. Yes, apparently, I knew one of the victims, and another took a class across the hall from where I teach around the same time."

"All the victims took a class across the hall from where you teach," Matt said.

Foster didn't bat an eyelash. "Coincidence. Nothing more. Yes, I have no alibi for Madison Scott's murder or for whatever related incident might have happened last night that you're also investigating. But what about motive? Let's say for argument's sake that I am the University Killer. What would have angered me or enticed me to kill after all this time?"

Another challenge. Testing them.

"Last month, you were passed over for tenure," Matt said. "I heard you didn't take it well."

Foster's expression went deadpan.

Hannah gave him a small smile. "Sounds like a motive to me."

"I'm an esteemed professor and was given assurances that I'd make tenure next time. If that's all you've got, let's see how you two fare getting a warrant." Foster took a couple more steps, stopped again and looked back at them. "You local cops, regardless of what city or small hick town, are all the same," he said with disdain. "Never recognizing when you're out of your depth, outmatched and outsmarted. Or when you could use assistance from an expert. Not working with me is your loss. But let me give you a piece of advice, not that your egos will allow you to take it—you could use help from a profiler. Otherwise, he's going to kill two more women and then go quiet again for a few more years. And when he does, you'll wish you had accepted my initial proposal for me to provide input." He hurried up the steps and out of the auditorium.

Matt folded his arms and leaned back against a chair. "What's your assessment of him?"

"Even if he's not the University Killer, I don't like him. He has this air of superiority. Too controlled, with that all-knowing smugness, which, by the way, are characteristics of a serial killer that he listed."

"Agreed."

"And the last bit about recommending we use a profiler felt twisted. Like he was using reverse psychology. Make us feel inadequate so we double down and prove that we can catch this guy without any outside assistance." *I see you, Bradford Foster—and your little mind games.*

If only they had a profiler on the Laramie PD. She'd go straight to them with the case file.

"Agreed," Matt said again.

She looked at him in disbelief. "Come on, you've got to have more thoughts than that. I can see it on your face that you do."

"Am I that easy to read, or have you made studying me your hobby?"

He wasn't easy to read. Not one little bit. "Your thoughts?"

"I think since he lives on campus, I'm going to have an officer tail him in plainclothes. May as well rifle through his trash while we're at it and get a sample of his DNA to be on the safe side."

Sometimes there were moments, such as this one, when they were in perfect sync instead of in opposition, and she wanted to give him something more affectionate than a high five or fist bump.

"I also think that, reverse psychology or not, the professor was right." Matt took out his cell phone. "We need a profiler."

Once again, they were of like mind. "You say that while you're dialing as though you have one in your contacts list."

By way of admission, he smiled and gave a small shrug.

This man never ceased to amaze her.

Chapter Seven

Wednesday, September 18
3:10 p.m.

“Thanks, Liz. You’re the best. Tell Sawyer I’m looking forward to seeing you guys at Thanksgiving.” Matt hit the disconnect button and met Hannah at the top of the steps in the auditorium.

While he was on the phone, she had done laps around the room, going up and down the steps countless times. The woman had boundless energy. But he’d noticed she still hadn’t eaten.

“Well?” she asked him as they pushed out the doors into the corridor.

“Success.”

Once they got outside the building, he explained. “My cousin, Sawyer Powell—”

“One of the four cousins you live with out on the Shooting Star Ranch?”

“Sort of, kind of.” That had come out of left field. “Anyway, Sawyer recently married Liz Kelley.”

“The famous FBI agent who was out here helping him investigate?”

Sawyer and Liz had been in the news almost every day during their investigation "The very same."

"She profiles serial killers?" Hannah asked.

"No. Would you listen?"

They strolled across the quad, headed back to his car.

"Sorry. My mind is racing a mile a minute. I thought doing stairs while you were on the phone would help, but it hasn't."

He understood that problem. Working until you were bone-tired—as a police chief and on the ranch—solved that issue for him. "Eating might help," he suggested, but she shook her head. Something was still off with her. "Sawyer and Liz are out in Virginia. She works at Quantico."

"Home of the profilers. She called in a favor for you." Hannah glanced at him. "Oh, sorry. Please continue."

"That's it exactly. She put me on hold while she squared it all away. Nancy Tomlinson has agreed to look at our case file because of the urgency of the situation since we know our guy is going to try and kill two more women soon. We just need to send her what we have and keep her apprised of all updates. No matter how small."

Hannah raised her palm and waited for a high five.

So help him, he wanted to wrap her in a big hug and give her a kiss. Instead, he gave her a high five.

"Okay, now elaborate on the *sort of, kind of* part," she said, and he gave her a puzzled look, wondering what she was talking about. "Your living situation. I'll admit, I've been curious since we worked together."

Curious about where he sleeps? "We don't all live under one roof. My aunt and uncle live in the main house. Logan moved into the apartment above the garage once Sawyer moved out. Holden lives with his wife in a house his parents built for them on the property. Monty also lives in a house on the ranch, but alone."

She quirked an eyebrow. "Also built for him?"

"Yep."

"What about your parents?"

Where were all these rapid-fire questions suddenly coming from?

The last time they'd worked together, she wanted to know as little as possible about him. "My dad lives in the bunkhouse. My mom…" He shrugged, annoyed. Not at Hannah. At the topic of the woman who had abandoned her family. Abandoned him.

"And you?" she asked, not pressing the matter of his mother.

Talking about himself was never easy. Talking about himself in regard to his family was, well…tricky. "The majority of the ranch will be passed down to whichever Powell son decides to run the place. But my aunt Holly wanted me to have something." To assuage her guilt. Although she had nothing to feel guilty about. The person responsible for the harm done to him and his father was his mother, Holly's twin sister. "They let me pick a parcel of land, a couple thousand acres, where I built my own house." Put his sweat and blood into that place.

"What?" Hannah stopped in her tracks. "How big is the ranch?"

"Sixty."

"Sixty thousand acres?" she said slowly, in an astonished voice.

He nodded with a grimace because he knew what was coming next. "And no, I'm not rich. Holly and Buck Powell are. Yes, I accepted the land they gave me." Albeit located as far from the rest of the clan as he could get, almost living in Bison Ridge. And only to stop his aunt from blaming herself for the pain and suffering he'd experienced as a child. "But I am paying for it." In more ways than one. "I'm creating another source of revenue for the ranch on the land."

"For the Shooting Star Ranch, on *your* land?"

Matt's jaw tightened. "It's complicated."

Her eyes were serious yet soft as she studied him. This time, it didn't make him uneasy. "This is your thing, isn't it? We've all got one. A soft underbelly. This is yours."

She was exactly right. His family, his mother, his relationship with the Powells—it was indeed his soft spot. His weakness. And his strength.

Alarm bells went off in his head. She'd been acting strange since Foster's lecture, and after they'd questioned the professor, she'd only gotten worse. Nonstop moving. Not eating. The sudden interest in him, asking a ton of questions about his living situation of all things.

Deflecting from herself.

"What's your thing?" he asked.

She rocked back on her heels, her body tensing.

"Come on, Hannah. Tit for tat."

"It's the same as yours," she said grimly. "Family."

He frowned at her honest answer, which didn't tell him anything more than he already knew.

His cell chimed in his pocket. He took it out and read the text message from Starkey.

Transit wants you to swing by to discuss your request in person.

"What is it?" Hannah asked, in that frosty, distant way of hers, putting the wall back up between them.

Matt sighed bitterly, his elation over getting help from a profiler now gone. "We need to go to Transit Services to get the names of the Secure Ride drivers."

"Then what are we waiting for?"

IN THE LOBBY of the Transit Services center, Hannah hung back while Matt strode up to the front desk.

He introduced himself. "I'm here to speak with someone about an official request for information my department made earlier today."

The person at the front desk nodded and picked up the phone. Matt glanced over his shoulder at her, sporting an inquisitive expression, but she averted her gaze.

Hannah had gone from firing a fusillade of questions at him to being brusque, all in a sloppy effort not to overshare.

Foster's lecture had left her on edge and raw, and combined with Matt's uncanny way of getting her to lower her guard—simply by being himself—she was in danger of spilling secrets she'd kept half her life.

A man with rosy cheeks and a receding hairline, wearing glasses, left one of the back offices and came into the lobby. "I'm Otis Ortiz, the supervisor."

Matt shook his hand. "Chief Granger, and this is Detective Delaney."

Now he omitted her first name.

Sweat beaded Otis's forehead and upper lip. "I received your request for information, and I wish I could be of help, but we have a policy not to give out information about our employees."

"We're investigating the murder of Madison Scott and the

attempted abduction of another student last night. The information I requested is vital. I'm sure if you fully understood the gravity of the situation, you wouldn't deny the request and subsequently obstruct justice."

Otis glanced around the lobby and met the prying gazes of the employees seated behind the front desk. "Why don't you come on back into my office?" Spinning on his heel, he hurried down the hall.

Matt and Hannah followed him into the office.

"Close the door," Otis whispered, and Hannah shut it. "Sit down."

Exchanging a glance, they both took seats, facing the desk.

"I already have the information you wanted printed, but I had to make a big show out there of not complying."

"Why is that?" Hannah asked.

Otis wiped his forehead with the back of his hand. "I'm in good health and I want to stay that way."

Matt's brow furrowed. "I don't understand. Care to explain?"

"Oh yeah, I was getting to that," Otis said in an exasperated way. "I cross-referenced the times Madison Scott and Jessica Atkinson used the Secure Ride with our drivers. Two names came up." Otis picked up a couple sheets of paper. "Bobby Evers and Shane Yates. Bobby has been in the hospital for the past four days. Since you mentioned an attempted abduction last night, I take it you probably don't still want his information."

"Why is he in the hospital?" Hannah asked.

"Appendicitis. They had to operate. He should be out in a day or two."

"Then you suppose right that we won't need his information," Matt said. "But that still doesn't explain your little act in the lobby."

"Yes, yes." Otis took a deep, shaky breath. "That brings me to the second driver and the reason for my ruse. Shane Yates," he said in a whisper.

"Is he here?" Hannah asked. "Are you afraid he'll overhear you speaking about him?"

"He's not in right now. Shane was supposed to work tonight, but he called in sick again. He does that whenever he feels like it."

Irritation ticked through Hannah. She pushed for a clear explanation. "Then why are you whispering?"

"I don't want any of the other employees to hear and then run back to him, saying I was a snitch."

Matt heaved a sigh, undoubtedly annoyed as well. "And you're afraid of him because..."

Otis stared at them like the answer was obvious. "Because snitches get stitches."

"If he's threatened or assaulted you in some way," Matt said, "we can write up a report, and it would be grounds for dismissal."

Pushing his glasses up the bridge of his nose, Otis shook his head. "I can't do that."

Matt took off his hat and ran a hand through his hair. "Why not?"

"Shane is with the biker gang."

Hannah pinned him with a glare, wishing he would simply tell them what they needed to know. "The Iron Warriors?"

That didn't sound like something their leader, Rip Lockwood, would allow. The guy was prior military and kept a tight leash on his men. He never made trouble for law enforcement. A tough guy for sure and undeniably hot if one was drawn to an edgy, bad boy on a motorcycle, but from what she knew of him, he didn't permit harassment and intimidation.

"If only." Otis shook his head. "I know Rip, the president of the Iron Warriors. We went to high school together. He even served in the Marines for a while. Good guy. Decent. He finally cleaned up the club, though it caused a big rift. All the guys doing illegal stuff broke off and formed a new club under Todd Burk. The Hellhounds."

Other than Todd Burk being a scumbag, the rest was news to Hannah. "When did this happen?"

"Last month."

"They've kept it pretty quiet," Matt said, clearly uninformed as well.

"They don't want to draw any unwanted attention." But Hannah was surprised she hadn't seen any new biker cuts around. Maybe she'd been too busy to notice.

"Where does the new gang hang out?" Matt asked.

Otis sat back in his chair with a grim expression. "Rip gave them the clubhouse of the Iron Warriors."

Whoa. The clubhouse was a single-story building that took up almost half the length of a city block. Rumor had it that every member had his own bedroom there so when they partied, they each had a private place to crash. It was her understanding that they had a bar, game room, armory, conference room, gym and dance area, complete with stripper poles. Handing over control of the facility was no small matter. "Why on earth would he do that?"

"To prevent bloodshed, I guess." Otis shrugged. "Todd didn't want to form a new club, and he didn't want to abide by Rip's rules," Otis said. "A lot of threats were made. Rip gave the Hellhounds the clubhouse to make the transition a peaceful one from what I've heard."

"And you're afraid to report or fire Shane because you think the Hellhounds will cause trouble for you if you do?" Hannah asked.

"Heck yeah, I'm afraid. And I don't *think*. I *know* they will."

"Then we'd bring them in," Matt said. "You'd press charges, and we'd put them away."

Otis flattened his lips into a grim line. "They would send a couple of prospects looking to earn their patches, wearing hoods, to bust the windows of my house and harass me. Even if you did catch them, the Hellhounds would make the next punishment even worse. It's just easier to keep Shane, not let anyone know I snitched and spare myself the misery."

"Give us his home address," Matt said.

Otis handed them the paper he was holding. Not only did it have Shane's address but also his schedule and his picture at the top of the page.

"Yates didn't work last night," Matt murmured.

Hannah stood. "If anyone asks whether you gave us any information, simply tell them you were forced to comply with a court order, and you'll be fine."

Otis's demeanor told her he was unconvinced. "For my sake, I hope so."

Matt took out a business card and grabbed a pen. "I'm giving you my personal cell number." He scrawled on the back of the card. "Call me day or night if you get any blowback on this." Putting his hat on, he stood and walked over to the door. "Thank you for your assistance."

They left the office and strode toward the lobby. Matt handed her the sheet on Shane Yates. She folded it and put it in her pocket.

One of the employees behind the desk eyed them as they pushed through the double doors, exiting the transit center. She looked over her shoulder and spotted the guy picking up the phone, his stare still glued to them.

"It's a good thing we drove over here," she said, headed for his campus police SUV.

"Why is that?"

"Because I have a sneaking suspicion that if we have any chance of catching Yates at home, we'll need to hurry."

Chapter Eight

Wednesday, September 18
4:05 p.m.

As Matt turned down Blackberry Lane, the street where Shane Yates lived, a motorcycle went roaring past them, the rider wearing a Hellhound biker cut, with long, curly hair flapping in the wind.

"Do you want to bet that's Yates?" Matt did a U-turn, tires screeching.

"No need to bet." Hannah glanced down at the picture of their suspect. "It's him, all right."

"How did you know he was going to bolt?" Matt asked. Hannah was good and had great instincts, but that bordered on clairvoyance.

"I saw the employee at the front desk that you spoke with make a call while he was watching us leave."

Matt pressed down on the gas pedal, speeding after Yates. "Might've been nice of you to mention it."

"Hey, I told you we needed to hurry over here."

She had, but still… "Full disclosure would've been better."

"Duly noted," she said, with an underlying tone of displeasure.

He could always tell when she disliked something he'd said to her. This time around working together, calling her *reckless* and uttering *duly noted* were on the list.

Yates glanced back at them and picked up his pace. He took the next corner hard and fast.

Whipping the steering wheel to the right, Matt stayed after him. "I'm sorry I called you reckless. You *can* be—" no doubt about that "—but you weren't last night. To go undercover, alone, to catch the University Killer was gutsy." Still, it irked him, but he couldn't question her bravery or commitment. "And I shouldn't have used such a harsh tone with you when I said 'duly noted' about Farran back at the hospital. I can be overly protective of my people." He took another sharp turn and gunned the gas pedal to keep up with Yates.

Matt flicked a glance at Hannah.

She'd shifted in her seat, facing him, eyes wide, she gaped at him.

He looked back at the road and at Yates. "What? Shocked I'm capable of apologizing?"

"Actually, no. You're the type who would. You care enough about other people. You're empathetic and believe an apology can make a difference. I'm just surprised you noticed those things bothered me."

"I'll make you a deal," he said. "I'll try harder to be less offensive if you try to be less passive aggressive." Yates turned into the parking lot of the Hellhound's clubhouse, and Matt cursed.

Hannah turned to see what had made him swear. "Oh, great. Instead of questioning one Hellhound, now we'll have to deal with all of them."

Yates had parked his bike and ducked inside the building

by the time Matt pulled into the lot. He put the SUV in Park, killed the engine and grabbed the handle to open the door.

Hannah placed a hand on his bare forearm, stopping him, her fingers warm against his skin. "I'm sorry, too. For being passive aggressive. When you called me reckless, all I heard was you saying that I was a lousy detective."

"Far from it." He gave her a half grin. "You're the best I've worked with." He thought about Joe, the partner he'd lost, and a pang cut through him. Shoving it down, he got out of the car.

Hannah climbed out and popped some gum into her mouth. She offered Matt a piece, and he declined, not in the mood for bubblegum.

They strode toward the front door, but before they reached it, Todd Burk pushed through, stepping outside, along with two other Hellhounds carrying shotguns.

Todd had been in trouble with law enforcement since they were in high school together, and Matt wasn't too proud of a period when he'd hung out with some of the Iron Warriors. But even as a teenager, no charges had ever stuck to Todd.

The Iron Warriors had given him the fitting nickname Teflon.

"I believe you're lost." Todd gave a Cheshire cat grin, his black hair slicked back, looking every bit the part as leader of an outlaw motorcycle gang. He checked out Hannah, his gaze sliding over her with a sleazy look, and then licked his lips. "It'd be best if you got back in the vehicle and got off our property."

The other two men leered at her as well. Her face and body were lean and honed, but with enough curves to turn heads.

"Not lost." Matt put his hands on his hips. "Here to speak with Shane Yates."

"Don't know anyone by that name," Todd said. "Do you, boys?" He turned to his buddies, and they shook their heads.

"Knowingly lying to a law enforcement officer during an investigation is a Class 1 misdemeanor, punishable by up to twelve months in jail and a $2,500 fine," Matt said. "You might want to reconsider your answer."

Todd smirked. "I don't even bother to contact my lawyer unless it's a felony charge. Mr. Friedman is way too expensive. And if you haven't learned by now, I don't do jailtime. It's not conducive to my social life."

Matt tipped up the brim of his hat. "I saw Yates run inside through the front door less than sixty seconds ago. I need him to come out and answer a few questions. It's not even about club business. That's all."

With a sneer, Todd shook his head. "You Powells may run this town but not my clubhouse."

Matt took two steps forward. "I'm not a Powell."

"Keep telling yourself that." Todd winked at him. "Now, you look, high and mighty campus police chief, you've got no authority here. Scurry on back to the university before I make you leave. Go on. Get gone."

The other two Hellhounds pumped their shotguns.

Hannah laughed. A great, big, loud chortle rolled out of her as she came up alongside Matt. "That is the most impressive display of testosterone I've seen since the last time I watched *WWE SmackDown*." She pushed back her blazer, unclipped her badge from her belt and held it up to Todd's face. "I'm Detective Delaney, and I *do* have authority here. Send Yates out. Now."

Todd hiked his chin up. "Or what?"

Hannah blew a bubble with her gum, letting it expand in his face until it popped.

She was good. Really good. As they were getting out of the car, she had expected things to be difficult and planned this little bit of fanfare.

"Or," she said slowly, with that piercing stare of hers that had a way of dissecting someone layer by layer, "I'm going to haul your two sidekicks into jail for obstruction and intimidation of law enforcement officers. And I'm not going to bother with you directly, since you'll simply wiggle out of trouble, as you're prone to do. But I will be back. With lots of other officers. And even if we get to speak to Yates at that point, I'm going to hold a grudge for all the extra effort and paperwork you made me go through. Then it's going to be my mission in life to make things miserable for you and the rest of the Hellhounds." As usual, her voice and mannerisms were clear and direct. Her husky tone was not dulcet, but strong and razor sharp, like barbed wire. "There are going to be raids. Lots of them. When you're riding around, cops are going to pull your guys over if you are this much—" she held her thumb and index finger apart one inch "—over the speed limit. We will invent reasons to search your vehicles, especially those vans that come in and out of this lot. And let's not forget that nettlesome little law that we usually turn a blind eye to—since it *is* the Cowboy State we're living in—that forbids a felon from possessing a firearm. We'll be shining a bright spotlight on you hence forth."

Hannah took Matt's breath away. She was glorious.

One of Todd's buddies, a burly guy with a beard, set his shotgun on the ground and backed up with his palms raised.

Matt loved watching her work—a sight to behold.

"I don't take kindly to threats." Todd stepped up to her, and Matt put his hand on the biker's chest, making it clear he wasn't allowed any closer. "I might have to send a tantamount warning in return."

Hannah lowered Matt's arm and eased forward, going toe to toe with Todd. "It wasn't a threat. It was a promise. And here's a fun fact about me—warnings don't scare me off. They only make me angry."

"You've got spunk, I'll give you that." Todd smiled. "Because I like you and I'm feeling generous, you can have ten minutes if we happen to have anyone inside by the name of… What was it again?"

"Shane. Yates." Hannah gave him a lopsided grin.

"Okay." Todd jerked his head at the man who had dropped the shotgun. The guy with the beard hustled inside the clubhouse.

"And we want to speak to him alone," Hannah said.

"That can be arranged. But only for ten minutes. Not one second longer."

The clubhouse door opened. Shane trudged outside with his head bowed, puffing on a lit cigarette.

Yates fit the basic description of who had attacked Jessica Atkinson in terms of height and build. White. About five-ten. Matt guessed the guy weighed around one-ninety. Pinpointing his age could be difficult. Might be in his early thirties and had simply lived a hard life with too much booze and smoking too many cigarettes. Or he was as old as he looked, late forties. But since the assailant had worn a disguise, his true age was anyone's guess.

"You stay safe out there, Detective Delaney," Todd said with a smirk. "The streets can be rough. Especially for a woman." The Hellhound turned to Matt. "See you around, Powell."

Matt clenched his jaw at the veiled threat to Hannah and

being called a Powell. A nasty retort was on the tip of his tongue, but he swallowed the words. The dirtbag wasn't worth it.

"Nice to meet you, Shane." Todd put a hand on the guy's shoulder. "Don't say anything incriminating."

Once Todd and his henchmen were inside, Matt snatched Shane up by the collar with one hand, bringing the biker to the balls of his feet. "Why did your buddy at the transit center need to warn you that we were coming to ask a few questions?"

Shane shrugged. "Just looking out for me, I guess."

"Say we believed that—why the need to run?" Hannah asked.

Another shrug. "I don't know. Because cops don't like bikers."

Matt sniffed around the guy's head. "I smell a lie. Do you smell it?"

"Sure do." With a frown, Hannah waved a hand in front of her nose. "Quite the stench. The next answer you give us better smell a whole lot better, or we're going to continue this conversation down at the LPD. Do you want that?"

Yates shook his head. "No."

Matt let him go. "We've got two questions for you."

"Three," Hannah amended. "For starters."

"Get on with it." Shane took another puff from his cigarette. "What do you want to know?"

"Where were you last night between ten and eleven?" Hannah asked. "And don't tell me it was in this clubhouse, because I won't trust a Hellhound for an alibi."

His shoulders sagged as he squeezed his eyes shut for a second. "I can't tell you where I was."

Better than a blatant lie. But Matt suspected this was

where the incriminating part would come in. "Well, you had better, or you're about to become our number one suspect in the university murders."

Yates looked up then, his eyes wide, almost bulging out of their sockets, his face turning pale. "I didn't kill anybody."

Hannah gave a one-shoulder shrug. "Make us believe it."

"What if I was doing something illegal?" He took another drag. "Not anything like murder or rape."

Hannah's gaze slid over to Matt, and he nodded.

"Provided that's true, you've got little to nothing to worry about. Spill it." She glanced at her watch. "*Tick, tock.* We don't have all day."

"I was making my usual *drops*. On campus. Okay?"

Narrowing his eyes, Matt snatched him up again. "Drugs? You're dealing on my campus?"

Yates raised his palms. "They're not kids. They're all adults. Pay in cash. Good customers. They ask me for it. I'm providing a service."

"Let him go, Matt." Hannah put a hand on his arm, coaxing him to comply, and grudgingly, he did.

"Prove it," she said to Yates. "Show us your texts."

If he was dealing and making drops on campus, there would be a digital trail.

Yates took out his phone, unlocked it and showed them his text messages from last night.

It was all there: the requests. Messages that he was on the way. Announcements that he had arrived with their order. The usage of slang and emojis for hydrocodone, oxy, amphetamine, cocaine, Adderall, marijuana, mushrooms, ketamine and GHB.

"You've been selling date-rape drugs on my campus?" Matt asked. "To who?"

"The frat boys, mostly. Who do you think?"

"'Mostly'?" Hannah's brow furrowed. "Has anyone—a guy, older than your usual customers—purchased GHB? Maybe more than once?"

"Uh. Now that you mention it..." Yates nodded. "Weird guy. Real creepy."

That was saying a lot, coming from a drug dealer who associated with the dregs of society.

Hannah pulled out her phone and brought up the picture of the sketch the forensic artist had drawn. "Is this him?"

"Yeah." Yates pointed to the image. "That's 666."

"Why do you call him that?" Matt asked.

"He calls himself that. Wiped out my entire stash of GHB a couple of weeks ago, and before that I hadn't seen him in a while. It's been years."

Shane Yates provided the University Killer with the drugs he used to abduct his victims.

Matt's stomach roiled. He looked at Hannah. "I can't have this guy dealing on my campus."

Alarm swept over the biker's face. "If I don't deal because I talked to you, they'll know I told you, and they'll kill me."

"And we'll promptly arrest them for your murder," Matt said.

"You'd never even find my body. You wouldn't even care if I went missing."

"Don't worry." Hannah patted Yates's cheek. "You'll keep dealing."

"What?" Matt stared at her in disbelief. "No way."

"As my confidential informant," she continued. "You're my new inside man."

Yates shook his head *no*, with a terrified look.

The doors of the clubhouse flew open. Hellhounds began filing out.

"You will," Hannah whispered. "Because if you don't, Chief Granger will shut down your operation and I'll make your buddies believe you're a snitch anyway."

The message was clear. Either way would be a risk to his life.

The Hellhounds mounted their motorcycles—at least ten—cranked their engines and revved them up to a fierce growl. The noise was almost deafening.

Their time was up, and the conversation was over.

Hannah tipped her head in a silent question to Yates, and he gave a subtle single nod.

But neither the biker nor Matt was happy about it.

Chapter Nine

Wednesday, September 18
5:50 p.m.

Hannah couldn't believe she was still arguing with Matt. They had been over it, through it and around the issue ad nauseam.

"This is why no one will work with you," he said, his eyes ablaze with anger. "Because you go rogue."

"I prefer to be on my own because of blowback and grief like this. And others don't want me as a partner—which I'm good with, by the way—because I don't play politics. I simply don't care whose feelings get hurt, so long as I get the job done."

But she couldn't run from the fact that she did care about Matt's feelings and his opinion of her. She hated that he was furious, and she hated even more that she was the reason.

"I knew you were trouble," he said, the word stinging her in an unexpected way, like the lash of a whip. "But I didn't think teaming up with you would be trouble for this campus. Do you understand that I'm responsible for the safety and welfare of these students?"

The SAV members had started to arrive for the emergency

meeting and were huddled together in the lobby of the Student Union, watching them.

She tipped her chin up at him. "I do understand." Looking around, she took him by the arm over to a corner that afforded them more privacy. "Keep your voice down. This discussion could get a man killed."

"And that man is slowly killing kids at this school." Cheeks red, he huffed out a breath. "You decided to make that guy your CI with flagrant disregard for my job or the position it would put me in."

"That's not true."

He cocked his head to the side. "What are you going to say next? That day is night, the sun is the moon, the sky is purple—"

"And pigs can fly," she said, attempting to lighten the mood, but he only glared at her. "I did take you and your position into consideration. If we stopped that biker from dealing on campus, he would only be replaced by another using different methods. With him as my CI, he's under my thumb. I can make sure that, at the very least, he doesn't sell date-rape drugs on campus anymore. And as my inside person, we might finally be able to take down Burk's entire operation. Put an end to all their drug running and dealing in this town. In the meantime, you can make sure students, like those waiting for us over there—" she pointed to the SAV kids "—are aware that their drinks might be roofied. If I can do something, anything, to limit the sexual assault on campus, I will. I get that you don't agree with my methods, but you did say you'd do this my way. I never guaranteed you'd like it. We're on the same side, fighting for the same thing. I promise you."

Matt drew in a slow, deep breath. "You're right. I don't

like it. But they would simply get someone to replace Yates after they killed him for giving up information. He's nothing more than an interchangeable LEGO block to them."

"He's scum for being a dealer, but I protect everyone I work with. Even my informants. Once he sees that and trusts me, I can turn him against the Hellhounds. Against Todd Burk."

"You do realize that you put yourself in Burk's crosshairs, don't you?"

How sweet that he cared. She was touched. "He's not man enough to come after a cop himself. He'll send some prospect when he thinks I'll least expect it."

Little did the Burks of the world know that she always expected the worst to happen and could handle anything they might dish out.

"It's easy to think that because we're cops, we're untouchable," he said. "We're not. Dirtbags like Burk can still reach out and hurt us."

No one could ever hurt her more than her father already had. Not with punches and kicks—but he'd bruised and damaged her all the same.

"I know," she said. "I'll be more vigilant. Scout's honor."

He eyed her with mock wariness. "Were you a Girl Scout?"

She smiled. "No, I wasn't. If I had been, I'm certain I would've been kicked out for mouthing off to the troop leader."

"For that or not selling enough cookies. But for sure, they would've booted you out."

They chuckled, and it was nice. Making peace with him. Seeing a sparkle in his eye rather than anger when he looked at her. He had a nice laugh, rich and full and deep. Sexy. But beneath the grin and the light amusement, she saw a sadness in him, lurking behind the perfect facade. Something dark and painful that felt familiar.

And that's what scared her about him. The part of himself he kept hidden.

Looking down at her face, he brushed a lock of her hair behind her ear, stilling her. Gently, he cupped her chin and ran his thumb along her jaw, and she flinched.

Coming to her senses, she pulled away.

He considered her for a long moment. "I get it now," he said, his voice low and solemn.

She wasn't sure if she should ask or even wanted the answer, but the words slipped out anyway. "Get what?"

"That you're more likely to flinch at tenderness than at pain."

It wasn't a question. Simply a bold, insightful statement.

One she couldn't deny.

"Chief!"

They turned in the direction of the voice that had called for Matt and spotted Dennis Hill, looking frazzled, holding a stack of flyers and waving his Stetson at them.

"We should get the meeting started," Matt said to her.

"There's no *we* in this. This is your meeting. I'm just a humble spectator."

The corner of his mouth inched up in a grin.

They went over to Hill, who was wearing a black polo shirt with *SWU Police* stitched onto it and khakis—the same as the other members of the support staff she'd seen earlier.

"Doing okay, Dennis?" Matt asked.

Hill was winded. His cheeks were flushed, his sandy-brown hair, which was long enough in the front to brush his forehead, was disheveled and beads of sweat coated his face. “Sergeant Starkey,” he said, catching his breath, “had me running around campus, putting these up everywhere.” He lifted the remaining flyers in his hands. “By the time I remembered you needed some for the meeting, I was clear on the other side of campus and had to run all the way over.”

Matt clapped him on the back. “Good exercise.”

Not quite out of shape but with a bit of a belly, Hill wasn’t fit, either. Though he had a full head of hair, it was thinning at the top and flecked with silver along the edges.

“That’s what I kept telling myself all afternoon.” Wiping his brow, Hill smiled. Laugh lines formed around his weary eyes.

“I’ll go ahead and get started,” Matt said. “While I’m speaking, hand out a few flyers to everyone. Okay?”

“No problem, Chief.”

Matt welcomed the SAV attendees, a decent crowd of about forty students. She wished there had been more, but the meeting had been called at the last minute. Although the towns of Laramie and Bison Ridge were small, the university was quite large, drawing almost ten thousand students from Wyoming, across the country and from abroad. Tuition was on the lower end, but the students poured thousands of dollars into local businesses.

Someone cut through the gaggle and put down a one-step stool.

Matt stood on it, and everyone’s gaze was on him as he towered over them. He had what Hannah could only describe as *presence*. Any room he walked in, she’d bet everyone would not only notice but also stare a second or two.

A rather distracting trait.

She backed up and leaned against a column as she listened

to him speak while Hill handed out flyers for the students to give to others, spreading awareness.

From a distance, Matt didn't lose any of his appeal. Even if it was too much. It certainly had been minutes ago, when he'd touched her. The thought sent another frisson of heat through her, which was silly, considering he'd only caressed her face.

"Don't underestimate the seriousness of this threat," Matt said. "The University Killer has already claimed the lives of ten young women, and we believe he will try to take two more before the month is over. Thus far, he has been targeting petite blondes between the ages of eighteen and twenty-two, but that doesn't mean he won't get desperate and go for a different type. Tell everyone you know. Everyone you see on campus. The more attention and awareness we can bring to this, the better."

Late-day stubble made a shadow of scruff over his cheeks and square jaw. Everything about him was hard yet enticing, from his scruples to his sculpted muscles.

A young redhead raised her hand.

Matt pointed to her. "Go ahead."

She held up the flyer. "If this is a disguise that he's wearing, how are we supposed to know what to look for?"

"A man with his height and build. Possibly asking for assistance or using a different ploy to draw you close to his vehicle, where he can drug you and toss you inside."

Bleach.

Handcuffs.

Leg irons.

A shiver ran down Hannah's spine.

"If you get an inkling that you're being followed, get somewhere safe, with lots of people, immediately. If you find yourself in a situation that feels off in the slightest, get out of there. Above all, use the buddy system. No female student should go anywhere alone, especially at night, until we get this guy. In fact, staying inside your dorms and apartments at night would be best."

"Never going to happen, Chief," said a guy wearing a university hoodie. "This is rush week."

Recruitment week for the fraternities and sororities on campus. Hannah's gut clenched.

Dennis Hill finished passing out the flyers and circled around to her. "This is the chief's first rush week," he said in a whisper, and she recalled Matt had left the LPD in October last year, right after their assignment together, to take the position at the university. "He probably didn't realize because he's been focused on the murder. I'm surprised Sergeant Starkey didn't remind him."

The redhead raised her hand again.

"Feel free to share," Matt said.

"He's right. There's going to be a ton of parties. Everyone goes, whether joining or not. It's the biggest event on campus. Most people I know aren't even planning to attend class on Friday."

Hannah swore under breath. The University Killer went after girls with only a few friends, easier to isolate. It was doubtful he'd go for someone in a sorority. But most kids attended a party or two in college, and apparently, the ones occurring this weekend would have a huge draw for all types. This was going to be a nightmare.

"Then again," Hill said to her, leaning closer and keeping his voice low, "the sergeant is probably still peeved he was passed over for promotion to chief. This is the third time."

She turned to him, and the office manager nodded with a grimace.

"Why are they planning to skip class?" Matt asked.

The same kid in the hoodie laughed. "They'll be hung over, man. The parties kick off tomorrow night."

"Thursday is the new Friday," another student called out.

Nothing good happened after midnight. The kids were dewy-eyed optimists, unaware of the dark side to college parties, which had real consequences. Overdosing. Sexual assaults. Arrests. Blacking out. Driving under the influence. Getting roofied. And too many more dire things she didn't want to consider.

"In the office, we call rush weekend 'the blitz,'" Hill said. "Because it gets crazy with the parties, and the students get quite intoxicated. *Blitzed*. Get it?"

"Yeah." The dread inside Hannah deepened, wrapping around her. "I get it."

"Which reminds me," he said, "I need to get the espresso machine fixed ASAP."

"You might want to call a professional," Hannah suggested.

"I figured out the problem. Needs a new gasket. I'm picking up a replacement on my way home." Hill glanced at the clock on the wall. "I better go before the store closes. Also, I need to get home in time for dinner, or my wife will have a conniption. If she took the time and effort to make the meal, the least I can do is eat it while it's hot. Anyway, you can look forward to an espresso in the morning."

She pulled on a half smile. "Goody."

"There's something else that's come to my attention," Matt said to crowd. "Some of the students, some in fraternities, have been purchasing date-rape drugs. It's easy to slip into your drinks. I'd prefer you to stay home this weekend."

"Not going to happen," someone called out.

Fear of missing out was driving them to attend, when fear of murder should be keeping them in their rooms, playing video games.

Matt sighed. "Only drink what you have poured for yourself. Never leave your cup unattended. If you do, consider it trash and don't drink from it again. For a party, go in groups and leave in groups. There's safety in numbers. Designate someone to stay sober and to account for everyone. This is not the time to trust strangers or to start dating. Spread the word to as many as you can. Let's close the meeting with everyone repeating what I tell you every time."

"Stay alert, stay safe, stay alive," the students said in unison and then began to disperse.

A handful of pretty ladies, including the redhead, stopped Matt, demanding his attention. From the twinkle in their eyes and adoring smiles, they didn't seem to think his brand of appeal was too much. They were fearless in their flirtation.

Did that make her a coward?

Snap out of it, Delaney.

Once he finished speaking with them, Matt made his way over to her.

"You've got quite the fan club," she said, seeing how those girls could be in awe of a handsome campus police chief. A big difference, compared to the college boys.

He shrugged nonchalantly, not showing the slightest interest. "I guess so."

"Most men aren't capable of resisting that. Young, cute, eager to please." For some reason, she was glad he wasn't like most men.

"I sense a compliment buried in there somewhere. But just in case I read that comment wrong, let me set the record straight. If I wanted young, cute and eager to please, I'd get a puppy." His expression turned grim.

Hannah could see the same concern she'd felt earlier, thinking about the upcoming parties, heavy as a boulder in her chest on his face.

"I can't believe I forgot it's rush week," he said.

"You've been dealing with bigger issues, but someone in your office could've reminded you." She wasn't sure if this was the right time to bring up what Dennis had told her.

"It's going to complicate things. I don't know how I'm going to keep these kids safe. Especially this weekend." He ran his hand over the back of his neck. "I need to pop into the office and email Liz's contact, Agent Nancy Tomlinson, what we have so far. Afterward, why don't we grab dinner and hash over the case?"

"I can't. I need to clean out my dorm room and move everything back to my place. For someone who likes to travel light, I can't believe how much stuff I brought." She'd needed more creature comforts than she realized, and then she'd needed things a real college student might've had.

"How about this? You leave your mini SUV—"

"Crossover," she corrected. At least he didn't tease her, calling it a baby SUV like he had last year.

"Leave your *crossover* at the station. We'll take my pickup to the dorm, pack everything in, go to your place, unload it and discuss the case over pizza. Or Chinese. Really anything that delivers."

It had taken her two trips to haul all the stuff. She kept half the cargo space in her trunk filled with emergency supplies. Getting stranded in the middle of nowhere, with limited cell coverage and no essentials—such as bottled water, flares, extra ammo, MREs, blankets, a medical kit, portable charger, two spare tires and her 'go bag' with clothes and toiletries—was never happening to her.

"What about my car?" she asked.

"I'll swing by your place in the morning and pick you up on my way in."

She mulled it over.

"You need to eat," he added.

She did.

"And with rush weekend starting tomorrow…" He shook his head.

The blitz. "Okay," she said. "Since you're providing free labor, I'm buying."

Chapter Ten

Wednesday, September 18
8:45 p.m.

"Maybe you could speak with university administrators," Hannah suggested, seated on the carpet in her living room, resting her back against the sofa. "Explain the gravity of the situation and have the rest of rush week canceled."

If only it was that simple.

Sitting next to her, Matt swallowed the pizza in his mouth and washed it down with a swig of the beer he'd been nursing. His limit was half a beer if he knew he had to drive. "Canceling rush is one thing, which they won't do. Quite another thing to convince students to cancel parties. That's the real draw, not recruitment. The festivities, the music, the alcohol—probably the drugs, too." His gut burned again as he thought about Shane Yates dealing on his campus. But Hannah had made valid points.

The biggest being, this could lead to stopping Todd Burk, the Hellhounds, and their drug trafficking once and for all.

"What if you made it known that you were going to have cops circulating undercover and anyone caught drinking underage would get arrested? I can't think of a better buzzkill. Parties canceled. One problem solved."

She was thinking like an LPD cop, not one working for a university. "After I accepted this position, my limitations were made painfully crystal clear to me. One of the things I'm here to safeguard is the university's reputation. If the school became known as one that uses a campus resource to give students criminal records, enrollment will plummet. Then there's the practicality of executing such a thing. I'd have to arrest eight out of every ten students. I don't have the manpower, enough space in cells—then there's the logistics, overwhelming the court system." He shook his head. "It isn't feasible."

Hannah grabbed another slice of pepperoni pizza from the open box on her coffee table and picked off the pepperoni before taking a bite. "What about the reputation of having a murderer on campus? They can't be pleased with that. Get them to institute a curfew."

"I don't have enough to justify it yet. The administration is resistant to change."

"What more do you need? Another girl dead?"

He hoped not. "They view this as a failure on my part to do my job. They want this guy caught with minimal disruption to the campus, to the administration and to student life."

She rolled her eyes. "Unbelievable."

"This is my fault, not being prepared for some of the biggest parties of the school year. I should've kept my eye on this while trying to catch the killer. I shouldn't have let it slip through the cracks."

"Hey, there's plenty of blame to go around. I say share it. With Sergeant Starkey." She took a sip of her beer. "He's been with SWUPD for years. He's aware of the parties on rush weekend. Do you know your department even has a name for it? They call it 'the blitz.'"

No. He hadn't heard about "the blitz."

"What was Starkey's alibi?" she asked.

Not this again. "Okay, he didn't bring the parties to my attention, but that doesn't make him a murderer." But it did make him a lousy second-in-command.

"Starkey knows that young women will be extremely vulnerable while there's a killer on the loose. He could've taken steps to mitigate the problem and chose not to. Why?"

"That's a good question."

"Did you know he was passed over for your position?" she asked, eyebrows raised.

"I'm aware."

"Three times."

That, he didn't know. "How are you so well-informed?"

"I'm a good listener." She grinned at him, and he wanted to caress her face, but he also didn't want her pulling away again. "What's his alibi?" she pressed.

"His wife," he said. "She swears they were home together the night Madison Scott was murdered. She has no reason to lie for him. We need to take a closer look at Dr. Foster."

"There's no way he's getting through the winters here in a Z4. Not with all the snow we get." Hannah tipped her beer up to her lips and took a swallow. "I've got an idea, but it's a tedious one."

"Let's hear it."

"We get the DMV records for every dark-colored Tahoe and Yukon that's at least five years old registered in the area. The vehicle had wear and tear on it. Comb through the records and see if he has a second vehicle he neglected to tell us about that matches the description, or if anyone else affiliated with campus does. It's a two-for-one. While checking on him, we might get a lead on a different suspect."

"Do you have any idea how many people drive those vehicles around here and how long it will take to cross-reference whether they have an affiliation with the campus? 'Tedious' is right. I'll need to dedicate an officer to do it. Then I'll need another to tail Foster to ensure he's sitting at home alone and go through his trash when the opportunity presents itself. I barely have enough to patrol and now cover the campus parties, too." Man power was a serious issue.

She set her beer down and angled toward him, their knees grazing. "I might be able to help with that."

"How so?"

"Chief Nelson told me that whatever I need to get this guy and close the case, I can have. I'll ask for Kent Kramer to keep an eye on Foster."

The guy was a good detective. One of the few to survive the LPD purge of corrupt cops.

"If I can figure out how to be sweet and ask nicely, the chief might even give me an officer for the tedious task of going through DMV records."

Matt put his arm on the sofa behind him, easing closer. As he leaned toward her, his thigh brushed the holstered gun on her hip. "You're sweet. You just don't like to let it show."

"That proves how little you know about me."

He was trying to remedy that. "You have a softer side." He'd seen glimpses of it. "One I find sweet."

She chuckled. "Name one sweet thing I've done."

"You rescued a stray cat we found outside a meth lab and gave it to your elderly neighbor because hers had just died."

"Purely self-serving. Giving her the cat stopped her from knocking on my door whenever she saw my car parked in the driveway and striking up a conversation about drivel because she was lonely."

Hannah lived in a quaint, quiet neighborhood a short drive from the center of town. In stark contrast to the Shooting Star Ranch and its vast acreage, with no neighbors to be seen for miles, the houses on her street were within spitting distance.

"You keep me fed," he said. "You didn't *have* to get me that protein bar from the café." Some liked saccharine, cloying and in-your-face. He preferred the subtle, nuanced sweetness of Hannah Delaney.

"Once again, I was thinking about myself. I made the mistake of not feeding you later in the day, and you nearly tore my head off in the Student Union over Shane Yates."

He had gotten cranky, as she liked to put it, and had snapped at her. Said things he regretted. "I wanted the pepperoni pizza, so you ordered it, even though you clearly don't eat pepperoni." He gestured to the pieces she had picked off and tossed inside the box.

"You're reaching, Granger. Getting two pizzas would've been wasteful. I'm not sweet. I'm trouble. Remember?"

"You can be both. And some trouble is worth getting into."

She grinned at him. "I think that's the best non-apology I've ever gotten."

He met her honey-brown eyes. Amusement faded from her face, uncertainty taking over. As he took her in, really looked at her, the uncertainty in her expression mixed with awareness, and his throat grew thick.

Like earlier, in the Student Union, they were connected on a different level. Slowly, he grasped her chin and brought her mouth closer. She wasn't beautiful in the classic sense but nonetheless captivating. There was something about her features—the lines and curves of her body, the fierceness of spirit—that lured him in.

He drew closer, stopping a hair's breadth from kissing her. "Sweet trouble," he whispered, aching to taste her.

A soft sigh left her mouth, her bottom lip trembling. "I could use some water." She pulled away, jumped to her feet, and took a step back, both physically and emotionally. "Do you want—"

A crash outside—the sound of glass shattering—had her spinning toward the window and Matt leaping up off the floor.

He looked out the window. Flames danced over the hood of his truck, like someone had thrown a Molotov cocktail. "Stay here," he said, moving toward the front door.

"Like hell I will. This is my house." She cut in front of him, reaching the door first, opened it and stormed outside.

He was right behind her when he heard a rustle coming from the bushes that flanked her doorway.

Whirling at the noise, he faced a man, pouncing from the darkness. The guy charged him, wrapping his arms around Matt's waist, hitting him in the midsection with his shoulder, trying to bulldoze him down. But Matt braced, taking the full force with a groan, grabbed him by his biker cut and tossed him to the lawn. On the top rocker of the leather cut was a Hellhounds patch. The rest was blank. He was a newbie, not a full-fledged member.

From the corner of his eye, he saw a second guy lunge for Hannah. No way for her to stop the tackle; checking a larger, stronger assailant was tough.

At lightning speed, she flowed backward with the blow—using the momentum and his mass to her advantage—and drove her knees up into his abdomen as they hit the ground and flipped him over with her legs.

Before Matt had a chance to be impressed, the other guy charged him again. The same maneuver—head down, shoulder lowered, hitting Matt squarely in the stomach. This time the biker knocked him flat on his back. His attacker landed on top of Matt's chest. The guy got to his knees, quickly sat upright and hit Matt in the face with his fist.

"Nobody messes with the Hellhounds!" he screamed.

Hannah grunted as though she'd been struck hard.

Blocking the incoming blows, he glimpsed Hannah tussling with the other one. Her opponent managed to scramble on top of her and pin her down. She lifted a knee into the man's midsection, which made him gasp and gag. Hannah clubbed her hands together and smashed them against the side of his head, driving him off, and she rolled away.

The wannabe member of the motorcycle gang on top of Matt leaned back, reaching for something in his waistband, but he was having trouble, like it was stuck. Instinctively, Matt realized it was a gun, and if that man succeeded in getting the weapon out, he would die.

Matt reached for the holster on his hip, drew his Glock first and aimed at the biker's center mass. "Hands up!"

A gun fired, the explosive sound of the shot stilling his heart.

Hannah!

"Give me a reason not to put a hole in you," she yelled, and he exhaled in relief. She was okay. "Get face down on the ground with your hands behind your head, and if you so much as twitch, I'll shoot you."

Matt grinned, but a pang in his cheek made him dial it back. "You heard the woman. Down on the ground."

Chapter Eleven

Thursday, September 19
1:30 p.m.

"Thanks for agreeing to do this." Hannah stood in Matt's office in the SWUPD, sneaking glances through the top half of the wall that was glass, across the hall at Matt as he spoke with Sergeant Starkey behind closed doors.

"I didn't agree," Detective Kent Kramer said, sitting in a chair, holding a cappuccino from the espresso machine Dennis had fixed. Instead of wearing his typical frumpy suit, he was dressed down in jeans and a sweatshirt. Good attire for a stakeout or tailing someone. "I'm only following Chief Nelson's orders."

Between doing the paperwork on last night's events in front of her home, getting her request for additional man power approved, persuading her contact at the DMV to assist and reaching out to the homicide division at the Seattle PD—with the time difference, she was waiting on a call back—she'd spent the morning at the Laramie PD with Matt.

"Well, thanks anyway." She handed him a copy of Dr. Bradford Foster's schedule and glanced back over at the other office.

The conversation appeared to be getting heated, at least on Matt's part, as he was doing most of the talking, while Starkey sat looking bored, giving short responses and plenty of shrugs.

"That's quite the shiner you've got there," Kent said, shifting her attention, and he gestured to her bruised face.

The Hellhound had gotten in a few solid punches before she'd been able to draw her gun. Matt had insisted she put ice on the bruise. In fact, he had gotten the chilled compress himself and placed it on her face. And for a few seconds, she'd let him, accepting his tenderness—a vulnerability she didn't let others see. But despite the ice, no amount of makeup was going to hide her black eye. So she hadn't even bothered to try.

"You should see the other guy," she said. "Believe me, it's worse." She gave better than she had gotten, but she could use a couple extra hours of sleep and some more painkillers.

Kent sipped his cappuccino. "I heard those two 'acted'—" he threw up air quotes "—on their own accord and you can't charge Burk."

"You heard correctly." Their lawyer, Mr. Friedman, had miraculously arrived at the station about ten minutes after she and Matt had hauled them in. "Their story is that no one gave them any order to attack me in exchange for becoming full members."

"Don't you mean *kill* you?" Kent asked with a raised eyebrow.

She gave a one-shoulder shrug. "You say potato, I say potahto."

He wrinkled his nose. "I'd like to know how they got your address."

"They conveniently and cleanly had a ready-made answer for that," she said with a wag of her finger. "Found it on the dark web. Sure enough, there's a site out there with my information."

"Anyone else's from the department as a result of the breach, thanks to the dirty former lieutenant?" Kent asked.

"Oddly, no. Only mine. I guess we now know who bought the information." Todd Burk. "Just can't prove it." She couldn't wait to see that man rotting behind bars, right along with most of the town.

Movement across the hall caught her gaze. Matt was up on his feet. Then so was Starkey. Matt had a good four inches on him, but Starkey was solid, with a runner's build.

Kent sighed. "You know, if you throw a frog into boiling water, those suckers just jump right out. But if you place them in a pot full of water that's room temperature and slowly turn up the heat, the frog doesn't notice the temperature change until it's nearly at a boil. And by then...well, it's too late for the poor guy to jump free."

Looking back at the senior detective, Hannah considered what he said. "Am I supposed to be the frog here?" And was the increase in temperature the toll the job took?

He tipped his head to the side with a noncommittal expression.

Hannah appreciated his wisdom but never imagined she would suffer such a fate. "I'll know when the time comes to get out."

"Are you sure about that? By the look of your face, I don't think you do. We all believe we'll know when it's time. Here I am, still in the pot, too, when I probably should've gotten out a couple years back."

The door across the hall swung open, hitting the wall with a clatter. "Why don't you see how well you do without me helping you? Ungrateful SOB." Sergeant Starkey stalked out of the office, no longer wearing his badge or service weapon.

"I think that's my cue to leave." Kent finished his cappuccino and tossed the disposable cup into the waste bin. "It looks like the professor has office hours today." He stood. "Should be simple enough."

Matt came into the office. "Hey, Kent. It's good of you to help out by keeping an eye on Dr. Foster."

"Not really," the older detective said. "I wasn't given much of a choice. The chief told me to come. So here I am. Can I get a map of the campus?"

"Sure." Matt went around his desk and grabbed one. "Here you go. Also," he said, reaching over and getting something else, "this is a permit that'll allow you to park in designated faculty-only spots. By the way, Foster drives a light blue BMW Z4." He gave Kent the license plate number.

Hannah's cell phone rang. She took it out and looked at it. "Seattle area code." She answered, putting it on speaker. "This is Detective Delaney."

"Hi there. I'm Detective Trahern. I got your message about Dr. Bradford Foster. How can I be of assistance?"

"Yes. Thanks for returning my call. I'm here with two colleagues, SWU Campus Police Chief Granger and Detective Kramer. It's my understanding that Dr. Foster helped your department catch the Emerald City Butcher."

"That's not quite how I'd put it," Trahern said. "His assistance did lead to the arrest and conviction of a suspect, Sam Lee. But something felt off to me about the case."

Hannah glanced at Matt and Kent. "Like what?" she asked.

"We never linked Lee's DNA to any of the victims."

Matt scratched at the stubble on his jaw. "Then how did you get the conviction?"

"Trophies taken from the victims were found in Lee's house. He swore he'd never seen them and didn't know how they got there," Trahern said.

"What kinds of trophies?" she asked.

"Their ID cards, jewelry, sometimes underwear."

Matt folded his arms. "Do you think he was framed?"

"No prints were found on any of the trophies in his house. Felt strange to me, but at the time, we just wanted it to be over. I don't know. Sure hope not. If so, that's on me and my partner," Trahern said, his voice rueful. "That brings me to the next thing that hasn't sat well with me. The vast majority of repeat murderers will spill the beans in custody because of their ego—or definitely in prison because if you're a big, bad killer, life behind bars is easier. I've kept tabs on Lee all these years. To this day, he maintains that he's innocent."

"Foster published a book about his work with your division," Matt said, "and takes a great deal of credit."

"I'm well aware. Whenever I see a copy of it, I get sick and want to burn it."

"But the murders did stop once Lee was arrested, didn't they?" she asked.

"Yeah." Trahern blew a heavy breath over the line. "They did. But another way of looking at it is that they also stopped when Foster left Seattle."

Kent shook his head with a grimace. "Were any of the Butcher's victims raped?"

"They were," Trahern said. "But the perp used a condom, and they had all been killed by blunt force trauma to the head. Though there were ligature marks around their wrists, ankles and throats."

"Sometimes these serial killers who have been at it for a while evolve." Kent's mouth twitched. "Get more violent. More sophisticated. Bolder."

"Does this relate to a case you're currently working?" Trahern asked.

"The University Killer has struck on and off for the past ten years," Matt said. "Each time, he abducts three women. All blond and young. Rapes them and strangles them to death."

"The Butcher's victims were young, too—late teens to early twenties—but not all blond. How is Dr. Foster involved?"

Hannah stifled the groan rising in her throat. "He's a person of interest. The murders started a year after he began teaching at the university, at least one victim was a previous student of his, he's come in close proximity to all of them and he doesn't have an alibi. When we questioned him, he tried to flip the script on us and get us to enlist his help working the case."

"That's one slippery, shady dude," Trahern said. "Did you get any DNA from the victims?"

"We did," Matt said. "Our guy didn't use a condom."

Trahern swore. "Then your University Killer isn't the Emerald City Butcher. We found the killer's hair on one of the victims. You would've gotten a match in CODIS."

CODIS, the Combined DNA Index System, was a national database of DNA profiles from convicted offenders, unsolved crime scene evidence and missing persons.

"Even if you clear Foster for your murders," Trahern said, "I would never work with that pompous, self-aggrandizing jerk ever again."

Her thoughts exactly. "Thanks for speaking with us. We won't take up anymore of your time."

"No problem. If you have any other questions, don't hesitate to reach out." Trahern disconnected.

Hannah slipped her phone in her pocket, her mind spinning. Whether or not the professor was their guy remained to be seen. "My gut tells me we're doing the right thing and should still look into him."

"Agreed," Matt said.

"I'll stick to him tighter than a Rocky Mountain wood tick," Kent said, then turned to Matt. "Hey, I never did get a chance to congratulate you on the new job. One day, you were in the office. The next, you were gone. We didn't even get to throw you a going-away party."

Matt shook his head. "Parties are for retirements and promotions."

Kent extended his arms. "This is a promotion. One worth celebrating." He patted Matt on the back, and Hannah rolled her eyes with a sigh.

"Not to everyone." Matt lifted his head, his gaze meeting hers.

Kent waved a dismissive hand in her direction. "Don't let this sourpuss rain on your parade. She doesn't know how to be happy when it comes to herself. Unrealistic to expect her to be happy for others. Delaney will find the one dark cloud in the sky on the sunniest of days."

Wow. Could his opinion of her be any lower? "I'm standing right here. Where I can hear you," Hannah said. "And for the record, I know how to be happy." She just *hadn't* been in a very long time.

"Sure, you do. You wouldn't know happiness if it kissed

you on the lips, Delaney. You'd shoo it away, mistaking it for a threat."

She put her fists on her hips. "I believe the phrase is 'If it hit you in the face'."

Kent chuckled. "A Hellhound hit you in the face last night. Did it feel like love? *Poor thing.* Love isn't supposed to hurt."

Yet it did for her. Worse than anything else.

Kent looked back at Matt. "Give me a call one night, and drinks will be on me, Chief Granger. Well, I better get cracking." Kent left as quietly and subtly as he had entered.

"I see your chat with the sergeant didn't go well," Hannah said, desperate to change the topic. Starkey had called him in to show him the surveillance footage of the Mythology class right as Kent had arrived, and things took a turn.

"I'll get to that in a minute." Matt closed the office door and leaned against the desk, crossing his arms as he regarded her steadily. "Kent made a good point. I've worked hard to get to where I am. Why do you begrudge this promotion that I earned?"

Taken aback, she stiffened. "I don't."

"You do. Every chance you get, you undercut it. Imply that I'm some kind of coward for taking it. You literally accused me of *hiding out*."

Dropping into a seat, Hannah pressed her palm to her forehead. This was a conversation she'd rather not have, but if he insisted, then so be it. "You're the best detective I've ever worked with. Patient and dispassionate when necessary. Shrewd. Gifted at lasering in on perps in a way that I've never seen before. Like you sense the threat. That's exactly what we need out there in the streets. To take down the Burks and the cartels poisoning this town." She looked up at him. The paradox of Matt Granger was eating away at her. “You’re a war hero. The most decorated detective in the Laramie PD. What are you doing here if *not* hiding out?”

Chapter Twelve

Thursday, September 19
2:45 p.m.

This time, Matt was speechless. He had no idea she regarded him so highly. *The best detective she'd ever worked with?*

The answer to her question wasn't easy or simple and, now faced with it, wasn't one he was fully prepared to give. He sat in the chair beside her. Tipping his head back, he stretched his long legs.

"I was Special Forces. The job involved a lot of killing and seeing buddies die and others wounded. The job was necessary, and I was very good at it, but it took a toll on me. When I came back home, I joined the LPD. I still wanted to make a difference. Always. And I thought, as a cop here—not like in some major city with a seedy underbelly—that there'd be less bloodshed. That I wouldn't have to lose anybody I cared about to the job anymore."

"And then you lost your partner," she said, her voice soft.

He looked at her and nodded. "We shouldn't have split up. But we did, and a perp got the drop on him. When I got to him, he was still alive. I held his hand and watched him slip away while hearing the ambulance only a few blocks from us. I had to explain this to his wife and his children."

She placed her hand on his arm. "I'm sorry."

"I thought I could push through it—that's what I had been trained to do. But that loss hurt more than the others. Not because he meant more than other brothers-in-arms who died. But I can't shut off my emotions any longer. I lost the ability to go numb. Then we got paired up on the cartel case, and you came so close to dying."

Tightening her grip on him, she rubbed his arm with her thumb, and he appreciated the comfort she offered, knowing it was rare for her.

"I didn't want to go through that again. When this job opened, I jumped at the chance to take it. Because I thought it would be safer. Quieter. No chance of losing anyone else I cared about." Hearing the words out loud, he could no longer deny the truth. "I guess you're right. I *am* hiding out. Or at least, I was trying to. With the University Killer back, I suppose the joke is on me. There's just no escaping the darkness and death." For so long, he'd kept everything bottled up inside, unable to unburden himself. He couldn't talk to his family, and he'd figured he'd never share it with anyone. Until Hannah.

She moved her hand to his cheek. "Not everyone is cut out for this kind of work. But we are. It isn't easy and takes sacrifice. We pay a heavy price for it so that others get to look up at the sky on the sunniest of days without seeing any dark clouds."

That's when it occurred to him: Hannah Delaney had accepted not being happy, probably thinking it was simply a drawback of the job. Plenty of depressed, alcoholic cops to substantiate that belief, but it saddened and angered him at the same time to know that she would deny herself love.

"I was wrong about you taking this job," she continued.

"How so?"

"Yes, you're hiding out, but you didn't have to stay in law enforcement. You could've easily become a full-time rancher," she said, and he had considered it. "Instead, you were drawn to the position because a threat that has eluded everyone else for nearly a decade was coming back, and I think you sensed it. This is where you're supposed to be, right here, right now—to stop the University Killer."

He had been compelled to apply for the job, but he hadn't thought of it that way. Could she be right?

Her gaze slid from his to where her palm caressed his cheek. She dropped her hand, like she just realized that she was touching him, got up and moved away, breaking the connection yet again.

She deserved so much more than she was letting herself have. If only she could see it.

"Was there anything useful on the surveillance video?" she asked.

Shoving down the raw emotions he had allowed to surface, he pulled himself together. "Not really. There was no footage inside the class to see him interacting with Jessica Atkinson—only of him in the hall, hobbling in and out of the room."

She picked up a bottle of water and offered it to him, but when he declined with a shake of the head, she twisted off the cap and guzzled half of it. "What happened with Sergeant Starkey?"

He blew out a long breath. "We got into it after I brought up how he neglected to mention it was rush week, knowing another young woman could easily be taken with all the parties that are going to happen. There was a lot of back-and-forth finger-pointing I'm not proud of, but it became clear that he wants me to fail at this job."

"Did you fire him?"

Matt shook his head. "Nope. He took a leave of absence, effective immediately. Not that I approved it, but he's got a ton of vacation days saved up."

"Better that he's gone."

"This is an all-hands-on-deck kind of situation. The more officers, the better. Now I'm down one."

She finished off the bottle of water. "You don't want to hear this."

"Then don't say it."

"I'm obliged. If it's him, we don't want him to know where officers are going to be placed and what areas will be vulnerable."

"He already has some idea. But I don't think he's the killer. A jerk? Sure. What about his alibi? His wife swore he was home."

Hannah lightly touched her cheekbone and winced. "A person can be home with someone without them actually being home."

"How do you mean?" He got up, grabbed a bottle of painkillers from a desk drawer and tossed them to her.

She caught it. "Boils down to perception. Right? Maybe he was home, at first. They had dinner together. Then he decided to go to the garage and work on a car or into the basement or attic to focus on some hobby, in whatever space he's carved out as his alone. A sacred place. Not to be violated. And while he's in there, no one is to disturb him. Easy enough to turn on a radio or television to mask the fact that he snuck out. Perhaps used a secondary vehicle that he kept parked down the block and killed someone. The entire time, the wife thinks he's home."

He sat back down and stared at her. "That was very, very specific. Alarmingly so."

Averting her gaze, she opened the medicine bottle, popped a pill in her mouth and swallowed it dry. "Just a supposition that came to me. Anyway, it's possible. Don't you think?"

"Sure. It's possible. Crazier things have happened."

"He's got a hobby, something he's into. Doesn't he?"

Most folks did. "Watching baseball." Nothing suspicious there.

"Games can last late into the night, can't they?"

The latest game he was aware of had gone into eighteen innings and hadn't ended until four a.m. "They can, but she told me that they went to bed together."

"Is that what she said? Or was it more general, more vague? Sort of like, they had dinner, he watched some baseball and they went to bed. That could mean she had dinner with the kids. While he ate in front of the television in the space that's his, where he doesn't like to be disturbed, and she went to bed. When she woke, he was beside her, and she simply assumed that he joined her shortly after she fell asleep."

He honestly couldn't remember the exact wording from any of the statements he'd taken, but he recalled the gist, and Starkey's wife was confident he had been home. "Don't forget, he passed a polygraph test, too."

She shrugged. "Maybe he knows how to beat one. They're not one hundred percent reliable," she said, and he agreed.

"Being passed over three times and forced to help the person who has the job you've coveted is a lot."

"'Coveted'? You don't hear that word often outside of church."

"Before you got him riled up, you should've asked him to take a DNA test."

"Not helpful." He shook his head. Unfortunately, Matt would have difficulty getting a warrant for a DNA test at this point since Sergeant Starkey had passed a polygraph *and* had an alibi *and* there was no evidence to justify it. "Maybe we can get Kent to go through his trash, too."

"I'll send a text, asking." She took out her phone and started typing.

"There's something that you should know. I submitted the killer's DNA to a couple of those big, publicly accessible genetic-genealogy-testing services. About a hundred users matched as a distant relative, possibly as close as a third cousin." An ideal match in an ancestry search was a parent, sibling, half sibling or first cousin. It was the DNA equivalent of hitting the mother lode. "Logan Powell, my cousin who works for DCI, connected me with one of their retired investigators to research it, but it could take up to six months to narrow it down to a pool of people who could be the University Killer." The further back the matches went, the more branches on a family tree that would have to be built out. "No one else in the office knows about this. I wanted to keep it quiet. When this guy first started killing women, law enforcement wasn't using the public genetic-testing companies to track down suspects. Now, if our guy got wind that we have tracked down relatives somehow, he might bolt and disappear."

Something close to hurt flashed in her eyes. "But why didn't you tell *me* sooner?"

He didn't really have a good reason. It wasn't anything personal. She could be trusted with the information. "Everything has been happening so fast, one thing after another. Besides, we need to stop this guy before he kills two more women in a matter of days. Does it matter that I'm telling you now?"

Looking away, she shook her head. Her phone chimed, and she looked at the text. "Kent says he'll do it—but wants us to know no one has seen Foster for a few hours. Some students have been waiting to talk to him during office hours, but he's been a no-show. One kid claims he takes off sometimes to go fishing near Gray Reef or the North Platte."

"Have Kent check Foster's house," Matt said.

"Already on it. He's headed that way now." She set her phone down. "As for tonight with the parties, we should do something unexpected."

"What did you have in mind?" he asked, his curiosity piqued.

"Can you call in a favor with your other cousin?"

She would have to be more specific. "Which one?"

"Holden. In the sheriff's department. Nelson can't afford to commit any extra officers to this case. But maybe Holden can spare a couple of deputies tonight. We put them in plainclothes and have them circulate some of the parties."

"That's a good idea." Tonight, they needed as much help as they could get.

Chapter Thirteen

Thursday, September 19
6:10 p.m.

The tempting aroma of a hamburger and fries from the Wheatgrass Café wafted through the car. Parked down the street from the university hospital, where cameras couldn't capture him on surveillance footage, he tugged his gloves back on and pulled the top off the to-go cup of the fountain drink. Cola. He squeezed in a few droplets of tetrahydrozoline hydrochloride, decongestant eye drops easily purchased almost anywhere. In case the cop guarding sweet Jessica didn't drink soda, the water bottle in the take-out bag was his backup method of delivery, which he had already spiked. The top had been opened, but he doubted the officer would even notice.

If he had gotten the dosage right, the cop would only get sick—very sick—rather quickly, sending him to the bathroom to vomit. On the other hand, if he had used too much…

Coma. Seizures. Or even death. None were part of his plan.

Although he'd have to forego his hookup with Jessica, a

necessary sacrifice, she was still his prey. Claiming her life was essential. The first punishment for the undercover cop.

Detective Hannah Delaney.

He was going to teach her the hard way—his way—that once he had decided to take something, it was his. The only lives she could save from him were those he chose to forfeit.

Her interference would not be tolerated. And would not go with impunity.

He reached over and opened the glove box. Taking out the small envelope, he smiled.

Since he would not be able to enjoy Jessica in his usual way, she would never be one of his queens. Therefore, he couldn't leave his signature calling card.

Instead, he had something special, unique, just for the detective.

He slipped it into the inside pocket of his thin jacket, which already held the syringe with the lethal dose of GHB.

His cell phone rang. He glanced over at it in the cupholder and groaned. He'd never answer right before a kill, but he recognized the number and needed to take it. "Hey, kiddo."

"Hey to you, Dad. How are you doing?"

"I'm well." He scanned his surroundings. "You excited for your first rush weekend as a full-fledged fraternity member?"

"Yeah, can't wait," his son said. "So much better than being a newbie, jumping through recruitment hoops. But Mom is driving me crazy. She keeps calling, telling me not to drink and that I'm not at school to party but to learn."

"Give your mom a break. She loves you and just wants you to stay safe, that's all."

"Why can't she be cool about this like you?"

"Moms and dads are different. I trust you to make good

choices. You'll find a balance between getting an education and having fun. Only you can figure it out for yourself. We can't do it for you, as much as your old mom might wish we could."

"Talk to her. Tell her that. Get her to back off."

"I can't get her to stop loving you or make her not worry."

"Just wish she'd keep it to herself." Liam groaned. "Are you coming to my frat's parents' weekend?"

"Sure am."

"I'd prefer it if Mom skipped it."

"That's between you and her. I am not getting in the middle."

Another groan. "It's the last weekend of the month."

"I've got it marked on the calendar. I wouldn't miss it for the world."

"Great. I've got to go, Dad. I volunteered to be a sober brother tonight, keeping an eye on things, but first I have to go to a safety meeting called by the council."

"What are you talking about?"

"The campus police chief contacted the council because he's concerned about the safety of the students, specifically the girls," Liam said. "The council asked for volunteers to be sober brothers—watch dogs, really—circulating the party, keeping an eye on things, making sure everyone stays safe."

"Really? Interesting."

"Yeah, and they're beefing up the police presence on fraternity row this weekend."

Good thing he was already ahead of the game. No stopping him. Not tonight. He smiled. "I'm proud of you for stepping up to look out for others. You're a fine young man. Have fun this weekend. Love you, kiddo."

"Me too, Dad."

They ended the call, and he refocused on the task at hand. He needed to get back into character.

Looking in the rearview mirror, he checked his new disguise. He pressed down on the beard, ensuring it wouldn't budge, raked down the hair of the mousy-brown wig over his forehead and tucked down the bill of his cap. Patting his augmented fake belly, he made sure it was secure.

"Here you go," he said, practicing his altered voice. Not quite right. Needed a stronger hint of a Southern accent and to be an octave lower. He cleared his throat. "Here you go, Officer."

Perfect.

He got out of the car and locked the door. Lowering his head in case he passed any cameras on the way, he strolled to the hospital.

In the lobby, he breezed up to the front desk. "Hi there. I've got a delivery order for the SWU police officer on guard duty," he said, holding up the to-go drink and a bag with the words *Wheatgrass Café* written across it.

The attendant smiled. "One moment." She typed on the computer. "Room 411."

"Thanks."

Keeping his head down, he went to the bank of elevators and stepped onto a car behind an elderly gentleman. "Four, please."

The older man nodded and hit the button for him.

When it had reached the fourth floor, the elevator dinged, and the doors opened. He stepped off and got his bearings. Slowly, he walked down the hall, taking note of any rooms that appeared unoccupied. He passed the nurse's station and angled his face away. A few doors down, he spotted the cop, sitting in a chair, preoccupied with something on his phone.

"Evening, Officer. Here you go." He handed the guy the drink and the bag. "Dinner, courtesy of your friends at the SWUPD."

The cop's face lit up like a light bulb, and he smiled. "Thanks. This is better than eating hospital food again."

"Enjoy." He turned and retraced his steps.

Three rooms shy of the elevator, he glanced over his shoulder. The cop had taken the straw from the bag and was inserting it into the fountain drink.

Just as he had hoped.

He ducked into a room that looked empty and slipped inside the bathroom. Keeping his gloves on, he pulled out the clothes he had concealed under his shirt that had been strapped to his body. He slipped scrubs on over everything else he was already wearing, along with a white lab coat. The ballcap, he discarded in the trash. Brand new and purchased while wearing gloves, none of his DNA was on it. He raked down the wig once more.

In a few minutes, the tetrahydrozoline hydrochloride would kick in right around when the hospital would begin their shift change and personnel would be distracted. Timing wasn't just key; it was everything.

Then he'd pay sweet Jessica one final visit.

Chapter Fourteen

Thursday, September 19
7:17 p.m.

With a heavy heart, Hannah stepped off the elevator onto the fourth floor of the hospital with Matt beside her. Officer Carl Farran had been admitted for severe vomiting, blurred vision, difficulty breathing, elevated blood pressure and tremors. Something he'd ingested had most likely been poisoned. He was on the same floor, in room 424.

Hannah and Matt each showed their badge to a hospital security guard who stood outside Jessica Atkinson's room, controlling access as they'd instructed when they got the devastating call about what happened. The guard noted both their names in a log that tracked everyone coming and going. They stepped past him.

The room was so still, quiet as a grave. Hannah went over to the bed and stared down at Jessica's lifeless face. Her brown eyes open, frozen in death.

How?

Hannah gritted her teeth. How had she let this psychopathic killer get to her? Did Jessica know what was happening before it was too late?

There were no signs of a struggle. He must have pretended to be a doctor or a nurse and had injected her arm or the IV bag.

Guilt welled up inside Hannah, making her nauseous. She looked Jessica over, her gaze landing on a small white envelope that had been placed on her stomach.

Hannah glanced around for latex gloves. Matt already had some and handed her a fresh set. She slid on a pair, and he did the same.

As she carefully picked up the envelope, her hand trembled. That monster had rattled her nerves. Deeper than she'd realized.

They examined both sides of the envelope. The back flap hadn't been sealed. With a finger, she lifted it, revealing the edge of a piece of paper tucked inside. Not a playing card, as she had anticipated. Delicately and slowly, she slid the paper free, watching to see if anything fell out along with it, like a hair or anything else. But there was nothing. Only the slip of paper.

On it, three lines had been typed in all caps. It read:

DRESSED TO REVEL, HAZE AND RUN AMOK
CAN'T WAIT FOR SITTING DUCKS LINED UP
NO PALINDROME PALADIN DISRUPTING MY NEXT HOOKUP

"This psycho had the nerve to write a poem?" Her stomach turned, disgust filling her.

"A tercet," Matt said, and she looked at him in confusion. "A poem with three lines."

"A haiku?"

He nodded, staring at the paper. "A haiku is an example

of one, but this isn't that." His lips moved like he was counting. "Each line has seven words but a different number of syllables."

She scrutinized the words. "Revel, *haze*, run amok. He must be referring to the parties for rush. He's planning to take his next victim this weekend, maybe even tonight, and he's taunting us with it."

"Look at the last line. I think it's about you," he said, with concern in his voice. "Your first name is a palindrome, spelled the same backward as forward—and technically, you're a paladin. A guardian. A protector. A warrior."

A wave of anger and frustration rushed over her. "This message *is* for me. He's gloating. Even though I saved her, he still managed to get her in the end. He wants me to feel ashamed that *I*, a paladin, failed to protect her after I promised that I would."

And he had succeeded.

Tears stung her eyes. She swallowed the sudden lump in her throat and placed the poem and envelope in an evidence bag.

"I'm the one who promised." Matt put a steady hand on her shoulder. "This monster got through one of my officers, and that's on me. Not you. Don't you dare think it's your fault."

"That's how it feels." She stared at the poem again. "The way he phrased the last line about me. He's expecting me to fail. He's confident that no matter how hard I try, no matter what I do, somehow, he's going to be two steps ahead of me and grab another woman."

Her nerves tightened at the prospect of that happening. *Not another.* She couldn't bear to lose another one.

"Why didn't he leave a queen of hearts playing card?" Matt said, thinking out loud.

She clenched her jaw, cursing the cruel animal behind all this. "The poem is so much more effective, don't you think?"

"No, what I mean is, why didn't he leave the card along with the poem?" He stared at the paper, and she could see the wheels spinning inside him. "Almost as though he doesn't consider this to be one of his ritualistic three kills."

Hannah's gut twisted as her heart sank. "Then he only went through the trouble and effort of poisoning a cop and murdering her in her hospital bed, risking exposure and possibly getting caught, just to make me pay for saving her? Because I *disrupted* his *hookup* with her?"

Sweat formed at the base of her spine. Her mind flashed back to the adrenaline-fueled moments when she had stumbled upon him trying to take Jessica. In the hours after the attack, she had replayed the attempted abduction over and over. How she had fought not to let him get the young woman into the car.

All to what end?

She stared at Jessica's cold, pale body. "He's going to rape and murder two more women."

"No. We're not going to let him." He slid his hand from her shoulder to her back. "Do you hear me?"

"What if we are out of our depth, outmatched, outsmarted?" There was no hiding the fear in her voice.

Over the years, she'd learned that a good detective kept their emotions in check no matter how bad, how scary, how deadly things got. She never let anyone see her squirm. Instead, she had always done whatever she needed to do to hold it together and deal with it later, in private.

But standing there with Matt—looking at the woman she'd

failed to protect, holding the murderer's provocative message written to mess with her—she couldn't conceal the feelings bubbling over inside.

"This guy isn't as smart as he thinks," Matt said. "We'll get him. One way or another."

She nodded, knowing that it was only a matter of time because the killer had been overconfident and made the mistake of leaving behind his DNA for the past decade. But that sick poem had her second-guessing herself, questioning her next moves.

How was she going to prevent him from taking two more lives?

"While we're here, let's find Nurse Slagle and chat with her about her husband."

"Sounds good." Hannah left the room and went up to the nurse's station. "We're looking for a nurse who works here, Tina Slagle. Can you tell us where to find her?"

"I know Tina," one of the nurses said. "She's off today. My guess is, she's at home, getting in quality time with her kids."

"Thanks," Matt said. As they walked away, he turned to her. "Notice how she said quality time with 'the kids' instead of *the family*?"

"I did. We don't have much time before the meeting with everyone to prepare for the parties tonight. But I think we should make some to swing by the Slagle residence," she said, her thoughts still twisting and churning over that sick tercet.

Dread gnawed deeper at her.

"Hey." Matt caught her by the arm. "Did you hear what I said?"

She shoved the three lines of the poem from her head. "About what?"

"We can have hospital security drop off the surveillance

footage at the station. It'll save us enough time to speak to the Slagles." He steered her toward the middle of the corridor to the wall. "I can see that poem is messing with you," he said, and she sighed, unable to deny it. "Last night, you said that I didn't know you well. But there's something about me that you need to understand." Matt drew her gaze and held it. "When I set my sights on accomplishing something, I take dead aim and systematically go over or through everything in my path until I have reached my objective."

She appreciated his efforts to reassure her but was rattled by the idea that Atkinson's death was her fault. "Have you ever been in a battle you didn't think you'd win or survive? And fear wanted to curl you into a ball and try to wish the fight away? You ever felt that?"

"Plenty of times, in the military."

This was a first for her. To not only lose but to also have her nose rubbed in it. "What did you do?"

"Kept my finger on the trigger and my focus downrange, and fought through it. The same way you will now. You're not alone. We'll stop him. You and me, together. I need to hear you say it like you believe it, Delaney. Don't let him into your head. Don't allow him to undermine your self-confidence. Don't let him strip away one of the best parts about you. Your strength. Your will. The way you fight for justice. Because that's what he wants. For you to doubt yourself. You figured out something about him. Enough to run right into him. You did it once. You can do it again. We will stop him."

The other night she had been out on her own. This time, she had a partner. One who'd proven she could rely on him. One she trusted to help her get the job done, even if they had to go into hell and battle the devil himself. "You and me. Together."

AS MATT PULLED up to the Slagle residence, which was an easy walk to the university hospital and less than a five-minute drive, Hannah opened one of the buccal DNA test kits that they had in the truck. She tucked the sealed glass vial containing a swab in her jacket pocket.

"Remember," he said, "we'll get more flies with honey."

Hannah grinned. "Well, you said I've got a sweet side. I'll try to tap into that."

Then they went up to the front door. Matt knocked.

A few minutes later, a woman with a messy black bob opened the door. She wiped her hands with a dish towel and slung it on her shoulder. "Hello. Can I help you?"

"Tina Slagle?"

"Yes?"

"I'm Chief Granger." Matt indicated his badge. "This is Detective Delaney. Is your husband home? We'd like to speak with him."

"Actually, he just got back." She opened the door and waved them in. "Come inside."

Hannah offered a small smile. "Back from where?"

"Movie theater. On my days off, I try to give him a few hours of me-time since I'll get mine when everyone else is asleep." She closed the door. "Perry! The police are here." Turning back to them, she said, "May I ask what this is regarding?"

"We're investigating the murders at the school linked to the University Killer," Hannah said as Perry entered the room. "We're examining any possible connections between the victims and trying to eliminate any that we can."

Tina narrowed her eyes. "I don't understand what that has to do with Perry."

"Uh, all the victims had to take my HOPES class," Perry said quickly. "That's all. Nothing to worry about."

"Perry, where were you earlier, between six and seven?" Matt asked.

"Today?" He raised his eyebrows. "I was at the movie theater. Why?"

Hannah flipped to a new page in her notepad. "What did you watch?"

"That silly new action movie," Tina said. "I can't stand the franchise. So Perry always goes without me."

Her husband nodded with a tight grin. "Yeah."

Matt noticed the man wasn't nearly as at ease as he had been at the fitness center, or as talkative. "Were you alone?"

Perry nodded. "Yep."

"Can we see your ticket stub?" Hannah asked.

The guy tipped his head back and to the side. "Uh, you know what? I threw it away with the receipt. After the movie."

A telephone rang in the back of the house. "Elijah! Would you answer that please?"

"Sure, Mom."

Matt smiled. "That's okay. You can pull up your bank account information right now to show us the charge. These days, it pops up like that." He snapped his fingers.

"I can't." Perry stood a little straighter. "I paid in cash."

Tina chuckled. "You never use cash. When did you go to the ATM?"

"Mom, it's the hospital! I think they want you to cover for someone."

Tina sighed. "Excuse me." She left the living room.

Glancing over his shoulder in the direction his wife had gone, Perry stepped closer and then looked at them. "What if I didn't buy the ticket? What if I wasn't alone and I don't want my wife to know?"

"A lot of *if*s." Hannah slid a sideways glance at Matt. "Who were you with?"

"It's a student. I'd rather not say who."

Matt folded his arms. "We need to know so this person can verify your whereabouts."

Perry shook his head. "There has to be another way. Without getting Tina or the student involved in this."

"Unbelievable," Tina said, coming back into the room. "I have to cover for someone. Her boyfriend almost died, and she's an emotional wreck. He's a cop. One of yours, I think." She pointed to Matt. "Apparently, he was poisoned at the hospital, and a woman was murdered." Her eyes got big. "Is that why you're here? Asking where Perry was earlier?"

"We are here to confirm that your husband wasn't involved." Hannah put away her notepad. "Since you can't prove you were at the movies," she said, looking at Perry, "one simple option is to allow us to test your DNA. No one else needs to be involved, and when we speak to the media, we'll be able to say right up front that you aren't a suspect once we have the test results."

Perry glanced at Tina.

His wife shrugged. "Why not? You haven't done anything wrong."

"Sure." Shoulders sagging, he hung his head. "I'll do it."

"Great." Hannah pulled on gloves and opened the vial, and after Perry opened his mouth, she swabbed the inside of his cheek before resealing the swab in the glass tube.

"That's it?" Perry asked.

"That's it," Matt said. "We'll send it off to the lab, and you can get on with your life." For now.

Hannah and Matt left, and they hopped into his truck.

She held up the vial between her fingers. "I've seen perpetrators agree to a DNA test only to run as soon as they're out of our sight. We'll need to get this analyzed as quickly as possible, just in case."

STANDING BY THE large whiteboard at the front of the conference room, Matt was leading the briefing while Hannah sipped on her fifth espresso of the day. He didn't know how she could handle so much caffeine, but she'd shaken off her earlier self-doubt. At least outwardly.

Two of his officers who had worked earlier in the day had agreed to stay for an extra shift, four more cops were scheduled for the evening and Holden had come through with the sheriff's department, providing three deputies in plainclothes. Nine, not including Hannah and himself, was nowhere near enough, but they'd have to make it work. They had no other choice.

"As you know, Officer Carl Farran has been hospitalized, and Jessica Atkinson, the young woman who was attacked, has been murdered. The ME is examining Atkinson's body to determine the cause of death. Doctors have managed to stabilize Carl and are running blood work on him, but they suspect food poisoning. Detective Delaney and I—" he gestured to Hannah "—reviewed the hospital's security footage, and this is what we found."

Matt played the surveillance video on the screen to the right of the whiteboard.

Everyone watched as the University Killer, wearing a new disguise, walked onto the fourth floor of the hospital, handed Officer Farran a drink and bag of food, and then ducked into an empty room. Minutes later, Carl ran to the bathroom in the hall, and the killer then emerged and entered Atkinson's room, wearing scrubs and a white lab coat, and closed the door.

"He timed this to occur around the shift change for hospital staff. The nurses were unaware of what was happening. Less than one minute later, the killer left Atkinson's room. This leads us to believe he injected a drug in her IV."

Hannah stood and held up a photocopy of the poem. "He left this for us instead of his usual calling card." She handed it to the closest officer. "Take a look at it. He's taunting us, telling us that he plans to take his next victim this weekend, perhaps tonight, mostly likely from a party. We need to show him, even though he has been two steps ahead of us, how good we are at playing catch-up."

The law enforcement officers in the room nodded, giving verbal affirmations.

"Ballistics came back on the bullet the killer fired Tuesday night. We got a print but no match to it. This weekend, starting tonight, is another chance to get him. The sororities aren't hosting any parties," Matt said, "but six fraternities are. I've spoken to the Interfraternity Council, four young men who 'govern' the frats. Although they refused to cancel, they want to be a part of the solution. They've agreed to mandate that each fraternity must have five sober members, keeping a close eye on things. Now, I'm a realist. These are kids, not trained cops. I'm not expecting much, but any extra vigilance on their part is appreciated."

The council had also pledged to find out who was using date-rape drugs and put a stop to it, but Matt wasn't holding his breath. Instead, he was going to trust Hannah to do as she had promised.

"Okay, now we're going to go over the game plan and

where I want everyone stationed along fraternity row. This is going to be a long night. Parties have been known to last until four in the morning." Groans echoed around the room. "Everyone needs to be fully caffeinated and laser focused."

The conference room door opened, and the junior officer working the front desk poked her head in. "Chief! There's a reporter asking for Detective Delaney's side of the story regarding an incident at her house, and she'd like a statement from you about the murder of Jessica Atkinson."

Before he asked the question, he knew the answer. "Who?"

"Erica Egan."

His pulse spiked. "Tell her 'no comment.'"

The duty officer frowned. "Miss Egan told me to tell you that if you responded that way, I should inform you that you'll want to hear her questions to understand in what light her stories will be framed. She has to submit her story within an hour, and she wants you to have the chance to defend yourselves."

Defend? "Give us a minute," he said to the others in the room.

Matt and Hannah left the conference room.

Her phone chimed. She read the text. "Foster still hasn't gone home yet. Kent has no idea where he could be, but guess what?"

"Tell me."

"Today is trash day for Foster. Kent collected some samples before the waste-management trucks got to it."

"I'll take any good news I can get. I'll ask Logan to get it from Kent. Have the DNA fast-tracked at the DCI."

"But they're notorious for their backlog."

"The governor increased their budget, and DCI recently

hired more people so they could handle time-sensitive requests such as this."

"Finally. It's about time. I'll let Kent know." She fired off a quick text to him and shoved her cell phone back in her pocket.

They entered the lobby, where Erica Egan was waiting. The reporter was perfectly groomed, with her hair swept back from her angular face. She wore a low-cut, formfitting sweater the color of ripe mango, tight jeans, high heels and an eager smile.

"How do you know about the incident at Delaney's house?" Matt asked, disgusted.

"Reports of shots fired by the detective during an altercation with two members of the Hellhounds motorcycle club," Egan said, not actually answering the question. "According to the leader of the Hellhounds, Mr. Todd Burk, you instigated the incident after harassing members and trying to coerce them at their clubhouse by issuing unwarranted threats not within your authority. Would you care to give your side of the story?" She shoved a voice recorder forward.

Hannah leaned in, getting her mouth close to the recorder. "No comment. That's Hannah with two h's. Do you need me to spell Delaney for you?" She smiled then, and it wasn't nice.

He hated Egan, but he loved Hannah's style.

The reporter pursed her mouth hard, and lines marred her face. "Don't say I didn't give you an opportunity to set the record straight, Detective."

"'Straight'?" Matt spat the word, full of bitterness. "You slant record, regardless of quotes, and spin stories to influence the public, who you love to claim has a right to know."

"They do." Egan's mouth pressed tight, seemingly offended. "And I'm an objective reporter."

"Cut the bull. All you care about is the number of subscribers."

"My editor cares about subscriber numbers, which have only increased, not only for the paper but online as well since I joined the *Gazette*. Controversy and spice sell, and it keeps getting me bonuses. If you don't like it, take it up with the system." She shoved the recorder in Matt's face. "Chief Granger, would you care to comment on your failure to safeguard Jessica Atkinson, a student who your department was 'protecting'," she said, using air quotes, "and why the University Killer continues to evade capture?"

Matt swallowed the angry words on his tongue. "The University Killer poisoned a police officer, making him violently ill, and murdered a young woman in cold blood. My department, along with Detective Delaney, will not rest until this serial murderer is stopped."

"Is it true that you're unprepared to keep the student body safe during the blitz of rush because you were unaware this is one of the biggest party weekends of the school year?"

He had hoped that Starkey hadn't gone running to the reporter, but her use of the term *blitz*, was making that seem less likely.

"My officers and I are prepared," he said, "and we will be taking added precautions over the next several days."

"Are you saying that no other students will be abducted and murdered this weekend because of the safeguards you're putting in place?" Egan asked.

"I can't get into the specifics of the measures we're taking, but we'll do our best to keep everyone safe."

"Two women slain thus far with you as chief. Do you think

your best is good enough? Are you willing to stake your job on it? If the University Killer strikes again and goes quiet once more, should you resign?"

"We're not gamblers," Hannah said acidly. "We're police officers. Don't forget, the University Killer has eluded other campus police chiefs."

"Yes, that's true." Egan gave a sly grin. "But eventually, they all resigned or were fired from the position. I'm merely asking because readers will want to know if it will be resignation or removal for the current chief."

Matt didn't intend for it to be either.

Hannah's mouth tightened, and her eyes were stone cold. "You're assuming it will be one or the other. We're endeavoring, tirelessly, for a different outcome."

"Chief?" Egan's gaze slid over to him. "Care to add to that?"

"My sole focus at this time is on stopping this murderer and bringing him to justice. That's all I have to say."

Egan switched the voice recorder off. Her smile was feline. "Be sure to read my article. It'll be hot off the presses at three a.m."

Based on previous experience and the way Egan had treated his family in the press, nothing she printed would be good for him, Hannah or the university. "I'll be waiting for it, with bated breath, to use it as kindling for a fire."

Chapter Fifteen

Friday, September 20
3:59 a.m.

The night had gone better than he'd planned. *Flawless.* He had never intended to infiltrate a party and take his prize from there.

Sticking to the list meant choosing a birdie who would be predictably at home. And she had been, too. Her roommate was out, no doubt enjoying the festivities of rush. But he had not expected to find another young girl asleep on the sofa. Taking the blonde without waking the other had been impossible.

Complications were always a possibility. Fortunately, he had been prepared, as always.

He squinted as he scanned the headline of the *Laramie Gazette*. He was bone-tired. But sleep wasn't on his agenda anytime soon. Still too much to do before the sun rose, and then he had a full day ahead of him.

Chuckling, he flipped to the next page of the *Gazette.* They were the fastest with new stories, so he always started with their paper. The timing had given him the chance to get one, along with a coffee, from the last gas station on his way out of town. He needed to go up to the cabin in the woods and drop off his knocked-out cargo for safekeeping.

He glanced over his shoulder and grinned, his mouth watering in anticipation of the hookup to come.

There was time enough for him to take a break. Enjoy his coffee. See what the lovely Erica Egan had to say about him. Then he'd finish making his way to the woods, only to come right back to town. His busy, busy day was just getting started.

He perused the article, wanting to give that sexy crackerjack of a reporter a kiss. Not only had she covered his handiwork at the hospital so eloquently, but she had also bashed Granger and Delaney with electric writing that carried a powerful punch. He pumped his fist in the air.

Laughing, he couldn't wait for Blondie to take a gander. He'd given her a good blow with his poem, and this article would be a hefty bit of salt in the wound.

He sat a little straighter, invigorated, and stopped reading at the bottom of page four. The article delved into a skirmish outside the detective's house, where she had discharged her weapon at 720 Sagebrush Drive.

His jaw went slack. One didn't see that every day.

A police officer's home address printed in the newspaper! A detective's, no less.

Was this luck or serendipity or karma?

No. It was *fate*. He was becoming a true believer in it.

This presented a new opportunity. He cracked his knuckles, thinking. Debating.

Only a fool would pass up a once-in-a-lifetime opportunity like this. He glanced at the red numbers of the clock on the dash. If he was going to do this, in such an unexpected manner, he needed to hurry, even though he much preferred to take things slowly, drawing out his gratification.

But this would be worth it.

Throwing the gear into Drive, he was set on his chosen course. He pulled out of the gas station parking lot and headed back to town.

Chapter Sixteen

Friday, September 20
6:25 a.m.

Hannah was wiped out and running on fumes. "Thank goodness the night was uneventful," she said as they lumbered back to his office after finishing their after-action debrief with the rest of the officers.

"That we know of." Matt entered his office. "At least on fraternity row."

She followed him inside. "You don't sound pleased by it."

"I am, it's just…when we were out there patrolling, checking on the parties, I kept getting this tingle along my spine. Usually means trouble. Something bad is about to happen."

"No news is good news." They'd even had a couple of security guards posted at the computer lab and rec center as an extra precaution.

"Having the sober brothers circulate the parties turned out to be a good idea by the council. They kept two girls from getting roofied, and the boys who tried drugging those ladies will face charges." He sat at his desk and turned on his computer. "I need to send an update to Agent Tomlinson about Carl Farran and Jessica Atkinson. Once I'm done, want to grab breakfast?"

"I'm starving." She rolled her shoulders and stretched her neck. "Hash browns, scrambled eggs, bacon and toast would hit the spot. Then I need four hours of sleep. Maybe I can get by on two."

"Sounds good. The part about the food," he said, clacking away on the keyboard. "Why not place an order at Delgado's? Then we won't have to wait for it."

She took out her cell phone and called it in. "It'll be ready in ten minutes. The person who took the order recognized my name and kindly put a rush on it since it was law enforcement."

"Ah, the little perks of the badge."

A giant yawn made Hannah's jaw ache. "I'm tired."

"Me too." Matt was still typing at his computer with a slow, methodical rhythm.

He looked bright eyed and professional and not tired in the least.

A newspaper landed on his desk. The morning duty officer stood, glaring.

"What?" Matt asked.

"You're both in the paper."

"We expected to be," Matt said.

"You won't expect what was printed," the officer said in a singsong voice. "Page four, bottom right."

Matt's face tensed.

Hannah snatched up the paper. For a moment, she wondered what awful things the reporter had written about her, especially if the woman had referred to Todd Burk as *mister.* She flipped to page four, looked down at the paragraph on the right and felt the blood drain from her face.

"How bad is it?" Matt asked.

"Worse," she said, her voice barely a whisper. "Way worse than what you're thinking."

Rage spilled over. She fought the senseless urge to tear the paper into shreds and then go find Egan so she could pummel her into oblivion.

"I want to…" She swallowed the rest of the words: *kill that woman.*

First, her address had been posted on the dark web for every creep and criminal to find. Now, this violation. Making it public knowledge for everyone.

Calmly, Matt took the paper from her clenched hands and read it, but his jaw went tight and his eyes blazed fury. "She needs to be fired."

"The editor signed off on it. Allowed it. Printed it. Because the system sucks." She ran her tongue over her teeth. "The paper will hide behind the First Amendment. They can even say it was already posted online."

"That was the dark web." His eyes still flickered with anger. "Doesn't give them the right to pull a stunt like this."

"Egan is a menace."

Matt looked back up at her. "I wanted to talk to you about this anyway. Hannah, you can't stay at your place. I was worried before, with your information on the dark web, but this ups the ante. Every scumbag in town will be prowling around your house, waiting for a chance to do only goodness knows what."

"I'll hang a Welcome sign and set up a lemonade stand. Maybe I can make a few extra dollars."

"I'm serious, Hannah. You have to find a new place to live. Today."

"Not that anyone is asking for my opinion," the duty officer said, "but the chief is right. Ms. Egan painted a bull's-eye on you—or rather, your house. You get what I mean."

Matt nodded. "Yeah, we do."

"Got a genie in a bottle who can snap his fingers and make that happen? I can't just find a new place out of thin air that fast."

"You can stay with me until you do."

She grinned. "If this is your sly way of getting me into your bed, cowboy, it won't work."

He frowned. "I have a spare room."

"My job here is done," the duty officer said.

"Thanks for the heads-up," Matt said as the guy left.

"I can't stay with you."

"Why not?"

"It crosses a line. Or *blurs* one." The truth was that if she stayed with him, she'd be tempted to break her own rules: Never sleep with someone she worked with. Never spend the night. Never get personal. No strings. Ever.

She'd already gotten way too personal. And she came dangerously close to kissing him when they'd been at her place, discussing a case and eating pizza. And worse, she had wanted to kiss him. Imagined what his lips would feel like, how he'd hold her. She still did.

Dangerous.

"You've got a choice—my place or my family's ranch," Matt gritted out. He shut off his computer. "Let's pick up breakfast and swing by your house so you can pack a bag. End of discussion."

She shoved to her feet, not wanting to discuss it, knowing deep down that he was right.

Her face ached as she climbed into his truck, but she was careful to make sure Matt didn't see her discomfort. They'd been pretty attached at the hip during this investigation. She'd left her car at her house, and they'd been using his truck, which had sustained minor damage from the Molotov cocktail the bikers had used to draw her out.

After they grabbed their order from Delgado's, they went straight to her house without bothering to eat. Seeing her address publicized had a way of suppressing her appetite. Must've had the same effect on Matt, because he hadn't reached for the to-go bag on the center console between them.

He pulled up in her drive and parked. "You should follow me in your vehicle. Don't leave it here."

"I guess I need to decide where I'm going." She tipped her head back against the seat. "Are you sure your family wouldn't mind putting me up? I don't want be an imposition."

He frowned, casting his gaze down like that wasn't the choice he was hoping for. "Positive. Plenty of rooms. My aunt and uncle would put you in a separate wing from theirs."

"A *wing*? Is *main house* a euphemism for mansion?"

Clenching his jaw, he flattened his lips.

That underbelly was softer than she'd realized. "Why does your dad sleep in the bunkhouse instead of the main house?"

His fingers tightened on the steering wheel. "Because he's the help. He works there."

"But he's also family, right?"

"It's not what he wants," Matt snapped.

"If you don't want me to go to the Shooting Star, then say so."

"I don't want you to feel like I'm twisting your arm to

stay with me. I don't want to make you uncomfortable. The Shooting Star is a good option. It's just..."

"Just what?" Hannah studied his face, trying to understand.

"I hate asking my aunt and uncle for anything. I hate being beholden to anyone. For the job is one thing, calling in a favor to save a life. And I'd do it for you." He glanced over at her. "To make sure you're safe."

Something inside her cringed at putting him in such a position.

"Any man who tries to twist my arm will find it gets broken. And you don't make me uncomfortable." Only nervous. And terrified of making a mistake. "No worries about either. You offered your spare room. I'll kindly take it."

He didn't have to care. He didn't have to offer. But he did. What she wouldn't do in the face of that generosity and selfless kindness was insult him by asking him to call in a favor from his family on her behalf.

They climbed out of the truck and went to her front doorstep. She unlocked the door and stepped into the house. It was chilly inside. Had she forgotten to adjust the thermostat?

"Do you mind if I use the bathroom?" he asked, shutting and locking the door behind him.

"No, go right ahead. I'll throw a few things in a bag."

He headed for the half-bath in the hallway. As she made her way toward her bedroom, she noticed a draft in the house. Passing the guest room, she rounded the corner to get to her room and stopped.

Her bedroom door was closed. She'd left it open yesterday. She was certain of it.

She drew the service weapon from the holster on her hip. Raising it, she crept down the hall. At the door, she listened.

A slight *whoosh, whoosh* whispered on the other side, in the room. She grabbed the knob, twisted slowly, took a breath and threw the door open.

A crisp breeze slapped her in the face, and the curtains rustled from the window, which had been pried open.

In the center of her bed lay a young blond girl, spread eagle, her body bare and pale and bruised, her eyes closed. Ligature marks around her neck. A queen of hearts playing card with the eyes scratched out on her stomach. The decorative quilt had been ripped from the bed and the body on top of disheveled sheets, as though he had raped her here. In Hannah's house. In her bed.

Her skin crawled and her stomach clenched. She leaned back on the doorjamb, looking away from the corpse, her heart lodged in her throat.

Near the front of the house, the toilet flushed.

She took one deep breath, fighting against the shock and horror, the sheer revulsion. And then another.

The bathroom door opened in the hall.

"Matt," she called out, her voice steady but not sounding like her own.

"Yeah?" Footsteps hurried in her direction. "What's wrong?"

He came around the corner, and she stepped aside so that he could see.

"NO SIGHTINGS OF the SUV?" Hannah asked an officer with the Laramie PD over her cell phone.

"We put out a BOLO as soon as you called in the attack on Atkinson. We also went through all the street cameras in your area once we heard about the next victim, but it's limited," he said, and she gritted her teeth at the truth of that statement. Unlike major cities such as New York, Los Angeles and Seattle, which had thousands of traffic cameras, their town and the surrounding area had the bare minimum. "There's no sign of the vehicle. He must know where the cameras are and is deliberately avoiding them."

"Let me know as soon as—"

"Of course, Detective."

"What about the officer cross-referencing the records from the DMV with those of the university?"

"He's creating a list. He worked sixteen hours yesterday and has been back at it since five this morning."

"Okay. Thanks." Hannah disconnected.

The corpse of Kyra Adams being wheeled out of her house in a body bag. She and Matt had found her student ID card on Hannah's bedside table, along with a second one for a Zoey Williams.

They'd stayed at the crime scene for hours, watching bag after bag of evidence collected and removed.

A crime scene. That was exactly what it was now. Not her home, not anymore. The University Killer had taken that away from her. She didn't want the monster to take anything else.

Hannah paced back and forth while Matt was on the phone with the SWUPD. The waiting clawed at her insides.

"Okay. Thanks." Matt disconnected. "Sergeant Lewis finished speaking with Kyra's roommate, who had been out at one of the frat parties all night. They shared a first-floor apartment on campus. Apparently, Kyra and Zoey had been paired in the Student Support program. It's designed to ease the transition of new undergraduates. The system pairs an older second-or third-year student with a new one. Zoey is only sixteen. She graduated from high school early. According to the roommate, Kyra and Zoey really hit off. Kyra got her into a fantasy tabletop role-playing game and would let her sleep over on the couch if they played late so Zoey didn't have to walk back to her dorm alone at night. Zoey is confirmed missing. Cell phones for both girls were discovered in the apartment, along with their wallets."

That poor girl. To be caught in this sick game of cat and mouse that a psychotic killer was playing.

"Why would he take the other girl?" she asked. "She's not his type." From the picture on the student ID, Zoey had deep-olive skin and dark brown hair.

Matt shook his head. "I don't know. Maybe he was desperate. Didn't want to risk having to go through the trouble of kidnapping another girl later with us searching for him. A two-for-one, and he was willing to make do with a brunette."

Another idea came to Hannah. "Or maybe while he was taking Kyra, Zoey woke up and he had to make a choice—kill her there, subdue her or take her—and he preferred option three." She swore under her breath.

"Since he didn't kill her at the apartment, she's probably still alive. There are usually days between the time when he takes them and takes their lives." Matt put a comforting hand to her back, and she moved away from his touch.

She didn't want to be soothed. Holding tight to fury, frustration and control kept her sharp as a switchblade. And kept her from falling apart. "Tell that to Kyra Adams. She died within hours. Because of me. He saw a chance to do this." She pointed at her house. "To rape and murder another woman I failed to protect in my own home."

This was torture. The way he was terrorizing her by using these women like pawns in a game. One designed to hurt her.

Matt stepped around her, and she looked over his shoulder

to see why. He was blocking her from the newspaper photographers taking pictures. "This isn't your fault. It's Egan's. If she had never printed your address in the *Gazette*, Kyra Adams might still be alive. Come on. We need to let Forensics analyze the evidence and the ME examine the body. Standing here, giving the papers more fodder when we're exhausted, isn't going to help anything. Or anyone. Least of all Zoey Williams. We need to refuel and recharge. Let me get you out of here, okay?"

He was right. Yet again. The last thing she needed was to be provoked and pushed over the edge to the point where she hit a photographer.

"You lead the way," she said. "I'll follow."

Chapter Seventeen

Friday, September 20
9:30 a.m.

Matt showed Hannah into his house. To call it a *humble abode* would've been accurate. "Look around, and make yourself at home."

She dropped the 'go bag' that she'd taken from her trunk, on the floor near his living room since she couldn't take anything from the crime scene that was at her place and did just that, explored. "Anything off-limits?"

"Nope." He hung up his Stetson.

"Not even the drawers of your nightstand? Trusting me with your wallet is one thing. This could be something else."

A grin pulled at one corner of his mouth. He decided to view her curiosity as interest. "Knock yourself out."

The two-story cabin was simple. The front door opened to a spacious living room, which flowed into a dining room and kitchen. No walls separating the spaces. It was a large, open floorplan, with the exception of an office, powder room and a little den in the back. Upstairs was his bedroom with en suite. Two more bedrooms shared a Jack and Jill bath.

He'd built it not really thinking about the *why* behind the design. Until Aunt Holly had pointed out it was the perfect layout for a family. Maybe he did have a deep-buried hope—one he'd kept secret even from himself—to one day marry and have kids. Part of him wanted to. He just didn't know how to accept the constant state of vulnerability having a family would put him in.

All he knew was, this place was his, far from everyone else.

But after what had happened to Hannah, he was reexamining the exposure of this location. The one thing about the Shooting Star Ranch was its high degree of safety. The area with the main house, bunkhouse and where his cousins lived was practically a compound, with security cameras and every ranch hand armed.

No one was able to break in and leave a dead body there.

Out here in the boondocks, isolated and far from the Powells, was another story. His aunt and uncle had cautioned him about the choice. Warning him that the Powells had enemies and, by extension, so did he. Cautioning that a law enforcement officer would draw even more threats.

At the time, when he'd picked the parcel of land, he'd dismissed their concerns, only focused on his ego. His determination to stand on his own two feet. His need to carve out something separate from them.

There's safety in numbers.

He'd even advised as much to the SAV group, but here, he was not practicing what he preached.

Hannah waltzed down the steps into the kitchen, where he set out the food. "Nice digs. I wonder what the main house looks like."

"Nothing like this."

"I bet." She took off her blazer and tossed it on top of

one of the chairs that faced the kitchen island. "Got anything to drink?"

"Where are my manners?" He went to the fridge, opened it and pointed to orange juice, a pitcher of iced tea and beer.

"Anything stronger around here? I need a proper drink."

"I need a shower, and you need food before I show you where I keep the whiskey."

"Pretty certain I could find it if I looked hard enough, but I'd like to get cleaned up, too. So once I'm done with my drink, I can just crash for a couple of hours. Can we both shower at the same time?" she asked. "Any issues with water pressure?"

"None, if we're using the same shower," he said, half joking, half testing.

She gave him a soft smile in response, her gaze not leaving his.

"Beyond that?" He shrugged. "I guess we'll find out. I've never had anyone stay over."

"You? Never?"

"Why so skeptical?

"Have you looked in the mirror, Granger?"

He chuckled. "Sure. But what do you see when you look at me?"

Her smile spread wider, and she averted her eyes. "I expect a tumbler of whiskey waiting by the time I'm done upstairs."

He appreciated a woman who knew what she wanted. "Yes, ma'am."

They both hurried through their showers. To his surprise, his was a pleasant one. The water pressure and temperature had been fine.

When she came down to the kitchen, wearing a tiny pair

of shorts that exposed a tempting amount of skin, a tank top—sans bra—and with her hair damp and loose, he had built a fire in the living room and poured a drink for her.

"You clean up good," she said, picking up her glass, and he found it hard not to stare.

He gestured to his lounge pants and T-shirt. "If you say so." Then he poured himself a drink.

She eased closer and leaned against the counter. "I do."

"You never did tell me what you see when you look at me."

"A hot guy." Her eyes heated, and his heart turned over. "Who is overtop in the sex-appeal department."

That was unexpected.

He took a step toward her, testing boundaries. She didn't move away, holding her ground, but he could see her pulse flutter at the hollow of her throat. At her side, her free hand flexed and clenched, and he came to an astonishing realization: he made Hannah Delaney nervous.

"You should eat something. Drinking on an empty stomach can impair your judgment faster and could lead to regrettable consequences."

"I'm not hungry," she said dryly. "At least, not for food." Tipping her head up, she regarded him evenly. "Did you really want me to join you in your shower, or were you playing around?"

The moment stretched as he considered a response. Then he decided actions spoke louder than words. With one last single step, he erased the gap separating them. He slipped his hand around her neck, his fingers sliding up into her hair, and kissed her.

She wrapped her arms around his neck as she lifted onto the balls of her feet and kissed him back.

A shudder ran through him, as much from relief as release. It had been a while since he'd held any woman this way, tasted her lips, soaked in the sweet surrender of her response, and he'd wanted to do this with her for days. Careful of her bruised face, he kept it lighter, more tender than he wanted, much shorter than he wished.

Fighting against the coiled want in his gut, he ended the kiss but kept her close in his arms. "I wasn't sure if you wanted this. You've pulled back from me a couple of times."

She pressed her forehead to his chest, her arms curled around his waist. "Sorry."

The word left her so heavily that he drew back to look down into her face. "Why did you?"

Her gaze lifted, those honey-brown eyes glittering with desire as she smiled at him, a heartrending curl of her lips. It was like he'd been sucker punched.

"Because I didn't want to be attracted to you, to *want* you. But I am and I do."

Her response was ego-boosting and concerning all at once. "Why didn't you?" he asked.

"There are so many reasons." She sighed. "I don't know where to begin."

He stroked her back. "Start with the easy ones."

"I have rules. No sleeping with a coworker. No spending the night. No strings attached. But I realized that once this case is over—and it *will* end because we're going to catch him," she said, having regained her indomitable, confident balance, "you won't be a coworker. But you seem like the type of man who cares deeply. That you would for a lover, anyway. It would mean waking up in your bed and lots of strings attached, and things would be messy."

Gently, he cupped her chin between his thumb and index finger. "Messy can be worth it. Sort of like the right kind of trouble." He ran his hand over her hair. "You're a good judge of character, because that's exactly how I'll be with you." No supposition. No doubt. Only affirmation. Flings and casual sex never held much appeal for him. "I'm not looking to take the edge off here. When I'm with a woman, I'm with her. In a relationship. I give as much as I take, but I also expect as much as I give."

He didn't know how to be any other way. Once, things had gotten serious for him. His ex had wanted marriage, and the idea had terrified him. He couldn't commit. At the time, he thought he wasn't the marrying kind because of his mother and the damage of her choices. But holding Hannah, he didn't want to let her go. Funny thing was, he felt like he knew her better, trusted her more than he ever had his ex.

Hannah pulled back a bit. "Here goes the not-so-easy part. I'm not a good judge of character. I'm the absolute worst—in my personal life, anyway. And I've been dreading that you're hiding something. That everything I see isn't what I'll get."

In a weird way, she was proving how well she was able to read him. "I want to work through that. How do we solve it? What do you need from me?"

"Show me yours, and I'll show you mine," she said, and he understood that she meant his soft underbelly. "What's the deal with you and your family? With your father? And the Powells? Why does the subject stress you out and cause you pain?"

This was not a *stand in the kitchen* type of discussion. He grabbed his drink, took her by the hand and led her to the sofa. They sat close, with their thighs touching and her hand on his leg and his palm on her soft, bare knee.

Talking about his family, about the past, wasn't something he did. Easier to keep it locked away. But if he wanted this woman, he'd have to risk the very thing he feared most: being vulnerable.

"My childhood wasn't picture perfect. Things had always been dysfunctional to some extent, with my parents fighting a lot. But my father had been head over heels in love with my mother. No matter the argument or how bad, he made amends, kept the family together, until one day he couldn't. They'd kept the truth from me—that my mom was a gambling addict. She had blown through everything, putting the ranch in so much debt, it was worthless. Then she took off. With another man."

Hannah's eyes softened with pity. "How old were you?"

"Seven. Happened a few days before my eighth birthday." He drew in a deep breath, hating the pain that still surfaced when he thought of it. "Loan sharks showed up. Threatened my father. He offered them the cattle since it was all he had left. They told him that if he didn't get the money to cover my mother's debts, they would kill him and take me as payment. That I'd work for them for the rest of my life. So we left Texas. We ran in the middle of the night. Came here with no place else to go." He took a swallow of his whiskey, embracing the smooth burn down his throat. "My father was a broken man after that, ashamed—a ghost of himself, really." His mother had ripped out his dad's heart and thrown them both away like they were trash. "My aunt Holly took on some of the shame since my mother was not only her sister but also her twin."

"Identical?" she asked.

He gave a curt nod.

"I can't imagine how hard that must've been to be taken in by a woman who looked exactly like the one who abandoned you."

That was it exactly. "Same face. Similar figure. Almost the same voice. But completely different mannerisms and personalities. My mom had been flighty, temperamental, selfish. While Aunt Holly is fierce in her devotion, nurturing, steady, selfless. Her love and affection were a blessing and a curse for that very reason. Made it hard on my dad, too, to be around her. He refused to live in the main house. Grateful that they made him the cattle manager, he chose to live in the bunkhouse, like an employee, and forced me to live with my aunt and uncle in their house, being raised alongside their sons. In a way, he gave me to them and has held himself at a distance ever since."

"How awful." Her voice was thick with sympathy. "Seeing him but not being with him."

"Aunt Holly and Uncle Buck treated me just like I was their son. Anything my cousins got, I got, too. Sometimes they gave me more. Like giving me a parcel of land when only one of their boys will inherit the rest. That's why I'm developing an extra source of revenue—to pay for it in a way." Thinking of how much they'd done for him, given him, made him shake his head with remorse. "I was a fool for not appreciating their love. Instead, I grew up angry and hurt and resentful." If he was honest with himself, he'd admit he was still acting out by choosing to live so far from them.

"I think it's understandable," Hannah said, "considering the circumstances."

"Understandable for a seven-year-old, maybe. Not a teenager. Looking back on it, I regret that I was such a nightmare for them."

"You? I find that hard to believe."

"No, it's true. In high school, I fell in with the wrong crowd because I was stubborn as a mule and determined to distance myself as much as possible from the Powell boys. They were all into sports. I hung out with the Iron Warriors."

Her brow furrowed. "No way."

"Yep. Probably would have eventually joined the motorcycle gang, but when I was seventeen, I got into a bit of trouble. After an argument with my uncle, I ran off. Met up with some of the Warriors. Decided it was a good idea to get drunk. They ended up trying to rob a strip club while I could barely stand on my two feet. I actually passed out in the middle of it. Anyway, the judge gave me a choice because I didn't have a weapon and my blood alcohol content had been off the charts and he considered me to be a Powell, which meant special treatment. Jail or the military."

"That's why Burk kept calling you *a Powell*," she said.

He nodded. "The rest of them got nine years in prison while I got off scot-free."

"You joined the military. Plenty of soldiers have died serving this country," she said, and he had gotten close himself more times than he cared to remember. "You still paid a price."

Matt didn't see it that way. He recognized the leniency shown and the opportunity he'd been given. "I got a GED and enlisted. The army straightened me out fast. By the time boot camp was done, I was a different person. My aunt and uncle were thrilled. Hopeful. Then Special Forces gave me a purpose that I committed to fully." He drained the last of the whiskey from his glass, surprisingly relieved that he'd finally shared the things he'd had bottled up inside all these years. "What about you? Why is your family your soft spot?"

Hannah didn't pull away or try to hide. She simply held his gaze. "In five words? My father is Edward Ressler."

Ressler? Why was the name so familiar? He'd recently

heard it. Then it hit him. "The Neighborhood Killer…is your father?"

With grim eyes, she nodded. "I did have a picture-perfect family. At least, I thought I did. Dinners together every night. Church on Sundays. No fighting. My father was my favorite parent. We'd go hiking and fishing, and he'd take me for ice cream on a Tuesday just because. My mother was the bad guy, the one who made me clean my room and do my homework and criticized me for being a tomboy. My father's only rule, the one thing that he demanded, was that we not disturb him when he was in the garage, working on a project."

It was suddenly clear why her example of how Starkey's wife might not have known he wasn't home had been so specific. "Your father would sneak out, take a car that he had parked down the street and…" He let his voice trail off, not needing to say the words.

Sipping her whiskey, she gave a slow nod. "My father was my hero. I looked up to him. Thought he had a noble job, working for a big security company, keeping people safe. He installed security systems in houses. The same homes he later broke into after casing it and programming a backdoor code, murdering his victims."

"Foster said that you were the one to catch him."

"I went into the garage one day while he was out at work. I wanted to tinker around with his things. Be like him. I dropped something. A screwdriver. It rolled, and when I went to pick it up, I accidentally hit a baseboard that was loose. The piece of wood fell. I was going to fix it, but I saw things that he'd hidden behind it. Strange things. Small bundles of hair tied with red string. Driver's licenses that belonged to women."

"Did you understand what it was?"

"Not really. I mean, I was fourteen. At first, with the hair, I thought he had been sleeping with other women and he had keepsakes from them—but when I found the licenses, I knew something was wrong, that it was bad."

"What did you do?"

"I showed my mother. Explained how and where I found those things. For a long time, she sat at the kitchen table, thinking, staring at the stuff I had shown her. Eventually, she looked up the names on the licenses on the computer. She put it together that they were his victims. Then she packed a quick bag for each of us, grabbed food from the pantry and got me out of the house. We went straight to the police station."

He took her hand in his and held it. "That must've been unbearably hard. Grappling with the truth of what your father really was while dealing with the media frenzy at the same time."

She leaned over, resting her head on his chest, and he wrapped an arm around her. "It was devastating. Can't really explain it. Having my whole world collapse. But I guess you understand. Yours fell apart, too."

"It did but not like yours." There was no competition. He'd gotten lucky while she had gotten a raw deal.

"When we first went to the police, I kept telling myself it was a mistake and there had to be some reasonable explanation. Then they arrested him. I thought—as my life imploded and I discovered that my father, who I had idolized, who I thought I knew, became a devil, the true face of evil—that things couldn't get any worse. But they did. The police found a false-bottom space in the house where he stored sick drawings and kept newspaper clippings about the Neighborhood Killer. He confessed to the authorities. Boasted about what he had done. Told them that pressures of being a perfect father drove him to kill again."

"How could he do that to you?" If he had any love in his heart for her at all? "Did you blame yourself?"

"I did. To be honest, even after counseling, there's a little voice inside me that says if I had never been born, those other women never would've been murdered."

"You aren't responsible for his actions." He gentled his tone. "It wasn't fair for him to make you think otherwise." This explained so much about her: How guarded she was. Why she was always looking for a reason not to trust him. The way she so readily took the blame for things that weren't her fault. "You've saved countless people doing your job."

Atoning. For her father's sins and crimes. That's what she was doing, and his heart broke for her.

"The media claimed we must have known. No one believed that we hadn't. It seemed impossible, inconceivable, to them. Once we started receiving death threats, my mom filed for an emergency divorce. The court granted it with no delay. We moved, went by her maiden name after that. She added the h's to my first name to make it harder for anyone to figure out who I really was and dyed my hair blond." She sank against him, and he held her tighter. "Her health started to fail, and right after I graduated from the police academy, she died of a heart attack."

"I'm so sorry." He ached for her loss, for her grief, for the way she had to hide her identity and the worst experience of her life that had shaped her. "I'm glad you're telling me. Finally sharing it."

Knowing the truth of her past only made him that much more protective of her. Not that she couldn't defend herself—

Hannah was a force to be reckoned with—but he wanted to shield her from the University Killer's mind games.

The ordeal with her father would only make her more sensitive to his manipulative tactics.

It made Matt long to show that murderer what ranch justice looked like. Where fiends didn't make it to court and were strung up instead.

But then he reminded himself he was a man of the law.

"I haven't been able to let anyone get too close." Her voice was low yet tense. "Not trusting my own judgment. Always waiting for some horrible reveal. But something about you made me wonder if it might be different with you, if I could understand you better. Do you see why I need to be certain that you aren't hiding something terrible about yourself?"

"Absolutely." He put a knuckle under her chin and tipped her face up to his. "You don't know every detail yet, like I leave the toilet seat up and I'm a horrible cook and I've got a thing for beautiful women who rescue kittens," he said, and she cracked a sad smile. "Especially if they're in trouble. But you know everything big and important about me."

She pressed a palm to his cheek. "You swear no nasty surprises?" As she studied his face, a slight tremble went through her. "Because if we try to do this and there are, it'll break me."

His heart started pounding slowly in his chest. He couldn't explain it, how close he felt to her, the undeniable connection after only working on a case together twice. But for the first time in his life, he wanted to give himself completely, fully, to this…budding relationship. "I swear. You're safe with me."

Not taking her eyes from his, she slipped her hand to the back of his neck and lowered his mouth to hers. This time the kiss was savage and greedy. Unrestrained.

He wanted her. In his bed. Under him. Over him. Any way that he could get her. But he didn't want to bulldoze her into anything, either, if she needed to take this slowly. Mixing the physical with the emotional. A lot was on the line. He didn't want to blow it by rushing. So he pulled his mouth away.

She moaned, curling her fingers in his hair.

"It's been a long day, almost thirty hours with no sleep," he said, making his voice soothing. "If this is all you want right now, me holding you and kissing you, then I get it. I'm not expecting anything more than this."

Smiling and giving him a sexy, predatory look, she climbed onto his lap, straddling his thighs, and there was no hiding how aroused she made him. He groaned, clamping his hands on her hips.

She gripped the bottom of his tee and lifted it over his head. "Well, I'm expecting more, cowboy." Then she pulled off her tank top, tossing it to the floor, baring her full, exceptional breasts and pert nipples to him. "A lot more." She pressed the softness at the apex of her thighs down against the hard ridge in his pants and rocked her hips, making him throb for her. "And I'm willing to sacrifice sleep to have you. Right. Now."

Chapter Eighteen

Friday, September 20
Noon

Pushing up on her elbow in his bed, her leg draped over his, Hannah grinned down at Matt. "You realize we're going to be wrecks for the rest of the day."

"Complete toast." He lay limp and lax, looking sated, with his arm around her waist, keeping her close. Using his fingers, he drew circles on her hip. "But totally worth it. I didn't know how much I needed this."

She slid her palm up his taut washboard stomach to play in the curls on his chest. "How long has it been for you?" she asked softly.

His gaze flicked up to hers. "Four years."

Her eyebrows shot up. "Holy mackerel, that's a long, long time," she said, and he chuckled. She ran her fingers over his muscles, still exploring the lines and contours and every inch of his skin. "I needed it, too."

She had needed him. More than the physical release. A chance to unburden her secrets. To connect, for once. To enjoy this quiet intimacy that she usually denied herself.

But she kept those thoughts to herself. She wasn't ready to share everything quite yet.

He studied her for a long moment. "You deserve this. To be with someone who wants more than to sleep with you. Who wants to—"

"If you say *take care of* me, I'm going to gag."

His grip on her tightened. "I was going to say *care for you.*"

And she realized that he did. "While we're working, we have to be just colleagues. Nothing else."

The look he sent her was inscrutable. "Nothing else," he repeated. Then he surprised her by reaching up and kissing her with a fiery hunger that stole her breath.

Fresh waves of desire and need equal in surprise washed over her.

"But later, though," he said, "when we're back in bed, we'll be much more."

She was looking forward to that. Although there was no telling when that would happen.

His cell phone chimed. He reached over. "It's Kent. You haven't responded to his texts."

She swore. "My phone is in the guest room. I should've thought to check it." But she'd been distracted, too busy enjoying Matt Granger and all he had to offer. "What does he say?"

"Foster didn't go back home last night. But he's in class, teaching. Kent has to go home and get some shut-eye. He'll resume watchdog duties this evening."

None of them were machines. She and Matt would probably regret not getting any rest once the adrenaline and endorphins faded.

"How did the handoff go with Logan?" she asked.

"I forgot to mention that my cousin texted while we were waiting for Forensics at your house," he said. "The crime lab at DCI is working on it now."

"Maybe we should hedge our bets. Have someone follow Starkey, too. Just to be sure. The University Killer isn't going to be prowling the parties on frat row tonight or the rest of the weekend."

He nodded. "I think you're right."

"Could you also send one to LPD to help the officer who's going through the DMV records?"

"How about you have your guy come down to the SWUPD?"

She pursed her lips. "Sure."

"We should swing by the ME's office on the way into the station. See if Norris has anything for us."

"Wish we could call the guy."

"Yeah. It'd be nice if he answered instead of letting it go to voicemail. He must get lonely over there. Forcing folks to show up in person." Matt gave her butt a playful smack. "Come on."

MATT AND HANNAH found the medical examiner, suited up, over the body of Kyra Adams in the morgue.

"Hope you don't mind us popping in," Matt said, to be courteous.

Roger Norris always sent an email when he was ready for a visit. But Matt doubted the ME minded.

"Not at all." Norris waved them closer. Behind his forensic goggles, his green eyes were cool and hard. The ME was sharp, efficient and affable.

Matt only wished the guy would pick up the phone more often.

Music was playing; Norris rarely worked without it. Rather than listen to something somber and expected for work that required an admirable constitution, the bluesy, hard rock sound of Aerosmith came from the speakers.

"Here's what I know so far. She was nineteen. Best I can tell, five-three, five-four. Cause of death is the same as the other University Killer victims, except for Jessica Atkinson—strangulation. She was raped," Norris said.

Hannah shifted uncomfortably beside Matt. He didn't want to imagine what was going through her head. He only hoped she wasn't blaming herself.

"No signs of a struggle," Norris continued, "which would indicate she was heavily drugged and unconscious during the sexual assault and when she was murdered. I've ordered a tox screen. But my guess is, he used his preferred drug of choice, GHB, again. Like he did on Atkinson, with hers being the only lethal dose thus far. We'll know for certain soon enough. There are no secondary wounds or injuries."

Matt's phone rang. He pulled it from his jacket pocket. The weather had dropped about ten degrees, and he'd opted for a leather one. "Granger."

"Hey, Chief, it's Sergeant Lewis."

"Yeah, what's up? I'm at the morgue right now with Detective Delaney."

"Two things. First, the hospital called regarding Carl. He was poisoned with tetrahydrozoline hydrochloride."

"Tetrahydrozo-what?"

"Tetrahydrozoline hydrochloride?" Norris asked, looking up at him, and Matt nodded. "Eye drops. A common decongestant, like Visine or Clear Eyes."

"Did they say anything else?" Matt asked Lewis.

"His drink was spiked with a low dose."

"Could a higher dosage have killed him?"

"I don't know," Lewis said. "I didn't ask."

"Sure could," Norris said. "You know, there have been some recent cases in other parts of the country where a couple of medical professionals used it to off their spouses. A nurse and an EMT. Both caught. Tetrahydrozoline could also give someone seizures or put them in a coma."

Good thing they were here with Norris.

"What was the second thing?" Matt asked Sergeant Lewis.

"We received a suspicious delivery a few minutes ago. You and Detective Delaney should get back to the station as soon as possible."

Not only did a prickle flare down Matt's spine, but his skin also began to tingle. "We'll be right there."

Hannah was staring at him. "What is it?"

"Nothing good." Of that, he was certain.

SHOVING THROUGH THE front door of the SWUPD, Hannah was right behind Matt.

The duty officer stood. "Sergeant Lewis is waiting for you both in your office with the delivery, and an LPD officer is in the conference room with Farran, going through DMV records and the names of university personnel."

"Carl was released from the hospital?" Matt asked.

"They only kept him overnight. He came in. Says he feels awful about slipping up and wanted to get back to work."

With a nod, Matt said, "Thanks. I need to check on him when I get a moment."

They passed the front desk and headed back. Dennis Hill hopped up from his desk and hurried after them in the hallway.

"Whatever it is, can it wait?" Matt asked.

"I wish it could, but I held off yesterday."

Tension radiated off Matt. "What is it?"

"The bicycle-registration system is down. We can't print any new stickers."

"Students will simply have to wait," Matt snapped.

"You go through the effort of registering bicycles?" Hannah asked. She thought they would have their hands full with other things.

"Yes, we do," Dennis said.

Matt grunted. "Part of the job."

"Many bikes look alike, but identifying one with its serial number is the best way to protect property," Dennis said. "Speaking of which, we can't recover any lost or stolen bikes, either, because we can't access the serial numbers. Sergeant Starkey was working on getting the problem fixed until he left."

A groan rumbled from Matt. "I'll put Lewis on it."

"Thank you." Dennis turned around and went back down the hall.

Entering his office, Hannah spotted the delivery on his desk.

"What's urgent about a box of doughnuts from the Wheatgrass Café?" Matt asked, taking off his hat.

"No one here at the department ordered it," Lewis said, standing in front of the desk. "I questioned the delivery boy. He said that a man came in first thing this morning right as they opened. Placed the order, specified the time of delivery as three thirty-three and told them to include a thank-you card, which he provided."

"Why was the delivery early?" Matt asked.

"There was a lull in customers at the café. The manager told the kid better early than late."

"Did you get a description of the man?" Hannah asked.

"Yeah," Lewis said. "White. Five-ten, five-eleven. Brown hair. Dark brown beard. Baseball cap. Thinks maybe he had a Southern accent. Possibly Texan."

"Sounds like our guy, wearing the same disguise from the hospital," Hannah said.

Lewis nodded. "That's what I thought. When I opened the box, this was inside with the doughnuts." Wearing latex gloves, he handed over a small white envelope with the same dimensions as the one left on Jessica Atkinson's body.

"Oh my God," Hannah said. "It has my name written on it, and this time it's sealed.

Matt moved closer to her. "He wanted to make sure you were the one to open it."

Hannah straightened her spine, bracing for whatever tercet waited inside for her. Turning to the box of gloves, she grabbed some and handed a set to Matt. They both tugged on a pair.

She took the envelope, gingerly opened it and took out the card. Looking over her shoulder, Matt read the typewritten note along with her.

> TO SAVE ZOEY WILLIAMS AND HAVE HER RETURNED UNHARMED,
>
> MEET ME AT THE ETERNAL HOPE CEMETERY BY THE OBELISK TONIGHT.
>
> 7 PM. COME ALONE. OR THERE WILL BE CONSEQUENCES.

MATT CLENCHED A hand at his side. This madman was getting more and more personal with Hannah, dragging her deeper into his twisted games.

"Where is the Eternal Hope Cemetery?" she asked.

"Here," Lewis said. "In the middle of campus."

Confusion darkened her eyes. "Why would they build a graveyard in the center of a university? It's a bit somber for a college setting."

The explanation was a long story, which Matt had learned shortly after taking the job. "The graves were here first. When they decided to build the university, they relocated the bodies. As the school expanded, the graves were moved a second time to what is now the Eternal Hope Cemetery. Deals were made with the town to keep building the university grounds, eventually around it."

"Any significance to the obelisk?" she asked.

Matt shrugged.

"I think the monument is dedicated to young villagers who had died in a skirmish in the late 1800s," Lewis said. "It symbolizes lives cut short."

"Where is it located in the cemetery?" she asked.

"At the center," Lewis said. "Can't miss it."

Matt shook his head. "No, you can't possibly be thinking about doing this."

"He's offered to return the girl unharmed."

"Sergeant Lewis, would you excuse us? And get with Dennis about the bike-registration-system malfunction."

The officer left, shutting the door behind him.

"You can't possibly think he'd simply give her back."

"She's not his type. He wasn't expecting her to be there. But it gives him an opportunity to use that as leverage."

"To what end, huh? Just to meet you?" He shook his head. "I don't think so. There's more to it than that, and you know it."

Looking in her eyes, he could see that she did and simply wasn't concerned with the risk to herself.

"And why at seven when it's still light out?" Sunset wasn't until seven thirty, and the cemetery was a stone's throw from the quad. That early in the evening, the campus would have lots of activity, students walking about, though not through the cemetery. Most steered clear of it because of the ghost stories. "Why not at midnight? I don't like this. Not one little bit."

"Doing this is risky, yes, but if we have a chance to save an innocent girl's life, then we have to take it. *I* have to take it. Or I'd never be able to live with myself if something happens to her when I could've stopped it."

"Regardless of what happens to you?"

"Yes," she said, far too easily, like her life didn't matter.

He understood necessary sacrifice better than most, and this wasn't it.

The familiar prickle that warned him of trouble was now flaring hot. Felt like a live wire being raked down his spine. The last time the feeling had been this strong, his team had walked into an ambush, and he'd lost two buddies.

"This man is baiting you," he said, trying to get reason to sink in for her. "Using your guilt and compassion against you. It's some kind of a trap."

"Of course it is. But there's no other choice if we want to save Zoey."

"He's not going to give up something for nothing in return."

"A face-to-face with me is not nothing," she said, refusing to back down. "You agreed to do this my way."

"But I didn't sign up to let you go kamikaze."

She heaved a breath like he was the one not understanding.

"Step away from this case for a second and look at it in a different context. Have you considered that as we get closer to any moment of huge import—huge impact, huge challenge—that human nature tempts us to turn away from it? Sometimes that instinct serves us. But sometimes it's trying to protect what doesn't need protecting and instead is stopping us from taking that very risk we absolutely need to take."

Her point wasn't lost on him. In fact, there had been times in the military before embarking on a dangerous mission where it was easier to focus on why they shouldn't do it rather than why they had to. But she couldn't ignore how her instincts and choices were skewed, because they were going up against a monster that had been like her father. "I agree, but not about this. *You need protecting* when it comes to this guy."

If only she could see how her past made her more vulnerable.

"Why, because we slept together?" She put her fists on her hips. "Great sex isn't going to stop me from doing my job."

The barb stung. It had been more than sex to him. This was the start of something special between them that he didn't want to lose, even if it didn't mean the same to her. "I would never get in the way of you doing your job."

"If this guy wants to meet me in exchange for returning Zoey, then guess what? I. Will. Meet. Him. Getting her back alive is all that matters."

No, Hannah mattered, too. Every life did. But she was sharp and gutsy and made a difference in the world. He wasn't going to let anything happen to her.

"Fine. You'll go," he conceded. "But only over my dead body will you do it alone." His tone brooked no argument.

He would take every precaution conceivable to ensure her safety.

HANNAH WALKED DOWN the road that ran through the middle of the cemetery, the Avenue of Flags. At the center of the graveyard stood the obelisk, pointed toward the sky. It was quiet. No one was around except for the six officers in plainclothes, including Matt and Kent. Everyone had been given a section to cover. Since they had gotten Foster's DNA, Matt wanted to use Kent for this meetup.

The older detective was in his car, parked on the south side of the cemetery. Another officer was parked on the north end. Matt was concerned the University Killer would somehow lure Hannah to a vehicle, manage to get her in and take off. He was so worried, he'd insisted that she wear a GPS tracker.

No such thing as too careful.

At two inches in length by one inch in width and half an inch in height, the GPS tracker was smaller than a tape measure and fit tucked into her D-cup bra.

"I'm in position," she said into the two-way comms device in her ear concealed by her hair.

"I've got eyes on you," Matt said, his voice steady and husky.

She didn't know his exact location. Only that he had taken a discreet position behind a tree and was watching her through binoculars.

Part of her regretted telling him that it had only been sex for her and nothing more. The idea that their intimacy would change their working relationship had scared her, but she hadn't meant to hurt him. The other part of her understood Matt was a modern-day warrior. A natural protector. His instincts to safeguard someone he cared for would only be amplified, and the only way to prevent it would've been never to sleep with him.

There was no undoing it. Not that she wanted to.

Looking around, she spotted Sergeant Lewis dressed as a groundskeeper, pushing a wheelbarrow. Two more SWUPD officers, making up the rest of the team inside the cemetery, she couldn't see, which was a good thing.

Glancing at her watch, she checked the time. "It's four minutes past seven. Where is he?"

"Patience. He's out there somewhere."

A cell phone rang. But it wasn't hers.

Pivoting on her heel, she followed the sound. There was a burner phone at the base of the obelisk. Warily, she bent down and picked it up. The caller ID stated *Private*. She answered, "Hello?"

"Detective Delaney, how good of you to show up." The voice wasn't as deep as she had expected but was the same as the guy from Tuesday night. Slight Texan accent, barely perceptible.

"Where are you? I thought you wanted to meet."

"I wanted to send you proof of life first. Give me the number to your private cell phone."

"Why do you want my personal number? Send the proof to the burner phone you left."

"Don't give him your number," Matt said softly in her other ear.

"My game," the killer said. "My rules. Unless you don't want proof that Zoey is alive."

"No, I do." Hannah gave him her private number.

Seconds later, her cell phone chimed. A picture of the college student came through. She was seated in the front seat of a vehicle, sunlight filtering in through the window, trees behind her. The girl was dressed in a pin-striped pajama-shorts set that had strawberries on it. Tears filled her eyes. Her wrists and ankles were bound.

"See? She's fine. Not a scratch on her."

"I'd like to see her. In person. Why don't we finish this conversation in person? Isn't that what you want?"

"It is what I want. You were so, *so* close to setting sweet Zoey free," he said, and she cringed on the inside. "But you've hurt my feelings."

"What? How?"

"You're trying to trick me. Like I'm a fool playing your game and not the other way around. But I expected this from you, Hannah. Because you're deceitful and wicked."

"No, I'm not."

"Yes! You are. And now there must be consequences."

"I'm sorry. Please don't hurt Zoey."

"You're not sorry. Not yet. But you will be once you realize the unnecessary suffering you've caused." He disconnected.

No. What have I done? What will happen to Zoey?

There was no callback number. Still, she clicked on *Private*, trying to dial him back, and received a *not in service* message. Her gut twisted.

A gunshot cracked the air, making her flinch. The impact of the bullet spun Lewis forty-five degrees before he fell. Hannah drew her weapon as she spotted Matt lunge from his position, headed straight for her in a dead sprint.

No, no, no.

Another round whined in, this time hitting Matt, and Hannah's blood went cold.

Chapter Nineteen

Friday, September 20
7:40 p.m.

The EMT finished bandaging Matt's left arm in the back of the ambulance. "You're very lucky," she said. "The bullet went straight through the muscle. Didn't hit bone. Didn't nick an artery. No fragments left behind."

If only his other officers had been so lucky. Everyone in the cemetery hit had been shot except for Hannah. The murderer hadn't turned his sniper sights on her when he could've easily killed her. Kent and the officer parked on the north side of the graveyard had had their tires and windshields blown out, nothing more.

"Thanks," Matt said to the EMT, then climbed out of the ambulance.

As soon as his feet hit the ground, Hannah's gaze found his. The worry in her eyes was clear and unmistakable.

She was talking to Kent, who was wearing a Kevlar vest. The two headed in Matt's direction, and he met them halfway.

"I'm glad you're all right," Hannah said, her voice soft and somber, and he could tell that she wanted to say more.

But she glanced at Kent and took a deep breath. "Your three officers who were taken to the university hospital are going to be okay. Lewis was struck in the shoulder, the other two in the foot and hand."

Matt gritted his teeth, hating that his people had been injured and were in pain but also grateful that they were alive.

"Looking around, the only good sniper vantage from any of the surrounding buildings," she continued, "was the roof of the Animal Science facility and the Sweetwater Recreation Center."

"Laramie PD officers are checking out both now," Kent said, "since most of your guys are out of commission."

Matt shook his head. "This is on me."

"No, it's not," Hannah said. "The note was addressed to me. He gave explicit instructions that I was to come alone and if I didn't, there would be consequences." She was radiating more than anger, something like thundering self-blame. Her expression loosened for only a split second, but he saw what was beneath, how badly she hurt. "Now those men are in the hospital, and Zoey is still out there, trapped with monster."

The sharp-edged rage inside Matt shifted as he realized that he had been so focused on protecting Hannah that he had forgotten to watch out for the rest of his team. "I knew this was some kind of trap or an ambush. I felt it in my bones."

"I wish someone would've given me the heads-up about that," Kent said dryly. "I would've brought my ballistic helmet."

Preparing for something like this used to be Matt's specialty. This failure rested squarely on him. "The cemetery was the perfect location for it. With him having the advantage of the high ground, perched on a rooftop, sighting through his scope, he could not only see all of us but reach out and touch us, too. Pick us off one by one."

"He's got to be a deadeye to shoot like that," Kent said. "Probably a proficient hunter or someone with tactical training."

"Might not be tactical training," Hannah said. "Aren't there a few places within a two to four-hour drive that offer long-range precision-rifle training?"

Kent nodded. "I can think of three. But they're not cheap, if someone wants to learn how to shoot farther than, say, six hundred yards. People spend six to seven grand a day on that kind of training. Won't be paid for in cash, either."

"So they won't be able to give us the runaround about not having records," Hannah said.

Kent tapped his nose with his finger. "They're closed now, but I can make some calls. See if anyone with a university affiliation has been through over the years. I might have to pay them an actual visit to get any real traction."

Matt's phone pinged with an incoming text. "I emailed Agent Nancy Tomlinson about what happened while I was getting my arm bandaged."

"That's the finest example of multitasking that I've ever heard of," Kent said.

"She wants a virtual meeting ASAP. She's emailing a link." The SWUPD had a secure video–telephone software program that was shared throughout the federal government. "She wants to know how quickly we can get started."

Hannah turned to Kent. "Will you take the lead with the LPD cops checking out the rooftops and forensics here?"

"Sure. I can handle it."

Her gaze flicked back to Matt. "Tell Tomlinson ten minutes."

On the walk back to his truck, he sent the text.

Once they reached his vehicle, she held out her hand. "Give me your keys."

"I'm okay to drive."

"Keys," she repeated, her voice firm.

He dropped the keys in her palm.

They climbed into his truck and took off. She switched on the red and blue flashing lights, which gave her the liberty to speed toward the SWUPD while he was seated in the passenger's seat. A first for him. And he didn't like it. But this didn't seem like an issue worth fighting over. Not after the tragic events of the night.

Hannah's mouth was set, her full lips compressed into a thin line of displeasure.

"Something you want to share?" he asked.

"You don't want to know."

Whenever she said that, he'd learned she was right. He probably didn't want to hear what was on her mind. Still… "Just spit it out."

"You were a fool out there," she snapped.

"Come again?" He had been foolish for not doing proper reconnaissance and anticipating a sneak attack, but he didn't expect her to say it, especially not after he'd been shot.

"Running toward me to protect me while a killer is taking potshots with a sniper rifle. *Foolish*. You know better. You're smarter than that. You should've been taking cover. Not further exposing yourself. Did you think my training wouldn't kick in? Did you assume I'd freeze and need you? You didn't charge toward anyone else, hell-bent on saving them. Only me. Yet I didn't get shot."

He exhaled relief over the fact that she was all right. "No, you didn't." He would've preferred to be the one to take the bullet if it meant she didn't have to endure the pain.

"If I had known that you would've acted with such disregard for yourself or that those officers would've gotten shot, I never would have listened to you. I would've gone alone."

"And that would have been a mistake."

"Tell that to the wives and children of your officers who are in the hospital." She whipped the truck into the garage, parked in the spot reserved for the chief and cut the engine. "I told you, when we're outside of the bedroom, we had to be colleagues only. Strictly business. You pretended like you got it. Like you were on board. You lied! I don't want you risking your life for me. I don't need you to do that. I don't need you at all." She reached for the door handle.

"Hold on." He grabbed her wrist, stopping her, and gasped from the lightning bolt of agony that sliced through his bicep.

She winced as though she'd been the one to feel the pain.

"I messed up." On multiple levels. "I did make a promise that I failed to keep. When the gunfire started, the line between colleague and someone I care for evaporated. I've never done this before. It's harder than I expected."

"That's why I don't sleep with people I work with. This was a mistake." In the light from the garage filtering into the truck, her eyes turned impenetrable. "Maybe after this case, we can reassess."

Mistake? Maybe reassess?

He reached over with his good arm, slipping his hand around the back of her neck, brought her mouth to his and kissed her. Deeply. Until the tension drained from her and she softened against him. "I'm not running scared because I was shot. This—whatever it is—brewing between us is not a mistake. It's the first thing in my life that has felt right. Good. I don't need to reassess. Time is precious. People I care about have been ripped from my life without warning. Because they left or they were killed. I could've died today. We both could've but didn't. The fact that we're still breathing, not hospitalized, is a gift. We can't squander that. I don't want to waste one minute that I could be with you being apart instead."

Tears sprang to her eyes, and a shuddering breath left her lips. "I don't want you to die because of me."

"Well, me neither."

A hiccupping laugh came from her, and tears rolled down her cheeks. She wrapped her arms around his neck and tugged him close. "I just don't want anything to happen to you."

"Ditto. I don't want anything to happen to you, either." He pulled back. "No more talk about mistakes and reassessments. Let's just focus all our energy on catching this guy. Okay?"

Wiping the tears from her face, she nodded. "Yeah."

"You didn't mean it when you said that you don't need me, did you?"

She gave him a sad smile. "I don't want to need you. Because losing you would hurt too much."

He caressed her cheek and kissed her lips.

"Enough," she said, regaining her composure. "Agent Tomlinson is probably waiting by now."

She was right.

They hopped out, rushed into the building and hurried to his office.

He logged into his computer and clicked the link, dialing into the secure video conference. Hannah pulled up a chair and sat beside him.

A silver-haired woman with smooth ebony skin appeared on the screen. "Hello, Chief Granger and Detective Delaney."

"Agent Tomlinson," Matt said, "it's good to put a face with the name. Thank you for this virtual meeting. I'm glad you happened to still be at work."

"I'm always in the office. I keep promising my husband that I'll slow down so we can enjoy our golden years, but whenever I try, a pressing case finds its way to me. I wish I could've set up this virtual meeting sooner. The more information I receive from you, the clearer the picture. I appreciate the timely updates. Things have escalated far quicker than anything I've experienced in the past."

Hannah leaned forward. "What does that mean?"

"The problem is two-fold. Detective, you interrupted the UNSUB," Agent Tomlinson said, referring to the unidentified suspect, "during his ritualistic process. This has probably never happened to him before, angering and frustrating him. A major blow to his ego. Couple that with the fact that you look like his ideal victim. It's not only alluring to him but also quite vexing in a complex way. Based on everything that you have passed along to me, Chief Granger, I believe the University Killer has developed a fixation on you, Detective. A very dangerous one that he will go to extreme lengths to see satisfied."

Matt clenched his hand. "When you say satisfied, what do you mean?"

"Are you saying that he wants to kill me?" Hannah asked.

"Your death is no longer enough for him," Agent Tomlinson said grimly. "I wasn't certain of that until the unfortunate events of tonight occurred. But now I am. He wants to *eliminate* you in the same manner that he would one of his normal victims."

Disgust roiled Matt's gut. He was never going to let that happen. "We need more information in order to stop him.

Why is he only taking his victims from campus? With the attention from law enforcement, wouldn't it be easier for him if he expanded his hunting ground?"

"Easier? Certainly," Agent Tomlinson said. "But he isn't interested in easy. He's interested in besting you. The campus is a place that he loves, enjoys, that makes him feel safe. He's definitely someone affiliated with the university."

"Every time we get a description of him," Hannah said, "he changes his disguise."

"This man is a master at deception. I believe he goes so far as to wear a mask on a daily basis. And I don't mean literally with a physical disguise. I mean not showing his true persona at work or even at home. It's only when he is dominating his victims in his environment, in his lair, that he lets his true self show."

How were they supposed to know what to look for? Matt shook his head in frustration. "You're saying if our killer quacks like a duck and walks like a duck, he might not be a duck."

"As confusing as that may sound," Tomlinson said, "yes."

"Have you found any clues or developed any theories about who he could be?" Hannah asked.

"After what the UNSUB did at the hospital, poisoning Officer—" Tomlinson glanced at her notes "—Farran and then killing Ms. Atkinson without violating her, I had a suspicion. However, it wasn't strong enough to share yet. Although tonight's events have convinced me of my theory."

The back of Matt's neck tingled. An itching prickle that made him rub at it. "Which is what?"

"He is someone who has a love–hate relationship with authority. Specifically with the police. He could have used a lethal dosage of tetrahydrozoline hydrochloride, killing Farran. At the time, I realized it was also entirely possible that he may have guessed how much to use. That's why I kept my theory quiet. But tonight, he had your officers in his crosshairs. He made a choice not to kill any of you. The fact that he only inflicted relatively minor wounds was deliberate."

Matt had wondered about that, if the fact that they had been moving targets had thrown off the killer's aim. "But why, when he could have killed us?"

"I understand it may be hard to reconcile why, in your eyes, a cold-blooded monster who would take the lives of defenseless, innocent young women and not yours. There is a myth that serial killers don't love or care about others. The reality is that some of them often show loving and protective behavior over their own families and those in their inner circle even as they are slaughtering the children of others."

Hannah tensed, clasping her hands in her lap.

Matt knew that must be difficult for her to hear and wished the trauma of her past hadn't resurfaced, but he also knew it was impossible for her not to think of her father.

"That doesn't explain why he didn't kill us," Matt pointed out.

"But it does," Agent Tomlinson said. "You spare that which you care about, even if a part of you also holds it in contempt. His rage and disdain for the police—for the campus police, in particular—is exercised through his killings. Then the question becomes, how do you come to care about something, or someone, you despise? By being in close proximity. By pretending to care on a regular basis until he actually does on some level."

Hannah glanced at Matt before turning back to the screen. "Could it be a police officer? One high up in the ranks, who has been passed over for promotion to chief three times? Even if he passed a polygraph?"

"Most definitely," Agent Tomlinson said with a nod. "Sometimes serial killers are able to pass a polygraph because they don't view the world, the truth, the same way."

Hannah's phone chimed. She read the text. "It's Kent. Excuse me a minute." She got up and hurried out of the room, disappearing down the hall.

"That brings me to something else," Agent Tomlinson said. "Your guy has an obsessive compulsion around the number three. He's exhibited this in the timing of his kills, the number of his victims. Only choosing months that have exactly thirty days," she said, which was something Matt hadn't realized. "Asking for the doughnuts to be delivered at three thirty-three precisely. But I also strongly believe this will be exhibited in his personal life. Once you pinpoint the right man, it will become obvious on paper. He might have three cars. Three kids. Will use the number three in some deeply personal way that might not seem obvious at first glance."

"Thank you, Agent Tomlinson."

"Wait, wait, there's more. It's about his victims. His choice, blond and petite, is probably related to his mother, who was most likely an authoritarian figure for him. I suspect he tried to reconcile that in his dating life by choosing blondes. Then some woman—a girlfriend, between the ages of eighteen and twenty-one—hurt him, wounded his pride or ego in some way, and she was his first victim. It would explain why he didn't use a condom with his initial kill. He knew her. Violating her was his way of payback, and strangulation is a passionate, personal act. After that, he needed two more victims to fulfill his obsessive compulsion. And for him, there was no reason to use a condom at that point, since he'd already left his DNA on the first body. Look for a personal connection between him and the first victim. That link might not have been evident when he killed her. It's probably the reason he wasn't caught. You might have to go back three months, maybe even three years, from the time of her death to find the connection."

A spark of hope flared in him. "We'll go back over everything related to the first victim."

"Oh, I wish Detective Delaney hadn't left."

"Why?"

"Because I'm concerned for her welfare. Not only does she resemble the type of young woman he goes after and she interfered with his ritual, but she is also an authority figure. This makes her irresistible to him. Then there's the way he violated the sanctity of her home by taking his latest victim there. Raping the girl on the detective's bed," the agent said with a horrified look, "and then murdering her is alarming. Even more so was his elaborate ruse at the cemetery. It was a game. One specifically designed for Detective Delaney to fail."

"I don't understand. You mean he knew that she wouldn't go alone," he said, and as the words left his mouth, a chill snaked down his spine. Of course that monster had known. Otherwise, he wouldn't have been set up on the roof, already in position, waiting. "But why would he want her to fail? He wants to get up close and personal with her, and that was his chance."

"Once again, the answer is two-fold. He expected you and the other officers to be there. By shooting you, he effectively removed her protectors from the gameboard. Isolating her. Then she assumes the failure. The guilt. The responsibility. Not only for the lives of the officers but also for Zoey Williams. He wanted her to fail so that he could give her a chance to atone. To play his game on his terms. I believe Detective Delaney is in grave danger."

Chapter Twenty

Friday, September 20
7:55 p.m.
Ten minutes earlier

"Could it be a police officer?" Hannah asked Agent Tomlinson. "One high up in the ranks, who has been passed over for promotion to chief three times? Even if he passed a polygraph?"

"Most definitely." The senior agent nodded. "Sometimes serial killers are able to pass a polygraph because they don't view the world, the truth, the same way."

Hannah's phone chimed with a text. She glanced down and read it.

Say nothing to Chief Granger or anyone else about this or he dies. I swear it. Leave the SWUPD. Wait for my call. You have thirty seconds.

Her heart squeezed with terror. Pure fear for Matt. "It's Kent. Excuse me a minute." Not daring to look at him and give anything away in her eyes, she got up and hurried out of the room.

Once she had cleared the office, certain Matt couldn't see her, she ran down the hall, past the reception desk, ignoring the duty officer's quizzical stare, and shoved through the doors.

Her phone rang.

"I'm out of the SWUPD," she answered.

"Sixteen-year-old Zoey could still have a bright future. But that depends on what you do next. Do you want to save her?"

"Yes," she said without hesitation.

"Take off your badge and gun. Put both on the ground. If you don't, I'll know."

Glancing around the parking garage, she wondered if he was there, watching her. Hidden in one of the parked vehicles. The two entrances to the garage gave him a second exit so he wouldn't be boxed in. But there were cameras in here.

Instinct had her turning, looking beyond the garage. From where she stood, she could see the street and several parked vehicles. Which meant someone inside of one could also see her.

"Do it," he said, "or the kid will die screaming."

The last time she hadn't followed his rules, four men were shot, including Matt, and Zoey wasn't rescued. The only choice she had was compliance.

She did as he instructed, unhooking her badge and service weapon and then setting them both on the ground.

"Good girl," he said, like she was a dog. "Now, I want you to run to Millstone Cemetery. It's 1.3 miles away. Once you're off campus, take Fifth Street headed west, not Grand Avenue. You have nine minutes, thirty-three seconds to be there, or Zoey dies. Leave your phone. Your time starts now. Run!"

Hannah dropped her phone, pulled Matt's keys from her pocket, letting them fall, and then her legs were moving, pumping as they propelled her through the parking garage. She darted down the road, skirting Fourth Street as she made her way off campus. Taking a right onto Eagle Avenue, she went in the opposite direction of Grand Avenue. She bolted down the sidewalk, her arms pumping, her heart hammering.

Hurry.

Faster.

You have to run faster!

An avid jogger, she was not a sprinter. A ten-minute mile was good for her. Nine was possible. But making it to the cemetery, 1.3 miles away, in less than ten would take everything she had.

The small GPS tracker still tucked in her bra rubbed her skin with each brutal stride she took. In the aftermath of the shooting, she hadn't thought to remove it in the whirlwind of cries, blood, the sirens and then there was Tomlinson's urgent request for a video conference.

Matt would be furious with her for taking off without him. But now she was in the crosshairs alone instead of him being in harm's way. He'd remember the tracker and could find her once she saved Zoey. She didn't care what happened to herself, so long as that young woman survived.

She reached the cross streets of Eagle and Fifth and tore around the corner. Racing down the sidewalk, she dodged pedestrians and darted through traffic, not even slowing for moving cars.

Her lungs were on fire. She could barely breathe. But the one thing that mattered, the only thing, was getting to Millstone in time.

She'd failed Zoey once. Not again.

Hannah's legs were noodles, but a steely determination drove her. The cool night breeze nipped her lungs. Sweat beaded her forehead. Her heart swelled at the sight of Millstone just up ahead.

She dashed across the last street, reaching the sidewalk in front of the cemetery, and suddenly, her legs gave up, bringing her to a teetering halt on the edge of the pavement. She took huge swallows of air, trying desperately to catch her breath and steady her pulse.

A cell phone rang somewhere in the graveyard. She ran inside, down the center lane, searching for the source of the sound, desperate to find it before it stopped.

There!

On top of a headstone was a cell phone. And a capped syringe.

Her mouth went dry, but she grabbed the phone. "Hello?"

"Good girl. You made it with three seconds to spare. I like that. Shows you're committed."

"Where's Zoey?"

"Not so fast. Saving her comes at a price."

She took several more ragged breaths, preparing herself, bracing. "I'll pay it."

"I know," he said, and she could swear she heard him smiling. "A life for a life. Yours for Zoey's. Pick up the syringe, remove the cap, insert the needle in your neck and depress the plunger fully."

Her heart turned to a block of ice.

"I'm watching you very closely. If you try anything funny, if you don't do exactly as I've commanded, Zoey's blood will be on your hands."

"How do I know that you'll let her live? That you'll release her?"

"I wouldn't enjoy a hookup with her. I wouldn't enjoy hurting her, either. She's not really my type. But *you* are."

The words curdled her stomach. "Give me proof that she's alive."

"Zoey, say hello to the pretty detective."

"H-Hello," a shaky, young voice said. "Please help me."

"I will," Hannah said, her heart pounding. "I swear it."

"Describe the detective and what she's wearing," he said.

"L-long blond hair. You're w-wearing a blue jacket and b-blue jeans."

Squeezing her eyes shut for a second, Hannah took a calming breath. She glanced around. A few vehicles were parked on the street adjacent to the cemetery, but no dark SUV that resembled the body type of a Tahoe or Yukon.

"There. You have your proof," he said. "Do as I command."

A cold lance of fear stabbed her, but she shoved it aside. Freeing Zoey was what mattered.

Hannah picked up the syringe with a trembling hand, flicked off the cap and injected herself in the neck.

"Good girl. Now, take off your handcuffs and put them on, wrists behind your back, and wait for me. I'll even let you see Zoey because you've pleased me."

She set the phone on the headstone, took the handcuffs from her belt. Putting her hands behind her back, she slapped them on, loosely enough to be able to slide her wrists free.

With the GPS tracker, Matt would find her in time.

I'll be all right.

No matter what this monster dishes out, you can take it.

I'll be all right. And I've still got the knife hidden in my belt buckle. Given the chance, one split second of opportunity, I'll kill him.

Her vision blurred but then came back into focus. She swayed on her feet, her head growing heavy, her thoughts clouding. The drug was already taking effect. Quickly.

A white van emerged from the shadow of a building and entered the cemetery, heading slowly toward her.

Squinting against the glare of the headlights, she wobbled, struggling to stay on her feet. Everything turned blurry, her limbs growing numb. A feeling of sludge in her veins slowed down her thoughts, her blood flow, her heartbeat.

The driver's-side door swung open. A man hopped out. It was him. Different wig. No beard. But he had a fuzzy mustache.

She longed to kick his butt, to stomp his face in and make him swallow his own teeth, but as she took a step, everything spun, and she realized her legs had given out and she was falling.

She hit the ground, her head smacking hard against the pavement.

The man opened the passenger door and pulled someone out.

Hannah's eyelids were heavy, so heavy, but she needed to hang on. Long enough to see the girl was okay.

They walked toward her; the girl was crying and barefoot, wearing pin-striped pajamas with strawberries. He shoved her down to the ground on her knees.

Hannah looked up at Zoey's terrified face, and it was the last thing she saw before the darkness closed in.

A DEAL WAS a deal, and he was a man of his word. He picked up the cell phone from the headstone and handed it to Zoey. "Count to one hundred. Then I want you to make a phone call. There is one programmed number. Use it. Ask for Campus Chief of Police Granger. Tell him who you are and where to find you. He'll take care of you. Do you understand?"

"Yes." Sobbing and trembling like a leaf in the wind, the young girl took the phone.

"Fail to do as I command, and I will come back for you. Hurt you. Make you wish you were dead. Understand?"

"Y-y-yes."

"Now, say 'thank you.'" Young people had no manners anymore. He just spared her life.

Tears streamed down her cheeks. "Thank you."

He pulled an extra-long pushpin from his pocket that had a half-inch thick sharp steel needle and pricked the detective in her thigh to be sure she was out cold. Not so much as a twitch from her.

Good.

"Begin counting once I leave the cemetery," he told Zoey, and she nodded, clutching the phone to her chest.

He bent down and scooped up the detective into his arms. As he stood, he braced for the slight pain that flared up. An old leg injury from years ago. One that truly required him to wear a medical boot until it had healed. Sometimes it still bothered him. When it rained. When it snowed. When he had to pick up something heavy from the ground, like a body.

Adjusting her weight in his arms, he carried her to the van. A breeze blew through her hair, kicking up the scent of her shampoo. *Spicy.* Just like their hookup would be.

The detective was a feisty one.

He set her down in the passenger's seat. Then he opened the sliding door on the side. The crisp, powerful scent of bleach curled around his nose, comforting him. He grabbed the detective and tossed her into the van.

Climbing up inside, he looked her over and salivated. *Pa-*

tience. He removed her boots and patted her down, starting at the ankles, checking for any hidden weapons. This harpy was devious and wicked, and he wouldn't put it past her to have something dangerous concealed.

He ran his palms over her flat stomach and up to her breasts, giving them a nice squeeze. But he found more than supple flesh. Something hard.

What's that?

He pulled out a small, rectangular dark gray transmitter. A GPS tracker. He chained the detective up in the van. Instead of using GHB, he went for something different that wasn't as long lasting because he couldn't wait to party with her. She wouldn't wake up while he was on the road, but he didn't believe in taking unnecessary chances, either. Hence, the shackles.

Smiling, he took the tracker and placed it behind one of the rear wheels. He got into the driver's seat, threw the van in Reverse and rolled over the transmitter as he backed out of the cemetery with his prize secured.

Chapter Twenty-One

Friday, September 20
8:08 p.m.

"Thank you, Agent Tomlinson," Matt said, grateful for her insight. "But I don't think Detective Delaney can be persuaded to walk away from this case." He was almost certain of it.

"For her own safety, she must. The closer we get to the end of the month, the more aggressive and bolder the killer will become in his effort to achieve his goal. There's no telling how far he'll go. I would also recommend protective custody for her."

The one place he knew, without a doubt, that she'd be safe was the Shooting Star Ranch. "I'll speak with her." Although it would've been better for her to have heard it firsthand from a seasoned FBI agent. Then she might accept the gravity of this threat and not dismiss it as him being overprotective because of his personal feelings for her.

Where was she, anyway? Hopefully, Kent hadn't run into a problem.

"Good luck, Chief Granger. Liz was right to ask me to

look at your case. Don't hesitate to reach out if you need anything else."

They disconnected.

Where was Hannah?

He left his office, going down the hallway in the direction she had gone. In the lobby of the station, he looked at the duty officer. "Have you seen Detective Delaney?"

"She ran out of here like the devil was chasing her. Then she stood outside the front door for a minute and bolted."

"What?" He started toward the entrance to see if she had taken his truck. Stepping outside, he saw his vehicle still there.

Then his gaze fell, landing on her gun in its holster, her badge, cell phone and his keys. Disbelief rattled through him as he bent down and picked everything up.

No. Please, no.

"Hannah!" But he knew, deep in his gut, that he was too late.

She was gone.

Fear surged through him, complete and deafening. He reeled against it, his heart stuttering.

He rushed back into the station. "Secure these." He handed the duty officer Hannah's badge and service weapon and slipped her cell phone into his pocket.

Give me the number to your private cell phone.

The University Killer had demanded her personal number so he could continue communicating with her. The text she had received in his office must have been from the killer.

"Call Sergeant Starkey's house," he said to the duty officer. "The landline number, not his cell. See if he's home." This was the quickest, easiest way to see if Sergeant Starkey was a real suspect. The man couldn't be in two places at once. Either Starkey was innocent and at home or he might be the killer and have Hannah chained up somewhere.

With a nod, the duty officer picked up the receiver.

Think.

Think.

The tracker. Maybe she still had it on. Hurrying to his office, he took out his cell phone and dialed Kent.

"Kramer."

"Did you text Hannah about ten, maybe fifteen minutes ago?" he asked, needing to be sure. He sat at the computer and toggled over to the tracking system.

"No, I didn't."

Rage seared through his veins, and he struggled to keep his emotions under control. "That SOB took Hannah. He has her." The program was coming up.

"What? How? She was with you."

The words hit him like a dagger in the chest. "No time to explain. I need you to go to Foster's house. See if he's home. We have to find the killer. Tonight. Understand? We don't sleep. We don't rest. Not for a minute. Until we figure out where he's taken her and get her back."

"Yeah, okay."

Hanging up, he stared at the screen. No green dot. The GPS tracker she'd used earlier wasn't active.

He banged a fist on the desk. Taking a deep breath, he spun out of his chair and went to grab the file on the first victim.

"Chief," the duty officer said, poking his head down the hall, "Starkey's home. Now what?"

"Is he still on the line?"

"Yeah. But not for long. He's about to take his family for ice cream."

Matt raced down the hall and picked up the phone. "Victor, the University Killer shot three campus officers and me tonight," he said, bypassing any pleasantries and using Starkey's first name, to hit home that this attack on them was personal. "The others are in the hospital. I believe he's taken Detective Delaney. Your leave of absence is over, effective immediately. I need you here now. Uniform doesn't matter."

"On my way, Chief. I'll be there in ten."

Matt slammed the phone down on the receiver. As he was leaving to go grab the file, the phone rang.

The duty officer answered at the front and then called back to him. "Chief, it's for you. Sounds urgent."

Maybe it was him. The killer. Calling to gloat. To ask for something in exchange for Hannah. He put the phone to his ear. "This is Chief Granger."

"M-m-my name is Zoey Williams. He told me to call you. Only you. That you would make sure I was safe."

Grim calmness stole over him. "Detective Hannah Delaney. Did you see her? Do you know where she is?"

"He took her. The blond detective. He said 'a life for a life.'"

His stomach upheaved. Matt couldn't regret that an innocent teen had been released. But he also couldn't—wouldn't—accept this sacrifice that Hannah had made. He would do whatever necessary to get her back. "Where are you?"

"I don't know. A cemetery. Stone-something. I see a street sign for Grand Avenue."

"The Millstone Cemetery?"

"Yeah, I think that's it."

"I'm sending a cop to come and get you." While Matt would dig into the file on the first victim. "He'll be there in less than five minutes. In the meantime, I'm going to put the duty officer back on the phone. He's going to talk to you until you're in a patrol car. Okay?"

She sobbed over the line. "Thank you. Please hurry."

HE PARKED THE van at the cabin in the woods, which was only a thirty-minute drive from town, and slung Delaney over his shoulder. Walking past the front steps of the cabin, he went around to the side of the house. He squatted, grimacing against the ache in his leg. After removing the padlock, he opened the door to the soundproof, self-sealing concrete storm shelter. What he liked to call "the party room."

Balancing her weight on his shoulder, he eased down the steps.

Sometimes he brought his son out to the woods to hunt deer and elk, but no one was allowed down here. This was his special place, and only he had the key for the padlock.

He flopped Delaney on top of the fresh sheets and blanket covering the cot that was bolted to the floor. A proper hookup always had to start with clean white bedding. That way he could enjoy seeing it get dirty.

Snickering, he uncuffed her. But she wouldn't be unrestrained for long. He unbuckled her belt, unzipped her jeans, peeled them off, removed her jacket and T-shirt, undressing her down to her underwear. He ran his hands over her body. She would do nicely. When she woke up, she would realize her place in this new world—his world, where he would be her god.

"FOSTER IS HOME," Kent said over the phone. "He's watching a cooking show. Drinking pinot noir. I'm headed back to campus. Almost there."

Matt slapped the file in front of him closed. "Thanks. I rechecked the case file on the first victim, Paige Johnson. She was nineteen when she was killed. I spoke with her father. He said Paige didn't have any boyfriends."

"Do you believe him?"

"Paige liked girls, according to her father. So yes. He also said she got along with everybody. Never had any negative run-ins with anyone." Matt sighed. "Agent Tomlinson was confident there is a personal connection between the first victim and the killer."

What was he missing?

He was peeling away layers of the puzzle, but he didn't have the core. Not yet. It was only a matter of time. He just didn't know how much Hannah had.

Starkey flung open Matt's office door and rushed in with Carl and the LPD officer.

"Did you find something?" Matt asked.

"Possibly," Starkey said, his face grave. "There are quite a few people working at the university who drive a dark Tahoe or Yukon. But Carl noticed something odd."

Matt put his cell on speaker so Kent could stay in the loop. "What is it?"

Starkey handed him the DMV records.

Looking over the list, he zeroed in on the one line that had been both circled and highlighted.

"Dennis Hill," Matt said, the hair rising on his arms.

"According to the records, he owns a twelve-year-old granite-crystal metallic Chevy Tahoe," Starkey said. "But he's never mentioned it and has never driven it to work. Like he's hiding it. He's already got a Jeep, and his wife drives a sedan."

"Three vehicles," Matt said. "Tomlinson said that there

will be patterns of three's in the killer's life. Carl, grab his personnel record."

Farran hurried out down the hall.

"What do you know about Dennis?" Matt asked Starkey. "Anything involving three's in his life."

"Um, well, he married his wife three times. Does that count?"

"Why on earth would he marry her three times?" Kent asked.

"The first time was at the justice of the peace. Second was a big ceremony and reception. But his mother was sick or something. She's in the Silver Springs Nursing Home. The third time was over there so his mom could be a part of it. He's really proud of it, too. Celebrates three wedding anniversaries every year. His wife brags about how romantic he is."

Farran came back with the file.

Matt snatched it from his hands and opened it. Perusing it, he stopped midway. "He's got three kids, too."

"Oh yeah, he does." Starkey nodded. "Or did. I forgot. One of his daughters died. Meningitis, I think."

Matt looked for the date of death. "His daughter died three years ago. A month before the University Killer last struck. Hey, Kent. I need you to go to his house. Speak to his wife. See what she knows." He gave him the address. Hill lived in close proximity to the campus.

"Dennis has a son who attends the university," Starkey said. "Liam. We can find him at one of the frat houses. Alpha-something. He might know something, too."

Matt grabbed his hat and keys. "Let's find out."

Chapter Twenty-Two

Friday, September 20
9:20 p.m.

Hannah stirred, her heavy eyelids lifting. Her throat was dry. Her mouth felt like cotton. She stared up at a low gray ceiling. Soft amber light came from a lamp somewhere. As she sat up, chains rattled. She realized she was on top of a bed. Full-size. Wrought iron frame.

Her wrists were now in front of her but still cuffed, with a long chain locked to the top of the bed frame. She gazed down at herself. Her clothes were gone, except for her bra and panties.

She stood, barefoot, more chains rattling, and swayed on her feet. There was an iron shackle around each ankle with a separate chain connected to one of the lower corners of the bed. Sickening awareness struck her that he'd restrained her in a manner to make spreading her legs easier.

Bile burned her throat, and her stomach clenched.

Where were her clothes? Her belt?

She looked around. The room was small. A cell, really. Made of concrete. Maybe nine by twelve. The bed took up most of the space.

In a corner sat a table no larger than a nightstand. With a lamp on top of it. Beyond the table was a door.

She shuffled forward, only to be snatched to a halt. The chain connected to her handcuffs wouldn't let her make it past the bed.

Kneeling down, she looked under the bedframe.

Her clothes—and a bucket, but she didn't want to think about what that was for. She reached for the pile of clothes and dragged it out. Everything was in tatters. He had cut her pants, jacket, top and belt into pieces. The only thing intact was the buckle.

The fool hadn't checked it. And she was going to use that mistake against him.

She pulled out the short blade and shoved everything else back under the bed.

As she stood, the room spun. Turning slowly, she gazed at the walls. When she faced the one behind the bed, she froze. Polaroid pictures of women, bruised and still—murdered—covered the concrete like some sick wallpaper. Her skin crawled.

Each photo was of a different blonde.

And there were more than twenty.

MATT STOOD INSIDE the foyer of the Alpha Theta Nu frat house alongside Sergeant Starkey, waiting for Liam.

His cell phone rang. "Granger," he said, answering.

"Bonnie Hill didn't answer the door," Kent said. "I looked around through the windows. Saw her unconscious on the couch. An open bottle of wine on the table. I kicked in the door. She's got a pulse, but I can't wake her. I think her husband drugged her. The ambulance is on the way."

"Okay. Search the house. See what you can find that might point to where he's taken Hannah."

"Will do. I'll keep you posted."

"What's up?" Starkey asked.

Matt was about to answer, but a tall kid—eighteen years old, with dark hair and dark eyes; a younger, fitter version of Dennis—came down the stairs.

"Hey, Sergeant Starkey." The young man looked at Matt. "Hi, I'm Liam."

"Chief Granger."

"I was told you needed to speak with me."

"Son, we're trying to locate your father," Matt said. "It's of the utmost importance that we find him. It's a matter of life or death."

"He should be at home. With my mom."

"We checked there," Matt said gently. "Your mother was found unconscious and in need of medical attention."

"Oh my God. I'll call my dad." He reached for his phone.

"Please, don't." Matt raised a palm. "We're still piecing things together, and it would be best if we spoke with your father first."

Liam's brow furrowed. "Is he in trouble? You don't think he did something to my mom, do you?"

"We're not jumping to any conclusions," Matt said, not wanting to make the kid defensive, since they needed his help. "But it's imperative that we find him and speak with him in person." He kept his voice patient, his tone soft. "Is there any place that you can think of where he might go? A favorite spot? Somewhere he feels safe."

Liam nodded. "My grandparent's cabin. It's in the woods. In Wayward Bluffs." He gave them the address.

"Thank you." Matt turned to Starkey. "Take his phone

and keep him at the station. No phone calls. Make him comfortable and give him updates on his mother's condition."

Matt turned and dashed out the door, running to his truck.

Hang on, Hannah.

HIS PRIZE SHOULD be bright eyed by now and no longer groggy. He'd given her plenty of time to recover. Their first time together, he wanted her wide awake and fiery.

He removed the padlock, stuck the key back in his pocket and opened the door to the shelter.

Ducking his head, he climbed down and closed the door behind him.

Chains rattled as Hannah Delaney scooted back on the bed, bringing her knees up to her chest like she was scared. But fire burned in her eyes.

Was she up to something?

"Rise and shine," he said in a singsong voice.

Leaning forward a bit, she gaped at him. "You?" she asked, shock thickening her voice.

She didn't see the forest for the trees. Just like Granger and every other police chief before him.

No more disguises needed. He'd not only gotten rid of the wig, mustache and fake contacts but also the toupee he wore on a daily basis to hide his receding hairline.

He smiled. "These are the rules by which you live." And eventually die. "You will call me *Master*," he said, and she narrowed her eyes to slits. "Only by pleasing me during our hookups will you get food and water. If you make me angry, you will be punished. I own you now. The sooner you accept this, the better. For you." He waited to see what kind of response he'd get.

Sometimes they sobbed. Sometimes they argued. Sometimes they tried to bargain, promising that their parents would pay him money if only he released them. Inevitably, whether in the beginning or at the end, they all begged for mercy.

But Hannah didn't utter a single word. She just stared at him. If looks could kill, he would be ashes blowing in the wind.

He grinned.

She was strong and healthy and would last a long time. Longer than any other. Not mere hours or days but weeks. He was sure of it.

With her fighting spirit, he would have to hurt her. To teach her that she wasn't to try to hurt him. And in that lesson, she would also learn how glorious her pleasure could be after pain.

Like breaking in a wild horse, this would take a firm hand and patience on his part. He'd have to be careful, though. She was a threat, but only if he allowed her to be. Taming her would certainly be no easy task. He was up for the challenge.

She was special. Different. He would cherish her, even as he despised her.

Suddenly giddy, almost drunk with anticipation, he stepped to the foot of the bed. Watched her—his feral, quiet cat curled in on herself.

Grinning, he grabbed the chain connected to her right ankle and yanked it, forcing her leg to extend to the corner of the bed. He bent down and fixed one of the links on a hook on the floor to hold it in place.

As he stood, he sensed and then heard movement, the bedsprings creaking.

Hannah pounced forward like lightning and jammed something sharp in the back of his shoulder blade. Hot agony pierced him. But she didn't stop. She kept stabbing and slicing and drawing his blood while he tried to block her blows, howling and cursing in shock and pain.

He stumbled backward, away from the bed, out of her deadly reach.

Eyes full of rage, she was crouched, poised to lunge again, a blade in her hand covered in his blood.

Where had it come from? He'd been so careful.

"If you think I won't fight you until my last breath, then you had better think again! You took the wrong woman. Do you hear me, you sick, perverted monster?"

No. He took the right one. She was perfect. He liked it when they fought. When they struggled. "Breaking you will be that much sweeter. I think it's time for your first real lesson."

He stormed out of the shelter, leaving the door open. The cold night air would cool her off. He marched toward the cabin, realizing he'd forgotten to charge the cattle prod.

He swore to himself. While he had to wait for it to juice up, she would be that much weaker from the cold air, shivering, her teeth chattering, the deadly edge to her fighting drained.

But that wasn't enough punishment for Hannah Delaney. He was in agony.

Not only would he use the cattle prod, but he'd put her in a straitjacket, too. That would show her. Three days wearing that, and then she'd call him *Master.*

ABOUT A QUARTER of a mile down the road from the address Liam had given Matt, he pulled off to the side and shut the engine. From the back seat, he took a bulletproof vest, strapped it on and slipped his jacket over it. After he double-checked his Glock, he stuffed extra magazines, each containing fifteen rounds, into his pocket. He hooked two flash grenades on his vest, grabbed his night-vision goggles and flipped them down.

He set off into the woods, going the direction where the cabin should be. His shoulder ached something awful, but he ignored the pain.

Steadily, carefully, he moved, scanning for movement or anything that might give away his presence. Such as flood-lights or security cameras. He spotted nothing. Kept going. Stayed alert. He slipped between the trees like a shadow.

In minutes, he came upon the back side of a cabin. He prayed that this was the right place and that Hannah was safe.

Footsteps pounded down wooded stairs at the front of the house.

Fifteen feet before the back porch, he cut quietly to the left, tracking the footfalls over dry leaves. He peeked around the side of the house.

A man stalked toward a mound.

Dennis Hill. Holding a straitjacket—the buckles flapping—and something else, like a metal stick, but then Matt noticed the familiar U-shaped tip. Sparks flared, tiny bright flashes on the faint green tinge of his screen.

A cattle prod!

Matt ripped off his night-vision goggles and took aim with his Glock.

But Dennis climbed down the stairs that led below ground, grabbing hold of the door to close it.

Right before it slammed shut, Matt heard Hannah swearing.

She was alive, and she was fighting. The icy fear that had squeezed his heart loosened its grip a little.

He rushed over to the mound. Took a flash grenade from his vest. Pulled the pin with his teeth. Cracked open the door. Tossed it in and shut the door.

A deafening boom erupted in tandem with a bright flash of light. It would incapacitate Hannah just as much as Dennis for a critical moment. But she would recover. The same couldn't necessarily be said about Dennis.

Matt threw open the door and hustled down the steps with his weapon at the ready.

The sight before him made his blood boil. Hannah was chained to a bed, writhing from the effects of the flash bang, bloody hands covering her ears and more blood splattered on her half-naked body.

Rage overwhelmed Matt. He charged Dennis, snatching him up from the floor, gritting his teeth through the sharp pain in his arm, and thrashed the man with his fist until blood ran from his nose.

Matt shoved him to the ground, face-first. Hard. He put a knee on his back, keeping him pinned, yanked Dennis's arms behind him and slapped cuffs on him tight.

Standing up, he spotted the straitjacket and cattle prod. He had half a mind to string Dennis up, use the cattle prod on him and then put an end to that brutal beast. But ranch justice, a quick death, was too good for him.

Matt kicked the cattle prod away. He looked up, and his gaze snagged on the concrete wall behind the bed covered in heinous photos. Renewed fury rushed over him, but he needed to help Hannah.

He went over to the bed, sat down and reached for her.

Still squirming, she lashed out with a blade that came dangerously close to his throat, but he'd been expecting anything and pulled back out of her reach.

He caught her wrists gently with one hand and pressed a palm to her cheek with the other. Her eyelids lifted, and her gaze found his.

Relief washed over her face. He hauled her up into his arms, the chains jangling, and held her tight to his chest. Her cold body shivered against him.

He pulled back, took off his jacket and wrapped it around her.

"You're right in the nick of time," she said, her teeth chattering.

"I try to be punctual." Matt dug out a handcuff key from his pocket and freed her wrists. "There's so much blood on you."

"None of it's mine. It's his."

He got to work on the shackles on her ankles and released her. "You take too many chances."

She stood and rubbed her wrists. "Only when necessary."

He ripped the blanket from the bed and wrapped it around her waist. "You scared the hell out of me." He tugged her back into his arms, determined to never let her go.

Tipping her head up, she looked at him. "You say the most romantic things."

Epilogue

Saturday, September 21
7:30 p.m.

Hannah leaned against Matt, her head on his chest, his uninjured arm curled around her as they sat on his sofa in front of a cozy fire. She sipped her whiskey, grateful she'd made it out of Dennis Hill's lair alive. Relieved Zoey Williams was unharmed. Happy to have Matt at her side, willing to go into hell and fight the devil—not only with her but also *for* her.

Matt picked up her legs and draped them over his lap.

"I still can't wrap my mind around how many women Dennis Hill actually killed," she said, her skin crawling as she thought about the photos on the wall.

Twenty-four in total had been murdered. Hill had a type, and he never deviated from the profile. Young, under twenty-two, blond, fair skin, petite.

"If not for you, we never would have found his first twelve victims buried on the property of his cabin."

They'd thought Paige Johnson was his first victim, when in actuality, it was Nicole Noland.

"Agent Tomlinson was correct about the personal connection," Matt continued.

Nicole had dated Dennis when he was a kicker on the SWU football team. Number thirty-three jersey. Nicole had broken up with him after they got into a car accident, and he injured his leg and couldn't play anymore. He started dating Bonnie, his current wife, and waited three months to rape and kill Nicole. He'd used Bonnie as his alibi.

Hannah shook her head, horrified by what Dennis had done to his victims and his family. "For twenty years, he's been drugging Bonnie, making that poor woman think she has a drinking problem, so he could sneak out and kill women. The shame his wife must've felt when you questioned her about her husband's whereabouts the night Madison Scott was murdered. Too embarrassed to say she was drunk and had blacked out and couldn't remember, even though she had really been roofied."

"Dennis fooled everyone. He was so unassuming, lurking right under the nose of every campus police chief for the past twenty years."

After he'd graduated from SWU, Dennis tried to join the campus police department, but his leg injury prevented him from passing the physical, and he became the office manager instead, picking his victims from the students who came into the police station to register their bicycles.

He confessed that nothing in particular had triggered this latest murder spree. Only that he'd felt compelled to find a sense of release.

"Promise me something," Matt said.

"What?"

"That you'll never lie to me again," he said, referring to her telling him that Kent had texted her. "No matter how difficult. No matter how complicated. Not even to protect me."

She would always do whatever she could to protect him.

But she'd never lie to him again. "I promise. I'm sorry. You understand why?"

He nodded. There was no judgment or anger in his eyes. Only warmth. The knowledge that he understood her and accepted her, flaws and all, meant everything.

Matt rubbed her legs before taking her foot and massaging it.

"I should be massaging you." She kissed him on the lips, loving the feel of his stubble against her skin.

"You should, and you'll get your chance later, in the bedroom." He winked at her.

She couldn't help but smile.

He picked up his drink, took a swallow and went back to massaging her foot. "The university administration is impressed that we caught two serial killers."

Foster's DNA matched that of the Emerald City Butcher. Following a hunch, Kent had cadaver dogs search the state park situated in between the two spots where Dr. Bradford Foster liked to fish. They'd found four more bodies.

"Sam Lee will finally be released from prison," she said. "But nothing can restore the years stolen from him."

"At least his name will be cleared, and he can enjoy his freedom while knowing that the real Butcher will get what's coming to him."

Her thoughts careened back to Dennis Hill and his plans for her in that storm shelter. "I feel for Hill's children." His son, Liam, and older daughter, Susie. "And his wife."

She understood the unique agony of being the child of a serial killer. A nightmare she wouldn't wish on her worst enemy.

"Foster had kids, too."

It was hard to believe such men loved their children, their families, when they would leave them that legacy of evil.

"I have no control over what Erica Egan prints, but I have some influence with the campus paper. They've agreed to make it clear that the families of Hill and Foster didn't know the horrible truth and will ask for people to respect their privacy."

"That was really thoughtful of you."

He was the sweet one in this relationship.

"Hey." He picked up her hand and kissed her knuckles, and the tenderness in his eyes made her breath catch. "This might sound nuts or too fast, but what do you think about moving in here? Us making a home together?"

Stunned, she looked at him, totally blindsided and speechless.

"It's fast, but we both put in crazy hours on the job, and I do a lot of work on the ranch. It might be the only way to see each other with any sort of consistency. I want to build on this. This connection. And you said you were never sleeping in your place again."

And she wasn't.

When she didn't respond, he said, "I'm not trying to push."

"No. I want you to push. Sometimes we need a nudge out of our comfort zone for our own good." Funny how coming inches from being tortured and dying had made her realize how much was lacking in her life. "I want to be with you. See what *this* can grow into." Happiness swelled inside her as she studied his face.

The side of his mouth curved up. "Even if you fall madly in love and end up needing me?"

"I'm already falling, cowboy," she said, not mentioning

how hard she was falling, and he smiled fully. “And as for needing you? I’ve learned that’s not such a bad thing.”

She’d needed him throughout this entire case, as well as the one they’d worked on last year. But she hadn’t realized that she also needed his warmth, his understanding, his intensity.

His strength.

He leaned over and kissed her with tenderness and heat. This new relationship, this remarkable joy and lightness of being, was scary but wondrous. And worth it.

She smiled at him. “I guess you better get me a set of keys, because this is home.”

* * * * *

HUNTING COLTON'S WITNESS

ANNA J. STEWART

For the legions of Colton fans.

This one's for you.

Chapter One

"Can I get you another drink, Nate?"

Detective Nate Colton stifled a disheartened sigh and glanced at his club soda with lime. "No, thanks, Seb." He flashed a tight smile at the bartender/co-owner of Madariaga's before casting an even quicker glance into the mirror. Leave it to scam artist Dean Wexler to turn his free Friday night into one of alcohol-free surveillance duty. "I'm still nursing this one."

"Working, huh?" Seb's sympathetic expression did nothing to ease Nate's irritation.

"Afraid so." Nate paused, considered. He glanced around, trying to take some pleasure in the plethora of Christmas lights strung around, through and over the crisscrossing beams covering the ceiling. "Question, Seb."

"Shoot." The middle-aged man whipped a hand towel over the shoulder of his festive red vest. "Sorry." He grinned and had Nate chuckling. "Not a lot of cops come in here. Don't get many opportunities to use my well-honed humor. What's up?"

"This guy." Nate inclined his head toward the table at his left. The thirtysomething man wore simple jeans and a dark T-shirt beneath a black leather jacket. His hands flexed and relaxed in a kind of rhythm that had him alternating between grasping his half-filled beer glass and slicking back his straw-blond hair. "You see him in here before?"

"Don't think so." The gray in Seb's hair and full beard shimmered beneath the dim recessed lighting when he shook his head. "Why?"

Telling Seb the man in question was a convicted scammer and con artist probably wasn't the way to go. Instead, Nate shrugged. "He looks jittery."

"My guess? First date. Probably a blind one." Seb reached for a glass on the drying rack and set it aside. "Ever since we implemented our safe dating protocol, we get a lot of them."

"Safe…?" Nate shook his head.

"We put up a notice in the ladies' room," Seb told him. "They order a certain drink, we know they need help." Seb inclined his chin down the hall on the other side of the room that led to an emergency exit. "We call for a car, and they get picked up at the back of the building. Date's none the wiser, and the lady gets home safe and sound."

"Nice." Nate grabbed a pair of olives and tossed them in his mouth. "More restaurants need that kind of policy."

"It's definitely upped our business," Seb said. "Speaking of business, haven't seen you in here in a while."

"Been busy. Work and, you know…" Nate paused, ate another olive, this one stuffed with an almond. "Family."

He was still adjusting to the fallout of recent Colton family events and revelations. While he and his sister had always known of their too-close-for-comfort connection to the Colton line branching out of Owl Creek, that part of the family hadn't known either he or Sarah existed at all. Until recently, that is. The emotional fallout on both sides was still being assessed. It was one thing to know he had other siblings living not too far away. It was another to have to deal with them. And the role his mother played in the situation.

That needle-sharp prick of disdain caught as it always did and lodged like a bullet in his chest. Leave it to his mother to set off a familial bomb that resulted in near cataclysmic repercussions. Jessie Colton's calculated actions, as usual, bordered on cruel. But what bothered Nate most was that she never, ever did something like this without a bigger agenda in mind.

His mother was up to something. Something big enough to warrant blowing up a near thirty-year-old family secret.

Part of him didn't want to think about what was coming next. But he needed to do just that, if for no other reason than to protect his sister. He swallowed hard. Plus all ten of the half-brothers and sisters he now openly counted as family.

"Let me know when you're ready for another." Seb offered a sympathetic smile before he moved off to serve a pair of newcomers waiting at the bar for their table.

Pinning his gaze on the mirror to keep track of his target, Nate's stomach rumbled around the teasing promise of food. He'd made a mistake skipping lunch, but he'd been neck deep in planning how to deal with Dean Wexler, the aforementioned table dweller who seemed to grow increasingly fidgety as time passed. Well, Nate thought, he'd followed worse leads and trusted sketchier sources.

He took a deep breath and filled his senses with the familiar and intoxicating aroma of garlic, smoky paprika and saffron, which carried the sweetest hint of honey. The combination increased his crankiness and his hunger.

No one cooked a rib eye like the chefs at Madariaga's, but he couldn't count on Wexler sticking around long enough for him to finish eating. He'd have to make do with the selection of spiced olives and… He raised off his stool enough to grab a dish of mixed nuts farther down the counter. Judging by the way Wexler kept checking his phone for what Nate assumed was the time—or a message from his soon-to-arrive date—it was either going to be a quick wrap-up or a long, long evening. Either way, Nate was in it to the end.

Wexler was the closest thing he had to a lead when it came to his extortion and racketeering case against Marty DeBaccian. Since his release from prison two years ago, DeBaccian had been making his way up the criminal-element food chain here in Boise. Nate, along with a number of his fellow detectives, were determined to stop him before he got anywhere close to the top. Which was where Wexler—a smaller, less careful fish—came in. Nate had been working this case for going on six months. He was getting as antsy as Wexler appeared to be. He wanted this case closed. Now.

"Totally explains how you're spending your Friday night," Nate muttered to himself.

Friday nights on the Basque Block, an area of downtown Boise dedicated to the mix of French and Spanish culture, were notoriously crowded and energetic. The brisk December cold blowing through the city triggered temptations of warm, comforting food and drinks within the welcoming confines of the community. The streets were lined with countless lights and lanterns, windows displayed various images of the seasons, holiday sale signs were abundant and welcoming.

Add in extended Happy Hour at Madariaga's, a restaurant known for their clams Portuguese and in-house brews, and there were numerous festivities in which to partake. The snow had been somewhat gentle on his way in, but he could smell a storm coming.

As he lived a short distance away, Nate often found himself sitting right in this very spot, listening to various musicians performing on the small circular stage in the center of the dining room. Tonight, the usual weekend percussive sounds of drums, tambourines and flutes had been replaced by a solitary guitarist, who, if Nate was honest with himself, conjured a deep-seated envy as she plucked out familiar Christmas music with a finger-flying Spanish-inspired flair.

His lips twitched in unexpected humor. Growing up, he'd loved the idea of becoming a musician, but it soon became obvious the only talent he possessed where a guitar was concerned was stashing it in the back of his closet.

As entertaining as the place was, Nate bit back a self-pitying sigh as he rotated his glass. He'd really been looking forward to a night in, slugging down more than a few bottles of beer and binge-watching the latest in a series of ridiculous, over-the-top, high-speed vehicular action movies.

Seated on a corner stool at the bar, Nate ran through Wexler's rap sheet in his head to keep himself occupied and, more importantly, focused. There wasn't much Wexler hadn't been accused of in his thirty-three years. His first adult arrest had come two days after he'd turned eighteen.

Wexler's juvie record was sealed, but Nate would bet a year's salary the guy spent a significant amount of time locked down from a very early age. Now the guy had a tendency to mix things up and expand into whatever worked best for him. These days, burglaries seemed to be his preferred method of income. After going over numerous victim statements and reports, Nate strongly suspected Wexler was behind the rash of thefts that had relieved nearly a dozen single women of a significant amount of cash and property.

A streak like that had to have caught DeBaccian's attention, which gave Nate some solid leverage. Wexler's spine was as solid as straw. He'd bend over and kiss whatever backside he needed to keep himself out of prison. Or off DeBaccian's hit list. Nate planned on being the person who could make both those things happen. For a price.

Exhaustion crept up his spine. He hadn't had a good night's sleep since he'd gotten back from Owl Creek. Whatever switch that turned his brain off had been overridden by stress, circumstance and what probably amounted to an unhealthy amount of professional obsession.

"Heads up." Seb crouched to retrieve a trayful of clean glasses. When he popped back up, he jutted his chin toward the front door. "Your boy just went on full alert."

Nate's gaze shifted not so subtly to Wexler, who had indeed straightened up and was looking toward the door, which clicked shut.

Wexler's nerves didn't abate, Nate noticed. Instead, they intensified to the point of vibration. Like a cheetah poised to pounce on unsuspecting prey. Wexler stood, lifted an arm, and only then did Nate see the gleam of relief—or was it calculation?—on the man's face. Whatever it was, Wexler definitely had Nate's full attention.

Or at least he did until Nate looked to the door and saw her.

Her back was to him at first as she hung her coat on a hook. She wore a knee-skimming black dress and matching short-sleeved sweater. Her long, dark brown hair draped beautifully down her back. The knee-high boots spoke of practicality where an Idaho winter was concerned. She had curves where he preferred them and not an angle in sight. She was, Nate thought as she turned around and displayed a face worthy of a classical sculptor, the kind of woman who conjured carnal thoughts of endless nights spent in front of a fire while a winter storm raged outside their door.

"Beautiful," he murmured in a way that had him glancing around to confirm he hadn't been overheard. Impulse had his hands curled into fists before reality knocked him back down. He wasn't here for her.

But he wanted to be.

The woman paused, ran her hands down the front of her dress in a motion that spoke to her own bout of nerves. A thin gold chain around her neck displayed a solitary charm that, from a distance, Nate couldn't decipher. Rather than makeup, it was the cold that tinted her cheeks. Her full lips pressed together until they disappeared. Nate could all but hear the pep talk she was giving herself before she stepped shakily over to the hostess desk.

It seemed a cruel trick, or maybe it was a stroke of luck, when she was escorted to Dean Wexler's table.

Nate inclined his head, unable to pull his attention away. She stood beside her chair and offered her hand to Wexler, who immediately grasped it. He could see her mouth move, but couldn't, with the music and conversation bouncing around the restaurant, hear what she said. Her smile seemed strained when she pulled her chair back to sit. Polite. Reserved.

Nate gave Wexler's chances of a second date a whole one out of ten when the idiot neglected to play the chivalry card and pull out her chair for her. *Typical*, Nate thought with a silent snort. Why would Wexler act on something he probably couldn't spell?

Nate was so caught up in that observation he didn't realize she was looking directly at him.

Their gazes locked, and he couldn't, for what seemed

like a full minute, find his breath. His smile came without thought, and he felt a chill of accomplishment when she offered him one in return. Maybe he was fooling himself, but this smile, unlike the one she'd offered Wexler, appeared genuine. A flash of uncertainty illuminated her candlelit hazel eyes before she turned her attention to Wexler and the menu he handed her. Reaching into her purse, she pulled out a pair of round glasses.

Nate glanced away, cursing himself for being tempted to forget about the case and keep her in his sights. Darn if those glasses didn't add to her appeal. He'd never been into the librarian look. Oh, how wrong he'd been.

Focus, Nate told himself. If Wexler's pattern held, this woman could very well be his next burglary victim. Nate's hand tightened around his glass at the thought of anyone—Wexler in particular—taking advantage of her. Of eroding the trust and shadowy optimism he saw in those amazing eyes of hers.

"Seb!" As if taken over by someone else, Nate signaled for another drink. He couldn't risk surrendering to temptation and instead fixed his gaze on the mirror image of her.

Guilt had him shifting uncomfortably on his stool. He hoped he didn't look as pathetic as he felt. He needed to think about someone, anyone else, another woman he'd dated, met, talked with who had intrigued him more than this woman did. But it was a no-go. It was as if this woman, simply by walking into view, had erased every other woman from his memory.

"So?" Seb said. "What do you think?"

Nate took a too large sip of his club soda. "About what?" he choked out.

"Them." Seb tilted his head. "You think they'll make it to a second date?"

"No." Nate lifted his glass, toasted Seb with it. "I do not."

If only because Nate planned on having Wexler behind bars in the next few hours.

VIVIAN MAYLOR'S HEAD was spinning, and not in a good way. Why, oh why, had she let Lizzy talk her into online dating? Because Lizzy was her best friend and had rarely steered her wrong. Clearly there was a first time for everything.

Vivian's vision blurred as she tried to focus on the open menu in her trembling hands. Anxiety had grabbed hold, not when she climbed into her car or even when she'd parked a few blocks away. Oh, no, her old heart-stuttering friend had locked its twisty, suffocating bands around her back when she'd first clicked Accept on the online dating profile.

"Just jump in and rip the Band-Aid off," Lizzy Colton had told her a few weeks ago when Vivian made the mistake of lamenting feeling lonely out loud. "Just go out on one date and see what happens!" This from the woman who less than a month ago had been trapped in a blizzard only to be rescued by a man who may as well have stepped right out of one of Vivian's romance novels.

Of course, Lizzy's headline-making kidnapping around the same time had no doubt left her searching for an outlet for the residual trauma. As happy as Vivian was to serve as a support for her friend, she hadn't anticipated having to agree to a date in order to make Lizzy smile again. But she had. And Lizzy seemed relieved. About that at least.

"Leaving you to rip off the Band-Aid," Vivian muttered then suddenly realized she'd spoken out loud. She peeked over the top edge of her menu and smiled at her date. "Sorry."

She forced a smile before reaching for the ice water their server had delivered. "I live alone, so I talk to myself." She took a big swallow. "A lot."

"Who doesn't?" her date teased. But the glint in his brown eyes didn't lessen her unease. She had the feeling he was trying too hard. "Have you been here before, Vivian?"

"Ah, kind of?" She set the menu down and did her best to ignore the tingling racing down her spine. There was this—she didn't know how else to describe it—this force, pulsing out at her from the bar. Not the bar, she corrected quickly and glanced to her left and saw him looking at her again. But the man sitting there. She pushed her glasses higher up her nose, a nervous habit she had when uncertainty descended. He looked familiar, but she couldn't for the life of her figure out why. "I live a little ways away, but I've ordered from their delivery menu." She needed to focus on her date. He was, after all, why she'd made the white-knuckle drive into town. "So. Sam." She needed to give this an authentic chance. "Is that short for Samuel?"

"Nope." His eyes flashed. "Just Sam. Sam Gabriel."

"Right." She shook her head. "Sam Gabriel." Truth be told, she'd only retained a modicum of the information that had been listed on his profile. While she was at the top of her game in the PR department, socializing outside of work wasn't her thing. She wasn't...outgoing. Or adventurous. But loneliness was a surefire trigger to pushing someone outside their comfort zone.

She supposed it was a good idea to leave the house for something other than getting her mail. Since her cat Toby died last month, she'd spent an inordinate amount of time feeding the strays in her neighborhood, an activity that was quickly earning her loony cat-lady status. All that was missing was the bumper sticker on her car declaring herself a cat mom. Best to get out in the world before that became a reality.

She'd have thought all the cheery holiday decor lining the downtown Boise streets would have elevated her mood, but instead, it only reminded her of how alone she truly was. "You're a teacher, aren't you, Sam? What was it? Third grade?"

"Second." He leaned his arms on the table and grinned so wide she could see the fillings in his molars. He was good-looking enough, she supposed, but that smile. She couldn't help but suspect there was something else lurking behind it. "I just love kids, don't you?"

"I haven't spent enough time around them to say, honestly." She looked back at the dinner offerings, telling herself not to be paranoid. His questions were normal for a first date. Her instincts were out of practice and headed into overdrive. It was a simple dinner date. Nothing more. She was the fish out of water here, not Sam. "I think I'm just going to get the panzanella." Her stomach rumbled at the very idea. She'd been so nervous all day she hadn't had much to eat. The idea of a bread salad hit all the right notes. "How about you?"

"Haven't decided yet." He reached over and pulled her menu down with one crooked finger. "You don't have to be nervous, Vivian."

"It's my natural state." Her smile felt stiff this time, and that voice in the back of her head was definitely crying out more loudly to be listened to. She shouldn't have done this. Taking chances, doing the unexpected—that was Lizzy's way of doing things, not hers. Vivian shoved her hands under her legs and scrunched her fingers, felt the wood against her nails. "So, um." She glanced around, did her best not to let her gaze drift anywhere near the man at the bar. Even as her mind raced to place him. Thankfully, their server arrived and took their orders. The few minutes gave her enough time to get at least some questions lined up in her overactive brain.

The guitarist had taken a break, and to be honest, Vivian welcomed the silence. Or at least as much silence as the crowded restaurant allowed. A solitary votive candle flickered in a deep vessel, sprigs of rosemary pressed up against the glass, casting wintery shadows on the red tablecloth. "So, how long have you been using the dating app?" she asked when they were alone again.

"Not long." He was back to leaning on the table, a semi-smirking expression on his face now. "I like how it gets all the tedious stuff out of the way. I saw on your profile you're in PR. You own your own business, don't you?"

"Yes." She tucked her hair behind her ear. "PR Perfection. I represent a number of clients from various industries. I focus a lot on authors and entertainment figures."

"Sounds interesting."

It must, given the sudden spark in his eyes. "Social media is a big part of what I do," she said. "I guess a dating app didn't seem out of the norm by comparison." If only she was as good at talking about herself as she was discussing her clients. So far, the only word that came to mind regarding this date was *excruciating*. "It can be pretty long hours, unexpected work hours sometimes." A few of her clients had run into some rather scandalous situations as of late. How she'd handled them had earned her a few more clients in return. "But I like the challenge of staying on top of things for my clients and helping them expand their reach."

"I bet that pays pretty well."

The man at the bar coughed and shifted on his stool. Vivian couldn't help it. She glanced over and found him looking at her again. This time, the pretty blue eyes carried a bit of a warning. Vivian straightened in her chair. Was he… Was he listening to them? Her stomach knotted to the point of pain.

"I do okay," she said. "What made you go into teaching?"

Sam's smile widened. "I liked the idea of helping shape the minds of the future."

Vivian frowned. That sounded so rehearsed she could almost see a script sticking out of his pocket. "Second grade is, what, ten years old?"

"Thereabouts." Sam leaned back as his second beer was delivered. "So, this place is a favorite of yours, then?" He looked around. "It has a nice vibe."

"It has good food." It was one thing she indulged in. Some people had a weakness for aged whiskey or bookstores. Vivian held an affinity for cuisine. It was a safe way to be adventurous, especially these days with so many restaurants offering delivery service. "How long have you been teaching?"

"A few years." He picked up his beer. "Do you travel much?"

"No. Do you?"

"When I can. Gets a bit costly on a teacher's salary."

Vivian nodded, making note of the fact that that was the second time he'd mentioned money. Was it her imagination or was this guy digging for something? It didn't feel like a normal date. Not that she knew what that felt like. She couldn't recall the last actual date she'd gone on. She had to be overthinking this. She looked to the man at the bar, who offered an encouraging smile before he looked away again.

She silently sighed and tried to return her focus to Sam. He was currently talking up a storm, about what she couldn't really say, but the man at the bar? He hadn't said a word, yet she had this unsettling desire to sit beside him and strike up a conversation.

Vivian slid her gaze to the mirror behind the bar, found him watching her again. But instead of making her feel uncomfortable or targeted, that *whoomph* of a force field seemed to pulse in tempting rhythm.

Those eyes of his were so bright against the light brown of his hair. She'd never been one to like messy hair before, but on him it worked. She couldn't see much more than his face, hunched over his drink the way he was. He had wide shoulders, though. Strong shoulders, she imagined, and a broad chest to match. Beneath the long sleeves of his navy shirt, muscles bunched and tightened in a way that left her feeling a bit foggy-headed. She liked his smile. A lot.

"Vivian?" Sam caught her hand in his and gave her fingers a gentle squeeze. "You still with me?"

"Um, yes, of course." She waited for a spark, for some kind of confirmation that there was something between her and Sam. Instead, she had the sudden urge to retreat and pull back into her town house of a shell. Whatever she might have said next was scrapped when their dinner was delivered.

Relieved, she picked up her fork and quickly filled her mouth in order to avoid any other comment. Or any temptation to look back at the stranger who made her feel things she honestly hadn't thought possible.

Despite her intention to speed things up, dinner passed at an excruciatingly slow rate. She had to give Sam points for trying. Her date was nothing if not persistent with the questions and attempts to discover common ground. But there wasn't any. And there certainly wasn't heat between them, not even a spark.

They both reached for the check at the same time.

"I insist," Sam said with a bit of an edge in his voice.

So did she. "We'll split it." Vivian kept her voice light. "I think we can both admit this isn't going anywhere."

"Maybe we just haven't hit the right moment yet." His smile was tight as he reached into his back pocket for his wallet. He flagged down their server and waved off her determined offer to add cash to cover her meal. "Tell you what," Sam said. "There's a great little dessert café a couple blocks away. Let's take a walk, get some fresh air and you can treat. They have a great chocolate peanut-butter lava cake."

Proof he'd read her profile. She'd mentioned a weakness for anything chocolate. She did the calculations in her head. Twenty or thirty minutes more in exchange for lava cake? She shrugged, her sweet tooth activated. Seemed an appropriate price to pay for dessert. "All right."

She clutched her hands in her lap, her knees bouncing as she watched him fill out the tip amount on the credit card receipt. He clicked the pen shut and stood up.

"I'm just going to visit the ladies' room before we head out." She pointed toward the back of the restaurant. "I'll meet you out front?"

"You aren't going to go scampering out the back door, are you?" Sam teased.

She'd be lying if she said the thought hadn't crossed her mind. "I'll meet you out front." When he moved off, she dug into her purse, pulled out a couple of twenty-dollar bills and slid them into the bill folder just as their server reappeared to retrieve it. "Thank you for lovely service," she told him. "Sorry about his tip."

"I'm sorry about your date," the young man said with an understanding smile.

"Thanks." When she stood, she couldn't help but give in to temptation one last time.

The corner barstool was empty.

The man with the blue eyes was gone.

"Of course he is." On a scale of one to ten, she was hovering at about a minus two at this point where tonight was concerned.

Since the ladies' room was just an excuse to make up for the anemic tip Sam left—clearly her date had never worked in the service industry—it wasn't long before Vivian retrieved her jacket from the hook by the door and shrugged into it.

Regret over having agreed to dessert surged as she joined Sam outside. She really just wanted to go home and forget tonight had ever happened.

Sam was standing by the valet parking stand, looking at his cell, when she emerged. He straightened when he saw her, shoved it into his pocket in a motion that had her earlier suspicions resurfacing. She did a quick scan of the street in both directions and noticed a number of people around. The windows of other restaurants displayed plenty of customers amidst the holiday decor of garlands, lights and glistening, colorful ornaments.

Sam's smile was back in place, but his eyes were a bit jumpy, looking over his shoulder before he stepped closer. "All set?"

"Sure." Worst case, she'd head back to Madariaga's and use the escape hatch she'd seen posted in the bathroom. "How far is it?" She pointed behind her as he led her down the street at a rather hurried pace. "I'm parked in the other direction."

"Two, maybe three blocks?" He didn't sound nearly as

sure of himself as he had inside the restaurant. He dropped a hand to her back to hurry her along. "I promise this cake is totally worth it."

"Mmm." It would have to be a pretty fantastic dessert to get her to put tonight behind her. Snow drifted gently to the ground. Her lined boots kept her suddenly scrunching toes warm, and she grabbed the lapels of her brown down jacket. She'd forgotten to wear gloves, but the coffee she planned to order should take the chill off her fingers. Her boots clicked against the sidewalk as they walked. "I hope your next date goes better than this one," she said as a peace offering.

"This one isn't over yet." Sam, hands shoved into the front pockets of his jacket, gave her an encouraging smile. "But if you're looking for sparks, yeah." He sighed. "Looks like we're out of luck in that department."

Sparks like what she'd felt when she'd looked at the man at the bar? "I'm afraid so. Is that the place?" She pointed ahead to the lighted café sign two blocks on the left. At nearly nine on a Friday night, traffic was still humming alongside them. The rumble of engines cut through that winter silence she'd been longing for. If she never answered another question in her life, it would be too soon.

"Look, Vivian."

Sam stopped and reached out, caught her arm and brought her to a halt. The display cases in the jewelry store beside them showed off a modicum of offerings that glinted under spotlight bulbs. Sprays of holly and tinsel decorated the windows, along with spray-on snow creating a framed effect.

In the street, a beige car occupied by two men drove by at a crawl. The passenger in front slid down, almost in slow motion as she glanced over her shoulder.

"Maybe we should give this another try?" Sam suggested.

"This could have just been first-date jitters, and, well—" His eyes went wide as a pop sounded in the air. She jumped, looked toward the car. Something gold glinted in the back seat. The sound of breaking glass tinkled in the air followed by another pop. And another.

Sam caught her around the waist and knocked her to the ground, driving the air out of her lungs. She hit shoulder first. Her head bounced against the cement. Her glasses snapped, the jagged edge cutting into her face. Whatever scream she might have offered was caught by the whoosh of Sam's body landing heavily on top of her. Now that she could, she couldn't form the thought to cry out.

The weight of Sam's body pushed down on her to the point she could feel the ground pressing against her side.

More glass tinkled, another pop echoed. An alarm went off, blaring into the night as people cried out and tires screeched. Footsteps raced past and around her. Unintelligible conversation picked up speed to the point it became white noise.

Vivian lay there, frozen, the cold of the ground soaking through her jacket and making her shiver. A sob caught in her throat as she tried to move and got one hand up to her shoulder in order to shove Sam away. She kicked her legs in an attempt to extricate herself. "Sam, get up. Get off." She shoved again, only he didn't move. She felt an odd warmth trickle down her neck and spread beneath her jacket. "Sam?" She pushed harder.

The growing crowd didn't seem to know what to do any more than she did. "Help, please," she cried, her voice muffled by Sam's shoulder. "Someone…help!"

"Back! Everyone stand back!" The male voice that exploded through the crowd brought her an unexpected moment of relief before Sam was rolled off her.

Suddenly feeling as if she could breathe again, Vivian tried to sit up. When she did, she saw the man from the bar, crouched behind her, that handsome face of his marred with controlled fear and concern. She lifted a hand to where her glasses had been, where her face hurt. "You." It was the only word that came to mind. The only thing she could think to say. Her ears were ringing, and her head throbbed. She lifted her fingers to her temple. "What are you—?"

"Are you all right?" The man shifted slightly, reached into his pocket for his cell. "Don't move too much."

"I'm—fine." Her mind raced, trying to catch up with whatever had just happened. She looked around. The parked car didn't have windows anymore. Shattered glass littered the sidewalk. She clutched her hands to her chest, took comfort in the hand resting on her shoulder.

"That's not your blood?" The man asked in such an urgent way he left her blinking.

"Blood?" She looked down, saw the glistening red liquid coating her jacket and her neck. She touched a hand to her skin, drew away sticky red fingers. "N-no. It's not mine." Realization shot through her, and she felt her face grow cold. "Sam." She scrambled onto her knees, but the man from the bar shifted to keep her where she was. "Is he hurt? Why isn't he—?"

"Yeah, this is Detective Nate Colton, Boise Police." The man spoke into his phone. He clicked the speaker feature on, placed the phone on the ground beside him. "Stay right there," he ordered Vivian, who could only nod and stare. He turned his back on her, but the second she could move, she was on her knees beside him.

"You're a policeman?" she asked the detective as he pulled open Sam's jacket, pressed two fingers against the side of Sam's blood-spattered neck.

"Dispatch," Nate continued as if she hadn't spoken. "Requesting backup and patrol. And an ambulance to…" He glanced around and recited the address. "I've got a gunshot victim, at least two to the chest. Rapid pulse, but he's alive. I need to keep him that way. Over."

"Request received, Detective Colton. Assistance is on the way. Over."

"Great." He reached out a bloodied hand and clicked off the speaker. A number of people raced out of a nearby restaurant. "You!" Nate yelled over the heads of the crowd creeping closer. "I need towels or tablecloths or napkins, something to help stanch the bleeding."

"I can—" Vivian started to stand, but her knees folded immediately.

"You stay right there," Detective Colton ordered. "And you all, turn those stupid phones off," he snapped at the crowd, who all but ignored his order. "This isn't anything that needs to be shared."

Vivian shivered and tried to breathe regularly. Her head spun. Her stomach churned. For a moment, she feared she might throw up. She pressed a hand against her mouth and tasted bile in the back of her throat.

"Hey." Detective Colton nudged her knee with his foot. "You're okay, right? You still with me?"

"Yes." She nodded, feeling both useless and helpless, which only irritated her. "I don't know what happened. One thing we're walking down the street, and the next thing I know he knocked me down."

The detective gave her a blank look, but if he was going

to ask her anything, he was prevented by the restaurant employees returning with a stack of towels and napkins.

"Great, thanks." Detective Colton inclined his head. "Grab some of those will you?" he told Vivian. "And keep one for yourself." He nodded to her face. "You're cut. From your glasses probably."

Her glasses. She looked around but couldn't focus enough to see where they might have ended up. She'd have to get her spare pair from home. Her hands shook as she accepted the offerings and quickly handed the detective one so he could slip it between his blood-soaked hands and Sam's open wounds. "Don't you die on me, Wexler."

"His name is Sam," Vivian corrected. "Sam Gabriel."

The detective leaned forward, pressed down so hard with his hands Vivian winced. "I need you to stay quiet right now," he told her, looking as if he didn't want to be saying what he had. "Just…trust me, okay? I'll explain everything I can soon, but not now."

It was a request Vivian often had trouble with. Trust was a big reason why she lived alone. Why she worked alone. But with this man… She couldn't explain it. "Okay." She said it in a whisper and reached for another towel. "Yeah." She swallowed hard. "I trust you."

Chapter Two

Nate had long ago lost track of the number of nights he'd spent in a Boise emergency room.

His years as a uniformed officer had made visits an almost daily occurrence, from getting unhoused people looked after to overseeing the transport of accident victims, or overdose victims in a sometimes futile effort to get them help before they succumbed to their addictions. Early on, he'd developed that necessary emotional detachment that kicked in every time he stepped through the swinging doors, whether trailing behind a gurney or having hauled someone out of the back of his patrol car. Nate had always been able to keep himself detached and logical in a crisis.

Tonight, however? Tonight was a very different, not to mention unnerving, story.

He'd left the restaurant the second Wexler's date reached for the check. Seemed an apt signal of the end of his target's dinner, and Nate hadn't bothered to dismiss the relief he felt at the encounter tanking. He needed his focus on what Wexler could do for his case, not what plans the scam artist might have for his date.

After signaling good-night to Seb, he'd made his way outside and waited in the alley between Madariaga's and the dry-cleaning business next door. Out of sight. But close enough to pick Wexler up as soon as he was on his own, once his suspect finished the cell call he accepted.

Only Wexler wasn't on his own. Somehow, he'd managed to convince her to join him for coffee and dessert.

That odd, primal wave of protection surged as Wexler and his date walked past. There had been enough distance between the two that Nate could take comfort in the knowledge there wasn't anything close to a love match. Not that that mattered. That wasn't any of his business.

He needed Wexler to talk, which meant Nate needed to keep his target in sight, approach when he could be assured of privacy. He'd stepped out from the alley, waited until they'd crossed the first street before following.

Even now, Nate was kicking himself for not noticing the beige sedan creeping slowly up the street just behind the pair. He'd increased his pace, was only a little ways behind when the passenger window rolled down and the gun appeared.

What was happening should have dawned on him sooner and not after the first shot shattered the parked car's driver's-side window.

He was running as the second shot sounded and the jewelry store window exploded. Wexler dived forward as glass rained down like a deafening winter snowstorm. More shots. Tires screeched, and Nate leaped into the street to try to catch a glimpse of the plate number as the car raced around the corner and disappeared from sight.

Shouts of shock and terror reverberated before Nate gave up and shoved his way through the instantly forming crowd. He couldn't hear anything other than a low, dull buzzing in his ears. He thought for sure she was dead. She had to be, his mind screamed at him as he'd dropped beside them. For an instant, he let himself feel the fear and the dread, accepting, however reluctantly, the truth of what had happened.

Wexler was on top of her, unmoving. Blood seeped out and spread across the glistening frozen pavement.

His heart stopped. She'd moved. Only a little at first, then with enough of a determined cry he dared to hope…

He rolled Wexler off her. Seeing her blink up at him settled the unfamiliar panic that had surged inside him. She was covered in Wexler's blood as she pushed herself up. Her eyes were glassy with shock, and she was shaking so hard he was afraid her bones might snap, but she was alive.

And so, miraculously, was Wexler.

Now, standing outside the second pair of double swinging doors in the ER, Nate stared through the glass window. He flexed his tight, blood-stained hands. It felt as if he were wearing gloves. His heart pounded. He should have drawn his gun. He should have fired at the car, but there were so many people around and the car had been speeding so fast, it was just as well he hadn't.

"Detective?" A nurse from the registration desk approached. She was older, her silver-streaked hair worn in a long braid down her back. The badge she wore identified her as the duty nurse. "Are you all right?"

"I'm fine." The statement didn't sound like it came from him. "What's his status?"

"We won't know for a while. Why don't you come with me?" She took him by the shoulder and led him behind the desk. "You can use the locker room to clean up. I'll let you know when the doctor's available to speak with you."

Nate stopped outside the door as if he'd hit a wall. "There's a woman who was brought in. Pretty. Dark hair, brown jacket. She's being checked for injuries."

"I'll see what I can find out. Please." She motioned to the door. "Take your time. I'll make sure there's some coffee waiting for you."

Nate almost laughed at the idea of adding caffeine to the situation.

It was only when he was standing at the sink looking at himself in the mirror that he realized why the nurse was so intent on getting him out of sight. His hands, the front of his shirt, even part of his face were covered in blood. At least the dark fabric would hide most of it, once it was dry anyway, but the clothes and probably his jacket were toast after today.

He gave his hands a quick scrub, dried off, then cleaned off his phone and the wallet he'd dragged free to show his badge when the ambulance and other cops had arrived.

By the time he thought himself presentable, his anxiety over Wexler surged afresh. As selfish as it sounded, he really needed the guy to pull through. He needed him. His case against DeBaccian couldn't be made without him.

The nurse was back at the station when he walked past.

"Detective." She held up a large paper cup. "Dr. Billings can speak with you in a few minutes. In the meantime, the woman you asked about, she's being examined right now." She inclined her head toward the hall. "Third room, second bed on the right."

"Thanks. Can you…" He paused. "Did you happen to get her name?"

"Vivian Maylor." The nurse smiled as if understanding something he didn't. "And just so you know…" She leaned forward and lowered her voice, a soft smile on her lips. "She asked about you, too."

He moved away, ducking his head before she or anyone

else saw the heat in his cheeks. Just what his evening needed, a matchmaking nurse.

Rehearsing what he was going to say to her would be a lesson in futility. There wasn't anything he could utter that would make any kind of sense, at least not yet. Right now, all he cared about was seeing that she was all right.

He stood outside the drawn curtain, heard her soft murmur of a voice. It was the same murmur he'd listened intently to and for at the restaurant. He closed his eyes, blotting out the words she spoke but listening to the tone. It was a tone that comforted him in a way he'd never quite experienced before.

The curtain was ripped open, and a woman stepped out. She wore blue scrubs and her blond hair up in a messy knot on the top of her head. "Ah. Hello. Dr. Preston." She held out her hand. "You must be Detective Colton."

"I must be." The sooner he got his sense of humor back on track the better. "Is she okay?"

"Near as we can tell." Dr. Preston nodded. "She has a bruised shoulder, so we're waiting on X-rays, and she got a pretty good knock on the side of her head, but no signs of a concussion. We took care of the cut near her eye." She reached up and grabbed hold of the stethoscope hanging around her neck. She'd clipped a sparkly harp-playing angel to the metal center. "She'll be sore for a couple of days and probably have a headache, but other than that, she's okay. I'm going to get her discharge paperwork started for once we see the X-ray's clear." She stepped aside. "Go on in."

"Thanks." Nate didn't know what was more embarrassing—the nurse's romantic coddling earlier or the fact he felt like a teenager picking up his first date.

He peeked around the edge of the curtain. She sat there, sitting up in the mechanical bed, her gaze pinned on him the second he stepped clear of the fabric. They'd put a small butterfly bandage on the cut by her right eye. Dried blood coated part of her face and the side of her neck. Her eyes seemed slightly dazed, the shock no doubt. Even with all that and very pale skin, she still struck him as beautiful. He felt like he could breathe again and yet…not. "Hey."

"Hey, yourself." Her smile was quick and more than a little confused. "Detective." She eyed the cup in his hand with the ferocity and longing of a fellow caffeine addict. "Is that coffee?"

"Supposedly." His first sip hadn't been promising. He removed the plastic lid and handed it to her.

"My hero." She accepted the cup with both hands and drank nearly half of it down. "For the second time tonight." With a sigh, she sat back. "How's Sam?" Nate hesitated long enough for her to roll her eyes. "His name isn't Sam, is it?" The calm acceptance had him frowning. "That might be one thing about tonight that actually makes sense."

"Bad date?" He blinked in feigned innocence, but that only earned him a judgmental glare.

"You know it was." She eyed him dubiously. "You called him Wexler back on the street. Who is he really?"

"Not anyone you need to be concerned with from here on." Nate came into the cubicle and reached for the metal-frame chair in the corner. "Is it okay if I sit?"

"Sure." She shifted on the squeaking mattress. "Trust me, you're getting the better end of the comfort deal." She tugged at the collar of the pale hospital gown. The monitor in the corner beeped out her vitals, which, in Nate's limited experience, still seemed a little high. "My butt's already asleep. You didn't answer my question. Is what's-his-name okay?"

"I'm waiting to hear." From his vantage point, he could

see the hallway and the thin bits of tinsel strung in the hall. "Your doctor says you're fine."

"Oh, I'm just great," Vivian said with more sass than he expected. "But I think I'm officially off online dating." She laughed, but it sounded more pained than amused. Her hands were shaking, just enough to signal the shock hadn't yet fully set in. "As if I wasn't already inclined to swear it off completely. I don't think there's ever been a bigger first-date disaster on record."

He sat back and chuckled in an effort to put her at ease. "I once had a date that ended with me mistaking her brother for a burglar. Planted the guy face-first into her refrigerator. Broke his nose," he admitted. "And about a dozen butterfly magnets."

She looked doubtful, but there was a glimmer of amusement in her hazel eyes. "You're making that up."

"Oh, how I wish I was." Funny. For the life of him, he could not recall that woman's name.

"Verbal first aid for the heart. Who knew that was a thing?" She took another drink of coffee before handing it back to him. "Thanks. That jolt should be enough to get me home." Her eyes went wide. "Eventually. My glasses." Her sigh was heavy and resigned. "They broke back on the street." And she hadn't had the wherewithal to attempt to locate them.

"Where is home?"

"Here we go with questions again," she muttered. "Must be inquisition Friday and no one told me. I live about halfway between here and Owl Creek. Am I supposed to give a statement or something? That always happens on cop shows."

"One of the few things they get right," Nate observed

wryly. Oh, if he could only list his pet peeves on that front. "There will be another detective to take yours."

"Not you?"

Maybe it was his exhaustion talking, but she sounded disappointed. "I was there, so no, not me." He would, however, have to give his own account.

"Well, I'm not going anywhere for a while, so." She pointed to a sign that listed how long various tests took to complete. X-rays averaged two hours. Vivian sighed in evident frustration. "Let's have it. Tell me exactly who it was I had dinner with tonight. How bad is he?"

"I don't think—"

"You can follow that tidbit of information with why you were running surveillance on my date," she said as if he hadn't spoken.

"I wasn't running surveillance on your date. Exactly," he added at his own doubt. "I didn't intend to, anyway."

"Yeah, well, lucky for me your intentions changed." She was getting fidgety, plucking at imaginary threads on her sweater and trying to keep her hands occupied.

Nate often played fast and loose with the truth. Faking out suspects, questioning witnesses and putting them at ease was necessary in his job. So was assuring people who had witnessed something borderline horrific that there was nothing for them to worry about. He possessed a talent for skirting that thin line of truth that most people only crossed in desperate times.

But there was something about the way Vivian Maylor looked at him that snuffed out that natural tendency and left him uttering the truth. "Long story short?"

"Don't shorten it on my account." She looked completely resigned to hearing the absolute worst. "Going to be here awhile."

"Your date's real name is Dean Wexler. He's a convicted con artist. His last stretch in prison was eighteen months for stealing an elderly woman's life savings shortly after she was put into a nursing home."

Vivian sat up, wide eyes filling with something akin to rage. "Nu-uh."

"Afraid so." He cringed. "He's currently a suspect in a string of burglaries targeting successful single women using various dating apps."

"Of course he is." She leaned her head back and sighed. "So that's why you were following him? To get an eye on his next victim?"

"No, actually." He looked down at his almost empty coffee cup. "That's not my case, unfortunately. But I've got a few leads that link him to another one I've been working on." He might be feeling chatty, but he wasn't about to add to her already overburdened and bruised shoulders by telling her about Marty DeBaccian. "Suffice it to say, I have reason to believe he's connected to a much nastier individual." He spotted the nurse from earlier standing in the doorway. She leaned over, caught his eye and waved him out. "I'll be back in just a minute."

"Sure. Gives me some time to absorb all that." Her tone was completely indecipherable as Nate left to meet the nurse in the hall.

"Dr. Billings has an update for you." She led him back to the nurse's station, where a rather rotund, middle-aged man tapped his finger on a tablet computer. "Dr. Billings?"

The doctor looked up, shifted his gaze from the nurse to Nate. "Detective Colton. Dr. David Billings. I'm a trauma specialist here in the ER." He set his tablet down and held out a hand. "Thanks, Lorna."

"You bet." Nurse Lorna shot them both a smile before ducking around the desk.

"Is Wexler alive?" Nate forewent any pretense. It was the only question that mattered at the moment.

"He is." Dr. Billings nodded slowly. "There's no guarantee he'll stay that way, however. Two bullets caught him in the chest. One went straight through, the other's lodged so close to his heart it's a miracle he's still breathing."

"Any chance I can question him?"

"Not for a good while. We've had to put him in a medically induced coma. Could be days or even weeks before it's safe to bring him out of it. He's semi-stable for now. He won't wake up again until after we get that bullet out. And for that, we need to wait."

"Right." Nate scrubbed a tired hand across his forehead. "Okay. I'd like to be kept apprised of his condition. And I'm going to see about assigning an officer to his room."

Dr. Billings frowned. "Is that really necessary?"

"Someone drove by and opened fire on him in the middle of a crowd," Nate said as he pulled out one of his cards and passed it across the counter to Lorna. "It's a miracle no one else was seriously injured." Last he'd heard, there were some minor injuries, bumps, bruises, scrapes and cuts from flying glass. "That tells me they hit their target. If word gets out he's still alive—"

"Say no more." Dr. Billings held up both hands. "We'll cooperate however we can."

"Is there a room you can put him, away from emergency exits? How's your security system?" Nate took a quick look in both directions. The round rotating cameras gave him some peace of mind. "Recent update?"

"Last year," Dr. Billings confirmed. "I'll alert our security office to pay close attention to the area around Mr. Wexler's room. One last question, Detective."

"Sure."

"Other than an ID for Sam Gabriel, we didn't find any other information or ID on him. Regarding his next of kin, do you happen to know—"

"He doesn't have any that I know of," Nate said. "I'll double check the file we have on him once I'm back at the station." Criminal or not, Wexler deserved someone to be responsible for him. "In the meantime, put me down as a contact."

VIVIAN REALLY, REALLY needed to stop watching so many cop shows. Obviously, they'd implanted shockingly unrealistic expectations in her psyche. Or dulled her to the realities of actual crime. Was that even possible?

It had been a shooting. Had to have been. All the broken glass and panicked racing about, not to mention the gunshot wounds in Sam—Dean's chest; there wasn't any other explanation.

"Wait until I tell Lizzy about this," she whispered and heard the growing hysteria in her ragged voice. "One date in four years and *bam!* I get shot at." She shook her head, thinking of her childhood friend. Well, her *only* friend. "She'll probably think I'm making it up to get out of trying again. Who doesn't pretend to be shot at to get out of dating?"

Was she ever not going to feel as if she wanted to jump out of her own skin?

Vivian's mind raced like a broken-down sports car,

speeding up one minute, stuttering and stalling the next. Thoughts didn't seem to be completing themselves before another started, and they all sent her down winding, dead-end roads of panic and fear.

The coffee had probably been a mistake. She looked down at her trembling hands, feeling as if somehow, she was hovering above her own body, unwilling to retake possession in order to cope with the fact she'd nearly been killed. She squeezed her fingers into fists, tried to focus on the sensation of her nails digging into her palms.

How funny was it that the only thing that seemed to be holding her together was the thought Detective Nate Colton would be returning to her bedside?

Detective Colton, who had been the first person she'd beheld after the shooting. Handsome, messy-haired, blue-eyed Detective Nate Colton, who, when he'd peeked around that ER curtain, had acted as an instant balm and a kind of unexpected refuge.

Refuge. She squeezed her eyes shut, shook her head. What on earth was going on in her head that she even thought to use that word where he was—?

"Ms. Maylor?"

She nearly sighed at the sound of his voice. In that instant, the jagged edges of her thoughts smoothed, and she opened her eyes, unclenched her fists. "Vivian, please. Detective."

"Nate." His smile was easy.

"Nate." She must have knocked her head harder than even the doctors thought. Just saying his name made her feel better.

His hands were now devoid of the coffee cup. Probably a good thing with the way her heart was racing. Not that she could hide that, given the monitors that kept *beep-beep-*

beeping overhead. And the good-looking detective wasn't helping. "Did you find out anything about…" She nearly got his name wrong again. "Dean Wexler?"

"He's alive," Nate said. "They've put him in a coma until he's strong enough for surgery. It could go either way."

"Oh." She didn't know how to feel about that. As off as the date had been, as suspicious as she'd been about Sam, Dean, whatever his name was, she certainly didn't wish anything like this on him. Or on anyone. "That's just…horrible. Do you know who—"

"Not yet," Nate said, then stepped back and motioned to someone behind him. "Vivian, this is Detective Jim Sullivan. We work together in the Boise PD. He's been assigned to the case."

"Ms. Maylor." Detective Sullivan gave her a friendly nod. He was on the short and stocky side—nowhere near as tall or fit as Nate—and had ginger red hair. She figured him to be about forty years old with a cool, almost jaded awareness in his eyes. "I'd like to ask you a few questions about the incident tonight if you don't mind?"

Incident? So that was what they were calling a drive-by shooting? "Yeah, sure." She pushed her hair behind her ear and managed a flickering smile. That headache the doctor had warned her about was beginning to pound, dully, loudly, on both sides of her head. "I want to help however I can."

"I'll just leave you two—"

"No, stay," Vivian said, cutting Nate off and reaching out a hand that she immediately tugged back and held against her chest. "Please. If it's okay?" she asked the other detective. "He was there. He probably saw a lot of things I didn't." It made her feel slightly less dependent to make an excuse for him to be there. Other than her just wanting him to stay.

Sullivan didn't look particularly pleased at the request. "Sure." He motioned to the chair, but Nate urged him to take it while he leaned back against the cabinet of medical supplies beside the bed. After Sullivan took down her information—full name, phone number, address, occupation—he started in. "How do you know Dean Wexler, Ms. Maylor?"

"Vivian's fine," she said. "And I don't really know him. We connected on a dating app. We messaged a couple of times. A friend of mine told me to take a chance and say yes to a date. So I did." She smoothed her hands across the strangely rough and heavy blanket. "I don't think I'll be taking her dating advice again."

"Detective Colton said you know him under a different name?"

"Sam Gabriel." She rattled off the name of the dating app they'd used. "I'm thinking their vetting process isn't as secure as they state in their ads." How stupid could she have been, putting her faith in anything connected to the internet? Stupid, naive. Her mouth twisted. Lonely. She'd just become a statistic in the lonely to desperate ratio. "We agreed to meet for dinner at Madariaga's. He'd never been there, but I order from them occasionally when I want to treat myself. And I knew it would be crowded."

"Smart thinking," Detective Sullivan said as he scribbled in his small notepad.

"I was thinking it was a good test for temper," she said. "You know, how irritated someone gets around noise and chaos. I wanted to see if he was quick to trigger."

"Never would have thought of that," Nate said.

"You're not a single woman," Vivian said, but rather than the comment sounding or feeling snarky, it felt more conversational. "You've never had to. I'm not a big dater. Honestly, tonight was a complete fluke." One she was probably never going to forget. "Felt more like a game of truth or dare, and I stupidly chose dare."

"There's nothing stupid about going out on a date," Nate said.

"Seriously?" Vivian arched a brow and looked at Nate. "You're a cop, and you're going to say that, in this day and age? I let myself forget the world is full of psychopathic whackadoodles."

"Sneaking past defenses is what people like Wexler do," Detective Sullivan said. "An attitude like yours tends to be a pretty good shield these days."

"Always the exception to the rule. Anyway." She took a deep breath and sighed. "He let me choose the restaurant, which I took as a good sign. I arrived on time—"

"Did you see anything out of the ordinary before you went into Madariaga's?" Sullivan asked. "Anyone lurking or a strange car parked somewhere?"

"No." She shook her head and thought back. "But then I wouldn't have known if they were strange, would I? I parked in the lot across the street. I remember thinking it looked like it was going to storm and that I hoped to get home before it got going." She hesitated. "I don't like driving, especially at night. Add in the weather, and…" She was already dreading the drive once she got out of the hospital. "Honestly, it was just a simple, no-go date."

"Any particular reason it failed?"

"He didn't pull her chair out for her," Nate muttered.

Vivian's gaze flew back to his, and she saw in the way his cheeks tinted pink that he hadn't meant to say that out loud. "No, he didn't. I don't know that I expected him to, but…" She lost her train of thought. "You noticed that?"

"I noticed a lot of things," Nate said, then, after a look from Sullivan, he shrugged. "Sorry. I'll keep quiet."

"He lied to me. S— Dean," Vivian told Sullivan. "Almost from the start. About his job. He told me he taught second grade, but then said his students were ten years old."

Sullivan's brow arched. "Second graders are seven or eight. Good catch."

"It was a little thing," Vivian said. "But it was so strange. If you lie about small things—"

"What's to stop him from lying about bigger things?" Nate held up both hands. "Sorry. Last time."

Sullivan frowned, as if he didn't quite understand Nate's behavior. "Anything else strike you as odd?"

"He kept mentioning money in different ways," Vivian said. "That I must make a really good living with my business. That he liked to travel, but it costs too much. And a lot of what he said just felt rehearsed. Like he had a script."

Sullivan nodded, made another note. "You aren't the first woman we've heard this from about him. Looks like your instincts about Wexler were right, Nate." He poked his pen into the paper and glanced up at Nate. "I'm going to recommend we look deeper into Wexler in connection with those burglaries."

"As long as I get first shot at him for my case." Nate winced. "Wow. Sorry. Really bad choice of word."

"Walk me through after you left the restaurant, if you can," Sullivan prodded Vivian.

She shrugged. "He talked me into going down for a dessert at a café," Vivian said, wanting to get this over and done with. "A few blocks from the restaurant. Proof I'll do just about anything for chocolate," she admitted quietly. "We were maybe two blocks from Madariaga's when he stopped me. I heard what I thought was a kind of pop." She narrowed her eyes, tried to recall exactly what had happened. "I heard the glass in the car break before I realized what it was. I remember looking over my shoulder in the direction it came from and seeing this car. Light brown, like beige maybe? I remember thinking that the headlights were strange. The shape of them. More angular than round. And there was this face—"

"Face? You saw the shooter's face?"

She squeezed her eyes shut. "I'm not sure if it was the shooter or the driver? Sorry." She shrugged. "I didn't realize that was what I was seeing at the time. I remember seeing something bright, shiny. Something that glinted. Then there was another pop, and another. The next thing I knew, Sam, I mean Dean, knocked me to the ground. I remember being irritated because my glasses broke." She lifted a hand to her temple and rubbed it with her fingers.

Nate cursed, and Sullivan shot him a look of irritation.

"How about a description of the man you remember seeing?" Sullivan asked.

"Dark hair, weird…something." Vivian considered. "I feel like there's something odd about him? But it's not there. Not yet anyway. Maybe it'll come back."

"You said Wexler knocked you to the ground," Nate said. "Are you sure about that?"

"Absolutely." She nodded, a chill racing down her spine. "At the time, I was asking myself what he thought he was doing, then I realized…" She looked back to Nate. "The full weight of him landed on me. He was so still. I tried to shove him off of me, and then he was gone, and I was all… wet." She swiped her hand across her neck, which one of the nurses had scrubbed clean. "Oh." Her stomach rolled. "This was his blood."

Nate reached out and pulled her hand down. "It's gone now. Worry about that later."

"Easy for you to say." Vivian shuddered. She'd never wanted a shower more urgently in her life.

"Sounds like Wexler might have saved your life," Sullivan said.

"Yeah," she whispered in fear and awe. "I think maybe he did."

"And you?" Sullivan turned his attention to Nate. "How much of this did you see?"

"After the date? Beige car, late model." He almost snapped out the words. "No plates on the back. The quick look I got at the gun, I'd say 9 mm."

"Techs recovered a 9 mm bullet from the broken glass of the jewelry store window," Sullivan confirmed. "It had blood on it."

"Probably hit Wexler," Nate said. "The doctor said one shot was a through and through."

"We'll get it tested at the lab to be sure. If I put you in touch with our department sketch artist," Sullivan said to Vivian, "would you be willing to come in and work with her? Get an image together? She's good at helping people remember details they think they can't."

"Oh." She blinked, processing. "Sure, yeah. I could do that." Was it wrong to think that was kind of cool? She'd seen artists used before on TV, of course. And read about the process in books. What did that mean about her that she was anxious to see how it worked in real life?

"You don't have to do that," Nate said cautiously.

Sullivan cleared his throat and glared.

"I'm just saying—" Nate tried again.

"I know what you're saying," Sullivan said sharply. "Vivian? You up for it?"

"Yes." While she appreciated Nate's attempt to protect her, she was going to do everything she could to catch the person responsible for such a brazen act. "I want to help find whoever did this."

"Okay, then. I'll give you a call in the morning." Sullivan stood and set the chair aside. "Nate? Can I have a word before I leave?"

"Sure."

Vivian didn't know anything about Detective Nate Colton, but that one-word answer, to her at least, seemed to convey both dread and irritation. The combination fascinated her. "Could you get me some more coffee?" she asked Nate when he started to follow Sullivan.

"If you can wait," he said, "how about I get you one once you're released?"

"Oh. I thought maybe you'd be—"

"I'm off duty. Kind of. Unless there's someone you'd like me to call?"

She shook her head and thought of all the people he might be considering. Parents, siblings, friends… "There's no one."

"Well, someone needs to get you to your car. That lucky person is me." That smile was back, and she wondered if he was aware of the power it held. "Don't go anywhere."

"Okay." She nodded and breathed easier. Not so long ago, heck, even yesterday, the idea of sitting back and letting a man show even the slightest amount of care for her would have left her laughing in dismay. Instead, she found herself counting the seconds until Detective Nate Colton returned to her.

Chapter Three

"Here you go, Detective."

Nate, keeping one hand at the small of Vivian's back as he escorted her out of the ER, caught the keys the patrol officer standing at the sliding glass doors tossed to him.

"Thanks, Coop." The younger officer, with only two years on the job so far, was one he'd met during a training seminar at the academy. Since then, Nate had found himself as his unofficial on-the-job mentor. Cooper was definitely in the breaking-in stages. The job hadn't tarnished that one-time debate team captain shine yet. Sometimes the kid smiled so brightly it was like he was made of sunshine.

"Your car's in drop-off parking," Coop said. "Thanks for recommending me for guard duty."

"Don't thank me yet," Nate told him as they passed by. "Cool it on the coffee, or you'll spend most of your time in the bathroom. No one but doctors or nurses with ID get in to see Wexler, okay? Learn their faces and their names. Anyone unfamiliar, don't hesitate to question. And remember to look at their shoes."

Cooper's light blond hair fell over his eyes when he nodded. "Got it."

"Shoes?" Vivian asked once they stepped outside.

"Doctors and nurses wear certain kinds of shoes. Soft soled. Practical."

"And someone coming in off the street probably would wear something different." Vivian nodded. "Interesting." She wrapped her arms around her torso and shivered.

"Here." Nate shrugged out of his jacket and draped it over her shoulders. He felt the need to remind her that chivalry did still exist in the world. Besides, he could practically hear her teeth chattering. "Sorry we took yours for evidence."

"Not like I wanted it after tonight." She touched fingertips to her chest and the edge of her dress. "I guess I should be grateful you didn't take everything. I'd hate to have to drive home in my underwear."

Nate felt that comment all the way to his toes. "Yeah," he managed on a slightly strangled note. "Wouldn't want that." The second they stepped clear of the ambulance bay, Nate cringed. "Looks like you were right about that storm." The snow was coming down in steady curtains now. Not blizzard conditions, not yet at least, but that could change on a dime.

"The perfect end to the perfect night. Even without the storm, I'd have been stuck. Can't drive at night without my glasses." She drew the lapels of his jacket close. Something about the way she turned her face into the lining, as if she were breathing him in, had parts of him tightening into complete discomfort. "I think there's a motel near the restaurant. I'll grab a room—"

"You can stay with me." The offer came out of nowhere and apparently surprised both of them. He inclined his chin toward the dark SUV parked in the second space over. "We can talk about it inside. Come on."

"Ohhh...kay..." Her drawn-out response indicated both

reluctance and curiosity. He could definitely push back on one of those emotions.

Sullivan had made it clear he believed Nate had a bit of a conflict of interest with this case. Nate couldn't blame him. He'd been vocally protective of Vivian—without really thinking about it. It had just been…instinctual. Arguing would have only made the situation more difficult, so he'd silently agreed to disagree if only to be kept in the loop moving forward.

Once inside, Nate turned on the engine so he could raise the heat up to full blast. At least with the snow the temperatures would calm a bit and the cold wouldn't feel quite so biting. "I've got a guest room," he said without preamble. "Nothing fancy, but it has its own bathroom. You can shower and get some sleep. Sullivan's going to try to get the sketch artist in tomorrow. Might as well get it all over and done with before you head home."

She leaned back in her seat and slid her arms into his jacket. When she flipped her hair free of the collar, he had to stop himself from reaching out to see if her hair was as soft as he imagined. "Part of me is thinking this could be an extension of my bad decision-making tendencies for the evening," she said and looked out his snow-covered windshield.

"Or it's the chance to start making good ones," he suggested. "I promise, you'll be in safe hands. That I can keep to myself—"

She leaned across the console and pressed her mouth to his.

Nate wasn't a man prone to surprises. He prided himself on being able to expect just about anything that could possibly come flying at him. But Vivian Maylor proved yet again she was capable of sneaking past his defenses and straight into his heart.

Her lips trembled against his, as if she hadn't quite thought things through. When he angled his head and moved to deepen the kiss, he felt her hesitancy. Right before her hand slid up the front of his chest and grabbed hold of his shirt.

With the engine rumbling, he slipped his hand up to grasp the back of her neck, held her against him as he dipped his tongue in to taste her, tempt her. Tease her. The curving of her lips had him almost cheering in triumph, but that would mean releasing her, and as he continued the kiss, he couldn't imagine a time he would want to stop.

When he did pull back, it was only far enough to press his forehead against hers. She was breathing heavier than before. She licked her lips, pressed them together as if trying to capture the taste of him.

"Well." He slipped his hand to her face, stroked a finger down her cheek as something unfamiliar and strangely welcomed bloomed inside him.

"I've spent a good part of the night trying to remember where I've seen you before."

"Oh?" Panic swirled, but he kept his gaze steady and even. He could only imagine where she'd seen his name, or even his picture over the past few months. Being outed as one of Robert Colton's illegitimate heirs was something no one would want on their bingo card. "Figured it out yet?"

"No. But then I'm having trouble deciding if kissing you was another bad decision," she murmured, her brow knitting slightly in confusion. "Or a good one. Maybe my brain was a bit scrambled tonight."

"You can think on it for a while." It would be easy, he thought, so easy to make one gentle push that would probably topple her right into his bed. But tonight wasn't the night. For either of them.

She was going to experience the emotional upheaval that always followed a traumatic event, and he had no doubt it would hit with both barrels. While he… He took a deep breath and inhaled the faint fragrance of flowers drifting off her skin. When the time came for him to partake in what he had no doubt was the wonder of Vivian Maylor, he wanted to be fully present, awake, and…prepared.

"So, my place or would you like me to find a hotel for you for the night?"

"So long as I can get home in time tomorrow for an online meeting with one of my clients." Her smile curved her swollen lips and almost reached her eyes.

"What time would that be?" he teased.

"After lunch. One thirty."

"That should be doable," he assured her.

"Then I will accept your offer of the guest room. If that's really o—"

He kissed her this time. A quick one, just fast enough to convince her he understood but also give her a hint of what a promise between them might hold. "That's perfectly fine. And before you ask…" He hit the windshield wipers and cleared the view. "I have more than enough coffee to get both of us through to tomorrow."

"How did you know, Detective?"

He chuckled and shifted the car into Reverse. "Lucky guess."

AS NATE PULLED his SUV into the driveway of a darling little cottage of a house on the very edge of Boise, Vivian realized she might be attempting to deal with the evening's events by diving into something even more outrageous than a blind date.

But there was no need to rationalize Nate's invitation to use his guest room for the remainder of the night. It was closing in on one in the morning. The first dose of OTC painkillers the nurse had given her before she had been discharged was already wearing off. She'd felt a bit of a buzz the second she'd stepped outside into the cold December air. Almost as if she'd been given a second lease on life. Whatever else had happened, she'd literally dodged a bullet, and for the next few hours at least, she was giving herself permission to go with impulse.

Impulse had worked well so far and helped her to answer the one question that had been floating around in her mind since she'd first seen Nate Colton sitting at that bar: what would it be like to kiss him?

She pressed her lips together again. Well, she had her answer.

The only problem was she wanted to ask the question again. And again.

Some inquiries took multiple investigations to come to the correct and accurate conclusion, she decided and had to cover her mouth to stop herself from giggling. Man, she was really out of it.

"Well, here we are." Nate turned off the engine and rested his hands on the steering wheel. "Ready to make a mad dash?" He leaned forward to examine the snow that had consistently fallen during their drive. "No," he said when she started to shrug out of his jacket. "Wait until we get inside. I'm used to the cold."

"Okay." It seemed to be her favorite word around him. Was there some kind of cosmic force at work? Even before they'd spoken a word to one another, she'd felt comfortable with him. As if she instinctively knew he was someone safe. But how was that possible? He was a stranger.

A stranger with a badge, but a stranger nonetheless.

Once she got some sleep and some distance from everything that had happened, she was probably going to come to a different conclusion or admit that her irrational reactions and actions were nothing more than spur-of-the-moment coping mechanisms. That said, there was nothing wrong with enjoying the moment, was there? Chances were that after tomorrow, she'd probably never see him again.

She wasn't the least bit surprised that, after climbing out of the car, he hurried around to open her door. Vivian couldn't shake the feeling of intimacy that struck her when he slipped his hand into hers and tugged her toward his front porch.

In the dim light of the porch lamp, she couldn't get a good look at or feel for the interior of his home. It seemed the second he opened the door the sky opened up and dropped a full blanket of continuous snowfall.

Once inside, a blast of warmth set her frozen cheeks to stinging as he drew the jacket off her and hung it on a hook by the door.

"Hang on. Let me get the lights." He left her in the entryway as he moved down the hall. A moment later, light blazed to life. Nate leaned out and waved her back. "I'll get the coffee going. Unless it's too late for you?"

"I have stratospheric caffeine tolerance," she said. It might make her jittery at times, but it rarely kept her awake. Especially when an adrenaline crash was coming. She strode down the short hallway to the kitchen, which she found surprisingly comfortable and practical. "Nice place."

"Yeah?" He shot her a surprised smile as he set his coffee

machine to gurgling. "It serves a purpose. I'm fixing things up as I go along. Only been here a couple of years."

"Handy around the house, are you?"

"Well, I wield a mean paintbrush. The little touches are more my sister's doing. She's much more attuned to things than I am."

"Sister, huh?" She hugged her arms around herself as she wandered across the marble tile, nodding approvingly at the shiny black appliances and gold-flecked black marble countertops. "Younger or older?"

"Younger." He retrieved one mug from the dish rack by the sink and another from a cabinet. "We had a kind of complicated upbringing, but one thing we always had was each other. How about you? Brothers and sisters?"

Regret and that all-too-familiar pang of loneliness chimed inside her. She pulled out one of the two barstools at the counter and sat while he rummaged around in the refrigerator. "I was an only child. And not the best at socializing."

"Doesn't seem that way to me." He set a sealed container on the counter before going back in. "Let's see. I've got some leftover pizza in here. And some salad that..." He popped off the lid, then grimaced. "Okay, yeah, that might send you back to the hospital."

Vivian laughed. "Pizza sounds great, actually. And what's this?" She pointed to the first container.

"A neighbor across the street uses me as a guinea pig for his baking experiments. I thought you might appreciate them since you didn't get your promised dessert. Go ahead." He gestured for her to open it.

She did and felt some of the tension she'd been struggling with ease. "Chocolate chip cookies?"

"Double chocolate chip cookies," Nate corrected. "He has a secret ingredient."

"Espresso powder?" Vivian guessed and earned an arched brow. "I might not be the best baker, but I read a lot of books about food. The espresso's supposed to enhance the chocolate. I'll know for sure when I eat one. Later." She left the lid off and slid it out of reach. "Chocolate's best at room temp."

"Funny." The cardboard pizza box replaced the cookies as he went to get plates. "I've never been patient enough to prove that theory. Anything for your coffee?"

"Straight's fine." She could feel her energy beginning to drain. That adrenaline crash was barreling straight for her, no doubt coming on faster because of how comfortable she felt, both with Nate and in his house. "Can I ask you why you were following Wexler tonight?"

"You can ask me anything." He bit into an ice-cold piece of pizza, the corners of his eyes crinkling as he chewed and swallowed. "Doesn't mean I'll tell you."

"Why not?"

"Because you've had enough to deal with, and—honestly? I don't want you any more involved in this situation than you already are."

"So you're protecting me." Should that idea both appeal to and annoy her?

"Yes."

"I'd argue that I can take care of myself, but considering I couldn't find the courage to drive myself home tonight, I guess that argument's moot." She didn't think she could convey how relieved she'd been not to have to get behind the wheel of her car in the dead of night.

"You must have had high hopes for your date if you made the drive into Boise."

"Not high hopes." Surrendering to the rumbling in her stomach and wanting to give her pain pills somewhere to land when she took them, she reached for a slice. "But I did have a friend who wouldn't let me back out. Can't wait to tell Lizzy how wrong she was." That, at least, would be one silver lining to the night. She nearly had the pizza to her lips when the thought struck. The pizza clattered on her plate with a disturbing stale thunk. "Colton. Your last name is Colton."

"Yes." Nate frowned, concern rising in his eyes. "Are we starting over?" He reached out, touched a finger to her bandage and looked into her eyes. "Your head okay?"

"My head's fine." But her heart was racing so fast it nearly jumped out of her chest. "Nate Colton. Boise PD. Are you..." She swallowed hard as certain pieces fell into place. "Your sister's name? Is it Lizzy?"

His face went blank for an instant, as if her question had flipped a kind of switch. He gave a halfhearted nod and ducked his head. "One of them is."

"Oh, wow." She leaned back on the barstool, relief and shock tumbling through her. She laughed, pressed her hands against her cheeks before she jumped off the stool and raced around the counter. "This explains it." She grabbed hold of his arms and turned him to her. "Oh, my gosh. This... I don't know, this thing I feel with you. This ease. This..."

"Spark?" Nate said in a way that had her wondering if he'd heard that part of her conversation with Dean Wexler.

"How many Lizzy Coltons could there be?" Vivian challenged.

"Hopefully, only one," Nate said. "She's a bit of a firecracker, for want of a better term."

"You're her brother." She grabbed his face between her hands and looked more deeply into those blue eyes of his.

"The brother she only just found out about. I don't know if I can see it, but I can feel it."

"Can you?" He looked a bit flummoxed at her comment. "What do I feel like?"

"Lizzy's the best friend I've ever had. Ever since grade school, she's just... She's always been there for me. No matter what. She's solid, you know?"

"Can't really agree or disagree." The humor in his eyes had been replaced by what she could only describe as pain. "I don't know her well enough to say."

"Oh." It was only then she remembered what Lizzy had said. "You and your sister." Her mind searched for the right name. "Your other sister, Sarah. You and she share the same mother with Lizzy and her brothers."

"Yep. Good old Jessie Colton. Fracturing families and setting the whole root system on fire." He extricated himself from her hold and ducked down into a lower cabinet. "Suddenly, I'm feeling the need for something stronger than coffee." He added a big splash of bourbon to his mug.

"I'm sorry." She didn't like the expression on his face, the way his entire body had tightened up, as if her realization had somehow unlocked a secret part of him he wasn't interested in sharing. "I should have realized the media coverage and fallout must have been horrible for you. Lizzy said things were complicated. *You* said they were. I'm prying. I'm sorry." She stepped away from him.

"No reason for you to be." Was his response more obligatory than polite? "Didn't think I'd be traversing that particular minefield of family history tonight is all. I'm glad Lizzy's your friend. I can call her if you want? I bet she'd be happy to—"

"No, please." Vivian held up both hands. "With everything that happened to her recently, I don't want to be another thing for her to have to worry about. Besides, last I heard, Ajay was taking her away for a little while to help her…decompress." Was that the right word when it came to being kidnapped?

"Good." Nate nodded and looked relieved. "That's good to hear."

"This is so strange." She returned to the chair. "From the second I saw you at the bar, I couldn't shake this feeling like I knew you. Even though I don't. Didn't. Does that make sense?"

"I'm going to say yes and leave it at that."

"Right. You don't want to talk about it."

"It's not that." Confusion filled his voice. "It's more… I don't know how to talk about all that, actually. I'm assuming Lizzy told you about me and Sarah and our…place in the family."

She nodded. "Yes. A few weeks ago, I think? She was trying to process finding out she had two siblings she knew nothing about."

"Yeah, well, Sarah and I always knew," Nate said, and it was then she was able to decipher what it was she was seeing on his face. In his eyes. It was definitely pain. But also sadness. "That whole Coltons of Owl Creek, the branches of the family who built that town into something greater than anyone believed it could ever be? Sarah and I found out a long time ago that we're related. So we've had a bit more time to adjust to the idea than Lizzy and her brothers and cousins. There's still a bit of…tension among us."

"You said you've had time, but you haven't adjusted," Vivian observed. "Have you?"

"Don't get me wrong." He started to play with his pizza

rather than continuing to eat. "I've met most of them now, and I like them all well enough. They're good people. They have every reason to distrust us, especially given who our mother is. Maybe I can see a time in the future when we're closer." He shrugged. "But not now. I spent a good portion of my life accepting the fact I was never going to be one of them. It's a hard shift to make when you're suddenly presented with an opportunity you didn't think you'd ever have."

"I'm sorry." She reached out, grabbed hold of his hand and squeezed. "And here I am going all cheerleader on the situation."

That smile of his returned, if not a bit less bright than before. "I'm sorry, but there's no way you were ever a cheerleader."

She laughed and squeezed harder. "See? You know that about me already. I'm thinking we were most definitely destined to meet." She surprised herself by yawning. Her eyes went wide as her cheeks went hot with embarrassment. "Oh, geez. Sorry." She covered her mouth, shook her head and pulled her hand free. But not before he clung to her for a few seconds more.

"I'm going to take that as a hint to show you the guest room. Give me just a sec."

"Okay." She nibbled on her pizza after he disappeared, then quickly cleaned up and put things back in the fridge and finished her coffee. She wandered around a bit, cookie in hand, looking for the bits and bobs of character that turned a house into a home. He didn't seem to be a collector type of person. Everything she saw projected a lifestyle of practicality and purpose.

Photographs were sparse. There was no mistaking the people in the few she found—one of whom she'd bet good money was his sister Sarah. The affection between them was palpable and made her smile. The man she'd been dealing with tonight seemed no different than the one in the picture. Whatever niggling doubt she might have regarding her current situation vanished.

"Okay, bedroom's good to go," Nate said from where he lounged in the door frame, watching her examine the photographs on the TV stand in the living room. "I set out some towels for you, and there should be other things like a toothbrush and stuff in the cabinet drawers. Sarah left a load of laundry last time she stayed here. T-shirts and stuff. You're about the same size, so take your pick."

"Thanks." That urge to shower returned with an unexpected ferocity as she finished what she had to agree was a pretty great double chocolate chip cookie.

"Help yourself to anything in the kitchen. I'm a light sleeper, so if you need anything, just knock on the door." He pointed to the one on the other side of the living room. "I'm usually up around six."

"Me, too." Nerves she thought she'd banked surged afresh. "Ah, I really am sorry. Bringing up all that stuff about your family."

"It's fine, Vivian." There was no animosity in his eyes. "I should probably take it as a sign that it's time to start dealing with it all head-on. They're family after all."

"Yes, they are." Vivian felt a pang of envy so sharp she nearly lost her breath. "Grab hold of it, of them, Nate. Trust me. I've been alone most of my life. There's nothing more important than being a part of something that's bigger than you are."

"As much as I'd like to continue this conversation," Nate

said, "I think you're questioned out by now. For tonight, at least."

"I really am." The last thing she wanted to do was unload her particular tales of woe. "Whatever else you're struggling with..." She walked over to him, rested a hand on his chest and curled her fingers under ever so slightly. She wasn't certain if it was she who shivered, or if it was him. "You're a good man. That's what I picked up on when I walked in the bar. You radiate it. You glow with it." She lifted her other hand to his cheek. "Believe me, that is a very rare trait indeed."

She resisted the urge to kiss him again. Afraid that if she did, it would lead to something neither of them was ready for. "I'll see you in the morning." She moved past him, forcing herself to look straight ahead and avoid looking at him again as she closed the door.

Chapter Four

Nate lied. He wasn't up at six.

He was up at five thirty. Getting through today on a whole three hours of sleep was going to be so much fun. It wouldn't have been so bad if those three hours had given him a degree of rest. Truth was, he tossed and turned, his mind racing first around his options surrounding Dean Wexler, and then around the fact that Vivian Maylor slept only a few steps down the hall from his bedroom.

He couldn't recall the last time he'd started his day with an icy cold shower, but since first seeing Vivian, he'd been doing—and thinking—a lot of things he wasn't used to.

What were the odds that this woman would consider Nate's half sister to be her best friend? He shook his head as he set a fresh pot of coffee to brew. The universe must be having a serious laugh at his expense. Clearly, he hadn't been paying enough attention to the shift in his family dynamic. His stomach tightened. What would Lizzy think when Vivian told her about their meeting?

It was obvious his siblings hadn't decided if he was guilty by association just yet—his mother's antics and actions, including her recent involvement with the Ever After Church and its leader, Markus Acker, had been the cause of much of the distress the Colton family was going through.

If he were to look at things from his siblings' side, he'd definitely be suspicious, not to mention cautious. Whatever he might be feeling about the situation, their reserved behavior had hurt Sarah more than anyone. His sister had always longed to belong to a big family, and it had been difficult when they'd discovered they had one that they couldn't reach out to. Wanting Sarah to have that now meant Nate would do what he needed to make that happen.

"Morning."

The sound of Vivian's sleep-husky voice triggered a smile Nate couldn't have stopped even if he'd wanted to.

"Morning." He turned and his knees went weak at the sight of her standing in the doorway, clad only in a rainbow-centric T-shirt that skimmed the tops of her thighs. "You, um, sleep okay?" His voice sounded a bit choked. He cleared his throat, tried to reboot himself into thinking clearly.

He'd spent a big portion of the night not imagining what her legs looked like. Now that they were on full display—those long, toned legs—he was forced to admit his imagination hadn't come close. Never in the history of the female form had a woman filled a T-shirt to the absolute perfection of Vivian Maylor. Judging from the slightly dazed expression on her face, she didn't have the first clue as to the effect she had on him. And the effect was…for want of a better word, *stimulating.*

"I slept great, thanks." Sleepy-eyed, she walked toward him. "Coffee going already?"

"First thing." He shoved his hands into the back pockets of his jeans, rocked forward, his bare feet scrunching into the hardwood floor. "Wanted it ready for you when you got up."

"Sweet." She touched a hand to his arm but didn't, as expected, come over to watch the coffee appear. Instead, she popped open the container of cookies. "My first shot of the day." She bit in and closed her eyes, sighed in a way that left Nate feeling oddly jealous of a chocolate chip cookie. "That shower in your guest room worked wonders." She leaned back against the cabinets.

"Glad to hear it." He cleared his throat again and distracted himself by putting away the dishes from the drainer.

Those kisses they'd shared in his car last night had been a pressure release, a way of coping with an adrenaline-spiking event neither of them could have prepared for. At this point, it would be unprofessional of him to pursue any kind of relationship or push for a quick encounter that could, in the end, cause her more emotional harm. It wasn't the time.

Or the place.

"Everything okay?" Vivian asked.

"Everything's fine." He'd never felt so grateful to hear his cell phone go off. He all but dived to where it sat on the counter across the room, skimmed the text message. "It's Detective Sullivan. He said he texted you, but you haven't answered."

"Oh!" Her eyes went wide. "I totally forgot to charge it when I got here. Geez." Muttering to herself, she hurried out of the kitchen, the T-shirt skimming higher up the backs of her thighs with every step.

"Heaven help me," Nate muttered to himself even as his jeans became increasingly uncomfortable. "I'm not going to make it another hour with her around."

"Did you say something?" She was already back, cell phone in hand. That wide-eyed, innocent expression on her face was more alluring to him than a classic femme fatale's come-hither look.

"Nope. Not a thing."

"I've got the message." She squinted at the screen. "I really need my glasses." She sighed. "Can you read it?" She held out her phone.

"Sure." Their fingers brushed when he accepted her cell. A zing of energy shot through him, from his fingers, straight down to his toes, then back up to where it settled significantly south of his heart. "Ah, he says the sketch artist can come in this morning. Time's up to you. She's free until noon."

"That makes two of us," Vivian said. "How about...nine?"

"How about eight?" The sooner he got her out of his house, the better. The longer she was here, the more his thoughts circled things other than work. Inappropriate things. She was his witness. He needed to remember that. "We can stop for breakfast on the way. This early, we'll miss the main weekend crowd."

"Sick of leftover pizza?" she teased.

"Something like that." He answered the message, then texted Sullivan on his own phone confirming the time. The message he received back was a simple smirk emoji that told Nate he was in for some serious ribbing from his fellow detectives and officers. "Okay, eight's good. There's a twenty-four-hour diner on the way, one of my favorite places, actually." But that didn't stop him from pouring them each a cup of coffee. "You hungry?"

"Always." Accepting the mug, she smiled and tilted her head, which sent her hair cascading out of its loose knot down around her shoulders. "I'll be quick." She grinned over her shoulder at him as she walked away. "Promise."

SHE'D DONE SOMETHING WRONG. Sitting in the passenger seat of Nate's SUV quicker than promised, she nibbled on her thumbnail. What was it? He'd been acting nervous from the jump today, like every word she said grated on his nerves. The tension radiating off him had been alluring at first, tempting. Even seductive, but the way he'd all but danced and dived away from her to get to his phone had left her wondering if last night's interaction had been a fluke. She hadn't dreamed kissing him, had she? Or that he'd kissed her back?

Oh. She frowned, panic grabbing hold of her heart. Last night hadn't been some weird hallucination. Or had it?

"Hey." Nate's voice broke through her circling doubt. "You okay?"

"Yeah, sure." She rested her hand against her stomach. His sister Sarah had a fun, quirky sense of fashion, at least when it came to her casual clothes. The bright, colorful T-shirt collection had given her a surprising choice. The jeans she found in the dresser were on the snug side, but at least the zipper had gone up.

Vivian's favorite all-purpose black dress was wadded up in his bathroom trash can. The second she'd tried to wash out the blood, the red in the water had set her head to spinning and her chest to throbbing. She'd never be able to wear it again without remembering the shooting. Best to toss it and move on.

"Why?" she asked Nate impulsively. "Everything okay with you?"

"Yeah, sure."

She caught her lower lip in her teeth and might have gnawed straight through if she hadn't stopped herself. "I appreciate everything you've done for me." She hugged her purse against her chest. "I'll be out of your hair pretty soon."

"You're not in my hair, Vivian."

"Tell that to your face." She'd meant it to be a joke, but even to her own ears it didn't sound like one.

He pulled into the parking lot of a throwback diner. Vinnie's boasted twenty-four-hour breakfast and a selection of cakes and pies that were, supposedly, second to none. The fact he had to circle the lot to find a space spoke of a dedicated clientele. She considered that an acceptable endorsement. As if it had a mind of its own, her stomach growled.

Once parked, Vivian scrambled to grab hold of the handle. The sooner she had a fork in her hand and food in her face, the faster she'd put some distance between them. She didn't jump when he gently grabbed her arm. But she did sigh silently at the way her body wanted to melt toward him.

"Vivian." He tugged her back before she could open the door. "I'm sorry if I'm making you uncomfortable."

"I think I'm the one doing that," she argued, determined not to look at him. She promised herself to stare out the window or at the floor. Anywhere that wouldn't force her to admit to the embarrassment flooding through her. "I'm sorry I kissed you last night."

"I'm not." His response sent chills racing down the arm he still held in his strong fingers.

"I didn't mean to—"

"I spent most of the night wishing I didn't have a guest room."

Her lips twitched and hope flared.

"The thing is…"

"Right." She sank back against the seat, and this time her sigh couldn't be stopped. "Of course there's a thing."

"I don't do well mixing business with pleasure. You're part of a case, however indirectly, and honestly, I'm worried

I won't be able to do my job if I'm distracted by...you. And if I don't do my job, people get hurt. I definitely don't want one of those people to be you."

She blinked. Then frowned. His words soaked in, but she didn't quite accept them. "I distract you?" She broke her promise to herself and looked at him, unable to hide her disbelief. No one, certainly no man, had ever said that to her before.

"From the second you walked into Madariaga's." Nate released her and rested his arms on his steering wheel. "This can't come as a surprise. I didn't stop staring at you all through your dinner."

Her face warmed. So she hadn't imagined it.

"Add to that you're friends with Lizzy and I'm not entirely sure how she'd feel about us...connecting."

"Considering she encouraged me to go out with a con artist," Vivian observed, "I think me liking you would be an upgrade."

"Yeah, one would hope."

It was the first time she heard disappointment in his voice. Whether it was about her or his newly formed relationship with his siblings, Vivian couldn't be sure.

"For now, we have to keep things professional," Nate insisted. "I can't taint my case, and I don't want you getting more involved in something that could hurt you."

"What about after? Your case," she added when he seemed confused. "Can we see each other after you close it?"

"I—" Another shrug. "Well, yeah. I don't see why not."

"Be still my heart," she muttered. "What every woman longs to hear." But still she smiled. If only because she'd struck a nerve with him—a raw one, it seemed. And that was something that left her feeling more than a little bit powerful. “Okay. I’ll leave it up to you if and when we… reconnect. Later.”

“What every man longs to hear,” he echoed with that charming smile of his. “You still hungry?”

“If I can’t have you, at least I can have…” She leaned over and scanned the writing on the bank of windows. “A bacon buttermilk waffle with real Vermont maple syrup. Shall we?” She pushed out of the door before he could stop her again.

Or before she attempted to seal their pseudo-friendship deal with another kiss.

“EIGHT ON THE DOT.” Detective Sullivan was waiting for them at the Sergeant’s desk on the first floor of the Boise Police Department. The fluorescently lit lobby boasted uniformed officers pinballing their way from door to door to staircase to elevators, some offering Nate a wave of welcome. Shoes squeaked on the linoleum floor that had probably been installed decades before he was born. “Looks like you got some sleep, Vivian.”

“I did, actually. Thanks.”

Nate hadn’t known Vivian for long, yet he couldn’t help but think she’d offered the other detective one of the most forced smiles he’d ever seen on anyone’s face.

They stepped out of the way of a pair of officers dragging in a barely responsive suspect. Weekends might slow things down for everyone else, but for law enforcement, they went into overdrive.

“Thought you’d want to know,” Detective Sullivan said to Nate, “patrol found a car about three hours ago, few miles away from the shooting. Burned out, but the VIN comes back to a beige sedan reported stolen two days ago in Conners.”

“You think it’s the one used in the shooting?” Nate asked.

"Fits the description, and it was completely torched. Whoever did it knew how to do it effectively. And they didn't try to hide it. We've taken it into evidence, but we aren't holding out any hope for prints or DNA."

"Right." Nate shook his head. Professional or not, like Sullivan implied, they'd probably done it before. "Hopefully, there's something to be gleaned from Vivian's sketch."

"Sure hope so. You ready to do this?" Sullivan asked Vivian.

"More than ready," Vivian confirmed. "Let's get it over with. Thanks for breakfast, Nate. And the guest room."

"Ah. Sure." Nate started to follow, but Vivian turned, held up a hand and shook her head. "I'm good from here. Thanks for everything." She looked down at her T-shirt. "I'll get Sarah's clothes back to you as soon as I can."

"No rush. Let me know when you're done. I'll drive you back to your car." It hadn't taken him long to realize he'd completely messed things up. True to form when it came to women he cared about, he'd stuck his foot in his mouth. Only in Vivian's instance it seemed as if he'd wedged both feet—along with half his shoes—into the mix.

"That's okay. I don't want to be a bother."

"I can have a patrol car drop you off," Detective Sullivan offered.

"Perfect," Vivian accepted immediately. "We're all set then."

"We can have a patrol car follow you, just to be on the safe side." Nate wasn't ready to say goodbye. "Are you sure you don't want me to—"

"I'm sure." Her too bright smile was back in place. She did surprise him by rising up on her toes and brushing her lips against his cheek. "I'll be fine. Thanks for everything."

He had no response. Instead, he stood there, in the middle of the lobby, and watched Detective Sullivan hold the elevator door open for her. Nate was still trying to ease his disappointment when he got up to the third-floor bullpen where the criminal investigation department was housed.

"Colton!"

Nate turned as Lieutenant Luke Haig stepped out of his office. His commanding officer held up two fingers and circled them in the air to indicate Nate's presence was requested.

Just as well. He could already smell the over-brewed coffee spiking its way out of the break room. Peak distribution time had passed him by, probably back when he'd been trying to salvage something positive out of his time with Vivian. The fact he was already regretting how he'd handled things did not bode well for the rest of his day. Or weekend.

"Close the door," his superior officer suggested and gestured to one of the two hard-backed chairs on one side of his desk. The shelves behind his desk were lined with photographs of his superior, most of which showcased his close-knit ties to the community at large.

His focus on the Armenian community, the community he'd grown up in, connected him to various neighborhoods in ways other officers couldn't replicate. His successful years working undercover in the criminal investigation unit had given him his choice of commands and he'd chosen to remain here, in Boise. His home.

That said, his detectives called him the Mob Whisperer, and not only behind his back. The fiftysomething immigrant considered the moniker a badge of honor. "The desk sergeant tells me you requested Officer Cooper for protective detail at Boise General."

"Yes, sir." Because it was expected, he sat, even though

the last thing he felt like doing was staying still. "Dean Wexler's condition is unchanged. There were enough cell phones recording the scene last night that it wouldn't be difficult for someone to assume he may still be alive."

"You're convinced someone will come after him?"

"Whoever shot him was willing to make a very public attempt to take him out," Nate said. "If they think there's a chance to finish the job, we should be ready for it."

Haig nodded. "Agreed. And any progress connecting him to DeBaccian?"

"I'm going to do some more digging," Nate said. "But everything I've found so far leads to a connection versus not. Wexler's been maneuvering his way up the criminal success ladder for years here in Boise. If what we're hearing about DeBaccian is true, DeBaccian would have his eye on him. Wexler can't get any further without going through him. Debaccian takes a percentage from most career criminals working the Boise area. Considering Wexler's less than subtle tendencies when it comes to his targets—"

"And this woman from last night, this..." Haig leaned forward, his chair squeaking beneath his six-foot-six-inch height and significant muscle mass and checked his notes. "...Vivian Maylor, was Wexler's latest target."

"She fits the victimology." Just saying that word made him cringe. He didn't like to think of Vivian as any kind of victim. "I know Sullivan and his team are taking a closer look at the women already on file. But Vivian matches up in a number of ways, not the least of which is she met him through a dating app. She's a successful businesswoman, owns her own home. Is financially secure." He couldn't attest to any belongings that might appeal to a burglar with more fences than a prison yard, but then neither could Wexler. "Their date was a bust. Wexler was trying to save it, but she saw through him. He slipped up a few times. She knew something was off." She'd have ditched him at the restaurant if it hadn't been for that promise of chocolate. *Something to keep in mind,* Nate thought, then mentally kicked himself.

Nate had burned that bridge. Best to stop trying to rebuild it.

"If only everyone had such radar," Lieutenant Haig said. "Sullivan's report stated she thinks she saw a driver and one passenger. He's setting her up with Stacy? Putting a sketch together?"

"As we speak, sir." If anyone could get Vivian to remember the micro-details of what she'd seen last night, it was Stacy Crum. The woman was a talented artist, but her degree in psychology often aided in guided exercises that enhanced victims' recall. Put the two things together, and she was one of the best weapons the Boise PD had at their disposal. "But that's Sullivan's case." Time to cut the cord.

Haig eyed him with unveiled skepticism. "Is there anything I need to be apprised of in regard to Ms. Maylor?"

"Only that she spent the night in my guest room. Alone," he added just to make certain his boss understood. "Her glasses broke during the shooting, and with the storm, she didn't feel safe driving home."

"Glad you were there to lend your…support." Haig gave a nod of dismissal. "Okay, then. Keep me apprised."

"Yes, sir." It always amazed him, Nate thought as he returned to his desk, how a simple conversation with his superior felt like an interrogation session. The man was as no-nonsense as they came, but he was also cognizant of the fact that every detective in his unit approached the job in varying ways. He gave a lot of rope to his people and rarely, if ever, did they hang themselves with it. "Give me time," Nate muttered as he surrendered to temptation and headed into the break room for coffee.

Considering the way Vivian Maylor had been seared into his brain, chances were he wasn't remotely done with the fallout of having met her.

"SO, I'M GOING to have you close your eyes, Vivian." Stacy, the sketch artist Detective Sullivan had put her in an interview room with, had placed Vivian in a chair directly in front of her. No table between them. Almost to the point of their knees touching. Stacy's red hair was pulled back from her face, and tiny springy curls bounced free to frame her bright eyes.

The large sketch pad sat on the table beside them, a series of sharpened pencils in easy reach. Vivian wasn't surprised by the nerves that struck, or that her hands were twisting themselves together like a frenetic acrobat troupe. She'd had a lifetime of learning to manage the anxiety that descended with any new situation. Anxiety that hadn't come close to appearing whenever Nate Colton was around.

She locked her jaw, shoved that thought out of her mind before it took hold. His explanation for backing off made complete sense. As disappointed as she was, she couldn't blame him. She could only imagine the dedication and single-mindedness it took to be a detective in this day and age. Becoming a clinging vine definitely wouldn't earn her any points.

"Why do I think this is going to be like one of my therapy sessions?" Vivian caught a quick smile on the woman's face before she closed her eyes.

"It's specialized therapy." Stacy's voice was calm, even

and gentle. "I've found this technique works really well when there isn't too much trauma involved. You seem relatively well-recovered from last night."

"It feels like it happened to someone else, actually." She focused on keeping her hands still and evening out her breathing. Truth be told, she was a master compartmentalizer. She hadn't let herself really dwell on anything that had happened last night, except her interactions with Nate.

"That may very well work to our advantage," Stacy said. "Did Detective Sullivan give you the information for our victim assistance department?"

"Detective Colton did." The card was wedged into the front pocket of her purse.

"I'd heard he was on-site right after this happened." The affection in Stacy's voice caught Vivian off guard. "He's a good one to have around in a crisis. Level-headed, cautious and a straight shooter. You always know where you stand with Nate."

"So I'm learning." The comment slipped out before she thought to stop it. She cleared her throat, shifted in her chair. "Do you know him well?"

"Well enough to have him on speed dial in case of an emergency." She paused. "Nate makes a habit of looking after strays. He doesn't limit his big-brother behavior to Sarah."

Vivian didn't know how to respond to that.

"Okay, so let's take some deep breaths and try to clear your mind," Stacy told her. "I'm going to talk to you for a little while, just to help you relax, and then we'll take small steps in getting you back to last night, okay?"

"Mmm-hmm." Vivian resisted the urge to nod. All she

wanted was to get this over with, put the entire incident last night behind her and move on with her life.

"Great. You're doing great, Vivian. Just keep listening to my voice, all right? There're no wrong answers. Everything is fixable. Details are my specialty, so I'm one of the few humans who likes change. Deep breath in, and out. In…and out."

Vivian instinctively focused on Stacy's voice and let herself fall into that space between full alertness and the brink of sleep. Stacy's questions gently guided her back, putting the memories into a kind of slow motion, but also kept Vivian separate from the action.

She walked behind herself and Dean Wexler. Her boots struck at the same place as her other self, and Vivian followed her motions, moving the same way. When Stacy asked what she saw, she talked about the store windows, the holiday decorations. The thick pine garlands winding up and around the lampposts accented with alternating tinsel bells and angel wings.

Her heart rate kicked up when she heard the car behind them. She turned in unison with her other self, seeing the bare details of the car.

"Tell me what you see, Vivian."

In the distance, Vivian heard the scratch of a pencil on paper. The sound was oddly soothing, she found. As if evidence of progress. Vivian knew as much about cars as she did NASCAR, meaning next to nothing. So color, the number of doors and the odd shape of the headlights were the only things she could mention.

"Who is in the car?" Stacy asked.

"Two men. Dark hair. Round faces." She squeezed her eyes tighter. "I don't know what I should say."

"Anything and everything that comes to mind."

"Right. Okay."

"Can you see them both?"

Vivian nodded. She hadn't realized that before. It was only now that she could see she'd originally merged her description into one person. "There's an older one driving. The passenger looks darker somehow. Meaner. Cruel. Sorry." Her lips twitched in apology. "I work in PR. I tend to pick up on personalities and intentions, even silent ones."

"That's good," Stacy encouraged. "Like I said, there's no wrong way to go about this. I want you to do something for me, okay? I want you to pretend to take a snapshot with your mind. Just like you do with your cell phone. Just click and store it for later. Can you do that?"

"I think so?" *Odd*, Vivian thought as she did just that. She even tried to zoom in and find more details that could help. A medal of some kind hung from the rearview mirror. A parking lot stub was wedged on top of the dashboard. The bucket seats were dark, almost black, and in the back seat…

Vivian gasped. Her eyes shot open. It took a moment to focus again, but when her vision cleared, she went wide-eyed when she looked to Stacy.

"What did you see?" Stacy asked.

"A third man." Her voice nearly broke from the tension winding through her body. "There was a third man in the back seat. He was wearing this big gold ring. That's what was glinting." He'd looked at Vivian and Dean when the gun fired. For an instant—a blink of one—she'd looked him directly in the eyes.

"Did you see his face, too?"

"Yes." She whispered now, tried to ignore the shiver racing down her spine. "Yes, I saw him." She swallowed hard. "I saw all of them."

Chapter Five

As glorious as Nate's updated waterfall shower had been in the early hours of the morning, the first thing Vivian planned to do when she got home was jump into hers and wash that man right out of her hair.

"That man. Last night. And everything in between." She cranked up the throwback '80s station on her satellite radio. It was obvious from the moment Detective Sullivan had joined her and Stacy in the interview room that Vivian's description of not one, not two, but the three men from the car in the drive-by had exceeded everyone's expectations.

Detective Sullivan had tried to hide his surprise, and there was a flash of anger that glinted before he covered it. But she'd seen it. It had sent chills down her spine.

He'd always been polite. But his more solicitous attitude when he'd escorted her back downstairs and handed her off to a pair of uniformed officers who'd driven her back to her car had definitely left her feeling both accomplished and unnerved.

Almost as unnerved as the trio of dark, dangerous eyes that all but glowed from inside that car. She shuddered, gave herself a hard mental shake and took a cleansing breath. Getting all those details out and into Stacy's talented hands had offloaded a lot of the anxiety that had been churning inside her. But not all of it.

A glance at her watch eased a bit of her anxiety. She had plenty of time to make the half-hour drive to Owl Creek, get cleaned up and jump on her call with Harlow Jones, a rather ebullient relationship-expert client who always managed to lift Vivian's spirits.

Taking the back roads always gave Vivian a bit of comfort. Getting behind the wheel was one of her least favorite activities, but a necessary one. Not that she'd be making her way into Boise again anytime soon. Detective Sullivan had insisted that should he have any follow-up questions, he was happy to come to her. Again, that solicitous attitude seemed a bit of a stretch from the no-nonsense detective she'd first met at the hospital in the middle of the night.

Weekend traffic was nothing like it was during the workweek. She was just happy for the daylight, however gray it might be. As her eco-friendly car hummed down the four-lane road, she breathed out and flexed her hands on the wheel, wincing a bit at the cars zooming past her on the other side.

She hummed along with the music, but within seconds was belting out, off-key and with wrong lyrics, her accompaniment as the cold air swirled outside.

Behind her, a dark SUV surged close, giving no indication of slowing down. She eased her foot off the gas, pumped her brake just to make certain to be seen. But the car kept its speed up.

Her stomach clenched. Her hands tightened on the wheel. Tailgaters were the worst, and her already shaky relationship with driving didn't make things any better.

"Just go around," she said as the music grew louder in her ears. "Go around, go around..."

She took her eyes off the mirror for a moment, checking for other vehicles that might be preventing the driver from moving over. Vivian slowed, debated easing onto the gravel shoulder, but there wasn't one for at least another half mile. The long, iced-over drainage ditches stretched endlessly.

The SUV was so close now she could see the muddied license plate.

"Go around!" she yelled, swerving to the right side. The left lane was clear. It didn't make any sense...

She screamed when the car hit her from behind. That deafening sound of metal against metal, that heart-stopping *bang*. Her hands gripped the wheel. She tried to speed up, but her little car wasn't having it. It stuttered a bit, then shot forward, but not before the SUV hit her again.

Every muscle in her body tensed up. She could feel each one of them from her shoulders right down to her toes. Terror tightened her throat and had her swiveling her head back and forth looking for somewhere, anywhere, to go. She could hear horns blaring when he hit again, but the sound didn't quite register before the SUV swerved around her and kept pace with her.

She pulled her foot off the gas. As if anticipating her action, the SUV rammed her from the side, sending her careening off the road before it sped off.

Her tires caught the top of the ditch and pitched the car up and over. She covered her face and, for a moment, felt as if she were almost airborne. The back of the car slammed down with enough force to flip one more time. The front windshield cracked and spiderwebbed, the horrific crackling echoing in her ears for what felt like hours.

It landed diagonally across the icy ditch. Water from beneath the frozen top layer seeped in below the door, freezing her boot-covered feet. Around her, brakes screeched and people shouted while a car door slammed and footsteps raced closer. She could only breathe in short, painful bursts. Her fingers seemed frozen around the wheel.

"Ma'am?"

She screamed again when someone pounded on her window. It was a bearded man wearing sunglasses. His red-and-black flannel shirt gleamed in the early morning, cloud-breaking sun.

"Are you okay?" He pointed down, indicating she should lower her window.

She did so. Her hands were shaking so hard she could barely see them.

"Call an ambulance!" the man called over his shoulder as more people raced over. She could hear people asking if anyone had caught a plate number, or if they'd seen the driver. Vivian released her seat belt and tried to stop sobbing. All she wanted was out of the car.

"Get me out." She pulled hard on the handle before realizing the door was locked. She unlocked it and, with the man's help, shoved it open. She grabbed her bag, held it against her chest as she shoved her legs out of the car.

A couple of people grabbed her and pulled her free, immediately sitting her on the level ground above the ditch.

"Ma'am?"

"I'm okay." She touched a hand to her head, expecting to find blood, but she didn't. "I'm okay." Her memory fogged over as if protecting her from recalling the event.

"An ambulance is on the way," one person called as they raced over.

An older woman, silvery hair knotted on top of her head. "Hon, what's your name? Can you tell me your name?"

"Viv-Vivian," she managed. "Vivian Maylor." She shivered hard enough that someone noticed and draped something warm over her shoulders. In contrast to the malicious driver, she felt concern and gentleness from the growing crowd.

"I called the police," another woman yelled.

"De-Detective Nate Colton," Vivian managed as she drew in a shaky, lung-aching breath. "Boise PD. He's…a friend." Tears burned her throat. She'd gotten snippy. Petulant even. Rejection never brought out the best in anyone, especially herself. She'd wanted to pretend he didn't exist, so she hadn't bothered to say goodbye. Maybe if she had… "I have his card…" She blinked hard to clear her vision as she dug into her purse. When she found it, she held it up to whomever snatched it from her hand. "I'd be grateful if someone could call him for me."

NATE LEANED BACK in his chair, chin resting in his hand, a finger poised over his lips as he stared at his phone. The cell had buzzed a few times in the past couple of hours, but nothing came through of importance. Nothing from Sullivan about Vivian's session with the sketch artist. Nothing from the hospital about any change in Wexler's condition.

Just…nothing.

Irritated, he snatched the phone up and called Sullivan himself, only to get blocked by voicemail.

He swore, hung up, tossed his phone back on the desk and tried to refocus his attention on the file containing a list of Marty DeBaccian's arrests and his one conviction for armed robbery. Funny that was the only one, given his file was more than an inch thick. Since his release, he'd become as slippery as the lawyers who represented him. More so even.

He'd gone from being a one-trick pony to having his hand in everything from illegal gaming to loan sharking to felonious assault and, in at least two instances, attempted murder. But arrest-worthy proof was a completely different story.

Nate and most of the Boise PD had little to no doubt DeBaccian had committed far more crimes than he'd been arrested for, but that was only supposition, and supposition was not evidence.

At least Nate wasn't alone in thinking DeBaccian was one seriously bad dude. There wasn't a cop within a couple hundred miles of Boise who didn't have this guy in their sights. DeBaccian needed to be locked up, but even that might not do much to crush his growing criminal enterprise.

Nate was a realist if nothing else. He was well aware of the failings of the penal system. Oftentimes, convicts only became better criminals during their sentences, even to the point of continuing to run whatever organizations or rackets they had in place. But Nate was still of the belief that chopping off the head of the snake was the best way to kill the business and rid Boise of a good portion of organized crime. DeBaccian had become notoriously solitary. He didn't have a right hand or a number one. He had his favorites, but didn't completely trust anyone, which made the promise of information Wexler might possess all the more important.

Nate's fingers itched to call the hospital, but he'd already spoken to Cooper when the officer had returned to the station after being relieved at the hospital. Nothing out of the ordinary had occurred, no visitors, no strange happenings. As far as Cooper had been able to glean, there had also been no change in Wexler's condition.

Which left Nate standing completely still while the rest of the world kept spinning.

"Screw it." He pocketed his phone, grabbed his blazer off the back of his chair and took the stairs down to the second floor. He scanned the semi-empty bullpen for Sullivan, looking for that shock of red hair that always made the other detective stand out in a crowd.

"Hey, Nate." Stacy Crum headed toward him, bundled up in a bright purple down jacket and matching scarf. "I was just on my way out. If you're looking for Vivian, she left maybe a half hour ago."

"Left? Already?" He glanced at his watch. It was almost noon. Then he remembered she'd mentioned having a meeting with a client. "Where's Sullivan?"

"No idea," Stacy said. "Haven't seen him since he escorted Vivian downstairs. Your girl did great, by the way. Scary accurate, according to Sullivan."

His girl. Hearing that should have annoyed him, if for no other reason than it confirmed the department gossip mill was running smooth and steady. Instead, the very idea of Vivian being his girl left him feeling oddly...warm. And slightly dim-witted at how he'd left things. "I'm not surprised." Despite finding herself smack in the middle of chaos, near as Nate could tell, Vivian had weathered the shooting pretty well. "Anything come of her description?"

"Sullivan didn't call?" Stacy frowned. "Must have slipped his mind."

"I'm sure it did." Nate didn't believe that for a second. The detective had a rumored habit of putting ambition above all else and he definitely wasn't enthusiastic about Nate's involvement with his case. "Can I see what the two of you and

Vivian came up with?" He indicated the large, long-strapped artist satchel Stacy had slung over one shoulder.

Stacy shrugged. "I guess it'd be okay." She looked behind her. "Let's go back in Interview."

He followed, impatience hitting as Stacy took her time extricating her sketch pad from her bag. It took her flipping through a good half dozen pages before she got to the first one.

He let out a low whistle, shook his head. "Now that's some detail." The man's eyes chilled him to his marrow.

"I've never had anyone describe malevolence before," Stacy observed. "He looks real, doesn't he?"

"Yes, he does," Nate murmured.

"Here's the second one."

"The second…?" He flipped the page. "She saw both of them?" The Cyrillic tattoo on this one's neck would make him easier to trace. Chances were that was prison ink. "This clearly?"

"She saw all three of them," Stacy corrected and turned one more page. "She didn't remember until I took her under. Meet bachelor number three." Her smirk was one of pride, but the man looking back at Nate stole the air from his lungs. "Nightmare fodder for sure."

Something icy and slippery slithered up his spine as he looked at the face. And the ring on his hand. "Sullivan saw these?"

"Of course. Why?" Stacy frowned. "Or are you going to go all secretive on me and keep me in the dark? Who is this guy?"

Nate's mind spun. His instinct about Wexler being connected to Boise's latest crime boss was dead-on right. Had to be, otherwise DeBaccian wouldn't have come out to make sure the job was done himself.

"Thanks, Stacy." He turned and ran back up the stairs, beelined for his boss's office. Lieutenant Haig was getting to his feet when Nate's cell phone rang.

He checked the screen. Unfamiliar number, but no spam warning.

"Yeah. Colton." He held up a finger when Haig stood up and came to the door.

"Detective Nate Colton?" An unfamiliar woman's voice echoed. Beyond, he could hear sirens and shouts and rapid conversation. "I'm calling for a Vivian Maylor."

"Vivian?" He turned fear-filled eyes to his boss. "Why? What's happened? Where is she?"

The person gave him a location on the back roads between Conners and Owl Creek. "There was an accident. She's okay. Pretty shaken up, but a car ran her off the road. Straight into a ditch. The car did this flip thing—"

"Flip?" His lungs turned to ice. "But you said she's all right."

"Near as we can tell. Miracle if you ask me."

His cop brain kicked into gear at the last second. "What about the car that hit her? Did anyone get a good look?"

"Long gone. No question it was deliberate. Road rage, I guess you could say. Hang on." Silence for a moment. "The ambulance just got here. I'm pretty sure they're going to take her in."

"Ambulance?" Nate demanded in a loud enough voice to garner the attention of his fellow detectives.

"Precaution, I'm sure. The car's totaled."

Despite the fear clutching at his heart, he let out a sigh of relief. "Okay. All right. Tell her I'm on my way and that I'll meet her at the hospital." Hopefully, that alone would stave off any argument she might make against yet another ride in an ambulance. "I'm on my way now."

"I'll tell her." The caller disconnected.

"Report," Lieutenant Haig ordered in a way that jerked Nate back to reality.

"Vivian was run off the road on her way home. Sullivan..." Anger surged. "One of Vivian's sketches is of DeBaccian. Right down to that family crest ring he wears." She hadn't missed a single detail, and those details may well have almost gotten her killed. "He was in the car last night when they tried to take out Wexler."

"Ballsy," Haig said in that stern, detached way he had. "If that's true, that's a change in behavior for him."

"Indulgent," Nate said. "Arrogant." And proof DeBaccian had it in for Wexler. His gut had been right. "He's covering his tracks." Which put Vivian straight in the man's crosshairs. "Sullivan knew she'd seen him, and he still sent her home alone." His hand tightened around his cell phone. "I need to get to the hospital." He hurried to explain. "The person who called me said Vivian's car flipped into a ditch. She seems okay, but..." He hesitated. "We need her car in evidence." He was ping-ponging between cop and concerned... whatever he was to Vivian.

"There might be trace evidence we can link back to DeBaccian. Nice shortcut to an arrest, even if it is a Hail Mary pass." Haig nodded. "Okay. Paulson, Renard." He snapped his fingers over his head so loud nearly everyone in the bullpen shot to attention. The two detectives stepped out from behind their desks. "You two head out to the scene, control what you can and make sure every single witness is questioned. We want Ms. Maylor's car impounded, and I want Cassidy Barrett brought in to oversee the evidence collection."

Nate's fellow detectives quickly grabbed their jackets and, after giving Nate a reassuring pat on the shoulder, headed out.

"I need to—"

"Go," Haig said. "Let me know of any developments. And Colton?"

"Sir?" Nate skidded to a stop before reaching his desk.

"Consider Vivian Maylor in protective custody," Haig ordered. "Yours and yours alone. Don't let her out of your sight. She might be the best witness we've ever had against DeBaccian, and he clearly knows about her. I'm going to order surveillance on DeBaccian's known hangouts while we wait for a warrant."

"What about Detective Sullivan?" Nate demanded.

"Leave Sullivan to me." The chill in Haig's voice left Nate almost feeling sorry for the other detective. "Go. And report in when you can."

"Thank you, sir." He retrieved his gun from his desk drawer, strapped it into his holster. "Will do."

"ARE YOU SURE you're all right?" The desperate plea on the other end of the line only added to Vivian's anxiety. She'd gone her entire life without having ridden in an ambulance. Now, within the space of twenty-four hours, she was on trip number two. This was not an item she'd had on her meager and pathetic bucket list. At this rate, she was going to have a reserved bed in the ER.

"Harlow, I'm fine." She grimaced as the aches began to settle in. She was back at Boise General. Back in one of their triage rooms, only this time instead of the midnight glow of the moon, she got full-on sunlight. "I'm just sorry I missed our meeting."

"It wasn't a meeting per se," Harlow said with the teensiest edge of guilt in her voice. "I mean, it wasn't like official business or anything. You've already gone leaps and bounds beyond what I expected from a publicist. You hooked me up with Sandy Flemming, the queen of morning talk! I'm happy where I am at the moment." She paused. "Mostly."

Vivian frowned. "I don't understand." Harlow had been a bit cryptic in their last email exchange, mentioning some impulsive plans she was considering implementing. Vivian had assumed it was in regard to Harlow's ever-expanding audience for her online relationship advice. Whatever was beyond viral, Harlow had hit it in the perfect sweet spot. Hence her needing a PR person to help manage the cascade of offers and opportunities while trying to grab hold of even bigger ones. "So our call wasn't business related?" She sighed as the nurse tightened the blood-pressure cuff around her arm, forcing Vivian to switch her cell to her other hand.

She might have shot the nurse a look but found her own irritation mirrored in the older woman's face. Vivian glanced down, noted the woman's name was Helga and offered a strained, apologetic smile. "Cell phones really aren't allowed in here," the nurse said without bothering to try to keep her voice down.

"We're almost done." The familiar drab-blue curtains hung as limp as Vivian was beginning to feel. Talking to Harlow was at least helping her set aside the panic over losing her car and being run off the road by some reject from a bad *Mad Max* rip-off.

"You should go," Harlow said. "We can talk later."

"It's fine," Vivian lied. "What did you want to talk about?"

"Well." There was that pause again. "I think I'm going to come back to Owl Creek for a little while."

"Oh?" Harlow's career in Los Angeles was just beginning to take off into the stratosphere. Seemed an odd time to take a break. "You sure you want to do that?"

"I think it's time, you know? To finally put my folks' house on the market and get all that behind me. I was hoping we could get together in person once I hit town. I'll be there for a while, so I'm sure we can eke out some time?"

"Oh." The prospect might have brightened her mood if it hadn't been sitting at rock bottom. "That sounds great. Of course we can get together."

"Great. It'll be nice. Change of scenery, focusing on something other than…work."

There was that hesitancy again, a hesitancy that signaled something deeper was bothering her client-turned-friend. Given the *tsks* Vivian heard emanating from her nurse, now wasn't the time to question Harlow.

"I've got some things to tie up before I head to Idaho," Harlow continued. "But I wanted to touch base with you first."

"I'm glad you did. Seeing you gives me something to look forward to."

"You're sure you're okay?" Harlow asked again. "Car accidents aren't anything to laugh about, and it sounds like yours was a doozey."

"Could have been worse." Vivian blinked back the sudden rush of tears, but she refused to give in. She was alive. That was all that mattered. "But I'm really fine. I'll figure out everything that comes next. I just didn't want you to think I flaked out on our meeting."

"You're incapable of flaking. If you're sure, I'll let you

get back to the nurses hassling you. Take care, okay? You need anything, you know where you can find me. Seriously, I'm just a call away."

"Thanks, Harlow." It felt odd, Vivian thought after she hung up and stared down at her cell: she'd spent so much of her life alone. Other than Lizzy Colton, she could count the number of friends she'd had on maybe three fingers. At the rate she was going, she might be all the way to five pretty soon.

"I'll take that." Helga plucked the phone out of Vivian's grasp and plunked it out of reach on the table beside the bed. The satisfied smirk on her face seemed like overkill, but Vivian supposed nurses needed to find a way to make the most of a bad situation. And right now, Vivian was definitely on the precipice of becoming a difficult patient.

She hadn't wanted to come back to the ER. She wanted to go home and bury herself under her covers and sleep away the last couple of days.

"We've got a CT scan scheduled for you within the hour," Helga advised her. "You should rest until then."

"Great." A CT scan was going to take ages. She'd be lucky to get back to her cozy little town house before sunset.

The nurse left, pulling the curtain closed to give Vivian the spare bit of privacy possible in a bustling ER room. One bed over, the patient was dealing with some serious stomach pain that, unfortunately for Vivian's batlike hearing, was indicative of either a seriously infected gall bladder or ruptured appendix.

"All the more reason to be grateful," Vivian mumbled to herself as she scooted down in bed and curled up on her side. "At least you've only got bumps and scrapes." And one seriously aching body. At least she had a different cubicle this time, one with a gorgeous view of the loading dock at the back of the hospital. Still, it felt as if an avalanche of the past had landed on her full force.

She should sleep. She wanted to. But every time she closed her eyes all she saw was that black SUV barreling up behind her in the rearview mirror. She'd spent most of her life hoping, praying, that history didn't repeat itself and yet…

She turned her head, this way and that, trying to push aside the haunting, nerve-wracking sound of metal scraping metal. Hugging her arms around her body, she curled tighter, hating the tears and fear threatening to explode if she gave them half a chance.

She covered her eyes, repressed the urge to growl when she heard the rattle of the curtain being pulled back. "Please, just leave me alone." She was already shaking so hard her teeth ached. If she was going to fall apart, she needed to do so without an audience.

"Vivian."

She dropped her hand and looked over her shoulder. "Nate."

The tears she'd been trying hard to bank flooded instantly. She wanted to ask why he was here. What he was doing here. She hadn't wanted to believe the kind woman who had called him when she'd assured Vivian that Nate would meet her at the hospital. And yet…

He closed the curtain and approached the bed. Her gaze shifted to the chair in the corner, but he walked right past it to sit beside her on the bed, up close to where she could grab hold of him. Instead of clinging to him, she pulled herself up and slipped her arms around his neck.

She wasn't alone.

A sob lodged in her chest.

That he immediately responded by wrapping his arms around her and pulling her in so close she could hear his heart beating over hers had her closing her eyes again, this time in relief. And comfort.

"I was so scared," she whispered, hating the helplessness she heard in her voice. She knew how to take care of herself, but the last day had definitely left her wondering if leaving the house was worth it. Taking chances clearly wasn't for her. Except…

Except that it had led to where she sat now. In the one place that felt perfect.

"I never should have left you," he murmured against the side of her throat. "When I got that call, I'd never been so scared in my life." He caught her face between his hands, set her away from him.

The fear she saw on his face, in those blue eyes of his, made her feel, at least in this moment, that she mattered to someone.

"You aren't going to ask me what happened?" Her question came out slightly broken, hitched, as if her words couldn't piece themselves together any easier than the rest of her could.

"Not yet." He drew her back against him, cradled her head under his chin, against his chest. "I will. But later. I just need a few minutes first."

"I'm fine." Her fingers felt bruised, as did her forearms. From gripping the steering wheel so tightly she supposed. "They want to put me through a CT scan just to make sure."

"Good." He pressed a kiss to the top of her head, and it was, quite possibly, the most caring gesture she'd ever experienced. "I'm here. I'm not going anywhere."

"That's nice."

"You don't believe me." She could almost hear the smile in his voice.

She shook her head, still unwilling to release her hold on him. "You have a job to do. An important one."

"You're my job now." He shifted before he slid off the edge of the bed. "Lieutenant's orders."

"Oh?" That piqued her curiosity, and she sat back, just enough to look up at him.

"Definitely *oh*." He flinched and doubt rose in his eyes. "The man you ID'd, from the back seat of the car. His name is Marty DeBaccian." He paused. "He's the man I was hoping Dean Wexler could give me information on."

She blinked, processed. She blinked faster. "But…you told me the man you were after was a really bad guy."

"He is." He stroked his thumbs down her cheeks, before sliding one across her lips. "He's a very bad guy. I think that's who came after you this morning. I can't prove it yet, but unless you really ticked someone off while you were driving, I think it's a safe bet."

"I might have." He clearly thought she was joking. "I'm a terrible driver. I go way too slow. It's why I'm always going to the right. It's… I hate it. Driving. I've lost track of the number of tickets I've gotten."

"I don't think—" He nodded as if humoring her.

"My parents died in a car accident when I was nine." She chewed on her bottom lip, considered. "I was with them, but I don't really remember. One minute they were there, and the next…" She wanted to shrug it off as if that event hadn't defined the rest of her life. "I woke up in the hospital alone. All of this, it's just so surreal." And familiar. Far too familiar.

The sympathy on his face was almost too much to bear. "I'm sorry."

"I didn't get my license until I was twenty-two. Every time I climb into a car, I can't help but think it might be the last thing I do. And if I drive past an accident?" Her laugh was harsh. "It sends me spiraling back. I can't explain it any better than that. Nine years old and I was left all alone."

"Alone?" His brow furrowed. "You didn't have any family?"

She shook her head. "My grandparents were all gone by the time I was born, and my parents were only children. We traveled a lot and were spending the summer on a road trip. The crash happened in Boise. I spent the next nine years in and out of foster homes in and around Owl Creek. That's when I met Lizzy. Your sister. When I started school that fall." Tears filled her eyes again. "She made me feel as if life might be okay again."

"Yeah, well." He rested his hands on her shoulders. "We Coltons have a bit of an unofficial code. Family finds family."

She sniffled and nodded. "I really lucked out in that department." She lifted a hand to his face. "Twice maybe, it seems."

He kissed her, gently. Carefully. As if afraid of breaking her. Instead, it brought all the fear and panic back to the surface and gave it someplace to go. When she broke away, she scooted closer and hugged him, hard. For however long he was around, she planned to make the most of their time together.

"What happens now?" she whispered.

"First we're going to make sure you're in the clear medically," Nate said. "That'll give me time to make some plans. But fair warning—" he spoke as if he expected her to protest "—I'm not taking you home. Not for any length of time. Don't worry," he added when she sat back and gaped at him.

"We'll figure it out so your life isn't completely upended. Last night, you said you'd trust me. I need you to trust me again, Vivian. And know that this time I won't leave you behind."

"You promise?"

He nodded and pressed his lips to her forehead. "I promise."

It was, Vivian admitted silently when she closed her eyes in relief, the only thing she'd needed to hear.

Chapter Six

Guilt was a funny thing. Oftentimes, Nate thought as he waited in the registration area of the emergency room, guilt was also blinding. It descended with a familiar ferocity that shoved everything, including irrational thought, aside.

This was a roller coaster he'd been riding for as long as he could remember. Growing up with a less than stable influence of a mother—one who, while physically present, didn't come close to being emotionally invested in the children she'd brought into the world—meant growing up fast.

There was no defining the type of pain one carried upon realizing early in life that you aren't remotely close to being the center of anyone's universe.

He'd become an overachiever, a protector, especially where his sister Sarah was concerned. When Robert Colton, his father, had all but disappeared from their lives when Nate was around ten, Nate found himself instantly stepping into the caretaker role. It was a role that brought with it a particular resentment, one that grew with each calculated, cruel step Jessie Colton took away from her family. But with all of that came guilt. No matter how many years passed or how successful or accomplished he became, Nate could always find a way to feel as if he could have done something, anything, everything, better.

It was too late to reconcile with his father, or even have any kind of confrontation or conversation with Robert Colton. A stroke had ended his life earlier this year before any kind of emotional peace could be sought, for either of them. It didn't quite seem real, that his father was gone. It should have been easy enough to accept. Robert hadn't been around for most of Nate's life. But with all the questions Nate had, not to mention the family dynamics that continued to swirl into the realm of complicated, it also felt as if Robert was still smack dab in the middle of everything.

Even Jessie had seemed—what was the word?—*contrite* about the situation as a whole. Contrite to the point of…

Nate squeezed his eyes shut as if attempting to clear out his brain. His suspicious nature surrounding his mother's actions had no place in his thoughts. As far as he was concerned, Jessie herself had no place in them, but blood was blood. No matter how much he distrusted and disliked his mother, she was still his family. Whether he liked it or not.

Seated in a worn vinyl chair, he rested his elbows on his knees and stared at the linoleum floor. The attempt at festive decor didn't feel quite complete. Some windows were outlined with dollar-store threadbare tinsel garlands, while a pair of one-armed frolicking elves looked more demented than celebratory. Clearly, they'd been dug out of a holiday bin probably stored in the basement. He definitely wasn't feeling the holiday cheer.

He was being too harsh, no doubt. Internalizing what he should have been trying to find a healthy outlet for. But he couldn't help it. Dwelling on the *should haves* and *wished he hads* was pretty much a pattern for him.

He shouldn't have walked away from Vivian the way he had. He shouldn't have pushed her away and into Sullivan's irresponsible, self-centered hands. He'd built up her trust then turned his back when he felt himself getting too close. It would be so easy, too easy, to take that slide he could sense hovering before him and fall. A fall that terrified him far more than any dangers of his job.

He'd felt it the second she'd walked into the restaurant the other night. That pull that had only gotten stronger. That… gravitational force that seemed to have been created just for the two of them. And yet…

He couldn't let himself surrender to it. That attraction that had struck and settled dead center in his heart from the start. It had no place here, between them. Inside him.

Especially now that her life may very well depend on him remaining attentive, on guard, and most of all, ready. He needed to put her safety first. End of story.

If only he didn't know what it felt like to hold her in his arms…

The swinging doors bounced open. Nate shot to his feet as a young female nurse pushed Vivian's wheelchair into the open space. He hadn't noticed the bruises before, or the cuts and scrapes she'd received, no doubt, from the shattered glass. She had her arms wrapped tight around herself, as if cocooning against everything around her. A couple of new bandages had joined the one near her eye where her glasses had cut her during the shooting. She looked as if she'd gone a good three or four rounds in the ring with a less than sympathetic opponent.

"And here we are!"

Nate couldn't tell whether Vivian was embarrassed or annoyed, but the way she rolled her eyes at her escort's cartoony tone told Nate, more than any clear CT scan could have, that she was just fine.

"I can take her from here," he offered in an effort to spare the nurse any potential reaction. He could only imagine how frayed Vivian's nerves must be by now. She'd been shot at, questioned by the police, spent hours with a sketch artist and been run off the road. All that was beyond Nate's own capabilities of coping. "Really." He reached into his pocket and pulled out his badge. That action earned him another eye roll from Vivian, but he accepted her reaction as another good sign.

"Oh." The nurse straightened and looked a little disappointed. "Sure, of course, Detective. Just make sure you leave the chair in the depository just outside?"

"You've got it." He was well aware how effective a perfectly aimed smile could be for some people.

She settled her bag in her lap as Nate wheeled her outside into the sunny yet frosty day. She shivered.

"We need to get you another jacket."

"I just want to go home." Her grumble made Nate worry she didn't recall what he'd told her just a few hours ago in her cubicle.

"I'm taking you home to pack," Nate said in a way that he hoped left no room for argument. "Then we're headed back out."

"Is that really necessary?" She yelped a bit when he bounced over the metal threshold.

"Sorry. And yes," Nate told her as he steered her over to where he'd parked in the ER lot. "It is. I'm also going to need your phone."

"My...phone?" She made it sound as if he'd asked her to cut off her arm.

"Can't take any chances you're being tracked. Whoever ran you off the road—"

"It could have been an accident." She glanced over her shoulder at him, barely there hope swimming in her hazel eyes. "We shouldn't overreact."

Nate bit the inside of his cheek and remained silent until he had her in the car. Before he left to return the wheelchair, he pulled out his phone and tapped open the photos he'd been sent from Lieutenant Haig. "If you can look at these and still tell me you think it was pure coincidence this happened to you, we can discuss further. I'll be right back." He closed the door and grabbed the chair.

Showing her the photos wasn't something he'd planned to do. Personally, he'd have preferred not to show her the evidence of her own attempted murder, but they both needed to start looking reality in the face. If only to make some smart decisions.

By the time he returned to the car and slid in behind the wheel, he didn't have to ask if he'd made his point. She'd set her phone on the console between the seats. The tension swirling inside the SUV was more than enough evidence of that.

"You okay?" It was, perhaps, the dumbest question he'd ever uttered in his life. But it was the only thing he could think to ask. He quickly turned off her phone, popped out the SIM card and placed both in the glove box.

"Not really, no." She handed his phone over, and he pocketed it so he could use it again in an emergency. "I guess I'd convinced myself it wasn't as bad as it was." She sighed, sank down in her seat. "My car's totaled."

"Yes, it is." The images had been sent from their evidence station, where Lieutenant Haig had ordered Detective Sullivan to meet him. Nate's superior had wanted Sullivan to see the results of his dismissing a witness without thinking things through. Nate could only hope the conversation made some kind of impact, but he doubted it. Sullivan was a decent cop, but not the best human being. "But you weren't, so let's count that as a win."

"Go me."

Her sense of humor was intact, at least. "We'll worry about your car another time. Right now, let's get you home."

"What about you?" She looked over at him. "If we're leaving town, don't you need your stuff?"

"I keep a go bag in the back." He jerked a thumb toward the rear window. He reorganized the duffel every couple of weeks, just to be safe. He'd only had call to use it a handful of times since becoming a detective, but at least he knew it was reliable. Anything he might have missed they could pick up down the road. "I can live out of that thing for weeks if necessary."

"I still haven't given a statement about the accident." She took hold of the grab bar over the door and the center console when he reversed out of the parking space. "Sorry." Her eyes squeezed shut for a moment. "Getting back on the horse isn't easy. Stupid." She gave her head a hard shake and had him wincing.

"It's natural, not stupid. It'll get better. And I'll try to go slow." Truth be told, he'd considered having her drive his car to her place. Slapping fear in the face was usually his mode for getting past things. But she wasn't him. Vivian would have to be eased back into the driver's seat. Or at least be strongly motivated. Tiny steps, he told himself. "As far as your statement goes, we'll get that taken care of once we get to where we're going."

"And where is that exactly?" She hadn't released her grip on the grab bar. If anything, she'd tightened her fingers to the point her knuckles had gone white.

Because Nate wasn't entirely sure himself, he shrugged. "Does it matter?"

She went silent for a moment. "I suppose not."

"It's not going to be for long, Vivian. Just until we catch whoever is behind these attacks on you."

"Despite your best efforts to prove otherwise, you aren't a superhero," Vivian said. "You can protect me, or you can work the case. I doubt you can do both."

"Oh, ye of little faith." How she underestimated him. And it would be something akin to a pleasure to prove her wrong. "I'm capable of multitasking all sorts of things. Besides, I've got lots of friends in the Boise PD, and most of them owe me more than one favor. We'll get you home and back to your life soon enough."

She caught her lower lip in her teeth and turned her head to look out the window. The sun still shone, but a light dusting of snow fell from the gray clouds hovering overhead. Days like this felt like doom and gloom with the barest hint of light on the horizon.

"My lieutenant said there were more than a dozen people who stopped to help you." He was grasping at straws to help identify something positive out of all this. "They all gave statements and a description of the car that hit you. Most of them asked about you."

He couldn't see her reaction. "Do you think..." She stopped, took a deep breath. "When this is all over, do you think I could get their names so I can send them thank-you notes?"

It seemed both a ludicrous idea and so incredibly Vivian. “I think we can make that happen.”

She glanced at him. “That’s weird, isn’t it?”

“Incredibly,” Nate said without hesitation. “But more that you thought of it now, when you’re still reeling from what happened.” Her grimace told him she was doubting her own sanity. “Feel and think what you need to in order to get through.”

“I can compartmentalize better than most people.” Her voice was low now and carried a familiar sadness Nate could relate to. “Sometimes you have to do that in order to survive.”

Like she’d had to when her parents were killed. Like he did when his father had returned to his other family. His *real* family.

“Don’t ever apologize for being who you are, Vivian.” Because he couldn’t resist the urge, he reached over and laid his hand over hers. His heart jumped when she folded her fingers around his and squeezed. “You’re you. That’s the only thing that matters.”

“You missed your calling, Detective,” Vivian said softly. “You really should give poetry a try.”

He laughed, shook his head, and because she cast nervous eyes at his driving with only one hand on the wheel, he released his hold and put her mind at ease. “My expertise with poetry extends only so far as the naughty limericks one of my school friends used to recite.”

“You underestimate yourself,” she said in a tone that left no room for argument. “I think you have more talent in the word department than you realize. Can I ask a favor?”

“Sure.”

“Before we hit the freeway, can we please, *please* stop for some coffee?”

IT FELT STRANGE having a man drive her home. Strange in a good way, perhaps, but strange nonetheless. It was as if she'd left her home Friday evening one person and was coming home a different one. Maybe it was the fact that Nate was the man.

She didn't think it was the badge he wore or the job he did or even the last name he possessed, but perhaps it was the combination that made Vivian feel utterly and completely safe and content when he was around. Even while her entire world seemed to be falling off its axis.

For a woman who had spent the majority of her life alone, she wasn't completely pleased with the idea of feeling even the least bit reliant on another person for her emotional well-being but…there it was. Reality. And his name was Nate Colton.

Guided by his onboard GPS, he parked in front of her garden-gated town house and turned off the engine. There was an unexpected relief at seeing her house again. There had been moments before she'd crashed that she had honestly believed she wouldn't ever see it again.

"Can I have your keys, please?" Nate held out his hand.

She frowned, looked down at his empty palm. "Why?"

"Because I'm not taking a chance that they don't know where you live. They spent enough time looking at your license plate. Getting your address wouldn't take much more effort."

"Awesome." She hadn't even considered that. She dug into her purse, wincing at the slight dampness of the leather, to retrieve them. She hoped the bag wasn't ruined by its time in the icy water after the crash. "I suppose you want me to wait in the car while you check things out?"

"I'll only be a couple of minutes."

"More than five and I'm coming in." She was already mentally packing as he headed inside. She was also attempting to come up with some argument, any argument, to change his mind about letting her stay. She finished the last of her extra-large double-shot latte without the usual guilt at the caffeine level. Jittery was better than feeling helpless. At least, that was the idea she'd had when she'd placed her order.

Her home was her fortress, the one place she always felt untouchable and completely herself. What Nate was proposing was leaving all that security behind. As much as she trusted him, she wasn't completely on board with this idea.

Watching him approach her gate gave her an unobstructed rear view of the perfection of the male form. She let out a slow breath, appreciating the way he moved, even as he reached behind him and pulled a gun out of the back of his jeans.

"And there's the reality check." She was really getting sick of them, to be honest. She was not a fan of weapons. She didn't own a gun. Heck, she'd never even fired one! Now she found herself getting tangled up with someone who carried one for a living. As if a handful of steamy kisses equaled entangled.

The metal fence clanked shut, and he made his way up the short walk to her front door. He took a moment before sliding the key into the lock and disappearing inside.

Vivian's heart pounded hard against her ribs. What if someone was inside? What if Nate found them in there? Could she ever feel safe again after her space had been invaded? Or if he was hurt protecting her?

No sooner had she begun the internal debate than Nate reappeared and returned to the car. He pulled open her door.

"Everything looks fine to me." He held out his hand, and for an instant, she had an image of a particular glass-slippered princess being welcomed by her prince charming. She rolled her eyes, shook her head and wondered when her teenage self had been reawakened. Clearly the last couple of days had made a jumble of her thoughts and long-suppressed longings and dreams.

"It shouldn't take me too long to pack a bag." The sensation of his hand against the small of her back felt incredibly intimate. "How long should I plan to be gone for?"

"A week." His answer sounded as if he'd given it some thought. "We'll re-evaluate after that."

"Right." She left her purse on the floor in front of the small entryway table before heading up the stairs. "I'll be back down in a bit."

"Take your time," he called up after her. "I'm not going anywhere."

NATE CLOSED THE front door to Vivian's town house and, out of habit, snapped the lock. He'd only given a cursory glance to her home's contents on his initial entry. He'd been looking for disturbances, signs of someone else's presence. Not a reflection of Vivian's character and personality.

Since he'd found nothing disturbed, he relaxed and took in his surroundings. Not that there was much to take in. The ground floor mostly consisted of a spacious living area, where she had a small sofa, coffee table and rather large television set up in the corner beneath the stairs. There wasn't any art on the walls or knickknacks on the shelves.

Behind the sofa, taking up the entire back wall, was a bookcase crammed with titles of every sort, forced into precarious storage as she clearly read more than her system could contain.

A collection of blankets covered the sofa. One in particular, a black one over the back, near the window, had an indentation in it. He frowned, walked over, touched gentle fingers to the blanket, which was coated with cat hair.

He turned, looked around and spotted a pile of cat supplies in the corner by the front door. A cat perch with a cubby, a scratching post and a paper bag filled to overflowing with toys, food bowls and water dishes.

There were only a small number of framed photographs on display. One showed Vivian cuddling a beautiful, sleek white-and-gray cat with enormous yellow eyes. Another photo gave him a start as it was most definitely of his half-sister, Lizzy Colton. The two of them wore their caps and gowns at high school graduation. They'd been caught mid-laugh, and the sight stole his breath.

The other three were of Vivian as a little girl, being cuddled between two people he assumed were her parents. One during the summer, one at the holidays and a third at what appeared to be one of Vivian's birthdays. The light in her eyes was almost blinding with happiness as she blew out the candles on her cake. Those three pictures were more faded than the others, had folds and creases in them. Five pictures seemed a small and sobering number to represent thirty years of life.

In the corner by the window stood a round table on which a small, not even three-foot fake Christmas tree sat. Without the lights, it looked more than a little sad, with only a handful of ornaments on it, but there was one small, handcrafted paper angel sitting on the top with stringy blond hair. Other than that, there wasn't a hint of the holidays around her home.

"Hey, Nate?" Vivian came down two steps and leaned over. Her wet hair spilled over her shoulders. Heat and the fragrance of flowers wafted off her skin, a result of the shower she must have taken.

Gone were his sister's jeans and T-shirt. The sweater she wore now over faded jeans was a deep turquoise blue that accentuated her beautiful eyes. "We are staying in civilization, right? Electricity and everything? Internet?"

"We are if I have anything to say about it," he confirmed and earned a smile from her.

"Cool." She disappeared back upstairs.

He wandered through to the kitchen and small nook where a table and two chairs stood. Files and papers sat stacked in what he assumed was a system only she understood. Outside, a collection of empty bowls sat alongside the sliding glass door leading out to a small garden that contained nothing resembling plants. Instead, there were tumbles of rocks where grass or pots might have been.

He stepped outside, checked the back gate and noticed the garbage and recycling cans out along the back road where tenants parked. Deciding he might be of some help, he returned inside and rummaged through her refrigerator. He was shoulder deep into a collection of leftovers and takeout boxes when she came up behind him.

"Hungry?"

"Yes, actually." He grinned over his shoulder at her. The warmth of her hand on his shoulder had him once again needing to remind himself that he was actually working. Now wasn't the time for flirtations. "But I thought maybe we should empty this out just in case you're away longer than a week."

"Probably." She sighed. "Shame. There's some good food

in there. I found this new Peruvian place that… Where are you going?"

"I've got a collapsible cooler in the back of the car." He shrugged. "Like you said, it's a shame to let it go to waste." Because her smile of gratitude was almost more than he could take, he made a quick exit, taking deep, refocusing breaths as he retrieved the cooler. He'd no sooner slammed the back shut than he found himself coming face-to-face with an elderly man with glasses so thick he looked like a goldfish. "Hello."

"You visiting Ms. Maylor?" The man was a bit stooped and barely reached Nate's chest. He held a small package in one hand, a four-footed cane in the other. His T-shirt declared him to be a marine veteran, as did the steely, almost suspicious look in his bright blue eyes.

"I, well, yes, I am. Nate Colton." He held out his free hand, refrained from flashing his badge. "I thought I'd take Vivian on a bit of a vacation."

"A vacation?" His eyes went wide. "Well, land's sake. Never expected to hear that. Don't really see her unless she's coming out to get her mail. I'm Edgar Bartholomew. I live next door." He indicated the town house to the right. Potted poinsettia plants lined the walkway, interspersed with solar lights that no doubt cast a festive glow onto the red and white petals. His front window was filled with an enormous lighted tree twinkling bright enough to be seen from the space station. "Folks just call me Eddie though. Vacation. Huh." He frowned again, quirked his head in question. "Really?"

"Really." It shouldn't have surprised him that this news came across as unexpected. Vivian didn't strike him as the impulsive type. "Was there something you needed, Eddie?"

"Me? Oh, no." Eddie shook his head, then shoved the box

at Nate. "Delivery came for Vivian yesterday afternoon. It needed to be signed for, and I was out tending to my roses. Even in winter, they need tending to."

"Of course," Nate agreed, noting the line of blankets draped over the pruned bushes.

"I came over and rang last night, but no answer." His smile was quick. "Guess I know why now. Anyway. This is for her."

Nate accepted the box. "I'll make sure she gets it."

"Appreciate it." Eddie started to hobble away, then turned around and nearly toppled over catching his balance. "Nice to see she's found someone to take care of her. She's a lonely one, I think," he observed with a sad shake of his head. "Hate to see it. Put a smile on her face, would you? No one should be all alone. Especially during the holidays."

"I'll do my best," Nate assured him before he headed inside. He returned to the kitchen where he found her sorting containers and setting aside produce that wouldn't last much longer. The bowls that had been outside the back door were in the sink now. "I just met your neighbor, Eddie."

"Oh?"

"He accepted a delivery for you yesterday." He held out the box.

She accepted it with more than a question on her face. "I wonder what…" She read the label, then hugged it to her chest. She sighed and closed her eyes. When she opened them again, they were filled with tears.

"What is it?" Nate asked.

She grabbed a knife and sliced through the packing tape. Once open, she pulled out a small cedar box with *Toby* engraved on the top. "My cat's ashes. I had to put him down last month. Kidney disease." She sighed and touched her fingers to the polished wood. "I had him for over eleven years." Vivian attempted a laugh, swiped at the tears on her cheek. "Boy, when it rains, it pours. I wasn't sure when to expect this, but it makes sense it would come now. The hits just keep coming."

"Vivian." Her name was the only thing he could think to say. The toys and cat things in the corner made sense now. She was giving it all away because her cat had died.

"Thanks." She sighed. "Boy, I'm a piece of work, aren't I? Can't begin to understand why I'm still single."

"I, for one, am glad you are." He took hold of her shoulders and turned her to face him. "I'm sorry about Toby."

"Thanks." Her smile was both sad and sentimental. "He was the best cat. My best friend. My shadow. Never left me alone. Because of him I didn't feel quite so…"

"Alone?" Nate supplied when it seemed she couldn't.

"Yeah." Her voice was thick. "Geez, you don't want me blubbering all over you." She stepped away, bent down and grabbed a bag of cat food out of a cabinet. "I didn't want all this going to waste." She quickly filled four of the bowls to the brim, set them aside then did the same with water in the others. "I've been feeding the neighborhood strays in his honor. He was an indoor kitty," she said as if that explained everything.

"A fitting tribute," Nate agreed. "I've never had a pet."

"No?" She looked shocked.

"My mother had little interest in taking care of us. I didn't dare try to add an animal into the mix." As always, he didn't let that thought carry him very far. "Let me take care of loading up the food. You take care of the cats."

Her eyes were clearer now, and the two of them traded positions. Once she slid the back door closed again, Nate spotted two cats hopping over the fence and diving straight at the food.

"You all ready to go?" he asked, once he added a couple of handfuls of ice and zipped up the soft-sided cooler. She had her still damp purse on the counter, along with a different bag to transfer her things into. He didn't comment when she slipped the box containing Toby's ashes into the bottom.

"Just need to get my laptop and some files together." She did so in record time, and pretty soon he was carrying the cooler, one small suitcase and another smaller bag out to the car. She had her laptop bag over her shoulder when she locked up the house. "I'm going to ask Eddie if he wouldn't mind getting my mail while I'm gone," she said.

"Good plan." Nate stayed near the car while she did just that. That Eddie thought of Vivian as lonely had done something to Nate's heart. It wasn't fair, what life did to some people. The last thing Vivian deserved was to be pitched headfirst into this mess with Dean Wexler and Marty DeBaccian. Then again, if she hadn't gone on that date, then Nate never would have met her, and that, he realized as he pulled out his cell phone and stashed SIM card, would have been a terrible shame.

"Did you get a call?" Vivian asked when she appeared at his side again. "Is there any word on Dean Wexler?"

"No. I was just thinking about a call I need to make." One he didn't want to make in front of her. Mainly because he had no way of knowing how this call was going to go. "Why don't you get on in? I'll be there in a sec."

"Okay." It was obvious she knew why he was asking her to, but she didn't argue.

The now familiar dread that wound its way inside him when his thoughts turned to his siblings did so at extraordinary speed. His time in Owl Creek last month had been cursory and brief, but necessary given the events surrounding his sister Lizzy's kidnapping. He hadn't hesitated when he'd heard about the family dinner, but he'd also had to face a lot of truth by doing so.

Things had ended well, but it wasn't as if they'd all gotten to know each other very well. They were still, for all intents and purposes, walking on eggshells around each other. At least, that was the way Nate and Sarah felt.

Neither Nate nor his sister had summoned up the courage to call any of them to see if that truly was the case.

"Well, you've got a chance now," Nate muttered as he dialed one of the numbers he'd been given. His pulse kicked into overdrive as the phone rang.

"Detective Colton. Speak."

"Fletcher, it's Nate. Colton." He paused. "Your brother." Nate winced. Brilliant. "Sorry. You know that." He pinched the bridge of his nose and squeezed his eyes shut. "I don't know if it's okay that I called—"

"Of course it's okay." Fletcher's no-nonsense tone was, as far as Nate knew, his default and not to be taken personally. "What's going on?"

"I don't think there's a way to summarize." The last twenty-four hours spun in on him, robbing him of words but solidifying the one thing he knew to be true. "But I also don't think there's anyone else I can trust. I need your help, Fletcher." He paused. "More specifically, I think I need Colton help."

Chapter Seven

"Are you sure no one is following us?" Not for the first time, Vivian twisted around in the passenger seat to look out the back window. The snowcapped mountain vistas ahead really should have captured all her attention, but she was used to seeing them, having lived in the area most of her life.

How she envied the ease with which Nate—and just about everybody else on the planet—maneuvered the highways and roadways, especially in the wintertime. Snow drifted down and coated the car in a delicate dusting as she scanned the vehicles behind them.

"I'm sure."

"How do you know?"

"Because it's my job."

She gave him points for patience. She was on the verge of annoying herself; she could only imagine how her continued paranoia must be coming across.

"I'm watching for it, Vivian." He took hold of her hand and gave a gentle tug, one she took to mean she should turn back around. "You need to stop worrying."

"Apologies," she muttered. "It's my first time being targeted for death." She glanced over in time to see his jaw tense. "They say your sense of humor is the first thing to go when you're stressed."

"Mine just gets more obnoxious," he said, and when she tried to tug her hand free, he slipped his fingers between hers and squeezed. "You aren't alone in this, Vivian. I don't know what else I can say or do to convince you of that."

"I don't know, either." She stared straight ahead at the sign that said the turnoff for Owl Creek was only a few miles away. "Things like this don't happen to me, Nate."

"Things like this don't happen to most people," he assured her. "How about we get your mind off the possibility of being followed and play a round of twenty questions? Anything you want to know, ask me."

Bold move. Not one she would have made. Or would she? She looked at him for a long moment, pondering how he affected her emotional state. What was it about this man that had her thinking in completely different ways than she normally did? There was such ease with him, such comfort, that her life-long developed fears took an almost back seat to reality. "Anything I ask, you'll tell me the truth?"

"It wouldn't be much of a game if I didn't," he said. "Go ahead. Try me. Question one. Let's have it."

"How old are you?"

"Interesting way to start." His lips twitched. "Twenty-eight."

"Oh." She blinked, not sure whether to laugh or frown.

"For the record, I've always had a thing for older women."

She snort-laughed, covered her mouth in surprise when he chuckled. "I'm not that much older than you."

"Two whole years according to your driver's license."

"Yeah, well, that license also gives me permission to drive, and we both know how that tends to go."

"What did you do for your thirtieth birthday last month?"

She narrowed her eyes. "I didn't realize this game was reciprocal."

"How else am I going to find out more about you?" He tightened his hold on her hand. "Come on. Give. What did you do?"

"Ah." She sighed. "I met Lizzy at The Cellar in Owl Creek for some wine tasting."

"That's it?"

She shrugged. "I'm not big on birthdays." Birthdays always reminded her of her parents, and the fuzzy memories she did have of them faded with each passing year. "That's our happy place. I drove down, and we went there after… well, after she was back home."

"I hope Lizzy gave you a great birthday present, at least."

"She signed me up for multiple dating apps," she deadpanned and earned a gasp from him. "Kidding!" She laughed at getting one over on him. "Actually, she tracked down a rare edition of *Pride and Prejudice* for me. It's my favorite Jane Austen book."

"That explains why you have an entire shelf of copies in your living room."

She didn't know why, but the idea of him noticing things around her home actually warmed her.

"Okay, my turn again." She started to look back again, but he squeezed her hand hard.

"Every time you look back gives me an extra question."

She resisted temptation. This time. "Why aren't you married?"

"Wow. Going straight to it." He shook his head. A strand of hair fell across his forehead, giving him a bit of a rakish appearance with that smile of his. "I could go with the usual, just haven't found the right woman. Which is true. Being married to a cop isn't something most women aspire to." He shrugged as if it didn't much matter. "The truth is probably more in line with the fact that I have no frame of reference for the institution."

"Oh." She instantly regretted the impulsive decision to ask. "I'm sorry. I didn't mean to—"

"You ever notice how much you apologize?" he asked. "Honestly, Vivian. It's a perfectly fine question, and considering where we could have easily ended up last night, you should probably be brought up to speed on my familial situation. Not to mention we're headed right into the heart of Colton country." Nate gestured to the increasing signs identifying Owl Creek. "What all has Lizzy told you about the family?" His eyes were glossy and unreadable when he looked at her. "I'm not asking so I can decide what not to share. I just don't want to rehash what you already know."

"Okay." Vivian's mind raced. She'd always found the Colton family tree a bit…confusing. Overwhelming to be sure. Lizzy came from such a huge extended family while Vivian had well, Lizzy. "You, Sarah, Lizzy and her three brothers share the same mother, Jessie, and she walked away from that family when Lizzy was really young. Like three or four, I think. They were raised by their father, Buck Colton." She smiled. "I like Buck. He's a nice guy. Loves his kids. You can always tell, you know?"

"I've only met him a few times, but you're right. He seems like a good guy," Nate agreed. "Far more gracious than he has any right to be. What Lizzy and her brothers and cousins recently found out was that Jessie walked away from them to take up with Buck's brother, Robert Colton."

"Robert was married to Jessie's twin sister, Jenny, correct?" She really didn't want to get any of this wrong. It felt… disrespectful somehow.

"Yes. Robert and Jenny have six kids. Chase, Fletcher, Wade, Ruby, Hannah and Frannie."

"Frannie owns a bookstore in Owl Creek." She felt rather proud at remembering that tidbit.

"She does. Book Mark It," Nate said. "Should have figured you'd know that. I'm betting that's how Lizzy got hold of that rare book for you."

"Lizzy mentioned that Robert Colton died earlier this year."

"Yes, he did," Nate confirmed. "Unfortunately, my mother used that opportunity to make a familial comeback." His mouth stretched into a tight smile. "One of my dumber moves, believing she extended an olive branch on our behalf." His jaw tensed as if gnashing his teeth together. "She took his dying as her opportunity to tell the entire family about me and Sarah." He winced. "And no, she didn't give us any warning. And they didn't exactly throw out the welcome mat."

"Eeesh." Vivian cringed.

"Definitely *eeesh*. Personally, I don't think my mother took two breaths before she tried to stake a claim on Robert's money by presenting me and Sarah as two of his heirs. She literally used us as exhibits A and B."

"Oh." Vivian chewed on the inside of her cheek. "Wow. That's…" She tried to find the words. "I seem to remember Lizzy mentioning some additional unpleasantness about Robert's passing. So, Robert was your dad."

"Father," Nate corrected. "I don't recall him ever being a dad. He was gone a lot when I was younger, then pretty much vanished from our lives when I was ten. I saw him maybe a handful of times after that. The story goes he had a change of heart and went back full-time to Jenny and their kids." He winced. "Couldn't have sat very well with any of them knowing that Sarah and I were born at the same time Hannah and Frannie were."

"I suppose not."

"Sarah and I were teenagers when we found out our parents were never married. Then there was the fact that our father was *the* Robert Colton, who was primarily responsible for putting Owl Creek on the map."

Her heart went out to him. "That must have been a lot for a teenager to process."

"It's been a lot for everyone to process," Nate said with a hint of sadness in his voice. "Maybe more when you're an adult. One of the reasons Sarah and I drove out to Owl Creek a couple months ago, to break the ice and clear the air."

"Did it work?"

Nate shrugged. "Can't be sure. I'd say we're in a bit of a strained time of existence. Sarah wants so much to make a lasting connection with our half siblings. It's like a dream come true for her, the whole big-family thing. But given who our mother is, our newfound family isn't totally trusting. I don't blame them." He hit the turn signal and moved two lanes to the right. "I don't blame them one bit. Jessie is unpredictable at best, malicious and cruel at worst. My mother doesn't have the capacity to care about anyone other than herself, so whatever her motivations regarding exposing our existence, you can bet they're self-serving." He flashed her a look. "Which brings us back to your original question about marriage. My perception of the institution of marriage is all a bit… What's the word?"

"Skewed?" Vivian offered. "Tarnished? Tainted?"

"Those work well enough."

She couldn't quite reconcile why that sounded so sad. "So, between Robert and Jenny's kids and Jessie and Buck's kids, you went from having one sister to having…" She did the math. "Ten brothers and sisters?"

"Yep." He took the turnoff leading into downtown Owl Creek, circling around the off-ramp before veering off to the left. "You out of questions or did I shock you into silence?" He shifted his gaze to the rearview mirror as he'd been doing since they'd started driving.

"I guess I'm wondering what questions are appropriate. New ones have popped to mind since we started."

"Already told you, nothing's off-limits."

"Okay." Time to put that to the test. "So, Robert went back to Jenny. What happened with your mom?"

"Jessie? She spent a good few years playing the victim and the martyr. That takes real talent in case you're wondering. Despite none of us being willing to give her even the time of day."

"Lizzy's never talked about her," Vivian said. "She's only brought her up recently because of what happened after Robert died." Coming face-to-face with the mother who had walked away and never looked back must have been excruciating for her friend. She'd covered, of course, and played it off like it wasn't anything other than ridiculous family drama, but how could it not have hurt?

"Sometimes, I think Lizzy and her brothers got the better end of the deal." Nate made easy work of the traffic. "They had to deal with Jessie being gone. Sarah and I had to deal with her…well, *with* her. I readily admit which road I'd preferred to have walked."

Vivian frowned. There was a kind of detachment in his

voice, a tone that belied more than a tinge of resentment where his mother was concerned. It was, Vivian thought sadly, something she had no reference for. The vague memories she had of her mother, of both her parents, were so fragmented she couldn't piece them together. She'd tried to. For years. But they were just…ghosts.

"Hearing all this explains a lot about Lizzy. How she was growing up," Vivian said. Lizzy had always had serious trust issues and more than a suspicious nature when it came to anyone looking to the Coltons for a payout. "You said you were a teenager when you found out about your siblings."

"I was fifteen," Nate said. "I played basketball that year in high school. The team traveled to Owl Creek for a game. It was around the time some new construction project was getting off the ground. We were staying in this fancy—well, fancy to me—hotel in town. I went downstairs to work out and stopped in the lobby. There he was, my father, on the front page of the local paper. Along with his family. Jenny and all the kids." He hesitated. "His real family. Funny." Nate shook his head. "As shocking as that was—and believe me, I read everything I could about Robert Colton after that—seeing that picture, being in Owl Creek, walking through the town he was responsible for, everything about my own life suddenly made a lot more sense. It also made me a lot more self-conscious. I spent years worried about what would happen if the truth got out."

Her heart broke for the boy he'd been. How alone he must have felt in those days following his discovery. "But you didn't say anything to anyone."

"There was no point. I told Sarah a few weeks later. Once I'd worked everything out so I could answer her questions." A flicker of bitterness crossed his face. "I quit the basketball team first, though. I didn't need or want any more surprise trips to Owl Creek. We decided together to keep it to ourselves. We figured if our father wanted anything to do with us, he'd be the one to reach out. He'd already messed with the two of us. We didn't want to be the cause of destroying his other family."

Sympathy swirled through her. No. His mother had taken care of that, hadn't she? "I don't know that I'd have been that generous."

"It wasn't generous," Nate said. "It was survival. We had enough to deal with where Jessie was concerned, and honestly, if we had done things differently, who knows what might have happened." He frowned, gaze pinned to the rearview mirror. "Huh." He pulled his hand free of hers.

"What?" Forgetting the potential cost of looking, she turned around, scanned the steady stream of cars. "Do you see something?" Everything seemed to blur together.

"Maybe." He turned right at the next light without signaling. "Let's see what this might be about."

Vivian turned back around, gripped the seat in her hands and squeezed until her fingers went numb.

"Nothing bad's going to happen, Viv." He didn't look at her this time, just kept his eyes straight ahead or on the mirror as he drove. "We're in this together, remember? Do me a favor? Write down this plate number?" He read off the letters and numbers once she took her phone out of the glove box and began typing.

He took a left, bringing them through a residential area coated with a light dusting of snow and varying degrees of holiday cheer. One fence line in particular boasted oversize Santa hats perched atop dividing posts. When she let her gaze drift to the passenger-door mirror, an SUV similar to Nate's turned behind them a distance back.

"That car look familiar?"

"No." She shook her head. "It's not the one that ran me off the road."

"You sure?" He hit the gas, and they sped up. The car still followed, but maintained its same speed, and the distance between them grew.

"That one had a weird decal on the front window." She gasped. Stacy had been right. When her mind relaxed, it seemed to set things free. "I just remembered that. I'm—"

He shot her a look that included an arched and challenging brow.

"Not sorry I didn't tell you before," she corrected herself. He was right. She really did spend a lot of time apologizing for innocuous comments or thoughts.

"You remembered now. That's all that matters. We'll put a call in to my lieutenant when we stop. Bring him up to date. Get that information added to the case file."

"Are we going to stop?" She couldn't have stopped her voice from squeaking if she'd tried.

"Not yet." He took another couple of turns and got them back on the road they were previously on. He tapped on his dashboard screen, scrolled down a list of names. Vivian frowned when he hit Call for Fletcher Colton.

Nerves tangled around themselves in her stomach. As close as she was to Lizzy, she hadn't seen her friend's brothers in years. When it came to the extended members of her family, she must have been ten the last time she was around any of them. "I thought you said you don't talk to your brothers?"

"Not on a regular basis, I don't." Nate said. "Given the

situation we're in, couldn't really think of anyone else to ask for help."

"Nate." The deep voice bounced around the car like an echo. "You here yet?"

"We just got into Owl Creek. I've got you on Speaker with me and Vivian," Nate told him. "I'm pretty sure we've picked up a tail."

"Oh?" The alertness that came through on that one word added to Vivian's anxiety. "You close enough for a description?"

Nate rattled off the bare minimum. "And we've got a plate. Viv?"

"Hi, Fletcher." She swallowed the lump of anxiety lodged in her throat. "I'm sure you don't remember me—"

"Lizzy's friend from school," Fletcher said. "Sure. You spent Christmas at the ranch with us one year. You were what, fourteen?"

"Thirteen, actually." A very awkward, silent thirteen. Not that she'd ever needed to say much with Lizzy around. That was one of the reasons they got along so well. Vivian was always happy to let her take the lead. "It's nice of you to remember."

"That was the year Lizzy stuck a fake rattlesnake in my underwear drawer," Fletcher said. "I broke two of dad's favorite lamps trying to kill it."

Vivian's lips twitched. She'd forgotten about that.

"Every Christmas since," Fletcher went on, "someone buys me a lamp. The ugliest lamp they could possibly find. I hope no one shares that story with Kiki."

"Kiki?" Vivian asked before she thought better of it.

"She's a DJ here in Owl Creek. We're...dating."

Vivian shot Nate a look at the same time he gave her his

own. They grinned at each other but didn't say anything more until Fletcher asked for the plate number.

Vivian read it back and was answered by silence.

"Well." Fletcher coughed. "Okay, then. How about you come on by the station for a bit? I'll meet you outside, and we'll see what the driver does when he realizes where you've led him."

"Okay." Nate frowned. "Is something going on?" He looked back into the mirror. The car was backing off but still visible.

"Nope. See you in a few." Fletcher disconnected before Nate could push harder.

"Didn't take long to get strange," Nate muttered. "Okay, then. Owl Creek police station it is." He accelerated through a yellow light and sped up again. "And the sooner the better."

Chapter Eight

Nate's constant assurances to Vivian that no one would be following them had been uttered in good, solid faith. The chances DeBaccian's men would take another risk by running Vivian off the road twice in one day were, at least to Nate's mind, a million to one. And that wasn't even taking into account Nate's being along for the ride. Going after a cop was something DeBaccian wouldn't be stupid enough to do. Doubt niggled. Or would he?

That idea did not sit well. Still, lying to Vivian, intentionally or otherwise, was not something he ever wanted to do. Faith and trust were difficult enough to establish and build, especially with someone with Vivian's relatively solitary past.

"You're worried," Vivian said. Her voice was as quiet as he expected, as if she was worried about startling or offending him.

"A little." The full day was heading into the evening. Hard to believe things had been almost normal this morning when she'd walked into his kitchen wearing nothing but a T-shirt. What he wouldn't give to go back and take the day in a different direction.

"But going to the station is a good thing, isn't it?" The uncertainty rang loudly in Nate's ears.

"It is." He couldn't shake the idea that Fletcher knew something he didn't. It wasn't brotherly instinct—they didn't know each other well enough for Nate to claim that prerogative. But cop instinct was a completely different story. "You're going to be safe here, Vivian. I promise."

Her smile was almost wide enough to convince him she believed him.

Downtown Owl Creek opened up ahead and welcomed them like an old, festive frenemy. Nate's hands tightened on the steering wheel. He'd spent years limiting his trips here to official business and necessary excursions. Being this close to the Coltons was a lesson in tempting fate, and that was one thing Nate went out of his way to avoid doing.

Driving in like this, with his own trust placed firmly in the hands of a brother who would no doubt be happier not knowing Nate existed felt like a dangerous game to play. Especially where Vivian's life was concerned. But it was Vivian's life he was worried about, and—honestly? He couldn't think of anyone he could trust more when it came to her safety.

It was a bit like driving through a time portal, he noticed, as they made their way through town.

The town had developed into a year-round resort with skiing and other winter-centric activities taking center stage, yet during the warmer summer months, people flocked to the lake and consistent sunshine as a getaway. In February, the winter carnival would kick into high gear and feature incredible bigger-than-life snow sculptures, dog-sled racing and countless other events that would bring in a good deal of cash to the local economy. From the Tap Out Brewery that served local ales and pub grub, to Frannie's Book Mark It, the town had developed into a significant destination both for travelers and those looking for a laid-back, more relaxed way of life. Varying decor highlighted storefronts, walkways and lampposts. With the snowcapped mountains the perfect backdrop, it was like a kind of Christmas village had been plopped into the middle of civilization.

While the drive from Boise to Owl Creek was a good two hours, travel time—at least how Nate drove—from Vivian's town house was just shy of forty-five. Which meant the police station came up fast once they started down the main, business-lined thoroughfare.

"There's a space right in front of the station." Vivian pointed ahead of them. "Doris Day parking."

"What?" Nate glanced at her.

"You know, classic movies? How Doris Day always found a parking space in the front of wherever she was going? Sorry. I think of weird facts when I'm nervous." And with the way she kept looking at the car following them, she was most definitely nervous.

Nate shook his head. He couldn't recall the last time he'd watched a movie that didn't include explosions and car chases.

He pulled into the spot she'd pointed out, his attention partially divided and focused on the man standing with his back against the wall beside the entrance to the Owl Creek PD.

It was entirely possible, Nate thought, that Detective Fletcher Colton had a natural tolerance to the cold. With his worn jeans, thick, snow-friendly work boots and a khaki button-down shirt displaying his police badge, he may as well have been sunning himself in the middle of July.

"You look alike." Vivian's comment startled Nate back to reality.

"Do we?" Of course they did. Most of the male Colton offspring in these parts shared the brown hair and lighter color eyes. None of them could particularly look down on one another; height was another shared family trait. As was a natural propensity for athletic, fit builds and a low tolerance for bull. Yeah. Looking at Fletcher now, he definitely saw the resemblance.

Nate shifted, looked behind them as the car that had been following them pulled to a sudden stop in the middle of the street a few spots back. "Okay, here we go. Stay here."

Nate jumped out of the car, hand going to his back waistband for his weapon. He heard Fletcher yell his name, but it got carried off by the wind as Nate pulled out his gun and lifted it, both hands locked around the hilt, finger pressed against the side of the trigger. He aimed straight at the driver.

"Police!" Nate yelled. "Out of the car, now! Slowly!" He gestured with the gun as the man behind the wheel held up both hands. The sun visor obscured most of his face, but not so much that Nate didn't see the flicker of humor quirk his lips. A quick glimpse to the passenger seat told Nate that at least this guy was alone. Unless there was someone in the back seat…

"Nate—" Fletcher's voice sounded directly behind him now, but Nate wasn't going to take any chances. Not with Vivian's life.

"I said out!" Nate yelled again as he advanced.

Out of the corner of his eye, he saw Vivian push open the door and drop to the ground. She was bundled into the jacket she'd pulled out of the closet on their way out of her town house. Even from a distance, he could see her shivering.

"Nate, put the gun away," Fletcher said calmly.

"Not until he's out of the car." Despite the cold, he didn't shiver. He didn't move. He simply stared.

"Okay." Fletcher stepped around and motioned to the driver. "You heard him!" Fletcher called. "You'd best get out."

Nate stood there, staring as the door opened as he wondered why Fletcher was acting so nonchalant. Until the man stepped out of the car. Nate balked, glared and lowered his gun to his side. "Son of a— Max?" Max Colton, Nate's half brother through Jessie, slid out of the car, arms raised, an unfamiliar smile stretching across his mouth. "Did you skip surveillance-duty training back at the FBI?"

Max's expression came across as it usually did where Nate was concerned: guarded, suspicious and bordering on dark. But also, for the first time, Nate thought he saw impressed. That was a boost he hadn't expected.

"When did you spot me?" Max asked after he exchanged a hearty handshake and quick bro hug with Nate.

"About two seconds after you pulled out of the gas station parking lot just off the freeway." Nate holstered his gun, adrenaline draining. Only then did he begin to feel the December cold seep into his bones.

"We wanted to make sure you two were covered as soon as you hit town," Fletcher said on a laugh. "This is one for the books. Max Colton, serial-killer hunter, bested by his baby brother."

Nate froze. Baby brother? It took a moment to shake himself clear of all that thought encompassed. He was still a bit foggy when Vivian appeared and touched his arm.

"Everything okay?"

"Yeah." Her question had him nodding absently. "Fine. I might have overreacted." As Max and Fletcher closed the distance, cars crawled around Max's SUV. Out of instinct or protection or perhaps wanting to make a point he'd never anticipated making, Nate slipped his arm around Vivian's shoulders and drew her against his side. He immediately felt warmer. "Vivian Maylor, you probably already know my…" He stopped at the other two men's sharpened gazes. He swore, shook his head. "Well, hell. Fletcher already started it. Might as well start to get past it. Fletcher and Max Colton." He swallowed hard around unexpected emotion. "My brothers."

"Of course." Vivian held out her hand. "Fletcher of the rattlesnake Christmas."

Fletcher grunted and grinned when Max chuckled.

"And Max." She shook both their hands. "It's been a while. Lizzy said you only get back to Owl Creek between cases."

"True enough," Max said, and immediately shoved his hands into the front pockets of his jeans. "I've got some downtime at the moment. Fletcher said you two ran into some trouble back in Boise." He eyed Nate, then Fletcher. "Glad you thought to call. Looking forward to being read in."

It was on the tip of Nate's tongue to admit he was out of options, but there was no need to go burning down a just built bridge. He hadn't known what to expect coming to Owl Creek, but he was planning to make the most of it.

"I'm waiting on a call to make sure the house is ready for you." Fletcher motioned them to the station.

"House?" Vivian blinked. "What house?"

"Max, park that thing somewhere legal, will you? We'll wait on you." Fletcher slapped a hand on the back of his shoulder before he motioned for Nate and Vivian to follow him to the station house. "You two hungry?"

"Not really," Nate said.

"We have food in the car," Vivian explained as if she thought Nate's response bordered on rude. "I cook to relax, and I'm feeling ready for a distraction."

"Understood. And lucky Nate." Fletcher pulled open the door and waved them in ahead of him. "I have a bet with Wade that Nate lives on toaster pastries and root beer."

"Close," Nate said without missing a beat. "Brownies and Mountain Dew. You going to tell me why you thought the escort into town necessary?" Nate asked the second the door closed behind them.

"I am." Fletcher accepted a clipboard offered to him by a khaki-uniformed officer, scribbled his name at the bottom before handing it back. Another officer handed him a manila file folder, and he nodded his thanks. "Had a long talk with your Lieutenant Haig a little while ago. He gave me the rundown. Extra precautions seemed warranted. Our break room doubles as our conference room, so we can talk in there. Monroe?" Fletcher rapped his knuckles on the counter, and another officer, this one looking as if he'd just stepped out of high school, shot to attention. "Send Max back when he gets here, will you?"

"Sure thing, Detective." Monroe's baby face stretched into an eager smile.

Nate sighed. He remembered being that young, but had he ever been so…innocent?

The station house was nicer than Nate expected. Cozier, with its wood paneling and collection of framed photographs, it didn't have quite the harsh, sterile yet aged feel his own station house did. Images of Owl Creek officers over the years were displayed among other ones featuring town events both big and small. Funny—the place had an unexpectedly homier feel than most police stations he'd been in.

"I'm going to make a quick stop in the ladies' room." Vivian pointed to one of the doors they'd passed before disappearing behind it.

"Does Lizzy know what's going on?" Fletcher asked as he grabbed a couple of clean mugs out of an overhead cabinet. "Coffee?"

"Yeah, thanks." At the rate he was going, coffee would soon replace the blood running through his veins. "With Vivian, you mean? Not that I know of." He grimaced. "I suggested Vivian call her, but she refused. Mentioned that Lizzy had enough to cope with at the moment." He paused. "How is Lizzy doing?"

"Okay." Fletcher didn't seem of the mind to elaborate. "She's good at covering, though. She mentioned using Vivian as a sounding board on more than one occasion. That's good since the rest of us have kind of been hovering. Ajay's been good for her."

That bit of information didn't surprise Nate in the least. He'd been impressed with Ajay Wright, a K9 search and rescue agent. No doubt Ajay would view what happened to Lizzy from every angle and help her accordingly.

"How about you?" Fletcher eyed him with more caution than Nate felt comfortable with. "The last few months can't have been easy for you. How've you been doing?"

Nate couldn't tell if Fletcher was being polite, big brotherly or simply curious. "Okay, actually." He shrugged. "I'll be doing better once a psychopath criminal isn't chasing after Vivian."

"I hear that," Fletcher muttered. "We seem to be a magnet for psychopaths these days." He paused as Max strolled into the room. "Found your way back here okay, then?" he teased. "I thought about leaving some breadcrumbs..."

"Ha-ha." Max glowered, but in a way that had Nate laughing on the inside. An unexpected yet sadly familiar pang of envy struck him with pinpoint accuracy. He'd spent years wondering what it would be like to have a relationship with his brothers. The brothers who hadn't known Nate existed. Sure, it would have been easier on everyone if he'd remained an unknown Colton element, but even now he could feel those family ties knitting and forming. "This is where you fill me in."

"Just waiting on Vivian." Fletcher motioned for them to take a seat in one of the chairs around a large, circular table.

"Got anything to eat around here?" Max started yanking open cabinets that had more office supplies inside than munchies.

"Doesn't Della feed you?" Fletcher teased.

Max glowered again but gripped an open bag of nacho tortilla chips in one hand. "Our brother, the wannabe comedian," he said to Nate. "We don't starve," Max said in a way that made Nate wonder if Max ever gave a straight answer. "Fletcher mentioned a guy named Marty DeBaccian."

"Are you familiar with him?" Nate pulled out a chair as Vivian joined them, quietly sitting beside him. Without even asking, Fletcher poured her a mug of coffee and set it in front of her.

"No, not really…we've never crossed paths." Max shook his head, drank some coffee and winced. "Wow." His eyes almost watered. "Congratulations, Fletcher. Takes some major talent to make a brew worse than what I get at headquarters."

"Look at you with the compliments." Fletcher closed the door before joining them at the table. "Eat your chips. CliffsNotes version—" he said, looking to Max "—Nate and his fellow detectives in Boise have been building a case against

Marty DeBaccian. Wannabe crime lord with his hands in all kinds of dirty dealings."

"Up until last year, he'd made a name for himself loan-sharking and getting in on the local betting action," Nate added. "He's got a taste for things now. You name it, he's made a play for it. Drugs, extortion, protection rackets, which goes hand in hand with money laundering through local businesses whose owners aren't in a position to say no."

"Garden variety scum bucket, got it," Max said.

Nate glanced at Vivian. She had wrapped both hands around the brown coffee mug, but she'd hunched her shoulders and scrunched down almost into a shell of herself. Nate rested a hand on her knee, gave her a comforting squeeze. He'd needed it, but feeling the tension ease a bit in her body told him she'd needed it as well. She sat up straighter, offered him a quick smile that eased his mind a bit.

"DeBaccian's been building himself up as a kind of overlord of whatever criminal activity is running rampant in the city," Nate said. "I've had my eye on Dean Wexler for a while, trying to link him to a number of burglaries of single women. He's got a record that makes that possible. I thought if I could make the connection, I could use that information to flip him on DeBaccian."

"Apparently DeBaccian doesn't like it when people work outside of his purview," Fletcher added. "He likes to take his cut of the action."

"Which is where I come in," Vivian admitted. "Not the action part." She frowned, as if reconsidering her words. "I met Dean on a dating app. Seems I was his next planned target."

Nate didn't miss the ice flashing in both his brothers' eyes.

"Needless to say, our first date didn't go as expected." Vivian summarized it far more precisely than Nate probably would have. "Now Dean is in an induced coma, and I've become a material witness."

"Against Wexler?" Max's brows shot up.

"Against DeBaccian," Nate said. "He was in the car when Wexler was shot."

"And you saw him." Whatever Max had been thinking, his eyes turned to steel.

"Yes," Vivian said firmly. "I saw him."

"And he knows she did. Someone trying to run her off the road this morning proves that."

"It proves something, and I'm fine," she said at Max's suddenly sharp gaze. "Lucky, but fine. But Nate didn't think it was safe for me to be anywhere familiar or predictable for a while."

"Nate's right," Fletcher said. "And he was right to call. Lizzy would never forgive us if we didn't do everything we could to help."

"I appreciate that." Vivian's mouth curved. "And the trouble you're going to."

"It's no trouble, Vivian," Fletcher said. "If anything, Nate calling gave us all a bit of a kick. We're family. We need to start acting like it. We appreciate the faith, however tenuous."

Nate wasn't entirely sure what to do with that statement. So he did what he always did when emotions started clouding his judgment. He shifted back to the job. "You said you spoke with my lieutenant?" Nate asked.

"Yeah." Fletcher took a deep breath. "No change in Wexler's condition. He's continuing the protective duty you ordered in the hospital. No joy on the burned-out car they've identified from the drive-by."

"Awesome." Not a surprise, but still disappointing. That

meant Vivian's description of DeBaccian was the only evidence they had that he was involved.

"There's been a bit more luck with the SUV from this morning." Fletcher leaned back and retrieved the folder he'd been handed at the front desk. "He emailed this over so it was waiting for you." He set it on the table and flipped it open. "The car was found abandoned about ten miles from where they hit Vivian. Same MO as the first car."

"They didn't do such a great job, this time, did they?" So much of the car was still intact. A break for them for sure.

Vivian gasped, pointed at the half-worn decal in the bottom corner of the windshield. "That's what I saw. The sticker. That's what I remember seeing in the mirror."

Nate's hand curled into a fist. He'd known they'd gotten close enough to ram her off the road, but so close that she got a clear look at a sticker? He repressed a shudder.

"Your lieutenant recognized the logo from a strip club in downtown Boise," Fletcher said. "Place called Shake It Loose."

Nate's stomach tightened. "That's one of DeBaccian's properties." He'd spent an unholy number of hours parked across the street while Dean Wexler was inside. "He's either getting careless or desperate."

"Or arrogant," Max said. "Never underestimate the destructive power of ego. It takes a lot more of these criminals down than you think."

"True enough," Fletcher agreed. "Evidence is still working on the SUV, but they've got a couple of sets of prints so far. They're rushing it through the system." Fletcher looked to Max. "Anything you can do about that?"

"Sure." Max shrugged. "But I'd advise you to leave me in reserve." He pulled the file close and scanned the reports, flipping up the pages. "I'd want to do this on the up and up, and if I do that, you get federal interest, which could pull this case out of your control." He eyed Nate. "Unless you're looking for someone with FBI contacts to take the lead?"

Nate took his time answering. He wanted to make a good case against DeBaccian. Federal or state, locked up was locked up. His ego required a win. He'd worked this case a long time and had DeBaccian in his sights for months. He didn't like the idea of handing it off, even unofficially, without getting at least some credit.

Beside him, he could feel Vivian shaking. She was holding it together, but the longer this went on, the more anxiety and fear she was going to develop, and he didn't like the idea of being responsible for that—it was even worse than losing credit.

"I want DeBaccian taken down and out. I want Vivian out of the line of fire." He couched his words carefully. "Would I like a hand in that? Absolutely. But I'm more interested in seeing his operations shut down. Boise needs him gone." And so did Vivian. "If that means bringing the FBI in officially, I'm fine with it. Not my call, though." He looked back to Fletcher. "My lieutenant would have to take that up the chain in Boise PD."

Fletcher glanced at Max. "We're in a holding pattern for now on that front. He's got surveillance up and running on a number of DeBaccian's businesses and hangouts and his main residence. When he pops his head up, Haig will let us know." Something akin to admiration flickered in his brothers' eyes when they looked back at him. "In the meantime, it sounds like we're all on the same page."

Max grimaced, leaned to the side and pulled out his wallet. When he slapped twenty bucks into Fletcher's hand, Nate frowned. "What's this about?"

"That's about Fletcher betting you'd put the end result and Vivian's safety before your arrest record," Max said. "I was less…confident."

"Let me guess." Nate didn't have to hear more than that to understand Max's meaning. "Given who our mother is, you were thinking the apple didn't fall too far?"

He started to pull his hand away from Vivian's knee, but she dropped her own hand under the table and covered his. When she curled her fingers under and squeezed, he felt a boost of confidence and understanding surge through his system.

"More like birds of a feather," Max said easily. "But that's neither here nor there at the moment." His gaze slipped over Vivian, as if he didn't want to discuss their family drama in her presence.

"I know about your mother," Vivian said quietly. "I know the generalities of what she did going back to when you all were kids. Lizzy brought me up to date the last time I saw her. And, just so you know, Nate's been perfectly up front about his and Sarah's situation where Jessie Colton is concerned."

"Vivian—" Nate began.

"You all are Texas two-stepping around this, and no offense, but I've got enough to worry about without having to learn to dance," she said in a tone Nate hadn't heard from her before. "Nate's not his mother, Max. No more than you are. From the time this whole nightmare started for me, Nate has been the only consistent thing I could hold on to. Whatever else you might think of him, he's an honorable man who only has the family's best interests at heart."

The doubt in Max's eyes faded, not completely, but enough that Nate felt grateful to Vivian for knocking down at least one invisible wall between them.

"It's taking us some time to come to terms with a lot of what happened over the past thirty years," Fletcher said slowly. "We got blindsided when Dad died. It's obvious a lot of mistakes were made."

"Yes, they were," Vivian insisted. "But by Robert and Jessie. Not Nate or Sarah. Not that anyone asked me, but I think you're all lucky to have them as siblings. So either talk it all out or set it aside at least until I can go home and get back to my quiet, unassuming life."

Nate couldn't have stopped the wave of affection washing over him if he'd tried. "I was wrong." He squeezed her hand. "You would have made a fantastic cheerleader."

Her cheeks went bright pink, and her hand tightened around his.

"There's something else your lieutenant thought you should know," Fletcher said. "Regarding a Detective Jim Sullivan."

"Let me guess," Nate muttered. "He's complaining about my being involved with the case."

"No one knows what Detective Sullivan's doing," Fletcher said slowly. "He's disappeared."

"He's...what?" Nate frowned. "What does that mean?"

"Would you like the dictionary definition or—"

"Max." Fletcher glared at his cousin and shook his head. "All your lieutenant said was that they've been unable to make contact with Sullivan since he left the station after Vivian's session with the sketch artist. He'll get back to us when he knows more."

"Get back to *us*?" Nate hedged.

Fletcher didn't flinch when he met his confused gaze. "If DeBaccian and his men are looking for Vivian, then they're probably looking for you by now. The less communication you have with anyone back in Boise, the better. For the foreseeable future, what you're told, I'm told." He looked over to Max. "You have what you need?"

"Yeah." Max leaned forward again, reached into his back pocket and pulled out a flip phone. He slid it across the table to Nate. "This is untraceable," he said easily. "A few numbers programmed in. Your lieutenant's. Mine, Fletcher's. And Chase's." He paused. "I didn't include Sarah's. I didn't have it, and I wasn't sure how much she knows."

"Nothing," Nate said instantly. "She knows nothing, and I'd like to keep it that way."

Max nodded. "Understood."

Relief surged through him. His sister was a schoolteacher, for heaven's sake. The last thing he wanted to do was put her in the sights of a career criminal. The further away she was from all this, the better. He scrolled through the solitary page of numbers. "Chase." Chase Colton was CEO of Colton Properties. He didn't have anything to do with law enforcement. "Why Chase?"

"Because it's thanks to him you two have a place to hole up until this is all settled." As if on cue, Fletcher's cell phone vibrated. He looked at the screen, shook his head in mild disbelief. "Speak of the devil. Looks like we're all set." He got to his feet and motioned for them to follow. "Let's get you two settled in."

Chapter Nine

"You look like you've been caught in a whirlwind."

Nate's comment had Vivian pulling her attention away from the scenic, winding drive through the outskirts of Owl Creek and back to the reality of her current situation. "I kind of feel like it," she said. "From the outside, the Colton family feels like a force of nature."

"Newsflash," Nate said as he followed Fletcher's marked police SUV. "Doesn't feel much different from that on the inside." Behind them, Max followed, this time keeping a fair distance.

She wanted to smile, wanted to believe he meant that in good humor, but she couldn't be sure. The tension among the three brothers had been palpable. So much needed to be talked about, but she doubted it was ever going to happen where those three men were concerned. Not without a bit of a nudge. Which is what she'd been attempting to do by sticking her nose into something that was most definitely not her business.

"It's a pretty drive." She'd been to Owl Creek plenty of times over the years, mostly to meet up with Lizzy, but during the holidays, not so much. This time of year was always hard for her. It wasn't necessarily the being alone that triggered it, but the reminder that she was. Maybe it was being here with Nate or maybe the anxiety from the past few days, but she found herself feeling far more lighthearted about the season.

She loved how the dusting of snow cast the passing homes into a kind of exhibit in an art gallery. December in Idaho definitely put on a beautiful show. Add to it the festive outdoor lighting, the occasional decorated trees and decked-out front porches, and it was almost like stepping into a painting. The backdrop of snowy mountains conjured a longing for simpler, nature-focused times rather than the technological roller coaster the world found itself on these days. She had to remind herself, frequently, that it wasn't chance that had brought her to Owl Creek, or even that had put her in the vicinity of Nate Colton, but violence and danger that, even now, stalked her.

Surreal didn't come close to describing her current state. But she found herself wanting to push through the fear and embrace what had come to pass. Since walking into that restaurant the other night, she felt as if she were on some kind of self-awareness journey. One that was most definitely aided by the man sitting beside her.

Never in her wildest dreams would she have imagined finding herself traversing snowy mountain roads with someone who, near as she could fathom, might be responsible for reminding her she had a pulse. And a heart.

"Any idea where we're headed?" she asked.

"Not a clue." Nate did not sound happy about that, but she wondered if he realized the trust he'd displayed in the past few hours. He had, for all intents and purposes, placed both their lives in his brothers' hands, and that, she thought as her heart cracked open wide enough for a fraction of the Colton men to spill in, might make this entire situation worth it. "At this point, I wouldn't be surprised if it's a two-room shack with a padlock on the door."

She laughed, happy to pile onto the ridiculous suspicion, only to have every thought tip out of her brain. Fletcher veered off to the right and soon stopped at a guard post situated outside a large, iron-gated community.

"What the—" Nate's mutter only echoed her own disbelief. Eyes wide, she took in the vast area around and in front of them. The intricate welding of the gates offered both protection and elegant decor that stretched in both directions as far as she could see. "Guess the family business is doing pretty well."

The young, uniformed woman leaning out of the security office was pointing beyond the gate that was currently sliding open. She nodded and waved Fletcher through. Nate pulled up and powered down his window.

"Detective Colton." The woman offered a solid, welcoming smile. "Ms. Maylor. I'm Maya Baxter. Welcome to Colton Crossing."

"Nice to meet you, Maya." Because Nate seemed a bit tongue-tied, Vivian leaned across the center console and rested her hand on Nate's arm.

"Chase will give you the rundown for how to contact us here at the security office," Maya told them. "Someone will be here twenty-four seven. We've been made aware of your situation and will be on alert for anything out of the ordinary. If you have any questions or concerns, call the office at any time."

"Appreciate that," Nate said finally before he followed Fletcher's vehicle through the gate. Vivian checked her passenger-side mirror, saw Max stop for his intro then nip through the gate. "Apparently, I missed notice of this place in the family newsletter."

Vivian grabbed hold of his hand and squeezed. "This isn't easy for you, is it?"

"Entering Shangri-la?" His attempt at humor sounded strained.

"I meant dealing with your brothers. Your family." But he had a point. The sprawling homes that made up Colton Crossing ranged in size. Some were smaller, bungalow-type homes while others stood two stories with wide, wraparound porches. The complex was obviously in various stages of construction. She counted a few dozen homes that appeared completed, while other foundations were mapped out, and other cleared-out areas were no doubt going to begin construction once the snow stopped falling.

It was only when she looked past Nate and out beyond the security gate that she noticed all of them offered a stunning view of the mountains along with Owl Creek nestled into the valley below.

"I don't think they're taking us to a shack with a padlock."

"I think you're right." Nate waved at Fletcher, who after parking and climbing out of his car, indicated he should pull into the long driveway just beyond. When he stopped the car, they both leaned forward and gawked up at the house in front of them. "Am I the only one thinking both your place and mine would fit inside this place?"

"You are not." So much for cozy and close quarters. Disappointment and relief crashed against each other inside her. Something told her she and Nate could go days inside without seeing each other.

"I'll come back for our things." Nate pushed open his door and came around to open hers. "Looks like we aren't in Boise anymore." As if completely normal, he took hold of her hand, and they walked down the driveway side by side.

Fletcher and Max stood at the end of the walkway with another, slightly older man wearing a suit beneath his long wool coat. Vivian couldn't help but think he'd stepped off the cover of a men's quarterly magazine. Slightly lankier than his brothers and cousins, he had a professionalism about him that screamed competence and success.

"Nate." The man pulled one hand out of his coat pocket and extended it. "Good to see you again."

"Chase."

"Welcome to Colton Crossing." Chase's smile came a bit easier than either Fletcher's or Max's had, and she could feel Nate relax a little. "Ms. Maylor."

"Vivian, please."

"Vivian." Chase nodded in approval. "Welcome. I'm afraid the house is a little sparse furnishings-wise. We've got the bare minimum set up since this is going to be our first market model, but it should be enough for the two of you. On the plus side, there's a furnished office, and Nate mentioned you needed a place to work."

She probably looked a bit doe-eyed when she glanced up at Nate.

"Shall we?" Chase turned on his heel and took the lead.

"Like we're going to say no?" Vivian muttered so only Nate could hear.

They followed Chase inside, their footfalls echoing on the large porch landing. Up two steps and through an enormous, heavy wooden door. Inside, the foyer opened up and branched off into multiple hallways and directions.

"You met Maya down at the guard house," Chase said and led them straight ahead and off to the left. "The security company we've hired has been thoroughly vetted by multiple security experts, including SecuritKey and Max here."

"I love running background checks," Max said from where he trailed behind them. "Not that Sloan needed double-checking. I'm curious, Chase. Did you visit Versailles before you came up with the plans to this house or did you just wing it?"

"We call this the Colton-size house," Chase said easily. "Lots of room for a large, ever-expanding family. We've still got some touch-ups to do on the other finished homes, but this one is move-in ready. Permission to enter?" he called.

"Ack! Two seconds!" a female voice called back before a blond head popped around the corner. "Seriously. Just..." She held up a couple of fingers and had them stopping in the hallway.

"Ruby takes this kind of thing rather seriously," Fletcher said as he leaned back against the light yellow wall. "Especially these days."

"What kind of thing, exactly?" Vivian asked.

"Three things, actually," Max said. "Homecomings, the holidays and surprises."

"I'm guessing that makes us the family trifecta," Nate said.

"Okay!" A curvy, dark-haired woman with deep auburn tips and brown eyes jumped into view and waved them in. "Hey, Detective." She waggled her eyebrows at Fletcher, who moved in to catch her around the waist and pull her in for a kiss. "Nice to see you, too," she murmured and looked into his eyes in a way that had Vivian thinking they should all be someplace else. "You must be Nate." She held out her hand. "And Vivian. I'm Kiki Shelton. Ruby and Sloan recruited me to lend a hand."

"A hand for… Oh." Vivian blinked at the sight in front of her.

Not only was there a gourmet kitchen fit for a houseful of kings and queens, but the attached great room boasted a deep, comfy sofa, large-screen television and an enormous seven-foot Christmas tree in the corner. Lights had been strung to the point of setting it aflame with glowing white bulbs and a beautiful gold star sitting atop.

Two large plastic bins sat beside the tree, crammed full with colorful boxes and shiny ornaments.

"Hi. I'm Sloan Presley. We thought you could do with some holiday cheer." The woman stepped under Chase's outstretched arm and gave Vivian and Nate a wave. "There's more in the boxes if you want to play yourselves." She had her thick, curly dark hair pulled back from her round, friendly face. "Seeing as you're going to be stuck here for a little while, might as well pretty the place up."

Vivian was agog. The place was already prettied up near as she could tell. "The tree's a lovely addition. Thank you." The only other time she'd ever seen such a grand tree had been that aforementioned holiday she'd spent at the Colton ranch. "It wasn't necessary to go to so much trouble."

"No trouble at all." Ruby Colton, a familiar face from Vivian's childhood, came over and nudged Nate with her shoulder. If memory served, Lizzy mentioned Ruby recently had a baby boy. Named… Vivian's mind raced. Sawyer. Yes, that was it. And the baby's arrival also explained the new mother glow about Ruby. "We wondered what it might take to get you back to Owl Creek, Nate. Guess we know now, huh?"

"How about I show you around." Sloan stepped away from Chase and set her attention on Vivian. "Don't worry. We'll leave you two alone soon enough so you can get acclimated.

Let's start with the best thing about this house." She tugged Vivian by the hand through the kitchen and dining area to the glass double French doors. She pushed them open and flung them wide to give an unobstructed view of the mountain range. "How about that view, huh?"

"Yeah." Vivian looked back over her shoulder to where Nate remained standing amidst his newfound family. He looked both shocked and awed, but also, whether he wanted to admit it or not, exactly where he belonged. Vivian smiled and released at least some of the tension she'd brought with her in the car. "That is most definitely a great view."

Chapter Ten

Fletcher gave Nate his own tour well after Vivian's concluded. He'd also waited until well after Ruby, Kiki, Chase and Max had taken off under the guise of giving Vivian and Nate some acclimating time. Nate didn't need acclimating. He could settle in easily wherever he went.

But he had not missed the knowing looks that passed among his brothers. Looks that made the back of his neck prickle to the point of pain.

With the car unloaded and Vivian occupied with storing the cooler contents as well as going through the well-stocked refrigerator, freezer and pantry, Fletcher showed Nate the lay of the land, ending, to Nate's surprise, on the second floor and the balcony outside the massive bedroom suite that could have doubled as a ballroom.

"You worried about Vivian hearing whatever it is you're going to tell me?" Nate challenged.

Fletcher didn't blink. "More like I'm leaving it to you how much you want to tell her. Consider it my gift to you, offering a return of control you're going to be lacking for the next little while."

Nate almost grunted a reply. Seemed his new siblings really had thought of everything.

Outside, as it was coming up on five o'clock, the sun had begun its nightly surrender, and the chill factor dropped. The cold air blasting into the house was blocked by the bedroom door Fletcher had closed behind them.

"I'm guessing you all like your space." Nate twisted off the top of a beer bottle he'd grabbed out of the fridge and pocketed the cap. The house was beyond anything he could have ever imagined vacationing in let alone living in. *Tasteful elegance* was a phrase that came to mind.

"Colton Properties is Chase's baby these days. He's a fan of giving prospective buyers a wealth of choices." Fletcher pushed open a pair of French doors identical to the ones just off the kitchen downstairs and stepped outside. "He's hoping it'll offset some recent business blowback."

It didn't sit well, Nate realized, having this much space between him and Vivian. But Fletcher seemed to have a plan in mind, even if said plan meant turning them both into Popsicles. Good thing he'd noticed a stash of firewood by each of the fireplaces. He couldn't wait to get a fire started.

"Small homes, large homes, long-time residents, vacationers," Fletcher went on. "Chase has developed Colton Crossing for a myriad of income levels."

"It's called hedging one's bets," Nate countered and earned a nod of approval as Fletcher took a pull of his beer. "So, I give. What's with the cone of silence?"

Fletcher leaned back, sat on the edge of the banister and stretched out his legs. "I've been elected to broach a subject that might be considered a bit tricky."

"Elected by whom?" Nate needn't have asked. As much as he'd been hoping for an uneventful arrival, it was unrealistic to think it wouldn't come with a price.

Fletcher dismissed the question with a smile that didn't

come close to reaching his wary eyes. "What do you know about our father's death?"

Whatever Nate had been expecting to hear, it certainly wasn't that. "I read it was a stroke." He braced his feet apart, folded his arms across his chest, beer bottle dangling from two fingers.

"Read?" Fletcher's brow furrowed.

"Yeah, online. In the paper. Saw it on the news ticker." An unease he thought he'd left in Boise re-knotted low in his belly. This didn't have anything to do with Vivian's current situation as a target.

"You didn't hear about his death from Jessie?" Fletcher asked.

Why did everything have to come back to his mother? "Until Robert died, I hadn't seen or spoken to my mother in years. She wasn't thrilled with me becoming a cop, and when I made detective, I became persona non grata, for want of a better term." He didn't add that earning that status had been such a relief he'd privately celebrated. "I'd heard about Robert dying before she came knocking on my door a few days after it hit the press." At the rate he was drinking his beer, he was going to run through his supply pretty darn quick. "I know now she stopped by on her way to Owl Creek. She thought she had me, talking about regrets and how we'd lost the chance to mend family fences." He rolled his eyes, shook his head. "I didn't believe it for a second."

"Why not?"

"Because the only regret my mother is capable of feeling has only to do with her own failures. She tried to offer sympathy to me and then to Sarah. She tried to talk about the good times and bring back memories that, to be honest, I have no recollection of." Sometimes, he was convinced he'd lived a completely different life than the one Jessie recalled. "I remember him being around the first ten years of my life, but not really present, if that makes sense. He traveled a lot. For business, we were told." Business. Hardly. Unless maintaining two completely separate families was a new kind of Colton enterprise. The entire conversation was enough to turn his stomach sour. "I told her I didn't think it was a good idea for her to come here, but that fell on deaf ears. Next thing I know, she's back from having met with all of you here in Owl Creek, as angry as I've ever seen her, ranting and raving over being pushed out of the inheritance." He shook his head again. "As predictable as she is spiteful."

"*Pushed out* meaning you and Sarah?" Fletcher asked.

Nate smirked. "Hardly."

"So you're of the belief Jessie came to us because she expected a payout."

"Expected?" Nate shrugged. "Couldn't say. Wanted? Definitely." He shivered. "Is there a reason we're having this talk outside?"

"Extreme temperatures make it easier to tell when someone's lying."

"Huh." Nate had to give Fletcher points. The reality of being interrogated by his older brother hit him with a bit more force than expected. So much for happy families. He toasted Fletcher with his beer. "Thanks for living up to my very low expectations." Maybe he had made a mistake coming here.

"You and Sarah came out of nowhere, Nate." Fletcher's voice was even and calm. "Of course we were going to be suspicious. You have no idea the pain Jessie's inflicted on the family over the years."

"Fair." He nodded, but it didn't dispel the disappointment

he felt. "Just like you don't know what it was like to grow up in her house." Or to find out your father chose one portion of his family over another. "It might be easy for me to say, but don't paint me or Sarah with any brush connected to Jessie."

Fletcher glanced down. "You said it had been years since you saw Jessie. How long exactly?"

"I don't know." Nate frowned. "Three, maybe four years? Sarah sees her more than I do. My sister's a lighter touch when it comes to our mother's financial failings and machinations." Guilt he didn't like to ponder surged. "It hurt Sarah, more than me, to know Robert kept us secret from all of you. That we had this enormous family living only a few hours away. Sarah's always wanted to be part of something bigger than just us. When I found out about you all, I was terrified about what it all would mean. But Sarah? It was all I could do to stop her from jumping on a bus and coming out here to introduce herself as one of the family. Right now, I'm real thankful I won that fight."

If Fletcher took offense, he didn't show it. "Sarah didn't care that our father lied about everything?"

"Sure she did." Nate ducked his head, let out a soft laugh. "She just got over it faster than me. Sarah's far more forgiving. Which explains why she always lets Jessie back into her life. Despite knowing it won't end well."

"Hope's a dangerous thing," Fletcher said.

"Especially in the hands of someone who knows how to wield it," Nate agreed. "So." He took another drink. "What is it you want to ask me that requires a deep-freeze lie detector?"

"I guess I was curious if you thought Dad's death was… suspicious in any way."

"I hadn't seen the man in almost a decade," Nate said

carefully. "I'm not in a position to suspect anything about him." He paused, looked his brother in the eye. "Do you think it was?"

The clouds opened up and sent a heavy cascade of snow down upon them. Fletcher motioned him back inside, closed the doors, then led him into an alcove off the main suite that contained two overstuffed cream-colored chairs with matching storage ottomans.

"It's been discussed," Fletcher said as he got comfortable. "That there might be more to Dad's death than originally believed."

Nate tried not to react to the use of the word *Dad* where Robert Colton was concerned. Instead, he focused on putting the pieces of this conversation together. "If you're going to kill someone, especially a man as powerful and well-known as our father, there are better ways than to trigger a stroke."

"Unless someone is already prone to them. Then it would be—"

"Understandable and not wholly unexpected," Nate finished. His cop brain clicked on. "I take it his medical history proves that out?"

"He had a minor stroke a few years ago," Fletcher said. "And, okay, to be completely honest—"

"*Now* we're being honest?"

Fletcher looked at him. Really looked at him this time, then gave a slow nod. "Okay. I had that coming. We all had that coming, I suppose. Look." He let out a sigh. "I don't want you thinking we considered Dad some kind of saint or perfect father. Or a perfect man. He wasn't any of those things."

"Do tell." Nate took his last drink of beer.

"Jessie wasn't his first or his only affair. He had a lot of them," Fletcher said. "After Jessie, he stopped trying so hard to hide them. Near as we can tell, he didn't have any other kids."

Nate smirked again. "Time will tell."

"He was a hard-drinking, heavy-smoking, live-life-to-excess kind of man. His first stroke was a warning he didn't heed." Fletcher sounded both resigned and regretful. "The second one didn't come as a big surprise. Still, he was bigger than life, and it was a shock when he died. But then Jessie turns up. Out of the blue. And tells us all about their life together. Tells us about you and your sister." He rubbed a tired hand across the back of his neck. "Suffice it to say, none of us handled it very well. When we didn't acquiesce to her demands for an equal share of the estate, she talked to anyone who would listen. Papers, reporters, bloggers. She didn't just air out the family closet, she fumigated it."

"Yeah," Nate said. "I am well aware." He and Sarah had both needed to change their phone numbers multiple times to avoid the press's attention. At least the campouts on their front lawns hadn't lasted more than a few days. Small blessings, he supposed. Thank heavens for the media's short attention span.

"Chase has had to work nearly 24/7 to keep the scandal from destroying the family company," Fletcher said. "It took a while to stop the financial hemorrhaging, reassure our investors and shareholders. The rest of us just did what we could to wait it all out."

"He seems to have done a pretty good job of things. You all have," Nate added with some reluctance. "None of this answers the question you asked of me, though. About Robert's death. You haven't mentioned anything that argues the ruling of natural causes."

"That's because there isn't an argument. It's more a gut

feeling. On the surface, yes, everything points to a stroke. But then there are other things to take into consideration." Fletcher pursed his lips. "You ever hear of the Ever After Church? It's run by a man named Markus Acker."

"Of course," Nate said. "It's hard not to living around here. They have some kind of church compound, don't they? Near Conners? Although calling it a church seems a bit of a stretch."

"Mmm." Fletcher nodded. "You'd be right on that front. It's a cult, pure and simple to anyone on the outside looking in. Acker's a con man, plain and simple. This Ever After Church isn't the first time he's pulled this stunt, but so far it seems to be his most successful. He's got about a thousand followers living with him. Living under his rules, working his land, giving over their life savings in exchange for atonement, forgiveness, who knows what else."

"Free labor in exchange for the promise of redemption?" Nate supplied. "There's dozens of men like Acker working scams like this all over the country."

"True enough," Fletcher agreed. "Acker's especially insidious, though. He doesn't hide his love of money, or the power he thinks it gives him. He sucks everyone he comes in contact with dry, and once they are, he puts them into situations where they can get him more. And then there's his seduction ratio. He goes after what he wants, especially if he thinks it'll add to his coffers. Or if they're female." He paused, eyes shifting as he decided on his next words. "Jessie's one of his followers, Nate."

Nate blinked. Frowned. Opened his mouth to respond, then closed it. Tried again. "You're sure?" was all that came out.

"We're sure," Fletcher said. "From what we've been able

to find out, she has been for years. Maybe even from before Acker hit Idaho four years ago." Another pause. "One thing Acker's followers all do is confess to him. They tell him every detail of their life before they found him, and no doubt he keeps impeccable notes. Jessie wouldn't have been an exception."

Nate could only imagine how a man like Markus Acker would have reacted to hearing one of his devotees had her claws in Robert Colton. "You think she told Acker about Robert and their life together."

"She had to have. And if Acker's as dangerous as we think..."

It took Nate a moment to pull together the threads of their conversation. "You're thinking Acker might have somehow had Robert killed so Jessie could make a claim on his estate."

"That's part of what I'm thinking." Fletcher watched him carefully, as if poised for a fight once Nate caught on to whatever else lurked beneath the surface of accusation.

It was Nate the cop who needed to step up now. The cop who needed to stop lurking in the shadows and see this situation from the outside, taking into consideration everyone involved in the story. It took a moment to step away and look objectively, but once he did, the answer became more than evident. It became probable. "You're thinking it's possible my mother had a hand in killing Robert." He waited for the doubt or disbelief to land and steal the air from his lungs. But it didn't.

"As much loathing as there is for Jessie, we're struggling with that idea," Fletcher admitted. "We haven't brought the entire family in on this yet. It isn't time, and honestly, this isn't something any of us want to think possible. Right now, it's just you and me talking. Cop to cop." He hesitated. "Brother to brother."

For the first time, hearing that word didn't make Nate flinch.

"I think the timing of Dad's death is beyond coincidental," Fletcher went on. "Acker's rise to prominence, Jessie running out of cash, the companies' success. Given the resulting chaos Jessie's bomb created, it all feels a bit calculated. And cruel."

"My mother's specialties. Okay." His mind was spinning in a dozen different directions, not one of them good. "Okay, I'm not saying you're wrong, but I'm also not ready to say you're right." It should have hurt, far more than it did, to even consider his mother might be capable of murdering Robert Colton. But the truth was his days of predicting Jessie Colton's behavior had long ago passed. Given what he'd seen being a cop for as long as he had been, one thing was true in this life: anyone is capable of anything at any time. "That said, I'll agree this is something we should dig deeper into." He took a deep breath. "I hate to say it, but that should probably fall on me." As Jessie's son, it would be far less suspicious for him to go investigating the last few years of her life and any connection she had to Markus Acker.

Fletcher dropped his head forward as if in relief. When he lifted his chin once more, he had an odd grin on his face. "Max owes me another twenty bucks."

"Does he?" Nate didn't know why it mattered, but it did. Clearly Max Colton was going to take more time to be convinced about where Nate's lack of loyalties lay. "He doesn't have much faith, does he?"

"It's been hard on him, and Greg and Malcolm and Lizzy, knowing that Jessie chose to raise you and Sarah when she walked away from them. He was what, eight when Jessie left? That's a hard age to witness a family breaking apart."

Any age was as far as Nate was concerned. "And like I said before—"

"Yeah, I know," Fletcher agreed. "Living with Jessie wasn't a picnic. And I get it. I really do. But you've known about us for a while, haven't you?"

Half a lifetime, Nate almost admitted. Instead he simply said, "Yes."

"We've had months. Give everyone a bit more time to adjust. We'll get there, Nate. And believe it or not, we might all actually be worth it."

Nate wanted to believe that was true, but Fletcher didn't seem to be taking one thing into consideration. That Nate's mother may very well be responsible for what happened to Robert Colton.

And if that was the case, would Nate and Sarah ever truly be accepted?

"GOOD NIGHT, VIVIAN."

Vivian glanced up from her laptop screen, sliding off the barstool at the kitchen counter when Fletcher poked his head in to wave goodbye.

"Oh. Good night, Fletcher." She flashed him her best "not a care in the world" smile and lifted her hand. "Everything okay?"

"I've given Nate a crash course on the security system." He pointed to the keypad by the back door. "He'll fill you in on everything you need to know."

"Okay." It didn't escape her notice he hadn't answered her question, but it wasn't her place to push. Clearly what the brothers had to discuss needed to be addressed in private.

Didn't mean she wasn't curious about it, though. "Thank you, again, for everything. I hope..." She moved closer to him. "I hope we won't inconvenience you for long."

Fletcher's cool expression immediately shifted and, for want of a better term, opened. "You're the one being inconvenienced, Vivian. Your life shouldn't have to come to a screeching halt because you accepted a dinner invitation."

"No, it shouldn't, should it?" Easy enough to say, but at the same time, if she hadn't said yes, she might not ever have met Nate. And that, she knew without a doubt, would have been a terrible shame.

"Don't let all this family stuff get to you," Fletcher continued. "It's taking us some time to adjust to everything that's happened these past few months, but you were right back at the station. Nate's family. It's time we started acting like he is."

"I'm glad to hear it." Despite Nate's detached attitude about his place in the Colton family, she couldn't help but think that deep down, in places he didn't even know existed, he really did want to belong. But he also was preparing himself for disappointment. Something she could relate to all too well. "Nate will be glad, too. Especially for Sarah."

"Yeah." Fletcher nodded. "Yeah, I got the message on that. We'll get there. Eventually. I'll check in with you both tomorrow." He walked back down the hall, and a few moments later, the front door shut behind him.

The silence in the house was beyond deafening. Nate hadn't been wrong earlier about the size of this place. It was nearly cavernous and even echoed in places. Despite its beautiful decor and design, it didn't feel remotely homey to her. Or maybe she was just too comfortable with the way her life had been up until now. These last few days—despite the disastrous underpinnings of misadventure—had been a kind of awakening for her. Lizzy had been right all those times she'd worried that Vivian had locked herself away to stay protected from the world. Sure it was dangerous and scary, but it also contained wonders and excitement. Like a particular detective currently occupying the same house.

A detective who had her thinking about all kinds of activities the two of them might do together. Her face went hot, but instead of pushing the fantasies away, she embraced them. And settled them into the back of her mind to dwell on later.

"I smell something delicious." Nate's declaration as he walked into the kitchen startled her out of her reverie. He opened three bottom cabinets before finding the one housing the recycling bucket for his and Fletcher's empty beer bottles.

"Kiki suggested I break the kitchen in," Vivian admitted. It had been almost an hour since Nate had followed Fletcher upstairs, and she was dying to know what they had talked about. "I've got the leftovers sorted, and there's a whacky cake in the oven."

"A what cake?" He wandered around the large center island that housed a farmer's sink and extensive counter space, as if transfixed by the aroma emanating from inside the oven.

"Whacky cake." She flexed her fingers. "It's the first thing I learned to bake, actually. It's a kind of ritual for me. First night in a new house, I make it. My first foster mother gave me the recipe. It's from World War II, when rations limited store supplies. No eggs or butter, just pantry items, you know, like flour and sugar and… Sorry, babbling." She had to stop herself from twisting her hands into knots. "I'm nervous." She slid back onto the stool and tried to refocus on the emails waiting in her inbox. There wasn't anything urgent. Nothing that couldn't wait until tomorrow.

"Nervous about what?"

"Everything." Deflecting, she gave in to temptation. "What were you and Fletcher talking about upstairs?"

He pulled open the fridge, had his hand on a second bottle of beer, then changed his mind and shut the door without taking it out. "Trust me, you do not want to know."

"Oh." She scrunched her mouth. "Okay, sure. I understand." She closed her computer and stood back up, made a beeline for the remote. "How about we find something on TV to watch while we—"

He moved so quickly and quietly she almost yelped when his hand gently wrapped around her wrist. "Vivian."

She squeezed her eyes shut. She didn't want to admit how her name on his lips made everything inside her quiver. She didn't want to get any more attached to this man than she already was. She wasn't the kind of woman men noticed or gravitated toward, and she certainly didn't want to lean into the whole damsel-in-distress modus operandi. It took all her confidence to believe that the attraction she'd felt when she'd first kissed him, that *zing* of excitement that coursed through her whenever he touched her, wasn't one-sided.

"Do I make you nervous, Vivian?" He stepped closer, so close she could feel the heat of his body radiating through both their layers of clothing. He made her shiver, that baritone voice of his, that way he had of making her feel as if she were the only woman in his world.

"You know you do," she whispered. Her thoughts tumbled over one another as if caught in an avalanche of unchecked emotion. "I don't know how to do this, Nate."

"Don't know how to do what?" His thumb moved across the pulse in her wrist, tempting. Teasing. The slightest touch of his skin to hers, and she could feel herself melting.

"You know what. Interacting. I'm terrible at...this." Only now did she turn, if only because she had nowhere to hide. She lifted her chin, forced her gaze up to meet the eyes of the man who had stoked every fire inside her from the moment she'd first seen him at the bar.

"Well, Ms. Maylor." He released her wrist, threaded his fingers between hers and lifted her hand to his lips. "I think this deserves further investigation." He pressed his lips to the back of her knuckles, nudged her a bit closer as his mouth trailed across her hand. "You don't seem so terrible to me." His smile silenced her, emptied her mind of every thought except what it had felt like to be kissed by him. "Shall we see what else you aren't terrible at?" He let go of her hand, smoothed both of his down her sides, until they rested on her hips.

She whimpered behind pressed lips. Desire weakened her knees, and she clung to him, catching his upper arms in her trembling hands and willing herself to remain on her feet. When his lips brushed against hers, she sighed, opened her mouth and let him in.

Kissing him in the car yesterday had been pure impulse. A way to remind herself that she was still alive. But now, being here, in his arms, every cell in her being fired as his tongue swept in and engaged hers in a dance instinct led. He tilted his head, took the kiss deeper, and she rose up on her toes, stretched her body against his.

Her breasts tingled as he drew her in to him. She could feel every part of him pressing into her. He dipped down, wrapped those muscular arms around her waist and lifted her off her feet, his mouth creating a miracle of magic on hers. She could feel her arms move, as if on their own, up and around his neck. Her fingers tangled in the thickness of his hair at his neck. Silky, soft. Sensational. She sighed and sagged into him.

In the distance, she heard a buzzing, a ringing of sorts. Loud enough to break the spell, but not so intrusive that she unwound herself from around him.

"I think," Nate murmured against her throat when she dropped her head back, "your cake is done."

"Mmmmm." It took a moment for her head to clear, for his words to seep in. "Oh." Her smile came slow this time. "Right. Cake." She'd baked out of habit, and craving, only to find herself not the least bit satiated by the man in her arms. "I should get it out before it burns."

He nodded and the quirky smile that curved his lips felt as if it had been created just for her.

"I'll…just…" She let her arms drop and stumbled back. Her knees hadn't quite got their strength back, but given the self-satisfied expression on Nate's face, she wasn't going to add to his ego boost by falling flat on her fanny. Whatever else she might think, he was here protecting her; he felt responsible for her. And that cold splash of reality was enough to have the self-doubt surging afresh.

"I've got frosting to make." It was, quite possibly, the dumbest thing she'd ever said in her life. Nonetheless, she pushed her way around him and retreated.

She smiled to herself as something unexpected and powerful bloomed inside her.

For now, at least.

Chapter Eleven

While Boise wasn't sensory overload when it came to noise, the utter midnight silence of Owl Creek pressed in on Nate to the point of insomnia. He could feel the exhaustion creeping through his system, but every time he closed his eyes and tried to sleep, there was a kind of electrical zap that had him staring back at the ceiling.

He groaned, snatched one of the pillows off the bed and shoved it over his face.

How was it possible for a mind to travel multiple roads at lightning speed? It clearly wasn't enough for him to be worried about Vivian being targeted by a narcissistic Godfather wannabe, or what might happen should Dean Wexler, his best and only lead in the case, succumb to his injuries. Nor was his ever-expanding and confusing family dynamic happy to play second fiddle to the first worry. It wasn't even the fact that he had to consider that Fletcher was right and that Jessie, his own mother, could very well be responsible for his wealthy and estranged father's death.

He smushed the pillow harder on his face. Who was he kidding?

None of that was responsible for his inability to sleep.

What was keeping him awake was one beautiful, curvy,

slightly timid brunette who could kiss like a dream and made magic cake with a snap of her fingers. It would have been easy, so easy, he supposed, to nudge her gently up the stairs and into that spacious palace of a main suite she currently occupied by herself.

He'd always prided himself on following the rules. He had no doubt where it stemmed from—backlash against his parental examples who both excelled at making the world bend to their will. Rules were in place for a reason. It was inappropriate, unprofessional and irresponsible of him to even be considering getting involved with a witness, especially one connected to a case that could make his career. And yet…

And yet.

Nate tossed the pillow aside and grabbed the ridiculous toy-like flip phone Max had given him in place of his usual one. Two in the morning.

"Hour of the wolf," he muttered before he sat up, wishing, not for the first time, he'd surrendered to the idea of taking the bedroom next door to hers. Instead he'd sequestered himself downstairs. "This is ridiculous." If he wasn't going to sleep, he could work. Or at least stop circling the same mental track over and over.

Barefoot, and wearing only a pair of pajama bottoms, he grabbed the bag containing his laptop and whatever printed files he had on him and quietly padded down to and around the living room toward the kitchen.

He saw the glow of the Christmas tree well before he rounded the corner. Kiki, Ruby and Sloan had put enough lights on that thing for it to act as an airport landing strip. It had been sweet of them to add some holiday cheer, considering everything Vivian was being put through.

With only the tree lights on, the kitchen was cast in shadows. It wasn't until he set his bag on one of the barstools that he noticed Vivian sitting on the sofa, legs curled in under her, her hands cupped around a mug as she looked at the lights.

She turned her head, casting her profile in a shimmery glow that stole the air from his lungs.

"Did I wake you?" Her voice was as soft as the snow falling outside.

"No." All thoughts of work evaporated. "No, I couldn't sleep."

"Yeah." She sighed and returned her gaze to the tree. "Me, either. It's beautiful, isn't it?"

"Stunning." He wasn't certain he'd ever seen anything, anyone, more so.

"I made some hot chocolate. It's on the stove if—"

"I'm fine."

He sat down, purposely keeping some distance between them. He could smell the sweet cocoa steam drifting into the air. He'd been imagining what she might wear to bed. Somehow, the simple turquoise blue tank top and loose-fitting flowered pants hadn't come to mind. His thoughts had included…steamier selections. But with her hair tumbling free down and around her shoulders, her creamy skin gleaming in the dim light, reality won, hands down.

"That first holiday after my parents died," she said quietly, "I was living in a foster home with six other kids. The house was chaos, but in a good way, I suppose. It was… different. Shocking, actually." Memories clouded her eyes. "It was just me and Mom and Dad before that. To be suddenly in the middle of…" She sighed, shrugged. "Something strange is going on."

"Given the last few days, that statement is definitely a multiple-choice selection."

She laughed, just a little, but the sound took the clouds from her gaze. "For so long, I've felt like I'm sleepwalking through someone else's life. Like mine stopped all those years ago, and I'm just…adrift. Lost. Or, at least, I did feel that way." She looked up at the tree. "A tree like this seems like such a luxury. I used to dream about having one just like it. But as I grew older, it didn't seem…practical. As if I somehow wasn't worth the effort."

"Christmas shouldn't have anything to do with practical." Something his sister Sarah had said on occasion, usually when she was elbow deep in ornament boxes and trimmings.

"I didn't see a tree at your place when we were there." It wasn't an accusation, he thought. More of an observation.

"No." He shrugged. "No, I usually take extra shifts during Christmas so the detectives and officers with families can be home."

"Of course you do." She leaned forward, set her mug on the large, square coffee table. It was only then he noticed the small, wooden box sitting there. "It's funny. Before you came in, I was trying to convince myself you aren't as perfect as you seem to be."

He couldn't help it. He laughed. "Allow me to set your mind at ease," he teased. "I am not remotely perfect. There's a reason I cycle through partners the way I do. I'm difficult to deal with."

"Not from where I'm sitting." She uncurled her legs and scooted forward to the edge of the sofa. "I've never felt safer with anyone in my life, Nate. And I'm not referring to my physical safety." He looked for the uncertainty, the apology that had been hovering in her eyes since the moment he'd first seen her. As if she felt the need to apologize for existing. "I'm me with you. I don't have this…this need to put on a show or pretend to be something I'm not. I can't explain it."

"You don't have to explain it," Nate told her as his heart expanded to double its size. "I'll simply take it for the compliment that it is."

"You know what else I was thinking?"

Given that spark he saw in her eye, he had a pretty good idea. His fists clenched. She faced him, inclined her head.

"I was thinking," she went on when he didn't respond, "that I'm tired of living my life in the shadows. I don't want to live—or die—with any regrets." She stood up, smoothed her hands down her hips, took one, two, three steps toward him.

"You aren't going to die, Vivian." He leaned his head back to look up at her. Behind her, the tree's lights set her to glowing. "I'm not going to let you."

"Hmmm." She nodded, moved one foot then the other until she straddled his legs. "Then that means I'm going to live." She lowered herself, lifted her knees until she settled herself on his lap. He went as hard as stone in an instant, his breath hitching in his chest when she rested her hands on his shoulders, kneaded them gently with her fingers. "I don't think I've really lived much of a life, Nate." She leaned forward, placed a soft, nibbling kiss against the side of his throat. "Maybe it's taken almost dying twice in two days for me to see that. Maybe this is an awakening after all."

He squeezed his eyes shut, kept his hands at his sides as the scent of her washed over him, enveloped him. Her hair brushed against his face, his throat, as her lips moved ever so lightly, ever so gently, across his skin.

"Vivian, I don't think—"

"Don't." She sat up, caught his face between her hands and

waited until he opened his eyes before continuing. "Don't think. Not now. This is what I want. You. Us. Together. Tonight. For however many nights we might have in this… place. Our place."

He felt himself standing on the edge of a precipice he'd tried so desperately to avoid. "I don't know that I have anything to offer you, Vivian." He couldn't stop himself. His hands finally shifted, skimmed feather-light up her thighs, over her hips, fingers slipping beneath the hem of her shirt to caress her back.

"I don't need anything but you," she told him. "I'm not special, Nate. I'm not made of glass. I'm not…innocent."

His brow arched. "Aren't you?"

"I've had sex before." She inclined her head as if contemplating something he wasn't privy to. "What I haven't had is lo—" she stopped herself but didn't look away. "Intimacy. Sex is one thing." She brushed the backs of her fingers down his cheeks. "Giving myself over, letting go, actually being with someone is another thing entirely."

Love. Despite everything else she said, that was what he'd almost heard. The word shuddered through him and stole what was left of his breath. Was that what this was? Was that what he felt? This all-encompassing desire, the absolute determination to keep her safe, not only from what existed in the outside world, but from himself?

"You don't have to say anything," Vivian whispered. "I don't expect you to. I'm still trying to figure all this out myself. But it's there. It's here." She caught one of his hands, drew it around to her stomach, under her shirt and up to her heart. Her breasts. "I need to know what it feels like to have your hands on me. To feel you inside me."

She kissed him, drawing him forward as she took what she wanted, her core pressing against the hardness of him.

"Don't turn me away, Nate." Her breath was hot against his face, his lips. Her words singeing his heart. She moved his hand over until it cupped her breast, which filled his hand to perfection. "I don't want reason or rational thought or anything other than you. And me. Upstairs. In that big bed I can't bear to be in alone."

He stared up at her, unblinking. Transfixed.

She moved against him, let out a soft moan as his palm slid over her hardening nipple.

Seduced.

"Never let it be said I ignore a lady's request." Reason and restraint fractured. He surged forward, caught her mouth with his and dived in. Her thighs tightened around him as she folded herself around him, matching his kiss with one of her own that left him shaken to his core.

He pulled his hand free, and as if reading his thoughts, she leaned back far enough for him to draw the tank over her head. She moaned when he used both hands this time, cupping, teasing. Nate dipped his head, replaced his palms with his lips and drew one hardened peak into his mouth.

She gasped. Her head fell back as he circled her nipple with his tongue, leaving only to pay the same attention to her other breast. She clasped the back of his head, her hips rocking against him as she held him to her. She rubbed against him, the hot core of her against that which ached to be buried inside her.

"Stop." He gasped, struggled for control, and pulled his mouth free of hers. "Just…" He tried to catch his breath. "We need…" The word. What was the word he… "Protection."

She kissed him again, slowly, tortuously, slid off of him.

She stood, slipped her hands beneath the waistband of her pants and slowly lowered them down her legs.

He groaned at the sight of her naked, glistening body against the blinding glare of the tree lights. She held out her hand, took a step back. He followed, rising from the sofa as if caught in a spell. When their fingers entwined, the explosion threatening to undo him built again.

When they reached the stairs, she turned, taking his other hand in hers and drawing him with her.

"It wasn't only the pantry they stocked," she said, her lips curving into a beautiful smile. "I found a nice selection of condoms in the main bath." Her eyes glinted. "Made it very difficult to sleep after that. Thinking how they should be put to use."

Nate wanted to respond. He wanted to spout poetic words of perfection, but any capacity to utter a word had been stolen from him. The last steps to the main suite seemed to take both an eternity and a moment. No sooner had they crossed the threshold than he had her in his arms again.

Beside the bed, the table lamp glowed and the box she'd found sat open and waiting. With the mountains cradling them in their snowy wonder, he lifted her, kissed her. Devoured her. And lost himself.

She wound her bare legs around his hips, gasped into his mouth as he walked them to the bed. Kissing her, tasting her, should have been enough. It might have been enough if he hadn't already known what it was like to touch her. To have her touch him.

He lowered her, gently, until she was lying on the bed. He backed away, only enough to see her writhing on the mattress as she opened herself to him. "Nate, please." Her voice beckoned him with longing, but not yet, he told himself. Not until…

He knelt down, gently grasped her open thighs and drew her forward. Until he could feel the heat of her against his chin. His face. His lips. He licked her, one steady, firm swipe of his tongue before nibbling at that tiny nub of pleasure at the apex of her core.

She whimpered. Her hands grabbed his head, dived into his hair as she lifted her hips against him. Her back arched off the bed. Her breath turning into gasps that created a surge of power inside him. When she came, it was an explosion of unreserved passion that left her limp on the bed.

Even as her arms stretched out for him. For more.

He had never, in his entire life, seen a more beautiful sight than that of this woman laid bare before him, wanting him inside her.

Nate made quick work of discarding his pants. He had the condom on in record time, doing his best not to meet the teasing gaze of Vivian's oh-so-easily read eyes. Her hands reached for him, eager fingers clutching for him as he placed a knee on the edge of the mattress. She shifted back.

He moved forward, loomed over her, lowered himself and pressed his length against her.

"More," she whispered, bringing one leg up and around his hips, nudging him forward. "More, Nate. All."

He surrendered and sank into her. Her moan echoed in his ears, in his soul, as he moved, slowly at first, wanting her to get the feel of him, even as he held back. When she curled around him, her arms, her legs, he increased his thrusts, determined to set her climbing back toward release. There was no rationalizing what he felt being inside her. There was no way to describe the absolute bliss of joining with her. Her hips pumped in time with his. Their breathing came in gasps, even as he stared into her eyes.

"Come with me," she whispered when he felt the urge overwhelm him. Unable to hold back, unable to deny her, he erupted inside her.

And set her to soaring as well.

"WELL." VIVIAN HAD never felt so utterly relaxed and fulfilled in her life. "There's only one problem with us having done this."

"Only one?" Nate said on a sleepy laugh. He'd been efficient in the way he'd adjusted them in bed, had them snuggling beneath the comfy, warm down duvet once they could both move.

She lifted her head from the curve of his shoulder, rested her chin on her hand that was placed over his still rapidly pounding heart. "Well, only one comes to mind at the moment." She cuddled against him and felt her heart zing when he tightened his arm around her as if trying to draw her even closer. "One time isn't going to be nearly enough."

Vivian smiled and laughed at his arched brow. She traced a finger down his nose and allowed it to be caught in his teeth when she reached his lips.

"Did I mention I've always had a thing for older women?"

"You did," Vivian said seriously and moved her leg between his. She felt him stir, anticipated the minutes until they could try to outdo round one. "You're quite...adept for such a young man."

Nate snorted and laughed. "What do you think young men spend most of their time thinking about?"

"I don't have to think." She rose up, kissed him, all but melted into him. "I have firsthand experience." She tucked her head under his chin, closed her eyes against the sensation of his hand smoothing her hair, cupping her cheek. "Can I tell you something?"

"You can tell me anything," he assured her.

"Seriously. I don't want you to laugh."

His hand stilled. He tucked a finger under her cheek and lifted her chin so he could look into her eyes. "I will never laugh at you, Vivian."

"You know the first time I thought about this happening between us?" She hesitated. Exposing her body to him had been one thing. Exposing her heart? Well. She'd been wanting to take more chances with her life, hadn't she? "When I first saw you sitting at the bar."

"Yeah?" He looked inordinately pleased with himself.

"Yeah. It made focusing on dinner quite impossible, I can tell you." She trailed a finger across his chest.

"Tell me about it." He caught her hand and brought it to his lips. *Talented lips*, she thought as she pushed aside any regret or doubt. She was not going to let anything ruin this time she had with him. "You know when I first thought about this happening between us?"

She smiled, entertained at his amusement. "Tell me."

"When you took off your jacket at the restaurant." He blinked, and she searched for the teasing, for the lie. And found none. "It was like being hit by a lightning bolt." His hand sunk into her hair. "And that was before I even saw your face. Or your glasses." He tapped her nose and earned a laugh. "We should get bonus points for resisting temptation for as long as we did."

"Yes, well, you did your best to push me off. Didn't work though." She'd meant what she'd said earlier. Sex was one thing. Making love with Nate Colton had been entirely another. “I do believe almost dying…twice,” she added quickly, “might have finally taught me not to be quite so…timid.”

He kissed her, long and deep. Until her head spun.

“There is nothing timid about you,” he assured her when she reached down and grasped him in her hand. “Not one little bit.”

“No,” she said as she slithered down his body and lowered her mouth to him. “I don’t think there is anymore.”

WHEN VIVIAN OPENED her eyes, it took her a long moment to remember where she was. She wasn’t staring at dull white walls or a mirrored dresser she’d found at a yard sale shortly after moving into her town house. She didn’t feel the chill of the straining heating unit doing its best to spit out warmth on a cold December morning.

Instead, she was buried beneath a comfy, cozy down-filled duvet, looking out to the stunning mountain range encircling the town of Owl Creek. An unfamiliar yet welcome weight had settled over her, behind her. Around her.

The smile that spread slowly across her lips had her reaching up and resting her hand on the top of Nate’s head. Her fingers sank into the thickness of his hair as she drew her fingers down. He shifted, moved more snuggly against her in a way that both brought a tint of color to her cheeks and a slow boil to her blood.

“Don’t start something you might not have the energy to finish.” Nate’s voice rumbled against the side of her neck. He tightened his hold around her waist, pressed his lips against the pulse at her throat.

“Believe me,” she said on a half moan as his hand wandered down her bare stomach. “If we start, I’ll make absolutely certain we finish.”

Still, she found her gaze drawn back to the mountains as she clung to the memory of this perfect moment. A moment that only months before she couldn't have conceived of.

His stomach rumbled, and she laughed. "Hungry?"

"Starved." He nipped at her neck, and she gasped as he rolled her onto her back. He gazed down upon her as if he were an art aficionado looking upon a classic painting.

"I can cook," she offered, linking her hands behind his neck. "Unless you have someplace to be?"

"I do not." He kissed her. "Have any place." Kissed her again, longer this time. "To be." This kiss had her melting beneath him to the point of becoming utterly putty in his hands as the sun completed its ascent into the sky.

She hadn't lied to him last night, when she'd told him she'd had sex before. But she wouldn't necessarily qualify it as…rewarding. A quick tumble with a boy her first week of college had been the result of curiosity rather than passion. It certainly hadn't been anything that warranted a desire for a repeat performance either on the boy's part or hers. As a result, she'd added sex to the list of things she could live without.

She caught a giggle behind her still vibrating fingers.

She definitely couldn't say that anymore.

"Do I even want to know?" Nate lifted his head from where he'd been dozing against her breast.

"I don't think you do." This time, it was her stomach that rumbled. "Okay, that's embarrassing enough to warrant me heading down to the kitchen. After I take a shower."

"Mmmm." He nuzzled his cheek against her. "Couple more minutes."

She sighed. It was so easy to forget everything, including what had brought them to this place, this moment. And yet the threats hovered, as did the reality of needing to return to her actual life. They both needed to return. Once she was out of danger, he wouldn't be responsible for her safety any longer. His job would be done, and if there was one thing she'd learned about him the past few days, it was that his job always came first. "Nate?"

"Yeah."

"Are you going to tell me what you and Fletcher talked about up here last night?"

She knew asking would break the spell, but one of them had to be practical about things. Fairy tales were all well and good as a diversion, but she knew, better than most, that real life rarely brought a happily-ever-after.

"It doesn't have to do with you." He rolled onto his back but curved an arm around her when she leaned over him, catching the sheet between them. He pinched the bridge of his nose, squeezed his eyes shut.

"So it's none of my business?"

He dropped his hand, looked at her, and she wondered if it was possible to actually fall into the ocean blue of his eyes. "I didn't say that. It's…complicated."

"I'm a smart woman." Funny. It was something she'd always known, of course, but rarely was it anything she said. Out loud, at least. "Maybe I can help?"

"What makes you think I need help with it?"

"This." She traced a finger from his furrowed brow, down his nose, to his swollen lips. "It appears every time you start thinking."

"Then it must be permanently etched on my face." He stopped, sighed. "I don't know that I'd even know where to start."

"Anywhere." She hesitated, then plunged ahead. "If it doesn't have to do with me, does it have to do with your mother?"

"Okay, flag on the play." He sat up and scooted back against the headboard. "Let's not put you and my mother in the same sentence. Or mention her while we're in bed, okay?"

She knew he meant it as a tease, a joke, but there was definite pain behind the thought.

"Tell me." She sat up and crossed her legs, pushed her hair away from her face. "Talk to me, Nate. You've certainly listened to me enough."

He looked a bit lost for a moment, confused, and she caught a glimpse of a younger Nate, struggling with the truth about his complicated family life. When he spoke, it was with a resoluteness that made her heart ache for him.

"Fletcher thinks my mother might have had a hand in our father's death." His smile was quick and cursory. "Surprised you, didn't I?"

"Not…exactly." She frowned, frantically searching for the right words. But she didn't have a chance to say anything else before he went on.

"How about this, then? Apparently, for the past few years, she's been involved with this Ever After Church, and the guy who runs it. Markus Acker. You've probably heard of them."

"I definitely have." She nodded as her blood ran cold. "One of my clients, he runs a Fortune 500 company out of New York. He hired me to do some damage control when his son got caught up with Acker last year. Just press releases and statements to the media. He didn't want it to be full-blown news, but he didn't want his shareholders thinking he was being held hostage by the fact his boy was being used to essentially extort him."

"Did he get out? The kid?" Nate asked, a bit more alert.

Vivian ducked her head. "I don't know how much I'm legally allowed to say since I signed a nondisclosure agreement, but..." She nodded. "Without going into details, I can tell you my client hired a specialized team to get him out."

"Like an off-the-books mercenary kind of group?"

She shrugged, a non-answer. "The last I heard he'd had his son sent to a facility overseas that specializes in... I don't know if this is the right word...*deprogramming*." While she'd been relieved the boy was safe and out of the cult's reach, she hadn't found working that kind of job to be anything other than stressful and gut-wrenching. She much preferred working with authors looking to sell their books and brand, or actors and actresses hoping to up their profile. That particular client had helped her learn to set boundaries and not jump at every professional opportunity just because it might up her profile. "Do you think... Is it possible Fletcher's right about your mom being involved with this group? Does he have any actual evidence?"

As horrific as the stories were about Jessie Colton—and she'd gotten an earful from Lizzy as well as Nate—the idea Jessie may have murdered Robert came across as a little too *Game of Thrones* for her liking.

"Do I think it's possible?" Nate's brows went up. "Yes. As far as evidence? He doesn't have anything concrete. It's a gut feeling on Fletcher's part. Others, too, if I was reading him right. I don't know if he's talked to Max about it or not."

"I would think yes," she said and rested a hand on his thigh. "They might be cousins by birth, but they're brothers by choice. Something like this, if Fletcher truly believes it, enough to talk to you about it, then Max knows." She caught her bottom lip in her teeth. "That could explain why Max has been a harder sell on you."

"I told Fletcher I'd look into it. Later," he added quickly. "Once we're on the other side of this DeBaccian mess, and you're safe."

Once they were back to their real lives. Where neither one of them particularly fit with the other. When his job with her was done. "Then we'd best get to that." She tugged the sheet with her as she scooted off the edge of the bed. "I'm going to jump in the shower, then fix breakfast while you take one."

"Or." He caught her around the waist before she took two steps from the bed. He spun her around and kissed her breathless. "We could conserve water and shower together." The grin he gave her contained none of the hopelessness she'd seen shining in his eyes moments before.

"I do like conservation," she agreed, but her attempt to remain completely serious failed, and she laughed as he scooped her into his arms and carried her into the bathroom.

Chapter Twelve

Nate quietly stepped into the front downstairs bedroom that had been set up as a home office. It had made sense for Vivian to set up shop in here, where she'd have privacy to conduct whatever work she needed to take care of. When he set the fresh mug of coffee onto the coaster, he earned a thankful smile as she pressed a finger to her ear and the headphones for her online call.

"No, Wanda, this should work out fine. I'll send you my compiled list of agencies I think we should send your press release to, and we'll go from there. Uh-huh. I'm hoping to be back up and running sometime next week."

Nate offered an encouraging nod.

"Great. I'll check in with you then. Okay, bye." She clicked off and sagged back in the leather chair. "I could get used to this. Gorgeous view." She pointed out the front bay window that overlooked the sloping view of Owl Creek below. "Despite the constant run of construction trucks and crews."

Nate grimaced. The banging and buzzing of construction equipment had started right at eight. The fact that winter meant everyone was working on home interiors only made the noise echo louder, near as he could tell. "Could be worse." They could be dealing with cement trucks and paving equipment.

"I also have coffee at my beck and call."

"Not just coffee." He bent to kiss her, determined to keep it quick, but, as always seemed to happen, the moment he tasted her, he wanted more.

"Stop." She laughed and pushed him away. "I've got one more client to call and a ton of emails to answer." She gestured to her laptop. "Give me an hour, maybe ninety minutes tops, then I'll be all yours."

"Sounds like a plan." He walked backward out of the room. "I'll check in with Fletcher and my lieutenant. See if there have been any developments."

She nodded and spun around in her chair, but not before he saw a flash of sadness in her eyes. Before he could ask, she was clicking into her video system to make another call.

Later, he told himself. He'd ask her what was bothering her when she wasn't as focused on work.

He returned to the kitchen, where he'd set up his own makeshift workstation at the table near the door to the backyard. He was already getting antsy, being stuck in one place, but the view helped. As did the woman who would soon be joining him.

He'd spent the better part of the morning digging through police reports that contained any mention of Marty DeBaccian, going back the last few years. Even if Lieutenant Haig had someone doing this already, it was research that felt like they were making progress. More information was power moving forward. There was little that irritated him more than being bored and useless, so he'd take what he could get.

He was compiling lists of any businesses mentioned, any suspected co-conspirators and even the names of former detectives and officers who had come across him. Leaving no stone unturned was the only way they were going to catch this guy.

No stone... Nate pursed his lips, stared at the screen and the list of detectives he'd been making. "Sullivan." It didn't sit well with him at all that the detective assigned to Vivian's case had done a disappearing act. In his experience, that meant one of two things.

Either Sullivan had gotten too close to something and DeBaccian had reacted or…

"Definitely leaning toward *or*." He hated voicing it, hated the very idea of it, but there was no getting around the fact that Detective Jim Sullivan could very well be on DeBaccian's payroll.

Someone had to be, Nate reasoned. DeBaccian had been staying a good few steps ahead of law enforcement for a while now. Having someone on the inside of the Boise PD could explain that. Accusations like this were never made lightly, however. Even a false accusation of corruption could follow a cop around for the rest of his life, and if Sullivan was clean…

That thought didn't develop beyond that. He couldn't shake the feeling there was more going on, given Sullivan's recent disappearance. The timing couldn't be a coincidence.

Like Fletcher had said yesterday about their father's death: too many coincidences.

"Down the rabbit hole we go, then." He hunched over his laptop and got to work.

When his phone rang a little while later, he had to remind himself how to use a flip phone to answer. Distracted, he all but growled a greeting.

"Catch you at a bad time, Detective?" Lieutenant Haig's voice sounded surprisingly lighthearted.

"No, sir, sorry." Nate cringed, pushed his laptop back and blinked his eyes wide to clear the blur. "I've been doing some digging." Tapping his pen against one of the notepads on the table, he wondered how best to approach this.

"I just got a call from the hospital," Haig told him. "Wexler's stable enough for surgery. They're taking him in later today."

Finally, Nate thought. *Progress.* "What's his prognosis?"

"Fifty-fifty." Nate could all but hear his commanding officer's shrug. "If he comes through, we should be able to question him in a day or two."

A day or two. He gazed around the house that, because of Vivian, felt more like a home than his own ever had. It would be a shame to leave it. And her. "Sounds good, sir."

"Good to hear it. Now, tell me about your digging."

"Ah." Nate glanced over his shoulder as Vivian came in. Barefoot and with her hair loose and long around her shoulders, she wore silky, flowy pants that hung low on her hips, along with a short-sleeved shirt. The color reminded him of the syringa, Idaho's state flower. She looked like a summer oasis in the middle of a snowy, frigid winter. "I'm not entirely sure you'd approve of where I've been excavating, sir."

Vivian frowned at him, as if trying to decipher his code. She walked over to sit across from him, pointed to some of his notes as if asking permission. He nodded.

"Then it's a good thing this isn't an official call," Lieutenant Haig said. "Out with it, Colton."

"I've been looking for a connection between DeBaccian and Sullivan." Before giving his boss a chance to push back, he plowed ahead. "It's just a thought, and a rough one, but unless Sullivan's popped back up—"

"He has not. I sent a couple of patrol officers to his place this morning under the guise of a wellness check. His car's gone. No sign of him. We're hoping to locate his wife—"

"Officially separated as of last year," Nate said. "Near as I can tell, neither has filed for divorce. Haven't been able to track where she's gone."

"So he's rudderless," Haig murmured. "Okay, I'll get someone to track her down. Did you find the connection you were hoping for?"

Hoping wasn't exactly the word. Nate couldn't think of any police officer who hoped to find evidence of a dirty cop. "Maybe." He shuffled through his notes as Vivian rested her bare feet on the bottom rung of her chair. "Seven years ago, DeBaccian was arrested as a suspect in a string of electronics store burglaries. Sullivan was one of the investigating detectives."

"Is that it?"

Like Fletcher, Nate trusted his gut. And his gut told him there was something more. "The case was dismissed when one of the key pieces of evidence went missing. Security tape footage." He scrolled through the online evidence-storage database. "The assistant DA prosecuting the case had the evidence brought to her office. A day later, she had it sent back. According to her statement, she placed everything back in the box before it was picked up. When they retrieved it for court, the recordings were gone."

"Whatever it is you don't want to say—"

"Detective Sullivan was responsible for the transport, sir. According to the sign-in sheet, he was the last person to have access to the evidence box."

"All right, then." Haig lowered his voice. "Keep following this where you can. Put it together for me but keep it with you. Right now, there's no place safer for any evidence against DeBaccian than with you in Owl Creek."

"Yes, sir. Anything else, sir?"

"Not at the moment, no. I'll check in once I get word on Wexler's condition."

Nate slapped his phone closed. "You get all that?"

"I did." Vivian nodded as she flipped through his scribbled notes. "Looks like we're both making progress where our jobs are concerned. I've officially moved into the world of new client referrals."

"Yeah?" He wasn't entirely sure what that meant, but she seemed happy about it.

"Oh, yeah. Someone recommended me to this digital content company out of Texas. Their website certainly makes them sound promising." She frowned. "I had to email them and let them know I wasn't available for a consult for a while yet. But if they're really interested, they'll wait."

"Because you're the best at what you do," Nate said.

"Yes." She straightened in her chair, a hint of surprise in her eyes. "Yes, I am."

"Hopefully, we'll have you back to your life sooner than later. My lieutenant called to let me know Wexler is going in for surgery sometime today. If he wakes up and talks, I'm hoping we won't need your testimony against DeBaccian."

"A girl can dream." She flipped more of the pages of his notepads. "You really think Detective Sullivan is a bad cop?"

"The more I look into him, the more it looks that way." Despite needing to, this wasn't something he felt any pleasure in undertaking. "Personally, I just want him found so we at least know where he is." DeBaccian coming after Vivian was one thing. Like Max said at the station, criminals often let their egos get the better of them.

But having a trained cop hunting her? A person who knew the ins and outs of protecting witnesses, who understood how the police went about their jobs in the most detailed of ways? The very thought made the bitter coffee churn in his stomach. Her face tightened. The tension he'd been hoping would melt away for them surged. "You know what I saw out on the back patio?" He stood up, carried his coffee to the sink and set it to soak. "A hot tub."

Vivian looked out the window, into the graying, threatening sky, then back to him. "In December?"

"You've never been in a hot tub when it's snowing?"

"Ah, no." She laughed, shook her head. "Is that really a thing?"

"Let's find out." He returned to the table, held out his hand.

She didn't look convinced as she grabbed hold and allowed him to pull her up. "Funnily enough, I didn't think to pack a swimsuit."

He grinned and tugged her close, kissed her hard. "Neither did I."

Her brow arched, and she pulled her hands free, slipped them beneath the hem of his dark T-shirt. "Well, in that case..."

WHEN VIVIAN WAS LITTLE, before her parents died and before discovering the unpredictability of life, one of her favorite games to play had been "house."

She'd recruited her dolls and stuffed animals, lining them up on the bed while she cooked pretend food on the pretend cardboard stove her father had made for her out of an old shipping box. On occasion, she'd snuck into the kitchen, opened the cabinets she could reach and pilfered whatever items her mother had stashed away. A bag of rice. A potato. A dented can of tomatoes. She'd spent hours "feeding" her companions as she talked to them, telling them about all the fun things they were going to do together.

Funny. Vivian sliced through an onion and set to chopping. She'd never imagined playing house again since becoming an adult. But being here, now, with Nate, it felt exactly like that. She wouldn't outgrow it this time, but she would have to leave it behind when everything was resolved and life returned to normal.

Her eyes filled with tears, but she had the perfect excuse. She turned and slid the chopped onions off the cutting board and into the pan that had been heating on the stove.

Post–hot tub—and they'd definitely given it a workout in more ways than one—he'd returned to his computer, losing himself in chasing down the people who meant to do her harm. To prevent her from returning to that normal she'd existed in.

Normal.

The word didn't seem quite so defined any longer.

It hadn't taken her more than waking up in Nate's arms to realize that aching void of loneliness she'd lived with for so long was gone. She pressed her lips together hard, wiped the back of her hand under her eyes as she sorted through the meager selection of dried herbs.

She'd run on a handful of emotions her entire life, and never to extremes. Anxiety had tamped all that down and back to where, most of the time, she didn't have to acknowledge or deal with it. But being with Nate, loving Nate, she couldn't help but feel as if every emotion possible had jumped on board the spinning carousel that was her heart.

Loving Nate. She squeezed her eyes shut. She'd almost said it last night. Before she'd let herself think about it. Before she'd come to terms with it. It was one thing to fall in love with a man. It was quite another to admit it out loud and have him with no way to escape.

"So, what's for dinner?" Nate's domestic-tinged question had her thinking of her long-lost stuffed animals and dolls and how they'd remained silent. And forever perfect in her memory.

"Pasta." She had to assume it was Sloan, Ruby and Kiki who had stocked the kitchen, and they'd done so with an overabundance of attention to carbs. "I'm making my homemade meat sauce."

"Sounds great." He flashed her a smile. The way he looked at her—even as he plowed through the potential criminal activity of a fellow cop—had those unbelievable fairy tales surging to the surface of her thoughts once more.

"I'd have made bread, but I didn't have time." Time to get back to the teasing and playing of the relationship. "Someone distracted me in the hot tub."

"Totally worth it," he said. The humor in his voice sounded forced. His cell phone vibrated to the point of dancing across the table. He flipped it open. "It's my lieutenant."

Vivian turned the flame down on the stove, grabbed a towel and circled the island.

"Sir? Any word on Wexler?"

She stood beside him, tempted to touch him, but also worried it was too familiar a gesture. How was it she could share a bed with this man, make love with this man, and still be afraid? Not of him. But of what he made her feel. Even now, she could see the concern on his face, and she knew it was because of her.

He was a man dedicated to his job, so by extension she was his concern. And maybe, for a little while, a distraction.

"Okay. Great. Thanks for letting me know. Yeah." His gaze met hers, and in those blue depths, she saw a glimmer of hope. "I'm just about done with my report. I'll check in with you tomorrow. Yes, sir. Thank you."

He clicked the phone closed and sagged back in his seat. "Wexler's surgery went well."

"Yeah?"

"They got the bullet, but most importantly, he's stable. Lieutenant Haig thinks we'll be able to talk to him as early as tomorrow."

"That's great news." She let out a sigh she hoped would be heard as relieved. "That should make your job a little easier."

"We'll see. You know what's even better?" He collected his papers, stacked them up and, after hitting Save, closed his laptop. "I'm calling it a day. Just in time, too, since it's after five."

"Keeping bankers' hours now, are you?" She returned to the kitchen and searched for a cheese grater. She found one, on a shelf under the center island. When she popped back up, he was standing across from her, hands planted on the gold-specked black marble countertop.

"Can I help?"

"I don't know." She eyed him. "How good are you in the kitchen?"

That grin of his reappeared.

She was onto him this time. Even as she laughed, she held up both hands. "Oh, no. Not again. Not now."

"Why not now?" He challenged, stalking around the counter in a very precise and familiar way.

"Because nothing interferes with me making my meat sauce." She turned, tried to dive away, but he caught her around the waist, spun her around and straight into his arms. "Nate—"

Whatever else she was going to say was caught by his mouth. His wonderful, talented, undeniably tempting mouth. Bittersweet tears burned the back of her eyes. She felt so lucky, to be wanted by him. And he wanted her. There was no denying that.

When he lifted his mouth, and she blinked dazedly up at him, he reached out and turned off the stove. "What room would you like to try next?"

NATE'S EYES SNAPPED OPEN.

What was that?

He sat up, dislodging the blanket he'd dragged over them from the back of the sofa. Mind racing, he jumped to his feet, shoved both hands into his hair. "Vivian?" Her name all but echoed through the kitchen and great room.

The tree lights burned yet again. The remnants of the pasta dinner she'd finally found time to make for them still sat on the stove. Food didn't come close to satiating him, not since he'd gotten his first taste of her. But something felt…

Wearing only his jeans, he retrieved his gun from where he'd left it and his holster on the back of a kitchen chair. Something… He turned, scanned the room. Something was different.

He froze, listened. An empty house had an entirely different feel to it. The energy was lower but nonetheless heavier. As if the silence were pressing in on him.

"Vivian?" he called again as he searched the first floor. No sign of her.

He raced to the stairs, skidding to a halt with one hand on the banister. His keys. He'd kept them on the small marble table by the front door. They were gone.

He walked to the door, heart pounding.

It had been left ajar.

He swore, pulled the gun free and tossed the holster to the floor. He carefully placed his bare foot in the opening and pulled open the door.

The cold blast of air hit him like an avalanche. Locking his jaw, he stepped onto the porch, weapon poised at his side, ready to react.

"Vivian?"

He heard it again. A *click*. A *beep*. He swung toward the SUV he'd parked in the driveway. Gun raised, he made quick work of the path, circling down and around to the car, which, only now could he see, had its passenger door open.

Nate almost forgot to breathe until he saw two feet dangling from a pair of white pants. He grabbed the door and yanked it all the way open. "Vivian!"

She yelped, sat up and nearly slipped right off the seat. "Geez, Nate." She glared at him, pressed a hand to her chest. "Who needs a hitman chasing them when I've got you?"

"What. Are you. Doing?" It took every ounce of patience he had to quell his anger. "You aren't supposed to leave the house. Especially not without telling me."

"You wouldn't have heard me, anyway. You were snoring." She snapped the glove box shut and got out of the car.

"I do not snore."

She rolled her eyes. "I wanted to get my phone." She waggled it in front of him. "Okay?"

"Not okay." He snatched it from her hand. "Who were you going to call?"

"I wasn't—" She scrunched her mouth like a petulant toddler. "None of your business. Give it to me."

"No." He held it up over his head, well out of her reach.

"Give me my phone, Nate." She jumped once, twice, then growled and stepped back, slammed the car door so hard his teeth rattled. "I'm well aware of your sensitive areas, *Detective*, so unless you want them to meet my knee—"

"You don't have anyone to call," he reminded her. "Lizzy's out of town, and everyone else is a client. So I ask again." His patience wore thin. "Who were you going to call?"

She straightened, an odd, dim light flashing in her eyes that had him lowering his arm. "I wasn't going to *call* anyone."

With unnerving speed, she snatched the phone out of his grasp and spun on her bare heels. Head down, she turned on her phone. The glare of the screen cut through the darkness of the night.

Feeling ridiculous, he trailed after her. "Vivian, what is this all—"

"Here, okay?" She shoved the screen in his face. The screen that displayed a picture of Toby. Her cat. "I was missing him. I woke up and saw that stupid box with his ashes, and I was missing my cat, and I didn't have..." She stopped, tears glistening in her eyes. "I didn't want to wake you up and ask permission to see his pictures."

"Vivian." He heard it, the sympathy, the pity that had anger erasing the grief he saw on her face.

"There!" She stabbed a finger into his face. "Right there. I didn't want that. Just...forget it." She made it only a few steps before a car, headlights blazing, turned the corner.

His hand tightened around his gun. "Get inside."

"Nate?" He heard the fear, the uncertainty, but she didn't move toward the house. She moved toward him. The car stopped.

Nate shoved her behind him, feet braced apart; he watched, then gaped and rolled his eyes as he glared at the familiar face beyond the window as it slid down.

"Just checking the neighborhood to make sure all is calm." Max Colton leaned over, his expression, as always, unreadable. "'Tis the season, you know."

"Seriously, Max?"

"Della's working late, so I told Fletcher I'd just drive past." He shrugged. "I'd ask what the two of you are doing out here this late at night, but I'm not entirely sure I want to know."

Nate could feel Vivian shiver behind him. "Go on back inside, Vivian. Please." He could only hope his more solicitous tone would work better than his irritated one had. He didn't like to admit it, but scared was not a mode he operated well in. And finding her gone from the house had definitely scared him. "You want to come in?"

Max's eyes went wide with surprise. "You sure?" He watched Vivian make it up the path. "I've got time before picking Della up, but I don't want to intrude."

"Just park already." Funny how easily they'd fallen into the big-brother/little-brother routine. Nate wasn't entirely sure he was comfortable with that. Nate headed inside before his feet turned to blocks of ice.

"I put the coffee on." Vivian was already headed up the stairs. "I'm going to bed."

"Don't put the card back in your phone. We don't want anyone tra—" The second the words were out of his mouth he wanted to take them back.

"Thank you, yes." She gave him a look that had previously active parts of him withering. "As I have the IQ of a turnip, I was in need of the reminder."

"Wow." Max closed the door behind him as Vivian went upstairs. "Chilly in here." He detoured straight past him into the kitchen.

"It's December," Nate called as he retrieved his holster and keys and followed. "It's chilly everywhere." But his brother had a point.

Something told him he was about to experience his first-ever deep freeze where Vivian was concerned.

Chapter Thirteen

Vivian prided herself on not dwelling on the dumber things she'd done in her life. Picking a fight with Nate over her phone—and Toby's pictures—would no doubt remain at the top of that list for the foreseeable future. At least that was the thought she woke up to late the next morning.

That she found herself staring at the box containing her cat's ashes rather than debating how to extricate herself from her lover's arms didn't seem an ideal way to start the day. Like most people, she didn't do well with being embarrassed or being caught. Of course, she'd overreacted last night, but honestly, she hadn't expected to take more than a few minutes to retrieve her phone.

Still feeling cranky, she slugged out of bed and took a shower, got dressed and headed downstairs. She found Nate eyes-deep in his laptop, and while it didn't improve her mood, she was grateful for the distraction. And the delay in needing to apologize.

"Sleep okay?" Nate asked as she poured herself some coffee.

"Well enough." She'd slept like crap, but criminals weren't the only ones susceptible to ego. Hers had definitely been dented, but mostly by her own behavior. "I'm sorry I worried you last night."

"I'm sorry I overreacted. When I woke up to an empty house, I got scared. The things that went through my head—"

"Blame your car." She pulled open the fridge despite having no appetite for breakfast. "If the stupid alarm thing would have disconnected on the first try, you never would have known I was gone."

"I'll make a note to share that with the manufacturer."

She squeezed her eyes shut. She did not want to fall further under his charm. They couldn't afford for her to. "Nate—"

He was standing behind the fridge door when she closed it. "Yes?"

She had so many questions for him. What happens after she isn't in danger any longer? What happens if they don't catch DeBaccian? What happens if Wexler dies and she ends up having to testify in the murder trial?

What was going to happen to them when there wasn't a case pulling them together? Or ripping them apart?

None of those questions made their way out of her mouth. Instead, she retrieved her coffee and moved away. "How long did Max stay last night?"

"Long enough to clean up the kitchen."

"Oh." She frowned, hoisted herself up onto one of the barstools and sipped. "Dishes. Totally slipped my mind."

"Worked out okay," Nate assured her. "I told him he could eat whatever he wanted in exchange. You earned his seal of approval as far as meat sauce goes. And he might have taken a container of it home to share with Della."

"That's fine." There was always more sauce to be made. "I think we need to talk."

"I'm glad you're the one to say it." He leaned his arms

on the counter and pinned her with those blue eyes of his. "Or *am* I?"

She frowned, confusion finally taking hold despite her best efforts to avoid it. "What's going to happen when this case is over?"

He hesitated, but didn't pull his gaze from hers. "I'm going to assume you don't mean with DeBaccian and the justice system."

She inclined her head. "I don't… I don't know how to do this, Nate. Getting caught up in all this excitement and danger, it's been a bit of a mind-spinner for me. You have been. And I'm afraid we're becoming blind to the reality of our situations."

"Right." He nodded, then shook his head. "Nope, sorry. Not getting it at all."

"Do we just stop everything now, before it gets too messy?" she asked. "Or do we take it as far as we can go and then worry about it? If I have to testify, the DA probably won't like the fact we slept together—"

"It's none of the DA's business—"

"Nate." She dropped her voice and the shield of protection she'd been unwittingly wielding. "Of course it's his business. You don't want the case corrupted because you were sleeping with your main witness. But that's neither here nor—"

"I don't want to stop." He blurted it out so fast he seemed to have surprised himself. "Seeing you. Sleeping with you. Being with you." He shoved his hand into his hair and sighed. "I had a feeling I was going to botch this up. Okay." Nate took a long, deep breath. "Okay, let me come at this a different way. Once this is all over, however it ends, I would like to continue to see you. Socially." He frowned. "Why does it sound like I just stepped out of a Jane Austen book?"

She tried to catch the laugh behind her lips but didn't quite manage.

"Look." He leaned on the counter again, only this time he reached across to capture her hands in his. "I don't know how to do this, either. You're a new experience for me, Vivian. This…thing between us. It feels special. Like a gift. And I don't want to walk away from it before we find out if it's something serious, we can make a go of."

She wanted to believe him. All her life, she'd wanted to belong to someone, anyone, who was willing to put their heart on the line for her. But thirty years of life can tarnish even the most hopeful of dreams. "You're no Jane Austen hero," she said finally. "Mainly because none of them ever say so much at one time. I…" She'd told him the other night she'd felt as if she'd been awakened, thrown into a life she'd only been a passive participant in up until now. He was giving her a chance to embrace that fully.

What a fool she'd be to walk away from everything being offered to her. Even if it was for a fraction of time.

"I would like to continue to see you, socially, as well. Maybe even carnally," she added in a moment of inspiration. She earned a smile and his raised brows. "And maybe we'll both be more clearheaded about the future once we don't have this whole DeBaccian thing looming over us. Speaking of…" She looked over her shoulder to the kitchen table, which was once again a mess. "Did you finish your report for your lieutenant?"

"I did." He released her and turned back to the fridge. "I worked some things out with Max. He suggested I run it past Fletcher, too."

She wasn't going to discourage him from spending more time with his brother.

"You hungry?" He bent down and pulled a box of frozen waffles out of the freezer.

"Seriously?" She narrowed her eyes.

"Yeah, why?" Nate looked at the bright yellow box. "What's wrong with—"

"You want waffles, I'll fix waffles." She joined him on the other side of the counter, dropped the box back into the freezer, then grabbed his shirt and pulled him toward her for a kiss. It was, to her mind at least, a new start. A reboot, so to speak. Something she planned to use to keep the hope she was determined to cling to alive. "Go clean up the table while I try to remember where I saw a waffle iron."

"REMIND ME TO talk to Chase about the noise level around here," Nate grumbled as he tossed the remote onto the coffee table and gave up on whatever the plot might be of the movie Vivian had chosen. "Those trucks are driving me nuts."

"Just block them out." She sat beside him on the sofa, her bare toes tucked under his thighs as she typed away on her laptop. "I've got a pair of headphones in my bag if you think they might help."

"No. It's fine." He sighed and dropped his head back on the sofa. "Sorry. I'm just..."

"Antsy?"

"Frustrated."

"And bored?"

He rolled his head to the side, expecting to find her looking at him, but instead all her interest was on her screen.

"Go get your cell phone," she said. "You must have some kind of game or something on there you like."

"I don't want to play any games. With my phone," he added and earned a roll of her eyes.

"What time are you supposed to meet with Fletcher in town?"

"I'm not going."

"What?" She had something akin to panic in her eyes when she looked at him. "Why not?"

"Because you're here and I'm charged with protecting you. I'm not leaving you here alone."

"Are you suggesting I come with you?"

"No." They needed to keep her locked up tight until they had DeBaccian in custody, and last he heard, that wasn't remotely close to happening. "No, you need to stay here."

She sighed and closed her laptop. "Nate, go."

"Nope."

"If you don't—" her voice had an almost too sweet quality to it "—Fletcher's going to have another crime scene to worry about. One that involves your murder." Her smile promised much pain. "I've got plenty to work on getting ready to pitch to this next client. Plus, Harlow's got some new interest from a production company. I know how to operate the security system and the panic button. Plus, there's security down at the guard gate. If anything happens, I'll hit that first and call you second."

"On what?" he countered. "You won't have a cell phone."

"I have one." She opened her computer again. "I'm just not allowed to use it as anything other than a photo album."

He didn't move. But he was thinking.

"The faster you close this case, the sooner we can get started on a real relationship." How she could make perfect sense to him and keep typing away like that was a multitasking miracle. "Go meet with your brother. I'll be fine. I won't leave the house. I won't even use the hot tub if it makes you feel better."

A car door slammed outside, followed by the quick staccato sound of heels against the concrete. He was up and moving even before the doorbell rang. When he pulled it open, he felt both relief and uncertainty.

"Lizzy."

"Hi, Nate." His half sister, with her long, strawberry blond hair draped over her slim shoulders, flashed familiar, worried blue eyes at him. "Ajay and I just got home this morning. I ran into Sloan in town, and she told me…" She peered around him, her gaze frantic. "She told me Vivian's here? Where is she?"

"Lizzy?" Vivian stepped clear of the hall, a surprised smile on her face. "Yes, I'm here. It's okay. I'm right here."

"Oh, my gosh, Vivian!" Lizzy pushed past him and enveloped Vivian in a hug so tight Nate could feel it himself. "You're okay! When Sloan told me… I imagined all sorts of horrible things."

Vivian looked over Lizzy's shoulder at him, and he immediately regretted not pushing Vivian harder to call her friend. His sister.

"What on earth is happening?" Lizzy demanded. "What are you doing here in Owl Creek? In this house? Sloan said you were shot at? That you're some kind of witness to an attempted murder?" She swung on Nate. "Tell me what's going on, please? Why didn't you call me? You should have called me."

"Okay, Lizzy, stop." Vivian surprised Nate by grabbing Lizzy's arms and spinning her back around to face her. "Everything's fine. I will tell you everything, I promise. But all you need to know right now is that Nate's been watching over me, and I'm here and safe because of him. Okay?" She touched a hand to his sister's cheek. "No need to spiral.

Everything's fine. It's going to be fine." She looked to Nate again. "I promise."

He understood. She wanted him to know that he was an integral part of making certain her promise was kept.

"Okay." Lizzy sighed and sagged a bit. Nate closed the door and followed them back to the kitchen. "Okay, I'm sorry. I kind of freaked out after talking to Sloan. Sometimes, I swear it's like this switch gets flipped, and I—"

"You've been through a lot lately," Vivian assured her. "Which is why I didn't want to call you just yet. Sit down." Vivian pointed to the kitchen table.

"Should I make coffee?" Nate offered.

"Don't think she needs any caffeine," Vivian muttered under her breath. "How about some tea? We've got plenty of that, so hot water will do. Tell you what, Nate. Since you were worried about leaving me alone, why don't you take off and go see Fletcher, and Lizzy can stay here? Get this whole ball in motion, yeah?"

"You sure?" Nate eyed Lizzy.

"I'm sure," Vivian said as he gathered up his things. "I can handle this. And you need to get out of here before you go stir-crazy."

He both liked and didn't like the fact she recognized that about him. "Lizzy, can you stay with her until I get back?" Nate asked.

"Sure." Lizzy nodded and shrugged. "Sure. I'm not meeting Ajay at The Tides until five."

"Five, okay. Got it." Nate checked his watch. That gave him a few hours. "I'll be back by then for sure. Vivian?" He inclined his head to draw her over. "I've never seen her like this."

"You haven't been kidnapped before," Vivian said quietly.

"It comes in waves. Most of the time, I've been around for her to confide in. You Coltons are pretty good at keeping your feelings to yourself." She arched a brow at him. "Never show any weakness, right?"

"Tell me she's getting professional help."

"We've talked about it." Vivian looked back as Lizzy wandered over to look out the back glass doors. "We'll be talking about it again. And hey, we have a few more things in common now. Me with the flying bullets and killer SUVs. Her with… Yeah." She steered him to the door. "It'll all be fine. Just give us some time."

"Some." He was already counting the minutes until he could get back. "But not a lot."

IT TOOK TWO full mugs of tea before Vivian felt as if Lizzy was back on even keel. She'd bet just about every penny in her bank account that Lizzy Colton had kept things together for everyone else. There was an unexpected burst of pride in knowing that Lizzy felt comfortable enough to break down in front of her. But it also waved a red flag. Trauma was tricky and insidious and often snuck up to slap its victims when they least expected it.

A lesson for Lizzy, Vivian wondered. Or herself?

"I'm so embarrassed." Lizzy curled up in the corner of the sofa, a half-full mug clutched between her hands as Vivian dug out one of the many packages of cookies that had been left hidden around the kitchen. "I can only imagine what Nate might think."

"I can tell you exactly what he was thinking." Vivian pulled out four crunchy chocolate chip cookies, set them on a plate, then left those on the counter and brought the entire package over. "He's worried about you. Here." She handed

Lizzy the package and plopped down beside her. "Which means congratulations, you're now on his list of people to take care of." She snatched a cookie and bit in. "Welcome to the club."

Lizzy's eyes had stopped spinning more than an hour ago, once Vivian had gone through everything that had transpired since she'd first walked into Madariaga's. She'd felt odd rehashing everything, as if it were some kind of story she'd committed to memory.

"Is that a club I'm happy to belong to?" Lizzy's knowing look had Vivian squirming in her seat. "You and Nate? You're…together, right?"

"We are." Vivian had wondered how her best friend would feel about her getting involved with Nate. Given the strained family dynamic at the moment, there was no way to predict what was coming next. "Do you remember telling me the first time that you met Ajay?"

Lizzy ducked her chin, but not before Vivian saw the healthy pink tint to her cheeks. "I have a vague recollection of that conversation."

Considering the amount of wine that had been poured that evening, Vivian was impressed. "When I was sitting there, listening to you, all I could think at the time was that you were still caught up in the excitement of everything that had happened. That you were, I don't know, too susceptible to his charm. That you'd fallen as much for the romance of the situation as you had for him."

"You think being kidnapped was romantic?"

"No, of course not," Vivian said. She wasn't explaining this very well. "I think the end result has proven itself out though. You seem to have this, I don't know, calmness about you." Despite the anxiety that had sprung up. "As if you've stopped looking for something you were unaware you needed." Vivian sipped her tea, considered her words carefully. "The first time I saw Nate, sitting at that bar, that kind of warning in his eyes, like he was already protecting me, I don't know if I can explain it."

"Like finding your other half?" Lizzy suggested.

"No." She didn't need someone to complete her. "It was like being around him unlocked my other half." Her silent, intimidated half. Even now, the doubt remained. But since her conversation with Nate, her faith was stronger. "I'm not… afraid around him."

"Afraid? Oh, Vivian." Lizzy tilted her head.

"I mean I'm not afraid to be myself. There's no expectations. No show to put on. I don't have to impress him or pretend to be something or someone I'm not. He sees me." The admission lifted her heart. "Who I really am. And he has from the start. Everything I never thought I would have has clicked into place. Which brings me to a question I have for you."

"For me?" Lizzy frowned. "What about?"

"About Nate. And me. Lizzy, you're the best friend I've ever had. The only friend, really." She was already slipping into excuse mode, something she knew Nate would call her on. "But given everything that's going on with your mom and finding out about Nate and Sarah…" She screwed up her courage and just put it out there. "You're okay with me dating him, aren't you? I don't want to complicate things further."

"I could approach this question in a couple of ways." Lizzy ate another cookie, sipped her tea, looked at Vivian over the top of her mug. "But I'm not going to draw this out any longer than necessary. What's going on where Nate and Sarah and the rest of the family is concerned has nothing to do with you. There's only one thing I've ever wanted for you, Vivian. To be happy. And to be honest, until I saw you with him before he left, I don't think I ever have seen that side of him. You care about him, don't you?"

"I love him." The simple statement rocked the foundation of her life. "I haven't told him, of course." She laughed a little. Cried a little. "I haven't lost all my senses." But the time was coming when she would. She had to. If for no other reason than to put her heart out there one more time.

Lizzy's eyes filled. "Then take that ride with him, Vivian. Don't let go. Even when things get difficult or complicated or… I think he's probably worth it. You're right. About the family. Things are weird and frustrating, but everything I know about him—that he stands up for his family, even when he doesn't really know us? That's about as good a guy as you can find." She grinned. "That said, you might want to give him fair warning that he and I are about to become a lot closer because where you go, I go. End of story."

"Okay, then." Another weight she hadn't realized she was carrying lifted off her shoulders. "I'll do just that. And I'll go on that ride." For however long it may last.

Chapter Fourteen

Sitting across from Fletcher in his office at the Owl Creek Police Department, Nate watched his brother read through the report he'd put together on Detective Jim Sullivan and his plausible connection to Marty DeBaccian. The situation reminded Nate of his trips to the principal's office once upon a time.

Either his brother read at the speed of a comatose turtle, or Fletcher was committing every word Nate had written to memory. The only thing that made the waiting tolerable was Max, who, seated on the side cabinet by the door, kept rustling an open bag of chips that he'd found in the break room.

Nate checked his watch. The afternoon was ticking away, but he had plenty of time to get back to Vivian before Lizzy left. Storm clouds had accompanied them on the drive, which meant the snow would be coming in hard and fast. All the more reason to get all of this behind them.

"So, Lizzy," Max said between crunches. "How'd she seem when you saw her?"

Fletcher's gaze didn't flicker from the printed file Nate had run off as soon as he got to the station.

"Stressed." It was, Nate thought, the best word he could think of to describe their sister. "Worried. I think she might need some assistance dealing with what happened to her last month."

Max nodded, dug deeper into the bag. "I thought the same thing before Ajay took her away for some downtime. Good to know we're all on the same page."

"We'll make sure Lizzy gets whatever help she needs." Fletcher sat forward in his squeaky chair. "Vivian's always been a solid support person for her. It's good Lizzy showed up at the house. Means she's getting back on track. I appreciate you running this past me before sending it to your lieutenant."

"Figured it would be safer to send it from here on one of your more secure computers than from the house." Nate pointed to the pages Fletcher had insisted on printing out. "Took some finagling to track down all of Sullivan's logins for the past few years. Seeing the cases he was keeping an eye on tells me that when we get him into custody, we should look beyond DeBaccian. He's worked in a number of departments over the years, which means he's had access to more information than I feel comfortable with at the moment."

"No, I think you're exactly right," Fletcher agreed. "And I think the sooner we shoot this over to Boise PD, the better." He glanced at Max. "You've read this?"

"I have." Max chomped a chip. "Last night. Early this morning," he corrected.

"Thoughts?"

Max wrapped up the bag and set it aside. "I think, once Sullivan's been questioned, he might prove quite beneficial to a number of federal investigations currently on the books. Half the names DeBaccian has been in contact with are being actively investigated. More to the point, if you can flip Sullivan, you get him a deal to turn on DeBaccian and you remove Vivian from the equation altogether, which, let's face it, would be a major win for everyone involved."

"Not going to argue with that." Nate nodded. "I'm anxious to head back to Boise and try to put this whole thing to bed."

"Yeah, well, that isn't happening just yet," Fletcher said in a warning voice. "You're about to bust open what is tantamount to a nationwide organized crime ring. The longer you keep your head down, the better."

"Actually..." Max slapped his hands together before wiping them on his jeans. "I was going to recommend the opposite. Make some noise. Get down there and pull the attention off Vivian."

"Give DeBaccian a bigger target, you mean," Fletcher clarified.

"The second this report of Nate's hits the Boise PD system, all hell is going to break loose," Max went on. "Unless either of you can convince me that the server and anyone with access are locked down one-hundred-percent."

Nate considered it, and he didn't like the implied suggestion. "You're thinking Sullivan isn't the only one we should be worried about."

"Where there's one bad apple..." Max trailed off. "There's something to be said for scaring the crap out of people, even cops. Makes them do stupid things. Careless things."

"It also might push someone into coming forward with information you can actually use as evidence against Sullivan." Fletcher nodded. "It isn't a horrible idea."

"You do have a way with compliments, Fletch," Max said.

"I don't know." Nate's reluctance had more to do with the idea of leaving Vivian alone even longer than planned.

"I can have one of my deputies sit on the house, if that's

what's stopping you," Fletcher said. "Unless Max wants to take on protection detail?"

"Can't." Max slapped his hands together. "I'm going to Boise with our baby brother. Just to make sure he stays out of trouble."

Nate waited for the irritation. Or the embarrassment at his newly acquired nickname. Neither descended. But a smile lurked. A smile that came far more easily since Vivian had entered his life. One thing he'd learned in the past few days was that there was definitely a lot more to life than just work.

Fletcher laughed as his phone rang. He answered with a brusque "Detective Colton."

"Do people get confused, do you think?" Nate asked Max. "With all the Coltons in law enforcement."

"Nah," Max said easily. "We all sound different."

"Hang on, Lieutenant." Fletcher eyed Nate. "Let me put you on Speaker." He tapped a button on his phone, hung up the receiver. "You're on with me, Nate and our brother, Max Colton, who's a special consultant. You want to go through that one more time?"

"What's going on?" Nate asked his boss.

"We found a set of partials in the SUV that ran Ms. Maylor off the road," Lieutenant Haig reported. "I went with your gut, Nate. I ran them against Sullivan's. They're a match."

Nate swore. So Sullivan had tried to kill Vivian. "He must have followed her from the station house."

"Probably," Haig said. "I've got Renard and Paulson running the security footage from the station to confirm. I've got an arrest warrant in the works."

"What about DeBaccian?" Max asked. "Any sighting of him yet?"

"None." And Lieutenant Haig didn't sound pleased about

it. "But I'm not giving up hope. He's out there. We'll find him. In the meantime, Nate, I'm afraid your presence is required."

"In Boise?" He shook his head when Max opened his mouth, no doubt to tell Nate's CO they were already planning to head south. "Why?"

"You have a confidential informant on record who goes by the name Ferret Face?"

"Yeah." Nate frowned. "Real name's Colin Michaels. He's a hacker. Specializes in virus creation. Nasty ones that take down entire computer systems, but usually only for his own amusement. Did he call in with some intel?" Odd. He hadn't heard from Ferret in months.

"Not exactly," Haig said. "Someone tried to kill him a few hours ago."

"Tried?" Nate couldn't quite process. "And failed?"

"He's still alive. A bit crispy around the edges, though," Haig told them. "Said he did a job for someone, only instead of paying, they tried to shoot him. Bullet grazed his head, and he played dead. Then tried to put out the fire they set to take out his network with his bare hands."

"Ouch." Max winced.

"First I've heard of Ferret going commercial," Nate said. "Makes sense, I suppose. He's been putting his younger sister through college, and his mother's had medical expenses."

"Is that information in your CI file?" Fletcher asked.

Nate nodded. "Sure." He liked being able to use specific motivations when approaching one of his sources for information. Ferret might be one of the smartest computer hackers he'd come across, but compared to other criminals Nate had dealt with, the guy was a kitty cat.

"Did he say who hired him, Lieutenant?" Fletcher asked.

"That's the problem," Haig said. "He's not saying anything. He'll only talk to Nate. Either him, or he'll lawyer up. We've got him in an interview room, but he's going to start asking for additional medical attention pretty soon. I'd rather not take him out of the station until we have to."

"Ferret's always been wiggy," Nate told his brothers. "Makes sense he'd get more squirrely after something like this." If someone had tried to kill a rather insignificant hacker like Ferret, he must have taken on a really big job.

"Yeah, well, Mr. Wiggy underestimated our lab techs," Haig said. "They tapped into the security feed at his warehouse hideout." Haig paused. "Did Ferret ever mention Sullivan to you, Nate?"

"No." Nate couldn't make sense of this. "Cops don't poach other cops' CIs." What would Sullivan want with Ferret Face?

"Sullivan's not other cops," Fletcher said. "Lieutenant, I'm sending you the report Nate's put together on Sullivan. Right..." He turned his attention back to his desktop and clicked a few buttons. "Now. You should have it soon. In the meantime—"

"I'm on my way," Nate told his boss. "I can be there in—"

"*We'll* be there in a little under an hour." Fletcher hung up on Haig and headed for the door, grabbed his jacket off the hook. "Work out who's riding shotgun," he told Nate and Max. "Because we aren't stopping once we hit the siren."

"I SHOULD NOT have drunk so much tea." Lizzy straightened her pale yellow shirt as she came out of the bathroom. "I'm going to be lucky to make the drive before I have to pee again."

Vivian smiled, closed the door to the refrigerator, where

she'd been taking mental inventory so she could figure out what to fix Nate for dinner. "Yes, well, I'm sure you'll have a great night with Ajay, nonetheless."

"Oh, I know I will." Lizzy's cheery smile was back in place, a welcome sight compared to how she'd looked when she first arrived. "I'd say we'll have to compare notes in the morning, but seeing as it's my brother you're seeing..." She gave a little shudder. "Yeah, best not to have those images running around my head." Her cell phone rang from deep in her purse. "I bet that's Ajay now, checking in." She dug around, pulled out her phone, looked at the screen. "Huh. Totally wrong on that." She tapped Answer. "Fletcher? What's going on? Oh." Lizzy headed straight over to Vivian. "Sure, Nate. She's right here." She handed her phone over. "Nate needs to talk to you."

"Hey." She tried not to let the butterflies that had fluttered to life in her belly multiply. "Everything okay?"

"Honestly?" He sounded on edge, and the background noise surging through the phone included a siren. "I don't know what's going on. I'm with Fletcher and Max. We're headed into Boise right now. Something about one of my informants being in contact with Detective Sullivan. He's refusing to speak to anyone other than me."

"Oh." She glanced at her watch. Outside, the construction crew's trucks began heading out as a bright white van carrying custom glass drove in. "So you'll be later than you thought. That's okay." If anything, it was brilliant. She could get a jump start on her to-do list for tomorrow.

"You want me to stay?" Lizzy whispered.

Vivian shook her head, waved her off.

"Fletcher sent a patrol car to sit on the house until I get

home," Nate said. "It's a Deputy Jeff Bricks. You probably saw him at the station the other day."

She'd seen a lot of people at the station.

"He left when we did," Nate continued. "So he should be there any time now. Even with the storm that's coming in, I should be back soon."

"Okay." As she approached the window, she saw the patrol car pull up and park right in front. "I'll check in with him. I'll be fine, Nate. Do what you need to do. Be careful."

"You sure? Maybe Lizzy—"

"Lizzy is already on her way to meet Ajay for dinner." She wasn't about to ask her friend to change her plans. "We had this conversation before. I know how the security system works, and now there's a cop right outside. Focus on your job, then come home, Nate." She paused. "To me."

"Yeah." She could almost hear the smile in his voice. "Yeah, that sounds like a perfect plan. I've got the deputy's number. If I need to call, I'll reach you that way."

"Got it. Oh, and Nate?" Those butterflies swarmed to life, but this time she embraced it. "I've got something to tell you when you get here. Something…important."

Lizzy tilted her head, pressed a hand to her heart.

"Even better. Stay safe." He clicked off.

"You two are just so cute," Lizzy said. "Are you sure you don't want me to—"

"I'm sure." Vivian handed her back her phone and walked her to the door. "He won't be gone that long, and it's starting to snow. Go. Have a good evening with Ajay."

"Always do," Lizzy confirmed.

Vivian followed her outside, waved her off in her car before she headed to the patrol car. "Hi." She smiled as the young deputy powered down his window. "Nate called and said you were coming. Vivian Maylor." She held out her hand.

"Jeff Bricks." With his dark hair and boyish smile, he reminded her a little of what she imagined Nate had looked like shortly after becoming a cop. "I checked with the guard at the gate. Updated them on what's going on."

"I'm sure we're in for a quiet evening. I'll be working. You want anything? Coffee? Snacks?"

"I'm good." He patted the green thermos sitting in one of the oversize cup holders. "Hopefully, you won't have any need to see me again."

"Okay, then." She stood up, gave him another smile. "Thanks for doing this. You change your mind about wanting something to eat, just ring the bell."

"LORD LOVE A DUCK, Ferret looks like he spent this morning in an air fryer." On the other side of the two-way mirror, Nate stood bookended between his brothers and his lieutenant.

"We had him sign a waiver stating he'd postponed medical attention," Lieutenant Haig said, hands shoved into the front pockets of his slacks, gray-haired head shifting against the fluorescent recessed lighting. "EMTs did the best they could."

"He's got to be in pain." Even Max flinched.

"Which means whatever it is he has to tell me is worth postponing treatment." Nate shook his head. "Guess I'd best get in there and find out what it is."

A knock sounded on the observation room door. The four of them turned as it popped open. Detective Julia Renard poked her head in. "Sorry. Lieutenant, patrol just radioed in. They've got movement at Shake It Loose."

"Is it DeBaccian?" Nate demanded. There were only two

things he wanted right now: DeBaccian and Sullivan in custody, and to be back home with Vivian.

"Unconfirmed," Detective Renard said. "Our guys are too far away for a positive ID."

"I'm going to send two more cars out there for backup," Lieutenant Haig said. "Detective, get in there, and let's get to the bottom of this."

"Yes, sir." He looked to his brothers.

"You've got this," Fletcher told him. "But we're here if you need us."

"Thanks." Nate nodded. "Appreciate that." He didn't give himself much time to think. Thinking might lead to mistakes. He needed to be impulsive, even as he reminded himself how to deal with Ferret Face. He tended to be cagey, hyper and, more often than not, smarter than he looked.

He didn't knock, just walked right into the interview room. "Colin." Using his hacker name wasn't something he tended to do. He needed to talk to the man behind the moniker. "What's going on, man? I hear you need to talk to me." He couldn't stop his wince of sympathy at the sight of the burns on Ferret's face, neck and arms. A stark white bandage had been taped to his right temple, and his hands, both of them, were thickly bandaged and wrapped up. "Just looking at you, I can see you're in over your head."

Beady brown eyes, usually magnified behind thick glasses, widened as Nate took a seat across from him. "You're here. Nate, dude, I need your help."

"That's why I'm here." Hands folded on the table, he did his best to keep calm and maintain his patience. "You been working with Detective Sullivan behind my back, Colin? I thought you and I had a deal."

"We did, man, we did." Ferret leaned forward. "I didn't

want anything to do with this guy, right? I told him, I only work for you. Detective Nate Colton. Because you have my back. You always have."

"You'd best come out with it, then, just to make sure our relationship stays intact."

"But that's just it. I can talk now. Because you're here." The relief shining in Ferret's eyes seemed out of place. "This was part of the deal I made with him."

"Deal you made with who?" Something slimy and uncertain slithered in Nate's gut. "Detective Jim Sullivan?"

"So you know already?" Ferret squeaked. "Ah, man, does that mean Laura's okay? You've got her?"

"Your sister?" Nate glanced at the mirror, hoped Fletcher and Max got the message. "Sure, yeah, we've got her, Colin." Now wasn't the time to tell the truth.

Colin sobbed and lowered his head, banged his red, raw skin against the table. "Okay. Okay, I knew you'd get her. I knew you wouldn't let me down. He said he knew where she lived, that he could get to her anytime if I didn't do what he wanted."

"Detective Sullivan?" Nate had to be careful how he asked. It could just as easily be one of DeBaccian's henchmen, or even DeBaccian himself. "Colin? Look at me. Stop banging your head and come clean, okay? I can't keep helping you if you don't. Was it Detective Jim Sullivan? Describe him for me."

"Yeah, yeah, that's the name he gave me. Red hair, mean eyes. He shows up at my place a couple of nights ago, says he's heard about this new program I've created. Might have gotten too chatty at the Down and Dirty a few weeks ago in that poker game—"

"Colin," Nate warned. "Focus. What's this new program?"

"It's a virus that doubles as a tracker. Send an email with a virus, not as an attachment, but embedded in a link. Like in a sig line. It's mad brilliant, man. They click on it and *bam!* We can trace whatever device they use."

Nate nodded as if he understood completely. "So you did what he wanted, yeah?"

"Yeah, I sent the email that night. Told him I wasn't sure it would work. I'm still, like, beta testing it and everything, but he promised me ten K if I took the job. That's like a semester and a half for Laura's school. And sure, yeah, he threatened her if I didn't take the job, but ten thou!"

"I get it, Colin." Nate resisted flinching. "She's family. You do what you have to do for family. That's all he had you do? Send the email?"

"Yes. Well, no." His eyes shifted, and he sank back in his chair. "He came back last night. Man, I'm sorry. I didn't want to do it, but it was the only way he said he wouldn't kill me. The only way he wouldn't go after Laura. And my mom. He threatened my family!"

"You told the officers who brought you in that this guy tried to kill you." Nate pointed to the bandage on his head.

"I had to tell them something!" Ferret cried. "It was the only way they'd call you, and I needed to get you back here, to Boise!"

"Get me back…" The pieces fell into place as if in slow motion. "He didn't really try to kill you, did he, Colin? Colin? Ferret!" Nate slammed his hand hard on the table. Ferret jumped. Guilt swam in his watery eyes. "Was all this a setup? Did you set fire to your own place?"

"It was the only way, man! I'm sorry! I didn't want… You've always been—"

Nate looked up when the door swung open. Fletcher and his lieutenant stood in the doorway, looming. Brooding.

"What?" Nate demanded.

"DeBaccian's club, Shake It Loose?" Fletcher said.

"What about it?" Nate asked.

"We just got a 911 call," Lieutenant Haig said. "It's on fire."

"UNBELIEVABLE," MAX MUTTERED from where he stood beside Nate, across the street from the now smoldering building that housed Shake It Loose. The parking lot contained a handful of cars, two fire engines and one ambulance. The fact the strip club had been closed for the past two weeks had probably saved lives. DeBaccian knew how to run a successful—if sleazy—business. "They should rename this city Coincidence Central."

Lieutenant Haig had accepted Fletcher's offer to be a second pair of eyes and ears when speaking with the fire chief leading the charge to douse the remaining embers of the fire. The fire had been out for a good half hour, but the smoke continued to billow as water dripped into frozen rivers and streamed into the street.

"Patrol units at each corner around this place, and none of them saw who was inside?" Max said. "How does that even happen?"

"Nate!" Detective Kevin Paulson, Renard's partner, hurried over from where he'd been speaking with two of the uniformed officers. "Patrol officer in the third car on scene hit Record on her body cam. Not sure if she caught anything, but it's worth a shot. We've got the footage coming through anytime."

It was something, at least. He'd feel a heck of a lot better if he could speak to Vivian, but between spotty cell service and the frenetic activity, there hadn't been a chance. "Any updates on who was inside?" Nate had never prayed so hard for a dead body in his life. If DeBaccian was dead, that would kill any case the feds might be able to build against his associates, but it would put Vivian in the clear.

"Firefighters found three bodies in the back office." Fletcher joined them, his voice low and intense. "Just finished talking with the chief. Fire was started near the front, so it didn't get to them."

"Cause of death?"

"They were shot," Fletcher confirmed. "Close range."

Nate held his breath. "Tell me one is—"

"Chief's got a picture." Fletcher signaled the chief over, and she approached, still loaded down with equipment. She flipped up her face shield. "Chief Gibbs?"

"Detective Fletcher and Lieutenant Haig filled me in." The shorter, stockier woman handed over her cell phone. "Goes against protocol, but I took this. Hope it helps."

"There, bottom left corner." Fletcher pointed to the image. "Zoom in."

Nate took the phone and did just that. The familiar family crest glinted. "That's DeBaccian's ring."

"Looks like he didn't make it out of town after all," Max muttered before he swore and turned away.

"So he's dead." Nate couldn't quite let himself believe it.

"We've got the medical examiner's office sending out a team now," Lieutenant Haig said. "You should get back and finish with Ferret Face, Nate."

"Evidence tech is working with him at the moment," Nate said. "Ferret said he could access his cloud storage to retrieve the virus information."

"Probably go a lot faster if the guy could type quicker with those bandages," Max said.

Lieutenant Haig's cell rang. "Yeah." He turned away as he answered.

"So, that's it?" Nate looked at Max. "After all this, it's just over?"

"Sometimes that's the way a case breaks." Max shrugged.

"And all these coincidences?" Nate challenged. "They don't bother you?"

"Didn't say that." Max waited a beat. "They bother you?"

Yes, but his gut wasn't capable of overriding actual evidence.

Lieutenant Haig rejoined them. "Security at Boise Airport just stopped someone using Jim Sullivan's ID to board a flight to Mexico."

Fletcher, Max and Nate simply stared at him.

"Yeah." Lieutenant Haig smirked and ducked his head. "I'm not buying it, either. He'd know we'd have locked down the airports, train stations and bus terminals in the city. No way he's that careless. I asked the officers to send me a photo..." His phone chimed. "And there it is." He turned the phone around. "Definitely not Jim Sullivan."

"Misdirect," Fletcher said. "A stupid one."

"None of this explains Sullivan going to Ferret Face," Nate said, more to himself than anyone else. "What good would a tracking virus be...?"

"Was Sullivan tracking someone for himself or for DeBaccian?" Fletcher asked.

"Only person that we know of that DeBaccian would want found is Vivian," Max said. "Do we have a copy of the email he sent yet?"

"Still working on it," Lieutenant Haig said. "Apparently there are seven levels of security that need to be traversed in order to gain access to Ferret Face's cloud storage."

"No one's more paranoid than a hacker," Nate growled. Smoke continued to plume into the air from inside Shake It Loose. "Only three bodies inside. No one else?"

"As far as surveillance reported," Lieutenant Haig said. "No one else went in or came out the front or back in the past eight hours."

"What about the alley?" Nate asked.

Lieutenant Haig blinked. "What alley?"

"There's a narrow one between the club and the abandoned building next door. I read about it in one of the initial surveillance reports from a few months ago. It's not wide enough for a vehicle, but DeBaccian used it as a private entrance. And he had at least two security cameras working twenty-four seven."

Lieutenant Haig shook his head. "I just reread all those reports this morning. No mention of the alley or the cameras."

"That list of databases Sullivan accessed that you came up with," Fletcher said to Nate. "One of them was the official records files, right?"

"He could have deleted the mention from the report," Nate said. "I couldn't go deeper than a cursory examination without raising an alarm." He looked back to the club. "We need to get in there. There might be security footage. Proof of Sullivan getting away." Maybe even proof he was guilty of murdering DeBaccian.

"Chief!" Lieutenant Haig called to Chief Gibbs. "We're going to need your help. And a couple of helmets. We need to get inside."

WITH THE TELEVISION on for background noise—she preferred old Hollywood musicals to keep her mood elevated—Vivian made slow and steady progress on her always growing to-do list. Cyber-handholding had become her specialty. Selfishly, she preferred clients who liked communicating via email rather than spending countless hours on video or phone calls.

With the Christmas tree providing ambient lighting and the dim glow from over the stove, the house felt even cozier than before. Instead of tea—she'd definitely had her fill for a while—she had opened one of the bottles of wine she found in the dedicated wine refrigerator. Nothing rounded out the day quite like a bold Bordeaux. Sipping, she sighed and resisted the urge to check her watch for the hundredth time.

As the sun set and the night crept in, she couldn't help but feel anxious for Nate to return. Not just because she didn't relish being alone in this big house. Because she missed him.

Needing to stretch, she set her laptop on the coffee table and stood up, twisting and reaching her arms over her head to work out the kinks. She took a short walk down the hall to the front of the house. The patrol car hadn't moved. The now familiar shadow of Deputy Jeff Bricks shifted in the darkness. She waved, whether he could see her or not, and headed back into the kitchen.

She caught the oven timer before it started beeping and retrieved a pair of potholders to pull out the pork roast she'd set to cooking earlier. She tented it with foil, telling herself she could reheat it should Nate be much later.

With Bing Crosby and Danny Kaye singing on the television, she settled back onto the sofa and picked up her laptop again.

The second she started typing, the power cut out. The house went dark.

"GOOD THING THE fire inspector won't be here until tomorrow morning," Chief Gibbs grumbled at their backs as Nate and Lieutenant Haig made their way through the burned-out strip club. It had taken some convincing, letting any of them inside, but she'd eventually given in, probably just to get the lieutenant off her overburdened back.

They'd donned evidence booties—those lovely blue cloth shoe coverings that would prevent them from dragging any trace evidence of their own onto the scene. Nate was relieved she hadn't put them in hazmat suits.

The alley door had been left ajar. Ash and soot had spread outside the club. Fletcher and Max remained outside, acting as a point of communication should they need it.

It wasn't Nate's first fire scene. The charred, wet wood gave off its own particular aroma, and the smoke settled into his lungs like an unwanted resident. He'd be smelling this place for weeks, no doubt. Maybe the hazmat suit would have been okay. He could hear the *drip*, *drip*, *drip* of the hose water used to knock back the flames.

"At first glance, I'd say whoever started it hedged their bets. I've got traces in the front and back entrances," Chief Gibbs called over her shoulder, a hand keeping her bright yellow helmet steady on her head. "Be careful where you step, please. I really don't want to fill out a report about you two being in here."

"Consider yourself having earned multiple favors from the police department," Lieutenant Haig told her.

She stopped outside a barely holding together door frame. "I'll remember that." She stepped back. "Your bodies are back there, near the desk. What's left of the desk," she corrected. "I'm going to take another walk-through, make sure we didn't miss anyone. Ten minutes," she told them. "That's it."

"That's all we'll need," Nate assured her. Unable to choke down any more smoke, he pulled the collar of his T-shirt up over his nose, stepped carefully through the debris and burned carpet and flooring. "Well, I see three." He didn't know what he expected other than what had already been reported.

He crouched down, carefully lifted one of the three bright yellow tarps covering the bodies. The flames hadn't done enough damage to obscure the markings on both men's skin.

"These two match the description Vivian gave of the shooters." He flipped the tarps back up, stood up, turned and took four steps the right. The exposed hand, stretched out as if for help, displayed the now familiar ring that had, for years, represented DeBaccian's growing power. He'd wielded it like a weapon, frequently shifting it to his right hand in order to leave a lasting mark.

"Nothing surprising." Lieutenant Haig nodded to the large safe across the room. "That's been emptied out."

"Guns, no doubt. And cash," Nate said, shaking his head. "Chief Gibbs was right. This was a waste of time."

"I heard that!" Chief Gibbs called from outside the room.

Nate almost laughed. He pushed to his feet, slipped his foot free of the corner of the tarp that caught against his shoe. The tarp fluttered and settled, exposing part of the victim's face.

Shock cut through him like a knife. Nate dropped back down, ripped the tarp back and stared at the body, with its dead wide eyes. "Lieutenant? You seeing what I'm seeing?" He pointed to the red hair gleaming in the dim light of their helmet lights.

"It's Jim Sullivan," his lieutenant confirmed.

"Nate!"

Nate pivoted as Fletcher dived into sight.

"Hey!" Chief Gibbs stalked toward him, hands up. "I told you to wait—"

"Nate, we've got the email Ferret sent." Fletcher plowed right past her. "It was an inquiry addressed to PR Perfection."

"PR..." Nate's heart skipped a beat. "That's Vivian's company. Ferret was hired to track Vivian's laptop." He stared blankly at his boss, then turned to look down at the body. "Sullivan's dead," he murmured. "Which means DeBaccian isn't." Fear wrapped its talons around his heart and squeezed. "He's going after her."

"We have to get back to Owl Creek," Fletcher commanded. "Now!"

Chapter Fifteen

Vivian groaned and dropped her head back. The marvels of living in snow country. At home, she had a generator that would kick in when the power went out. But up here? She used her laptop as a light and untangled herself yet again from the sofa.

She heard a car door slam and quickly hurried to the window. The handful of street lamps that had been installed had gone dark as well. The only things casting any light were the moon and the interior of the deputy's car.

Deputy Bricks headed up the walkway, zipping up his jacket.

She set her laptop on the floor, hurried to the door and pulled it open. "What's going on?" she asked.

"No idea," the deputy said. "I'm going to take a walk around. There might be some crews working late… Maybe they tripped something." He offered a smile. "You okay in there?"

"Everything's fine." She shrugged.

"Let me take a quick look, just to be safe."

She shrugged and stepped back. "Okay. I think I saw some candles in the pantry."

"Great." He closed the door behind him and headed down one hall while Vivian retrieved her laptop.

"Oh!" She snapped her fingers, remembering her cell. It might be useless for calls, but it made a better flashlight than her computer. She headed upstairs to the bedroom, grabbed it from where she'd set it last night when she'd spent almost a half hour looking at pictures of Toby. She left her laptop on the bed, turned on the flashlight.

A soft thud echoed from downstairs.

She froze. "Deputy Bricks?" Taking slow steps, she moved into the hall, walked to the landing of the stairs. "Deputy?" The light wavered as her hand shook. "Hello?"

She cast the light around, eyes adjusting to the harsh light against the shadows.

"Deputy?" She yelled this time and winced against the echo that shot back at her.

Footsteps sounded. Dull, heavy.

Growing closer.

She shivered against a sudden chill and only now realized she could hear the wind blowing. Her mind raced. Everything she'd been told about the house seemed to tumble in her head. Alarm. Guard house. Panels.

She raced back into the bedroom, forced herself to be quiet when closing the door.

The keypad on the wall seemed to mock her as she flipped open the panel and hit the emergency button.

Nothing happened.

She pounded a fist against the console.

Frustrated tears burned the back of her throat. Blurred her eyes.

The footsteps were coming up the stairs. Slowly. Closer.

Her bare toes scrunched into the hardwood flooring. She

spun around, looking for something, anything, with which to defend herself. Moonlight shimmered against the glass door.

Swallowing her panic, she ran forward, threw open the doors, raced to the balcony railing, then forced herself to slow down, turn and return to the bedroom, placing her feet in the same prints she'd made in the snow.

She left the doors open, ran quietly tos the closet and ducked inside, pulling the door closed behind her as the bedroom doorknob rattled.

She killed the flashlight, hugged her phone against her chest. Moonlight streamed across the slats of the closet door.

She stepped back into the corner, into the darkness, as a large, shadowy figure stepped into the room.

"I'M NOT GETTING any response from Bricks," Fletcher said from the back seat. Max had reached the driver's side first and had them speeding out of Boise, siren blaring. "I'm calling the station now."

"We'll get there," Max said. "I promise, Nate, we'll get there in time."

"You know as well as I do that's an impossible promise to make." He was a cop. He'd been a cop for almost a decade. He was well aware of the realities of the job. "I shouldn't have left her."

"Don't go down that road," Fletcher ordered. "It doesn't lead anywhere good. If we can't get to her, I'll get someone who can. Yeah," he yelled into the phone. "Monroe, I want all hands on deck and up at Colton Crossing. We've got a wanted suspect on-site." He recited the address of the house. "Be on the lookout for Vivian Maylor..." He rattled off Vivian's description. "I'm about— Max! Watch it!"

Nate gripped the passenger seat with both hands as Max weaved his way in and around slowing traffic.

"We need to get there alive to help her," Nate ground out between gritted teeth.

"Doing my best," Max said as he pressed his foot even harder on the gas. "Don't worry. I'm motivated. Lizzy will never forgive us if anything happens to Vivian."

"*I'll* never forgive us." Nate stared into the snowy night and did something he hadn't done in a very, very long time.

He prayed.

TERROR, VIVIAN THOUGHT as she watched the figure pass, worked as a surprisingly effective mental reboot.

She knew what she didn't have at her disposal—the alarm and warning system she'd been told about time and again. No communication because her cell phone was little more than a door weight. She was currently a sitting duck. But hopefully a silent one.

Vivian stepped forward, angling her head to peer through the closet slats.

The man was following her footprints, stepping outside the bedroom. Onto the balcony. One step from the door. Two…three…

She pushed open the closet door and squeezed out. She couldn't risk closing it again for fear he'd hear. Moving as quietly as she could, she hurried out of the bedroom door toward the stairs.

She was three steps down when she heard him. No. She *felt* him. An energy of rage that pulsed through the house and nearly knocked her off her feet. She lost her grip on her phone, heard it skid away after it hit the floor.

Panic had her scrambling, tripping, nearly tumbling to

the landing, but she stayed on her feet, using the banister to propel herself to the front door.

He'd locked it. Bolted it. She tugged on the handle, tried to flip the lock, but he was coming down the stairs. Too close.

Too, too close.

Her feet slipped and slid as she scrambled toward the kitchen. There had to be something—anything—she could use…

"There's nowhere to run." His voice didn't echo through the house. It settled inside her mind like a dark mantra of warning. "No one to help. I'll make it quick. And painless."

She sobbed, feeling her way down the wall and imagining the path she'd taken countless times in the past few days. Vivian cried out when she ran straight into the corner of the kitchen island. She could already feel a bruise forming as she grappled her way around the stove, knocked over the salt and pepper shakers. Biting back a sob, her hands flailed almost desperately until she finally felt the curved neck of the oil bottle.

His presence pressed in on her. Moonlight shone through the doors, and her eyes adjusted enough for her to grab the bottle and douse the top of the stove.

He stood only a few feet away now, his height making her tilt her head back to see the top of him. He flexed his hands, the leather of his gloves creaking in the silence.

Braced with her back against the stove, she reached behind her and twisted the knob. *Click, click, click, hisssss…*

Vivian dropped to the ground as the gas burner flamed to life.

The flames exploded up, straight into his face. The man screamed, held up both hands to protect himself, stumbled back and crashed down onto the coffee table.

The fire alarm blared, the horrific screech cutting through her head like a hot knife.

Vivian didn't stop to evaluate her actions. Or the damage she may have done to the kitchen.

She raced around the island, down the hall, wrenched open the locks. She flung open the door and ran out into the stormy, snowy night.

"WHAT ON EARTH did they teach you at the FBI academy?" Nate demanded as Max took the off-ramp that would lead to Colton Crossing at nearly twice the legal speed limit. "Holy… Is that black ice?"

"Maybe." Max plowed over it anyway, leading Nate to believe, without a doubt, the tires of Fletcher's SUV weren't even touching the ground.

"My officers are four minutes out," Fletcher yelled over the noise of the engine, the storm and Nate's frayed nerves. "We had a multicar accident in town. They couldn't get away until that was settled."

Nate clenched his jaw tighter. Four minutes. A lot could happen in four minutes.

Max rounded the first corner on two wheels. The siren continued to blare. Nate had no doubt he'd be hearing it in his head for years to come. He should have let her have the stupid cell phone. He needed to talk to her again. Needed to hear her voice again. Needed to tell her…

"Almost there." Max raced down the road as the snow continued to fall. Another left turn and he zoomed up the final hill.

"There! I can see the guard house!" Fletcher pointed between their seats.

Behind them, more sirens screeched through the night.

Nate looked back. Down, in the distance, he could see three patrol cars making their way up the mountain.

Max screeched the SUV to a stop in front of the guard gate.

"Where's the officer?" Nate yelled as he jumped out of the car. He all but leaped at the door that swung open by the hand of a middle-aged man with a full, dark beard. "Open the gate!"

"Power's out!" the guard, whose badge identified him as Angelo, yelled back. "I've been trying to reset the generator, but it's not connecting. Must be the storm!"

"It's not the storm." Nate shoved his way inside, Fletcher right at his heels. "How do I…" He started flipping switches, anything that might trigger the eight-foot wrought iron gate to open.

A red light started blinking, and an alarm sounded.

"What's that? What did I do?" Nate demanded.

"That's a fire alarm," Angelo said. "There's only one house that's occupied."

"Vivian." Nate slammed out of the guard house and went for the fence, looking for a way to squeeze through the slats or pull open the lock.

"Get back!" Max yelled before he ducked back behind the wheel. He screeched the car back, set the tires to spinning and hit the gas full throttle. Nate dived out of the way seconds before Max ran the car straight into the gate.

It didn't open. But the crash jarred it enough to break the connection on the lock. Nate wedged his hands into the fractured opening, pushed with everything he had. His forearms burned with the exertion, but all he could think was that Vivian was on the other side of this gate. He had to get through. There wasn't any other option.

"Let me help!" Fletcher appeared, and sliding in behind Nate, he got his own hold on the frame. Together they shoved, crying out as the gate finally began to shift down the track.

Nate didn't wait to be sure he'd fit before he shoved his head through, then squeezed through the rest of his body. He tripped on the way out to the other side.

"Go!" Fletcher yelled when Nate looked over his shoulder. "We'll be right behind you! Max!"

Nate didn't have to be told twice. He turned and ran.

VIVIAN STOPPED OUT in the street, the house she'd escaped well behind her. She spun in a dazed circle. The thin fabric of her clothing gave even less protection than she would have imagined. Her feet had gone numb. The rest of her body was quickly following.

Above the gentle roar of the snow, she swore she heard sirens. But it could also be the alarm still blaring from the house. Which way to go? One way would take her to the guard house. The other…to the partially completed construction site. But which was which? She could barely see the sidewalks. But there…in the distance, whether her imagination or not, she saw lights.

She saw hope.

She only had one choice. Trust herself.

Ducking her head, she tightened her arms and, moving as fast as she could, headed into the snow.

THE DISTANCE FROM the guarded gate to the house was a lot longer on foot than it was by car. Nate didn't have the luxury to stop and reevaluate his route. He went by memory, hoping, praying he was headed in the right direction. He ran full out, lungs expanding to the point of catching fire. His legs had long ago gone numb, his feet hurting with each strike on the ground. He was having trouble seeing as the snow flurries whipped around.

He skidded to a stop. There. He squinted, tried to peer closer. He saw something. A flash of shimmering white amidst the white. Like a sharp slice through the night.

"Vivian." He knew it was her even before he saw the whip of dark hair. She was moving slowly, but in the right direction. "Vivian!"

He heard his name on the wind, a sob of relief, of desperation. He couldn't be certain which. Nate raced forward, only to feel his heart leap into his throat at the sound of her scream.

"Nate!"

He kept moving, his line of sight clearing just in time to see the dark shadow of Marty DeBaccian. He had one arm locked around Vivian's throat. And with his free hand, he held a gun to her head.

Nate reached back, pulled out his gun and held it up. He shook his head, tried to see through the falling snow. He couldn't get a lock. He aimed up, then down, to the side, shook his head. He couldn't get a lock.

"There's nowhere to go, DeBaccian!" Nate yelled as he did the only thing he could. He stepped closer. "You've got the Owl Creek cops and an FBI agent coming behind me. You're not getting away."

"There's more than one way out of here!" DeBaccian yelled back.

Nate was close enough now. Close enough to see the abject terror in Vivian's eyes as she struggled to breathe. As she clawed her hands at his arm to dislodge his hold.

"She comes with me!"

Vivian gasped as he lifted her higher, to where her bare feet dangled inches above the snow.

He felt rather than heard his brothers behind him. That charge in the atmosphere could only be one thing: backup. The sound of car engines, the reflection of spinning lights exploding against the falling snow released some of the fear coursing through him.

"She's coming with me!" DeBaccian yelled again, desperation in his voice now.

Nate released the safety on his gun. "She is not."

One more step and he was close enough to fire. He was poised to hit DeBaccian at point-blank range. One shot and it was all over. His finger tightened on the trigger.

Vivian shifted and blocked his shot. He pulled his finger away as she twisted and kicked until she could open her mouth. She kicked back hard, caught DeBaccian on the knee and sank her teeth into his arm.

DeBaccian howled with rage more than pain. He dropped her. Vivian hit the ground on all fours, but before DeBaccian reclaimed his hold, he aimed at Nate's head.

"Freeze! Police!" The voice wasn't familiar. Not to Nate.

DeBaccian spun, looked behind him, gun raised.

A shot rang out. Then another. And a third. Vivian remained crouched on the ground, shivering hard.

DeBaccian dropped to his knees, pitched forward. Landed face down in the snow.

"Vivian." Nate ran to her, had her up and off the ground and in his arms in seconds. He swore, he cursed, he held her as tightly as he could as she shivered so hard she practically vibrated out of his hold.

"Okay?" Fletcher came over with a spare coat and boots

from his vehicle for Vivian, then dropped a hand on Nate's shoulder as Max passed right by.

"Yeah," Nate whispered as Vivian nodded against his throat. "You're okay, right, Viv?" He pressed his lips to the top of her head, gratitude and relief flooding through him when she offered a choking whimper. "Is he dead?" Nate yelled at Max as his brother nudged a booted foot under DeBaccian's shoulder and shoved him onto his back.

DeBaccian groaned.

"Not nearly." Max bent down, ripped open DeBaccian's jacket. "He was wearing a vest. Fletcher, your deputy." He pointed to the staggering Jeff Bricks, who had a hand clutched against the back of his head as he made his way toward them.

"Son of a… He clocked me from behind." Bricks spat out the words as Fletcher grabbed him by the shoulders to keep him on his feet. "When I woke up, I swear I thought he was on fire."

"He was," Vivian murmured against Nate's neck. "I put oil on the stove and lit it in his face."

Nate couldn't stop himself. He laughed even as he held her tighter. "Watching all those murder mysteries finally paid off. It's over, Viv." Nate didn't think he could hold her any tighter. "It's all over."

"No," she said as he bent down and slipped an arm under her knees, swept her high into his arms. "It's just beginning." She pressed her lips to his. "I love you, Nate. I needed to tell you that, you know, in case something else happens."

"Nothing else is going to happen." He started walking back to the house. "I'm not going to let anything else happen to you. Ever. You hear me?"

"I hear you. Did you hear me?"

"Yes." For now, he left the fear, the anger and the cleanup behind with his brothers. "I love you, too." He'd always thought when he uttered the words they would come with a question, or with doubt. Or, at the very least, uncertainty. Instead he knew, without any hesitancy, that this thing with Vivian was one-hundred-percent right. "I want to take you out on a date. To celebrate everything," he told her. "How does that sound?"

"Madariaga's?" she asked as he rounded the walkway up to the porch.

"Where we first met?"

She looked up at him, a smile spreading across her lush, perfect lips. "Where else?"

Chapter Sixteen

Nate pulled open the door to Madariaga's just as a gust of wind and snow blew in ahead of him. He took a moment to stomp his feet and shake his head free of the weather.

"You're late."

"Yeah, I know." Nate offered Seb a quick smile as the bartender took the box containing Vivian's Christmas present off his hands. "She been here long?"

"Long enough you'll be glad you got her a gift."

"Awesome." Nate removed his coat, hung it up and slid a finger under his suddenly too tight collar. The flurry of activity that had taken place in the days following Marty DeBaccian's apprehension put the recent snowstorms to shame. But finally, the last piece had been placed, and he was officially on vacation.

"You want your usual?"

"Club soda?" Nate laughed. "Nah. Tonight we're celebrating. Scotch, on the rocks, please, Seb."

The bartender nodded. "You've got it."

"You weren't worried, were you?" Nate said as he slipped up behind a seated Vivian and brushed his lips against her cheek.

"Me? Worry?" She covered the hand he rested on her

shoulder and squeezed. “I figured you’d call if you couldn’t make it.” She didn’t look worried. But she did look nervous. Beautiful in an embroidered blue-and-white dress that made her look like a Grecian princess. “You look…” Her smile radiated the warmth of the dining room. “Wow, Detective. You need to wear a suit more often. Everything okay?”

“I’m going to give you the short version.” He sat, smoothed his tie down his chest. “Because I don’t want to spend to-night debriefing you.”

She reached over, slipped her fingers through his. “Well, that’s too bad.” Her smile lit up her eyes. “I was kind of hop-ing to be debriefed.”

That comment went straight to his groin. “Noted. DeBac-cian cut a deal.”

Her brow furrowed. “What kind of deal?”

“The kind that guarantees he’ll be in prison for life. He turned state’s evidence on multiple organized crime figures. In exchange, he gets a new identity and a private cell in a federal prison in Colorado.”

“Well, good for him. And us.” She lifted her glass of red wine as his drink arrived. They clinked in a toast. “How’d your Colton conference this afternoon go?”

“Colton conference,” Nate mused. “I was thinking it was more of a summit, but yeah.” He nodded. “It went well, I think. Chase said to thank you for putting their security sys-tem through the paces. He and Sloan are going to be making some changes after what happened with the power outage.”

“You ever figure out how DeBaccian did that?” Vivian asked.

“He stole a glass repair van and got in with the construc-tion crew. Early enough he gained access to the office and all the information he needed. He already knew what house you were in, thanks to that tracking email."

"Your ferret friend owes me a new computer," she grumbled. "But after the holidays is fine."

He wasn't the only one taking some time off. She'd put her clients on notice and said she'd be back in touch after the New Year. As for Nate, after the holidays, he planned to do a deep dive into his mother's reported connection to Markus Acker and his so-called church. He was not going to let Jessie ruin another holiday for him. "I'll get it taken care of," he told her. "So, about that summit, er, conference—"

"Before I forget." She held up a finger. "I stopped at the hospital today to visit Dean Wexler."

"Did you?"

"I did. He's going to be okay." She looked at him, narrowed her eyes. "You already knew."

"Lizzy told me this afternoon. Did Wexler tell you he's going to plead guilty to the robberies?"

"He did. And he apologized for putting me in danger." She ran her index finger around the rim of her wine glass. "I think he's had a change of heart when it comes to a criminal lifestyle."

"One can hope." But Nate wouldn't bet money on it. "So." He cleared his throat. "I have some, well, family news."

"Okay." She leaned her arms on the table and looked into his eyes.

"We've been invited to Christmas Eve dinner at the ranch in Owl Creek."

"We?" she teased.

"Well, Sarah and I have. And you have, too, but hopefully you'll be coming with me. As my date." He tightened his fingers on hers. "Does that sound like something you'd like to do? I know the holidays aren't the easiest thing for you."

"One thing almost dying does for you is help release the past." Her black hair glinted in the candlelight of the votive flickering on their table. "One of my happiest childhood memories is that Christmas I spent with Lizzy on the ranch. It only seems fitting our first Christmas together happen there as well. That's my long way of saying yes." Her smile was full and generous. "I would love to go with you."

He had no words. But he did have a gift. He looked over to the bar, caught Seb's eye and signaled to him. "Then we should seal this plan with a gift."

"Not a kiss?" She pouted. "You're really striking out tonight, Detective."

Maybe he was. But not for long.

"What's this?" Vivian asked as Seb appeared with the rather messily wrapped package topped with a big red bow. She accepted it with both hands, shot him a look. "Nate, what did you do?"

"It's why I was late. Ruby called at the last minute. I hadn't planned to do this until Christmas Day, then the whole invitation to the ranch happened and… I'm babbling."

"Happens to the best of us. Can I?"

"If you don't, we won't have anyplace to eat." The box took up a good part of the table.

"Okay." She smiled at the box, tears glistening in her eyes. "Other than from Lizzy, I haven't gotten a present for Christmas in a really long time." She rested her hands on the top of the box. "Thank you, Nate. Oh!" She started when the lid jumped. "What on earth…?" She popped open the lid, peered inside. "Oh. Oh, Nate." She reached in and pulled out the little black kitten. "Oh, he's— He?" Nate nodded. "He's beautiful."

Nate put the box on the floor as she cuddled the kitten against her chest. The tiny gold bell around his neck tinkled as the cat gave Vivian a good sniff, then licked her chin. "Ruby picked him out for you. He was the last in a litter and the only black one. She said they don't get adopted as often and are often lost." He inclined his head, reveling in the joy on her face. Tears streamed down her cheeks. "I thought you might appreciate that."

She shook her head, leaned out of her chair enough to brush a kiss across his lips. "You are the best thing I could have ever hoped for."

"Yeah?" He reached out, tapped the kitten on the top of his head. "You think?"

"I don't think," she murmured. "I know."

Epilogue

"You ready?"

Nate looked down at Vivian's hand, clasped around his. He'd needed a moment, after the drive to the Colton ranch, to get his bearings. It was one thing to have met most of his brothers and sisters in town or in Boise. It was another to be stepping foot on their land, into their home.

But it was time. He reached out and took hold of Sarah's hand. He could feel his own nerves in his sister's grasp, heard her nervous breathing as he tugged her close. He met her eyes and, for a moment, was transported back to that night he'd told her the truth about their father. Their family. Their brothers and sisters.

Back then, this day hadn't seemed possible. All the fresh pine garlands decorated with gold bells and bright red bows. The various trees decorated with lights and ornaments and the wrapping around the water vessels for the wildlife and ranch animals to drink out of. The snowcapped fences stretched to and fro, framing the picture-perfect setting in an image he didn't think he'd ever forget.

"We're ready, yeah?" he asked his sister. Sarah nodded.

The three of them walked up the path, hand in hand.

The closer they got, the louder the laughter and celebration sounded on the other side of the door.

Taking the stairs up, Nate's heart pounded.

He nearly stepped back when the front door burst open.

"Finally!" Lizzy leaped out and caught him in a huge hug. "We were wondering when you'd get here."

"I like to be on time," he said, glancing at his watch. "You said—"

"Yeah, yeah. Did you bring Jinx?"

"We left the kitten well tended to at Eddie's," Nate said.

"My neighbor," Vivian said. "He's declared himself an honorary grandfather."

"Fabulous." Lizzy beamed at Vivian, then turned her smile on Sarah, who, for the first time since getting out of the car, looked as if she might be changing her mind about coming. "Sarah. It's nice to see you again. I'm Lizzy."

"Yes, I remember. Oh." She found herself on the receiving end of another hug. "Thank you for inviting us."

"Of course. You're family, after all. No place else you should be. Come in." She stepped back inside and waved them in.

"They're here!" Lizzy yelled into the house as Ajay stepped out from where he stood with Chase and Wade.

"Forgive her," Ajay said as he closed the door behind them. "She started the eggnog at breakfast."

"Did not!" Lizzy called over her shoulder.

"Vivian." Buck Colton, standing slightly shorter than Nate, approached, held out his arms to her. "I feel like you should still be a little girl. Welcome back to the ranch."

"Thank you." Vivian shifted uneasy eyes to Nate. "Thank you for including us."

"Of course," Buck said easily. "You're family." He turned his attention to Nate and Sarah. "You're always welcome here."

It was on the tip of Nate's tongue to ask if Buck was sure, but he could see, with the lively humor and good intentions shining in Buck's green eyes, that he meant what he said.

"Jenny, Nate and Sarah are here." Buck stepped back, held out his hand. "I'm not sure you were properly introduced the first time we met."

Nate, still holding his sister's hand, felt it tighten around his. He knew immediately what she was thinking because he was, too. She was their mother's twin, but whatever resemblance they might have borne to one another no longer existed. Where Jessie was all harsh angles and anger, Jenny Colton radiated a warmth and maternal generosity that reached out and enveloped them.

This was, Nate realized, the moment he'd been most dreading. "I'm—" He was what? Sorry for actions he'd had no part in? Sorry for existing? Sorry for causing her and Buck pain he couldn't begin to fathom. Vivian leaned against him, wrapped her arms around his and gave him a gentle nudge. "Merry Christmas," he said instead.

Jenny lifted a hand to his cheek, then to Sarah's. She smiled. "Merry Christmas."

"Does this mean we can finally eat?" Max hollered and earned a combination of cheers and jeers. He hoisted four-year-old Justin, Greg and Briony's adopted little boy, over his head as Lucy Colton, only a year older, jumped up and down as she clung to her mother Hannah's hand.

"Let's get you something to drink, yeah?" Jenny pulled them farther into the room just as Frannie walked up a couple of stairs, turned and clinked her spoon against her wine glass. Her beaded white dress flared around her knees, and her blond hair had been sharpened into its usual bob.

"Before everyone goes nose down in the turkey..." She looked down, held out her hand and drew a man up beside her. "Dante and I have a bit of a surprise for all of you."

"No more surprises, please!" Lizzy called over the din. "We've had enough for the year."

"Well, then," Frannie said, then waited for quiet. "This should bring this year to a perfect close. Since we weren't sure when we could get the entire family together again, we figured we might as well make this day, a day when we're *all* here—" she toasted Nate and Sarah "—even more special. So..."

"We're getting married," Dante said, as if tired of waiting for her to get to the point. "Today." He glanced at his watch. "Right now, as a matter of fact."

It was impossible not to get caught up in the joyous cheers that erupted through the room.

"No one saw this coming?" Nate asked Vivian, who shrugged.

"And thank you to Hannah," Frannie yelled to get the family quieted down again. "We couldn't have pulled this off without her, especially since we had to have a cake!"

Hannah did a little curtsey, which her daughter copied. "Always happy to help with a wedding that isn't mine."

That earned another round of laughter.

"What do you say, Reverend Bostick?" Dante called to a middle-aged man wearing an ugly Rudolph sweater. "You ready to do this?"

"Me? Now?" Reverend Bostick seemed to choke on his eggnog as his eyes went wide.

"We're ready if you are," Frannie confirmed.

"Well, all right, then." The reverend patted his chest for his glasses. "I think I can wing this. Merry Christmas, indeed."

Ruby and Lizzy came over to draw Sarah away while Nate and Vivian made their way to a pair of chairs scooted together. Nate ran his hand down his tie, and when he looked at Vivian, he saw her beaming at him. She rested her hand over his.

"You know what this is, don't you?" she whispered.

"What?" He pressed a kiss to her lips.

"The best Christmas ever."

He pulled her close, tucked her head under his chin and watched his family swarm and settle and sigh. "I think you're right," he agreed. "You're absolutely right."

* * * * *